SLAVE TO LOVE

"Do you like that, princess?" Jamal whispered against Zara's ear. "Spread your legs and let me pleasure you."

"No, stop! Send me back to the stables but don't use me like this!"

Jamal went still. He seemed angry. "I'm not using you. I want to give you pleasure. We will pleasure one another."

"That's not at all what I want. Berber women are free to choose their own lovers. We are men's equals."

"You are a slave and slaves have no rights," Jamal pointed out. "I can take you here beside the pool, if I so desire."

"I will not submit easily."

Jamal stared at her. Her beauty was mesmerizing. Allah help him, for he did want her, but force did not appeal to him. Force had never been necessary in his dealings with women. *I will have her willing and submissive,* he vowed to himself, *without the use of force.*

"I will strike a deal with you, sweet vixen. Here's my wager. Within four weeks you will invite me inside your body. If you do not, I will set you free."

Other *Leisure* books by Connie Mason:

ICE & RAPTURE
LOVE ME WITH FURY
SHADOW WALKER
FLAME
PURE TEMPTATION
THE LION'S BRIDE
SIERRA
WIND RIDER
TEARS LIKE RAIN
TREASURES OF THE HEART
A PROMISE OF THUNDER
BRAVE LAND, BRAVE LOVE
WILD LAND, WILD LOVE
BOLD LAND, BOLD LOVE
TEMPT THE DEVIL
FOR HONOR'S SAKE
BEYOND THE HORIZON
TENDER FURY
CARESS AND CONQUER
PROMISED SPLENDOR
MY LADY VIXEN
DESERT ECSTASY
WILD IS MY HEART

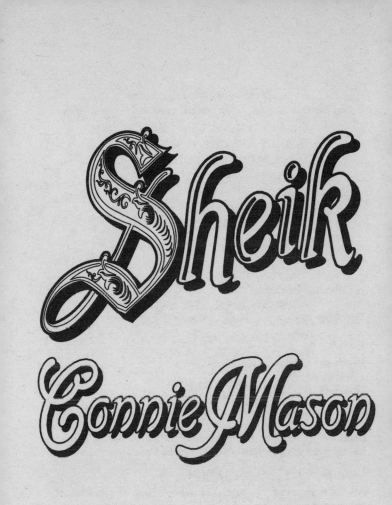

Sheik

Connie Mason

LEISURE BOOKS NEW YORK CITY

To my agent Natasha Kern.
You deserve a dedication for all your help and support.

A LEISURE BOOK®

December 1997

Published by

Dorchester Publishing Co., Inc.
276 Fifth Avenue
New York, NY 10001

ISBN 0-8439-4328-9

The name "Leisure Books" and the stylized "L" with design are trademarks of Dorchester Publishing Co., Inc.

Printed in the United States of America.

Prologue

Morocco, 1673

Sheik Jamal abd Thabit strode down the gang-plank of his pirate ship, *Plunderer*, and surveyed the amphitheater of hills rising above the great port city of Tangier. He was pleased to be home again after a year-long voyage to visit his mother in England. Jamal was not pleased, however, upon stepping ashore, to find himself quickly surrounded by a substantial number of Sultan Moulay Ishmail's soldiers.

"What is the meaning of this?" Jamal challenged with quiet authority. Those who knew Jamal best had learned to tread cautiously whenever the sheik used that coldly menacing, hushed tone of voice. "Am I under arrest?"

A large man whose skin glistened like polished

ebony stepped forward. "You are not under arrest, Sheik Jamal. Our great sultan, Moulay Ishmail, requests your presence immediately."

Jamal's dark gaze settled disconcertingly on the sultan's captain, whom he knew well. Ishmail's army consisted of over fifty thousand captured African slaves. His soldiers were renowned for their fierce loyalty to the sultan, their strength, and their fighting skills.

"I have just this minute stepped ashore after a long voyage, Captain Hasdai. I must first see to the unloading of my ship. Can this not wait?"

"You bring plunder?" Hasdai asked.

"Enough to satisfy even the sultan. I encountered three Spanish galleons, two off the shores of Portugal and one in the Strait of Gibraltar. All riding low in the water and rich with treasure. The sultan will receive his fair share."

"My instructions are to bring you to the royal city of Meknes immediately. Much has occurred during your absence and the sultan has need of your services."

Jamal thought of his luxurious white marble palace located just west of Meknes in a lush oasis he called Paradise. He hadn't seen his home in over a year. He closed his eyes and visualized the walled palace, the verdant gardens, the spring-fed lake whose clear blue water sparkled like a million diamonds. He pictured his concubines eagerly awaiting his return and was suddenly very angry at the sultan for demanding his presence.

"Tell the sultan I will come as soon as I can."

"You will come now." Hasdai was implacable;

he'd had his orders and to fail meant death. Sultan Ishmail was a man one did not cross. Mean-spirited and moody, Ishmail expected instant obedience from his slaves.

Jamal knew when to give in graciously. "Allow me time to change into my robes and issue orders for the transportation of my goods to paradise." Without waiting for a reply, he spun on his heel and returned to his ship.

Haroun, Jamal's lieutenant and the most trusted of all his men, met him on the quarter-deck. "What's amiss, Jamal?"

Jamal's dark brows knotted together in a frown. "My presence is requested in Meknes immediately. You know how the plunder is to be divided. See that the sultan's share is sent by caravan to Meknes immediately and that my share is delivered to paradise and stored in my vault. Divide the rest among the crew. Await my return at Paradise. I will notify you if I have need of my men-at-arms."

"It will be done as you say, my lord."

Twenty minutes later, Jamal strode down the gangplank to rejoin Captain Hasdai and his men. He had shed his European garb, consisting of tight trousers, linen shirt and waistcoat, in favor of a flowing white robe referred to as a *djellaba*, loose pantaloons and a shirt that laced at the neck. His thick, slightly curly dark hair was covered by a white turban.

"The sultan wishes to present you with a horse," Hasdai said as one of his men appeared, leading a pure black Arabian stallion. "He is called Kacem, the swift one. He is spirited but the sultan trusts you will be able to handle him."

Jamal eyed the prancing horse with relish. It was indeed a generous gift. Whatever the sultan wished of him must be important for Moulay Ishmail to part with such a fine animal. The tooled leather saddle was magnificent, as were the harness and reins studded with a dazzling assortment of precious gems.

Kacem snorted and pranced as Jamal mounted, flinging his head from side to side, but Jamal was equal to the task, and he quickly brought the horse under control. Hasdai eyed the horse warily, backing his own sturdy animal a good distance from the Arabian, whose wild-eyed snorting and stomping frightened his mild-mannered gelding.

Moments later, Jamal dug his heels into Kacem's flanks, leaving Hasdai and his men in his dust. His laughter reverberated behind him, earning smiles from his men. Most had been with Jamal long enough to respect his wild nature, his utter disregard for danger, his arrogance and his occasional ruthlessness. They also knew him to be fiercely loyal and unfailingly honest, and forgave him some of his harsher qualities.

With the sultan's army at his heels, Jamal entered the imperial city of Meknes. Passing through the triple protective wall, he entered the *medina*. Wending his way through the narrow streets of the old city to the imperial palace in the *Kasbah*, Jamal took time to savor the sights and sounds of the marketplace. Men playing drums, tambourines and flutes created magic sounds that he had missed these past months. Food cooking on braziers made his mouth water for spicy native fare, and he stopped to laugh at the antics of monkeys riding their masters' shoulders. How he had missed all this during his sojourn in England.

He entered the palace grounds through the *Bab Berdaine,* a gate of magnificent proportions. Captain Hasdai was beside him as he rode past Moulay Ishmail's granaries and the Christian prison where European captives, who worked on the fortifications, lived in a vast underground space. He did not pause to admire the fine mosques or elaborate gardens as he dismounted and passed beneath the carved and gilded entranceway into the palace.

"This way, Sheik," Hasdai said, leading Jamal through spacious rooms and long corridors, past guards standing at attention and supplicants waiting to see the sultan.

Jamal had been in the palace enough times to know that he was being taken to the sultan's private chambers instead of to the Hall of the Sultanate, where most business was conducted. His boot-heels clicked loudly against cool marble floors as he was ushered past tall Negro guards into the sultan's sanctuary.

Moulay Ishmail, a short, solidly built man of middle years with sharp features and a thick black beard, sat on a cushion surrounded by a bevy of beautiful women. His numerous wives and concubines were said to be among the loveliest women found anywhere in the world. Each was unique in her own way. Their skin tones ranged from milky white to ebony. But it was the sultan himself upon whom Jamal focused his attention.

"Ah, Sheik Jamal, you have arrived at last," Moulay Ishmail said, motioning him forward.

Jamal approached the throne, made his obeisance and asked, "Why have I been summoned without so much as an explanation? I had to leave the unloading of my ship to my men in order to comply with your demand. Could this not wait?"

Had Ishmail not been in desperate need of Jamal's help he would have been offended by his abrupt manner. But Jamal was a powerful sheik, a title inherited from his late father, and a faithful subject of Islam and the sultan. Though he carried the foreign blood of his English mother, he followed the teachings of Allah and was valued by Ishmail as an ally.

Jamal's activities on the high seas provided Ishmail with much-needed revenue. His escapades as a Barbary pirate were legendary. Ishmail had no reason to doubt or question Jamal's loyalty.

"I've been anxiously awaiting your return," the sultan said sulkily. "I need you, Jamal. The Berber *cadi*, Youssef Abu Selim, is making a pauper of me. He and his warriors attack every caravan going in and out of Meknes, then run to their walled fortresses in the Rif mountains to escape my army. In the meantime, I'm losing valuable revenue."

"The Berbers have been a thorn in the side of every sultan and caliph since the Arabs conquered their country," Jamal said. "Meknes once belonged to them. The city was named after the

Meknassa, the great Berber tribe that founded it. They want their territory returned to them. My own father lost his life fighting Berbers in your behalf."

With a solemn nod of his head the sultan acknowledged Jamal's loss. "We will take some refreshment while we discuss this matter. Leave us," he ordered his women. They scurried away, eying the handsome sheik with admiration as they backed out of the room.

Jamal sat cross-legged on a cushion facing the sultan as a servant brought a tray of honey cakes and set it between them. Then an old man shuffled in, bringing the charcoal, brazier and kettles necessary to brew fresh mint tea. After the elaborate ceremony ended, he filled tiny cups with the fragrant brew and bowed himself out of the room.

Ishmail sipped cautiously of the hot tea, then asked, "How did you find your mother?"

"In good health. She still misses my father."

"Is she as beautiful as I remember?"

"She grows lovelier with age. But you didn't call me here to discuss my mother."

"Indeed not. I know you hold no love for Berbers. That is why I chose you to help conquer them. I want you to capture the Berber *cadi* Youssef for me. You are cunning and experienced, just the kind of man I need to bring him to heel. My coffers grow empty while Youssef and his tribesmen grow rich."

"The Berbers have waged war against you for years," Jamal contended. "They resent the high taxes you levy on them. And they want their city back. If all the separate tribes banded together into one fighting unit they might succeed in recapturing their land. Fortunately, they fight in small bands."

"I'm obliged to expend time and money to keep them in line, when my energies could be better directed to enrich the lives of my people and establish trade with foreigners. Youssef Abu Selim must be destroyed. He is the chieftain. Without the *cadi*, his people will be left leaderless and without direction."

"I've yet to visit my home or ease myself with my women," Jamal complained. "My voyage has been a long one. Can this not wait?"

"Your women can wait but I cannot," Ishmail said. "You will be amply rewarded if you undertake this mission."

"I don't need your money. I have enough of my own. The three Spanish galleons that crossed my path were heavy with gold and plate. Your share will arrive in Meknes by caravan."

"Ah," Ishmail said, his black eyes glowing. "A rich caravan, you say? Youssef will be unable to resist so tempting a prize. My army is at your disposal, Jamal. If you cannot bring me Youssef's head, then find a way to stop him from attacking my caravans."

Chapter One

Beautiful as the sun and stars, Zara sat slim and tall atop her sleek racing camel, the distinctive blue robes of her people billowing about her supple form. As resilient as the stark brown Rif mountains, Zara was a proud example of the wild desert warriors known as the Blue Men. She possessed the heart of a lion, the soul of a staunch Berber freedom fighter, and the soft, rounded body of a woman.

Flanked by her father, Youssef, the *cadi* of their tribe, and her betrothed, Sayed, the chieftain's lieutenant, Zara fixed her bright green eyes intently on the caravan's progress as it slowly snaked through the winding trail below them. Against a backdrop of snow-capped mountains, the caravan traveled toward the imperial city of Meknes.

"There it is, Father," Zara noted excitedly. "It has to be the caravan carrying the pirate's tribute to the sultan, just as our spy told us."

Youssef, a darkly handsome man still in his prime at forty, smiled indulgently at his daughter's impatience. It was ever thus with his impetuous daughter. Zara, his golden-haired beauty, had ridden at his side since attaining the age of thirteen, and now, at twenty, she was as fierce and eager for battle as any of his seasoned warriors.

"Caution, daughter," Youssef warned. "Our success has always depended upon our being more cunning than our enemy. We must not act rashly."

"Heed the *cadi*, Zara," Sayed advised. "If our spy was right about the rich cargo, the rewards will be worth the wait. The pirate's plunder will provide our people with the means to continue our fight."

Zara quelled her eagerness with difficulty. Even her camel sensed her enthusiasm as he shifted restlessly beneath her. Zara pulled back on the reins, keeping her rapt gaze upon the caravan's progress.

"Nothing seems amiss, Father," Zara said as she glanced behind her at her tribesmen. Garbed in blue robes that had stained their skins the same hue as their robes, the Blue Men were armed to the teeth and eager for battle. "The men but await your signal."

Youssef and Sayed exchanged silent nods. Then Youssef raised his scimitar and brought it slashing downward. The signal sent the band of

16

fierce warriors racing down the mountainside toward the hapless caravan, brandishing scimitars and lances, their bloodcurdling cries a frightening forecast of doom.

"They come," Captain Hasdai said with relish.

"Mount!" Jamal ordered as he leapt upon Kacem's back. One hundred of the sultan's fiercest warriors reacted instantly to Jamal's order, eager to engage the Berber menace in battle.

No stranger to hand-to-hand combat, Jamal waited until the Blue Men were nearly upon the caravan to signal the attack. Had he given the signal a second earlier, the Berbers would have had time to retreat. The sultan's orders had been specific. He wanted Youssef dead and the Berber forces destroyed.

Kacem charged down the hillside toward the caravan, as eager for battle as his master.

Adrenalin surged through Zara. A heady rush of blood pumped through her veins. The scent of victory filled her nostrils. Actual fighting rarely occurred during an attack. Camel drivers were notorious cowards, unwilling to fight to protect the sultan's goods. The few soldiers sent along for protection usually broke ranks and ran when they saw the fierce Blue Men, mounted upon their racing camels and wielding their scimitars. Zara noted with satisfaction that this caravan appeared even less protected than most. Only six soldiers trailed behind the camels.

Racing neck and neck with Youssef and Sayed, Zara was confused when suddenly Youssef brought his animal to a skidding halt.

"Wait, daughter!" Youssef cried, scenting the danger that Zara failed to see. His warning came too late. By the time Youssef issued his warning, Jamal and his army were already upon them. They were vastly outnumbered; there was no escape for Youssef.

Youssef's first concern was for his beloved child. Though she had ridden with him countless times in the past, Youssef knew this was no simple taking of a caravan. This was an ambush. Deaths would occur, and he feared for Zara's life. "Ride, Zara, ride quickly!"

The unexpected resistance stunned Zara. Her father, Sayed and the Blue Men were already engaged in fierce battle with the sultan's soldiers. She heard her father's warning but did not heed it. How could she when her loved ones were fighting for their lives? Suddenly she saw a white-robed man on a midnight black stallion riding toward her father. Youssef's back was toward the man; he was unaware of his danger. Zara acted without thinking; her father's life was in peril and she had to save him.

Reacting instinctively, she rode her camel directly in the path of her father's enemy, thwarting the attack and allowing Youssef precious time to escape. Youssef's face convulsed in horror when he saw Zara riding into the middle of the fray. Fearing for his daughter's life, Youssef gave the signal for retreat. Though a call for retreat was rare, the Blue Men broke ranks, melting away into the surrounding mountains.

Jamal realized what was happening and spit

out an oath. "By Allah's beard, don't let them get away!"

Sheltered between Youssef and Sayed, Zara raced toward the protection of the mountains and their walled fortress. She heard the clamor of their pursuers and dared a glance over her shoulder. What she saw froze the blood in her veins.

A Negro soldier had managed to disable Sayed's camel by slashing the tendons in his hind leg. Sayed was tossed to the ground and the soldier leaped upon him before he gained his wits. The fight was ferocious but short. Through a red haze Zara saw the upward swing of the soldier's scimitar and its downward slash toward Sayed. Sayed was cut down unmercifully.

Zara let out a keening wail and her mind went blank, too filled with rage to think clearly. Sayed was dying! She couldn't let him die alone. Swinging her camel around, she raced back to her betrothed and leaped off the animal's back before he came to a full stop, landing hard. Gaining her feet, she gripped her scimitar and rushed at the soldier who had cut down Sayed.

Youssef, thinking both his daughter and Sayed were behind him, had no idea what was happening. With an army hard on his heels, he rode into the mountains with every expectation that Zara and Sayed would join him at their secret meeting place. Horses were no match for their superior racing camels, and he soon outdistanced the soldiers.

Jamal saw the Blue Man fall beneath Hasdai's scimitar, saw his companion ride to his defense, and couldn't help admiring the heroic act, rash though it might be. Jamal recognized the slim Berber as the same one who had ridden to the defense of the *cadi*. The courageous Blue Man had deprived Jamal of presenting the sultan with the head of his enemy.

Zara saw at a glance that Sayed was very close to death. Agilely ducking the soldier's blade, she threw herself upon Sayed, pleading with him not to die, willing her own life into him. The soldier snarled out a curse and raised his scimitar high above Zara's head. But Zara was beyond caring. Her childhood friend lay dying and she wouldn't leave him now, even if it meant her own life.

Something about that selfless act deeply touched Jamal. Racing toward the hapless Berber, Jamal ordered Hasdai to hold. Hasdai reacted seconds too late; his scimitar had already begun its downward swing. At the last moment he managed to pull back, but still dealt Zara a stunning blow to the back of her head with the flat of his blade.

Zara saw the blade swing toward her and placed her soul in Allah's hands. The blow she received, though not mortal, sent her spinning into oblivion.

Jamal dismounted and stared down at the stricken Berber. A strange feeling of destiny sent a shiver sliding down his spine. Yet he saw nothing unusual about the man. Slimmer than normal, perhaps, not quite as brawny as his comrades, he seemed much too fragile for the type of uncommon courage he'd displayed in defense of his comrades. Curiosity brought him to his knees beside the unconscious Blue Man, who sprawled across the body of his dead comrade. None too gently, Jamal flipped Zara over onto her back.

"He's naught but a bare-faced youth!" Jamal exclaimed upon close examination of the Berber's beardless countenance. His skin was fair and as flawless as that of a newborn babe. His eyebrows were the color of honey and finely arched; his lips were too full and lush to be considered masculine. His chin came to a delicate point below high, sculpted cheekbones. Jamal spied a strand of honey blond hair escaping from his headdress and had a strong suspicion that the Berber wasn't what he seemed. If Jamal wasn't mistaken, a woman's body was hidden beneath the blue robes.

Like many Berbers, who had emigrated to Africa from northern climes, Zara's Germanic heritage was evident in her fair skin, blond hair and finely chiseled features. Still unable to believe that a woman of such rare beauty rode with the fierce Berbers, Jamal needed to convince himself that his eyes weren't deceiving him. Reaching beneath her robes, he clasped a hand around a soft, unfettered breast, his fingers exploring its size and shape. He smiled and squeezed gently, noting that the firm mound was exactly the right size to fill his hand. He ventured further and found the hard, jutting nipple, sweetly erect and very much to his liking. He closed his eyes, imagining how perfectly it would fill his mouth. How delicious it would taste.

Heat. Zara awoke to a burning sensation that

had nothing to do with her aching head. It took a few seconds to realize she was being groped. Her eyes flew open, and she gasped when she saw a white-robed devil bending over her, his dark, sultry eyes smoldering with blatant sensuality.

The breath hissed through her teeth. "Take your hands off me, murderer!"

Jamal's searching hand stilled. "Ah, beauty awakens." His hand withdrew reluctantly as he stared into a pair of angry green eyes. "Who are you? How is it that a woman is riding with the Blue Men?"

Zara touched her head and groaned. She was surprised to find herself alive. She tried to rise and with difficulty managed to push herself to her elbows. Her gaze fell upon her fallen betrothed, sprawled beside her in the dirt, his life's blood draining upon the arid brown earth. She tried to crawl to him but Jamal held her back.

"He's dead."

"Fiend! Son of an ass! Camel dung! Sayed was too good a man to die like this."

Jamal frowned. He had no idea why this woman's friendship with the dead man should bother him. "What was he to you?"

"My betrothed. You've killed him!" She tried to grasp her blade, which lay just beyond her reach, but Jamal's booted foot clamped her wrist to the ground.

"I've killed many men, but not this one. Your betrothed knew the consequences when he attacked the sultan's caravan. Who are you? Your man was remiss in his duty toward you. Women don't ride with warriors."

Zara bristled with indignation. "Perhaps Arab women don't, but I am a Berber. Sayed couldn't stop me. Only the *cadi* has that kind of power, and my father was tolerant of my wish to accompany him."

Jamal went still, digesting Zara's words. Then he smiled. It wasn't a pretty smile. "Praise Allah for my good fortune. It appears I have captured Youssef's daughter."

Zara realized her mistake too late. By revealing her identity she had placed both herself and her father in grave danger. Her capture would likely bring Youssef running to her defense, and that could prove fatal. Her captor seemed too intelligent to accept a lie, so she didn't insult him by denying her identity.

"I am Princess Zara, daughter of the *cadi*, Youssef. Who are you?"

Stunned by her boldness, Jamal stared at her. Arab women never went out in public unveiled, or spoke to a man with such daring. But then, Berber women followed none of the rules that Arab men demanded that their wives, daughters and concubines obey. Finding his tongue, he said, "I am Sheik Jamal, loyal subject of Allah and the sultan. And you, Princess, are my captive."

Grasping her hand, he hauled her to her feet, surprised to find her so tall and lissome. Though he was much taller, she reached his chin. By contrast, Arab women were small and inclined to plumpness. Arab men liked their women round, curvaceous and submissive. This feisty barb-tongued Berber princess possessed none of those qualities; she probably didn't know how to be

23

submissive. Nevertheless, there was no mistaking her femininity. His questing hand had discovered a soft woman beneath her concealing blue robes.

Once on her feet, Zara swayed dizzily. Her head felt like a large melon about to explode. Recognizing her distress, Jamal swung her up into his arms.

Despite her injury, Zara resisted wildly. "No! You can't leave Sayed for the wild animals to devour! I won't let you."

Zara hated to display weakness before the arrogant sheik but she couldn't help herself. Tears welled in her eyes and spilled down her cheeks. She felt the wetness upon her face and blinked in dismay.

Handsome and brave, Sayed had been her best friend and protector for as long as she could remember. They would have already been married had she not delayed the wedding so that she might ride with her father a while longer. She had known that once she married, Sayed would have insisted that she remain in the village with the other women. And once she conceived his child, there would be no more riding with the men.

Tears were the last thing Jamal expected from this haughty princess. Then he recalled that the dead man was her betrothed and surprised himself by relenting.

"I will see that the dead are buried in a common grave."

Zara wanted time to grieve for Sayed, time to sit beside him and whisper her good-byes, but she would not beg favors from this arrogant Arab sheik. Once her people were in power again, she would make sure that Sheik Jamal received just punishment.

Zara's thoughts were interrupted when Captain Hasdai appeared to report on the fleeing Berbers. Since Zara saw no prisoners, she assumed her father had escaped. Hasdai's report confirmed her belief.

Hasdai spoke to Jamal but his gaze was on Zara, who still rested in Jamal's arms. "They all escaped, my lord, including Youssef."

"We haven't lost the day, Captain. The sultan's caravan is intact and his daughter is my captive."

"His daughter!" Hasdai's gaze swept over Zara with profound interest. Then he smiled. "The sultan will be pleased. Do we return now?"

"Aye, we return to Meknes. Leave enough men behind to bury the dead and collect the wounded."

"Let me remain behind with Sayed!" Zara begged, forgetting her pride. "I wish to mourn him."

Jamal had shown all the mercy he was capable of. After Hasdai hurried off to convey the sheik's orders, Jamal flung Zara atop his horse and mounted behind her. With one hand on the reins and the other pressing her tightly against him, he guided the prancing Kacem toward Meknes.

The warmth of Zara's slim body, the curve of her supple waist beneath his hand, and the imprint of her slim hips against his groin, made Jamal blatantly aware of her soft femininity. His arm tightened around her, bringing her even closer against him.

Zara held herself stiffly away from the arrogant

sheik, the angle of her body and tilt of her head a clear indication of her utter contempt for him.

Could she be broken? Jamal wondered, amused by her defiance. He sincerely doubted it, but he would like to try. Zara was too proud and insolent for a woman. She needed to learn obedience, to be taught to submit to her master. Jamal frowned, recalling that the pleasure of using Zara's sweet body belonged to the sultan. With no small amount of envy, Jamal wished him joy of it.

When Zara finally went slack against him, Jamal realized she had either fallen asleep or lost consciousness. She had taken a nasty blow on the head and could have been more seriously injured than he'd realized. The stubborn female would never give him the satisfaction of knowing how badly she was hurt. Holding her upright against him, he put his spurs to Kacem.

Zara awoke some time later to the rolling gait of Jamal's mount, still an unwilling captive of his superior strength. Allah forgive her, but she could kill him without a qualm for what he'd done this day. She glared at him over her shoulder and said, "You're holding me too tightly!"

He merely smiled and splayed his hand over her stomach so that the pad of his thumb rubbed back and forth against the soft underside of her breast.

"Son of a goat! Braying ass! You have no right to touch me."

"I have every right. You are my captive." That statement left a sour taste in his mouth. Technically, Princess Zara belonged to the sultan. She was not his.

What would Moulay Ishmail do with her? he wondered. Make her a part of his harem? He already had more women than he knew what to do with. Ishmail was a shrewd man; perhaps he would use her as bait to capture her father. Her life wouldn't be easy as Ishmail's prisoner. The sultan was an exceptionally cruel and vindictive man.

Zara dared another glance over her shoulder at Jamal. He appeared to be preoccupied with his own thoughts, and she took a moment to study him. His hair was concealed by a white turban, but judging by the color of his dark brows and lashes, she supposed it was dark also. His skin was more bronze than swarthy, and she suspected the dark color was due to the sun and was not his natural skin tone. His eyes were dark and impenetrable, not the murky brown of mud but the pure black of a desert night.

Her silent contemplation of his face at an end, Zara dwelled briefly on Jamal's other attributes, those she couldn't see but could feel. He was uncommonly strong; she could feel his strength in the hardness of his chest and thighs pressing against her, and in his hand splayed against her, restraining her struggling with such ease. He controlled his spirited mount with one hand upon the reins, as if born to the saddle. Sheik Jamal was a man to be reckoned with, Zara decided. She would need to employ cunning and guile in order to escape him, but, Allah willing, she would escape.

They rode across towering brown hills, through forests of mimosa, cork and olive trees, stopping briefly at a water hole to refill their goatskin water bags. Zara drank greedily when offered water, and accepted a handful of olives and a hunk of goat cheese from Jamal. Then they rode on, until darkness claimed the land and Jamal called a halt. A fire was quickly built to brew mint tea. Again they ate sparingly of olives, bread and cheese they carried with them, washing the food down with refreshing mint tea. Then Jamal placed his blanket on the ground and lay down, indicating that Zara was to lie beside him.

Nights were cold despite the sizzling heat of the day, and Zara would have welcomed the warmth of a blanket, but she neither trusted nor liked Jamal and wondered what mischief he intended for her this night.

"Come, Zara, lie down beside me. I'm tired, and keeping you beside me tonight is the only way I can be sure you won't escape."

"Your touch disgusts me," Zara said with a shiver. " 'Tis enough I'm forced to ride with you. I won't lie with you."

"Would you rather be bound hand and foot and made to sleep on the cold ground?"

"Aye, if it meant I wouldn't have to endure your hands on me."

Jamal's eyes narrowed dangerously. "Did you enjoy Sayed's hands on you?"

The breath hissed from her lungs. "Don't you dare compare yourself with Sayed. Aye, I very much enjoyed his hands on me."

"I understand that Berber women are bound by

28

few restrictions. An Arab man would slay his bride if she came to him without a hymen. How many men have you taken between your sweet thighs, Zara?"

"Do not judge me, prince of donkeys," Zara declared. "Berber women are free to love where they will. How many concubines do you have to ease your nights? How many love slaves do you keep in your household? I will be no man's slave. Berber women choose the men with whom they wish to share their bodies."

Jamal's mouth thinned. Never had he heard a woman speak so openly or with such passion. Zara's words shook the very foundations of Islamic teachings. In the Arab world women were taught to be obedient and submissive to men. Allah had placed women on earth for men's pleasure, and to bear their children. They lived in harems apart from males and covered their faces discreetly when they appeared in public. Their purpose in life was to pleasure their masters, and some, particularly concubines, were highly skilled in such arts. They did very little except indulge themselves with food and sweets and enjoy the luxuries provided by their husbands or masters.

Of course, his own mother had been an exception to the rule, Jamal reflected. His father had emptied his harem at her request and taken no other concubines or wives after she came to him as a young English captive. They had shared true love, and his father had desired no other woman. After his father's death at the hands of Berbers, his mother was free to do as she pleased. His father had willed it so. Lady Eloise had chosen to return to her people in England. Jamal had elected to remain in his native Morocco, sailing to England frequently to visit his mother.

Jamal felt a modicum of pity for the rebellious girl standing before him. But pity was not an emotion he dared to entertain. The sultan would have his head if he allowed Zara to escape. "Do you refuse to lie beside me?" he asked harshly.

"Aye," Zara said, tossing her head defiantly.

"So be it." Jamal called Hasdai to attend him. The captain appeared almost instantly.

"What can I do for you, Sheik?"

"Princess Zara has expressed a desire to sleep on the cold ground, bound hand and foot so she can't escape. See that her wishes are granted."

Grasping her arm none too gently, Hasdai pushed Zara to the ground and called for a rope. It was provided moments later and Hasdai seemed to derive great pleasure in binding Zara's wrists and ankles, then winding the rope ends around her slim waist and tying the ends securely behind her back. When he finished, he stepped back and looked inquiringly at Jamal.

"That will be all, Hasdai. Set the guard and see that the rest of the men settle down for the night.

"Are you comfortable, Princess?" Jamal asked with bland indifference. If she would but admit to her discomfort, Jamal would release her immediately. He wasn't cruel by nature and he didn't like to see women suffer.

Zara bared her teeth at him. "As comfortable as I can be amidst an army of jackals."

"Then I wish you pleasant dreams, Princess,"

Jamal said, rolling up in the blanket and facing away from her.

Cursing beneath her breath, Zara tried to squirm into a comfortable position, but the rocky soil beneath her became her enemy. Each hard pebble, every jagged twig, dug into her tender flesh despite the thick robes protecting her. And the cold! Blessed Allah, it seeped into her bones until she ached. She glanced over at Jamal lying a short distance away and wished him to Hades. Eventually, however, she fell into a fitful sleep.

Jamal awoke during the night feeling as if his back were against a blazing brazier. Rolling over, he found soft womanly curves planted against him, absorbing his heat. He smiled grimly. Prideful as the woman was, she had unknowingly gravitated toward the warmth of his body in her sleep. Surrendering to the dictates of his flesh, he pulled her against him, covered them both with the blanket and closed his arms around her.

Zara awakened and sighed, lulled by warmth and the pleasing scent that filled her nostrils. She tried to stretch, found she could not move her arms and legs, and frowned, suddenly recalling everything that had happened the previous day. Sayed was dead and she was the prisoner of Sheik Jamal. To make matters worse, she was being held snugly against his large body, the scent of him surrounding her, making her giddy.

Zara surged upright, dragging the blanket from Jamal. He opened his eyes and stared at her. "Good morning. Have I overslept?"

A sweeping glance around their campsite assured him that the soldiers had not yet begun to stir.

"How did I get here when I refused to lie beside you?"

He gave her a smug smile. "You must have changed your mind."

"Never! You're the enemy. I spit in your eye. I spit in the sultan's eye."

He clapped a hand over her mouth. His voice was cold and emotionless. "I wouldn't try it if I were you. The sultan isn't as lenient as I. I might not demand your head for such an insult, but the sultan would. Now, will you keep a civil tongue or must I gag as well as bind you?"

Zara gulped convulsively. She wasn't afraid of the arrogant sheik but at this point it might pay to practice caution, something she knew little about, or so her father had claimed. She nodded her head and he freed her mouth.

"That's more like it." He pulled her to her feet and untied her hands and feet. "There are some trees yonder, if you have need of them."

Zara nodded vigorously. Her bladder was about to burst. She started to walk toward the trees, then stopped abruptly when she found Jamal falling in beside her.

"Where are you going?"

"With you, of course, unless you'd like one of Hasdai's men to accompany you."

"There's no need."

Jamal grew weary of Zara's belligerent attitude and told her so. "You would do well to obey me. Your life depends upon my good will."

Once again Zara employed caution and withheld her sharp retort as she continued walking toward the trees Jamal had indicated.

"I'll wait here," Jamal said as he leaned against a thick tree trunk. "Hurry, or I'll come after you."

Zara did as she was told, wishing for a long, leisurely bath and something to eat other than olives and cheese. With Jamal and an army around her, there was virtually no way she could escape. She had to trust her father and his people to rescue her. And if that wasn't possible, she'd accept Allah's will with stoic resignation.

"It's about time," Jamal complained when Zara came out from behind a tree. "The men are anxious to be off and I am eager to go home. I've been away a very long time. If not for the sultan and his need to rid the world of the Berber horde I would be riding upon my own land, enjoying my women and eating food fit for a king."

"I pity your women," Zara said with a hint of contempt.

Jamal stared at her. "Why do you say that?"

"Are they not confined to a harem? Do you not summon them into your exalted presence so that you may use their bodies to ease your lust?"

Her words were harsh and condemning and didn't sit well with him. Who was she to tell him what to do and what not to do with his women? Not that there were all that many of them. He kept only three concubines and an older woman to see to their needs. He spent so much time at sea that he saw no reason to fill his harem with women. Neglected women would only make trouble in his absence. But when he returned he happily availed himself of their lush young bodies. His women were cosseted and spoiled; they lacked nothing in the way of material comforts. If they were lonely in his absence, he tried to make it up to them by bringing them back expensive baubles.

"Did no one ever tell you that men punish their women for being viper-tongued? You speak too boldly for a woman."

"Berber women are allowed freedom to speak and act as they please. They show their unveiled faces and are not confined to harems."

"No wonder Berber women are so brazen," Jamal muttered, sliding Zara a look that conveyed his contempt. Allowing women that much freedom was dangerous.

When they reached the main camp, the men were already mounted and waiting for Jamal to return with his captive. Jamal tossed Zara atop his horse and leaped up behind her. Moments later they were racing toward the imperial city of Meknes.

Chapter Two

The *medina* teemed with throngs of noisy people
and animals as Jamal entered Meknes with the
sultan's soldiers. Holding Zara possessively
against him, he passed through the narrow
streets which led to the *Kasbah* and imperial palace, a mighty fortress built on the crest of a hill
overlooking the *medina*.

Zara gazed in awe at the wondrous sights and
sounds surrounding her. The *souk*, a central marketplace within the *medina*, was a kaleidoscope
of vivid colors and pleasing scents. Children and
adults alike were grouped around storytellers and
magicians while nearby, dancers practiced their
graceful movements and monkey trainers and
water sellers mixed freely with vendors hawking
fruits, vegetables and meats.

Having lived most of her life in her own village

high in the Rif mountains, Zara had never seen such a colorful mixture of sights and sounds. Then the call to prayer by the *muezzin* in his minaret brought people to a halt as they fell to their knees, facing Mecca, the holy city and birthplace of Allah. The *muezzin's* cry echoed over the city, his chant in praise of Allah and his works repeated over and over by the faithful. After prayers, the sultan's party continued on to the palace.

Zara feasted her eyes upon the sultan's exquisite gardens, stunned by their extravagant beauty. A profusion of every kind of flower grew in a precise pattern of vibrant colors. When they reached the palace door, Jamal lowered her to the ground and dismounted behind her. Moments later the door was opened by two palace guards dressed in striped pantaloons, short vests and capes. When Zara would have paused in the doorway to gawk at the ornate walls and ceilings held up by tall marble columns, Jamal urged her forward.

"Have you never been inside a palace before, Princess?"

"Not one like this," Zara admitted. "Perhaps I might have lived in such a dwelling if the Arabs hadn't stolen our cities."

"Come along, I'm sure the sultan has been advised of my arrival and is waiting for my report."

"Where are you taking me?"

"To the harem. You can eat and refresh yourself while I speak in private with the sultan."

Zara stopped in her tracks. "The harem? I have never been in a harem in my life and don't intend to go there now."

No sooner had Zara uttered those words than a plump Negro slave shuffled up to Jamal and bowed low. He wore robes of the finest silk and pointy shoes of soft leather. His face was round, smooth and unlined, and his expression was anything but servile.

"I am Assad, chief eunuch. I will take the slave to the harem and bring her forth when Moulay Ishmail summons her."

Zara's chin rose mutinously. "I won't go!"

Assad gave her a look of stunned disbelief. Such behavior from a woman was unheard of. "The lady needs to be taught proper conduct, my lord," Assad advised. "Have you impressed upon her the fact that the sultan will not allow such disrespect from a woman? He is not an easy man to deal with."

Jamal grasped Zara's arm, pulling her aside. "Assad is right. You must do as you're told and keep a civil tongue in your mouth. Moulay Ishmail is so enraged at your father, 'tis unlikely he'll show compassion to Youssef's daughter."

Zara swallowed her angry retort, realizing she would gain nothing by antagonizing the sultan's household. "I thought I was *your* captive."

Jamal gazed into her vivid green eyes and wished it were so. "Nay, you were never mine. I merely held you in the sultan's name. After I make my report I will leave you in his care and return to my oasis home. I am not the master of your fate."

"I will take my chances with the sultan," Zara said haughtily. She nodded at Assad. "I'm ready. Take me where you will."

Jamal watched her walk away, her head held high, her pointed little chin refusing to lower, and a shiver of dread passed through him. The stubborn little wench didn't realize the danger she was in. As angry as Ishmail was with her father, Jamal wouldn't give a fig for her future. If he could but gag her he might have a slim chance of saving her life, but the brazen Berber vixen would have her say no matter what. The sultan had no use for women with cutting tongues, and Jamal feared that the consequences would not be to Zara's liking.

Zara found the harem beyond anything she'd ever seen: floors covered with thick woolen carpets, so colorful they hurt her eyes, walls hung with silks and satins, divans upholstered in rich velvets. And women. Allah, the women were too numerous to count. Short, tall, fat, plump, slim, they were dressed in vivid peacock colors and pale pastels, flowing silks, satins and brocades.

Some women lounged on divans or sat on pillows upon the floor. Others were bathing naked in a sparkling pool in the center of the main room. Several attendants dressed in coarse robes bustled about, catering to the demands of their charges. Assad beckoned to an older woman and she hurried over to them.

"Badria is the mistress of the bath. She will see that you are refreshed and fed something before you appear before the sultan."

Zara and Badria eyed one another warily. Badria found her tongue first. "You wear the robes of a Berber warrior."

"Aye, I *am* a Berber warrior," Zara proudly admitted.

Suddenly Badria snatched away Zara's headdress, releasing a cascade of hair the color of corn silk that reached nearly to her waist. Badria gazed in mute admiration at the combination of oval green eyes, smooth golden skin and hair that shimmered like sunlight.

"I know of no warriors who look like you and I've lived a long time," Badria contended. "Who are you?"

"I am Princess Zara, daughter of the great *cadi* Youssef."

Badria's breath hissed through her teeth. "You're the Berber chieftain's daughter? Allah save us."

The harem wasn't so isolated from the world that Badria didn't know what was taking place outside the walls. There were numerous ways of finding out things. Eunuchs and slaves could always be bribed to bring back news of importance.

"I am hungry," Zara said boldly. "Bring me food."

The women lounging within earshot snickered at Zara's imperious manner while secretly admiring her bravado.

"You'll bathe first, then food," Badria said, wrinkling her nose as if sniffing something offensive. "You reek of camel dung and dirt. Take off your robes. I'll find you something decent to wear."

Zara was reluctant to remove the badge of her people. Once she shed the distinctive blue robes, she would be just another woman. "You may shake the dust from my robes but I will wear them to meet the sultan."

"You're a foolish young woman," Badria contended. "Appearing before the sultan dressed like a man will surely anger him. If you wish to impress him—"

"I have no desire to impress the sultan," Zara claimed, interrupting Badria in mid-sentence. "I am Princess Zara, daughter of Youssef. I'm well aware of my fate. Do not badger me, mistress. I will bathe and eat and face the sultan in my own clothing."

Never in all her years had Badria met a more obstinate creature. So be it, she thought, disgruntled. At least she'd tried to save the Berber vixen. Defying the Sultan was not wise.

Zara allowed Badria to disrobe her, paying little heed to the woman's gasp of shock and outrage when she noted that Zara's body hair had not been removed.

"What manner of men are Berbers that they allow their women to keep their body hair?" Badria sniffed. "I will personally see that you appear before the sultan as smooth as a newborn babe."

In that respect, Zara knew Berbers and Arabs agreed. Berber men like their women smooth, hairless and clean, but Zara had found little time of late to groom herself properly. Besides, no man had ever seen her undressed. Not even Sayed. The proper time and place had never arrived for them to consummate their love.

Zara shrugged. "If you wish, for all the good it will do either of us. Never let it be said that Princess Zara met her death with an unclean body."

Zara was led to the pool, trying not to feel self-conscious as the sultan's wives and concubines watched with avid interest. She ignored them as Badria scooped soft soap from a jar and spread it over her body. Then the bath mistress took a flat tool and scraped off the lather, removing both dirt and soap at the same time. Next, her arms, legs and groin were spread with a pale pink substance that when rinsed off left her skin smooth and hairless as a babe's. Then she immersed herself in the pool, sighing with pleasure as the warm, scented water soothed her body.

Badria washed Zara's hair, scrubbing and rinsing several times before she was satisfied. When Zara emerged from the pool, Badria dried her hair with silk until it glistened and shone like the purest sunlight. Then Badria robed Zara in a diaphanous dressing gown and sat her on a cushion before a small table. Moments later a slave brought in a tray and placed it before Zara.

Zara ate heartily of *couscous* cooked with lamb, peeled green figs, newly made yogurt, fresh bread, grapes and oranges. The beverage maker came with his brazier, charcoal and kettles and brewed mint tea, which Zara drank in copious amounts. She ate her fill, then sat back, replete. After such a meal she was ready to face anything, even arrogant Sheik Jamal.

Jamal was taken to the Hall of the Sultanate, where Moulay Ishmail awaited his report. He made his obeisance and waited for the sultan to speak.

"I trust you met with success." It was a statement rather than a question. The sultan did not accept failure.

"The caravan will reach the city gates intact before sundown tomorrow. We met the Berbers and turned them back. I left men behind to gather the wounded and protect the caravan from further attack."

"What of that jackal Youssef? Have I seen the last of him?"

"Youssef escaped, my lord sultan."

Ishmail rose angrily from his ornate throne of carved ebony inlaid with gold and precious gems. "You failed? Surely not, Jamal. I've never known you to fail. I cannot tolerate failure. If what you say is true, then Youssef will continue his raids. He will strike again and again."

Jamal smiled, not at all intimidated by Ishmail's anger. Other men might quail in their boots, but not Jamal. The sultan had come to depend upon the plunder from Jamal's pirating.

"I hope you'll forgive me when you see the gift I've brought you. My gift will stop Youssef from raiding your caravans and keep his people in their mountain fortress."

Ishmail sat down, eager now to listen. "What game do you play, Jamal? I'm thoroughly sick of the Berber raids upon my caravans. What wondrous gift have you brought me?"

"Youssef's daughter."

Ishmail's face grew mottled with rage. "His daughter? *His daughter?*" he repeated shrilly. "Of what use is a daughter to a man like Youssef? Had you brought me his son I would have given you half my kingdom."

42

"Hear me out, mighty sultan. Youssef has no living sons. His daughter rides at his side and is as fierce as any son. Youssef highly values Princess Zara. Let her be your weapon against her father."

Somewhat mollified, Ishmail mulled over Jamal's words. "I would like to see this princess upon whom Youssef dotes. I will judge her worth for myself before determining her use to me." He turned to a guard standing nearby. "Tell Assad to bring the Berber wench to me."

Jamal felt his heart slam against his chest. He had known this moment had to arrive but now he felt an unreasonable fear. Zara wasn't a woman to hold her tongue, and the sultan wasn't a man to condone insolence in a woman. Fireworks were bound to occur when the two met face to face. A fierce protectiveness toward Zara welled up in him, one that both surprised and annoyed him. He prayed that Allah would take pity and strike Zara mute.

Zara knew the moment she saw Assad enter the harem that he had come for her. She had already donned her pantaloons, shirt and blue robes in anticipation of her summons and was waiting for him. She thanked Badria for her care and followed the plump eunuch through the lush interior of the women's quarters into the marble and mosaic hallways beyond the guarded entrance.

Zara was taken directly to the Hall of the Sultanate, past a pair of fierce guards carrying scimitars and wearing short knives strapped to their upper arms. Zara dragged in a shaky breath, lifted her head proudly and stared straight ahead into the vast hall as she approached the throne. Her gaze found Jamal and she faltered. He seemed to be conveying a silent warning that she chose to ignore.

"The sultan is waiting," Assad said, giving her a little shove when her legs refused to move.

Zara stumbled inside the huge hall, righted herself and walked on wooden limbs toward the dais.

"That's far enough," Ishmail said when Zara reached Jamal's side. Then he waited for her to make her obeisance.

"Pay homage to your sultan," Jamal hissed into her ear when she boldly glared at the sultan and showed no sign of prostrating herself before him.

"I will bow before no tyrant," Zara contended. Despite her courageous words, her knees were knocking against one another.

Jamal suppressed a groan. Did the vixen not realize she was flirting with danger? Did her life mean so little to her? He could see that Ishmail was becoming incensed and decided to defuse the explosive situation. Catching Zara by the scruff of the neck, he pushed her to her knees and shoved her forehead to the carpeted floor, holding it there with the sole of his boot.

"What manner of female is this who insults my imperial person?" Ishmail thundered. "No respectable woman would dress like a man and refuse to pay homage to her master. Release the Berber wench, Jamal. I wish to speak with her."

Jamal's foot eased on Zara's neck and she leaped to her feet, sending Jamal a searing look that singed the air around him. Then she whirled to confront the sultan, her hands clenched at her sides, her gaze defiant.

"What is your name, lady?" Ishmail asked harshly.

"I am Princess Zara, daughter of the great Berber chieftain, Youssef," she said haughtily.

"Have you brothers?"

"Nay, none that lived past infancy."

"Sheik Jamal tells me you are well loved by your father. He says that you ride at his side and fight like a man."

"Sheik Jamal does not lie. I have ridden at my father's side since the age of thirteen."

Ishmail's probing gaze slide the length of Zara's body with uncommon interest. "I do not believe you are a real woman at all, but an aberration. Remove your clothing so that I may judge for myself."

Jamal suppressed a groan, waiting for the fireworks. He didn't have long to wait.

"It does not please me to remove my clothing," Zara said with quiet dignity.

"It does not please me to put up with your insolence," Ishmail roared. "I've had men drawn and quartered for lesser offenses. Either remove your clothing, Princess Zara, or I will have it ripped from you."

"Do as he says," Jamal urged quietly. "Your life rests within his hands."

Realizing Zara meant to disobey, Jamal helped matters along by stripping away her turban, releasing a bright cascade of blond tresses. The breath caught in Jamal's throat; he was utterly

45

captivated by the shimmering curtain of golden silk floating about her shoulders.

Equally intrigued, Ishmail couldn't wait to see more of this unlikely female warrior. "Continue," he said with a hint of impatience.

Zara stood still as a statue as Jamal peeled off her *djellaba*, refusing to help him or even acknowledge the affront to her dignity. When Jamal reached for the ties on her shirt, she winced but gave no other other sign of her distress.

The shirt was whisked over her head and arms and tossed aside. A collective gasp from those in the hall brought a tinge of pink to her cheeks and throat but no other outward display of emotion. When Jamal made no move to release the sash holding up her pantaloons, Zara dared to breathe again.

"So you *are* a woman," Ishmail said, his gaze fastened on her full breasts. He stepped down from his throne to examine Zara more closely.

For some unexplained reason Jamal wanted to tear Zara away when Ishmail reached out to test the weight and size of her breasts. Ishmail's hands didn't stop at Zara's breasts but continued downward, across her torso and flat stomach, lower still, gliding over the material of her pantaloons to thrust between her legs. Jamal was on the verge of doing something entirely reckless, like snatching Zara away from the sultan, but Zara made his intervention unnecessary.

Screwing up her face, she shot a wad of spittle into the sultan's face. "Son of a pig! Camel dung! Take your filthy hands off me!"

Blood rushed to Ishmail's dark face as he flung

his arm back and delivered a stunning blow to Zara's face, sending her flying. She landed in a heap at his feet.

"Seize the Berber she-devil!" he cried, wiping spittle from his face. "The spawn of a jackal deserves no mercy from me."

Immediately two guards rushed forth, dragging Zara to her feet between them. The right side of her face had turned red and was already beginning to swell from the sultan's blow.

Panic raced through Jamal. He'd feared that something like this would happen. He'd tried to warn Zara against defying Ishmail but she'd chosen not to heed him. He searched frantically for a way to save Zara from a terrible fate but could think of nothing.

"The Berber wench is beyond redemption," Ishmail declared. "She would disrupt my entire harem should I decide to use her body for my pleasure. She isn't worth the effort. Cut off her head and hang it from the wall for all to see," he ordered brusquely. "Word of her fate will reach her father, and when it does he will realize Moulay Ishmail will not tolerate treason."

The guards started to drag Zara from the hall.

"Wait!" Jamal cried, growing desperate. It had never occurred to him that Ishmail might kill the Berber princess. He had assumed that Ishmail would either enslave her or keep her for his bed. "You're making a mistake. Killing Zara will enrage Youssef. Presently the Berber tribes are not united, but killing the wench will surely bring them together in a common cause, and that could be disastrous for you. Think of the vast number

47

of Berbers scattered throughout the Rif and Atlas Mountains, and imagine them uniting under one leader."

"Perhaps you're right," Ishmail allowed as he halted Zara's progress from the hall with a wave of his hand. The guards obeyed instantly, dragging Zara back to the dais.

"Think carefully, my lord," Jamal intoned solemnly. "Spare the Berber wench. Keep her as a slave and make it known that her continued health depends on Youssef's obedience. Word will reach Youssef that his daughter will live only if he ceases his raids upon your caravans."

"Hummm," Ishmail said, rubbing his chin in contemplation. "I see what you mean, but I don't want the wench in my household. She has the body and face of an *houri* but she is a menace. She is undisciplined, brazen and defiant and would disrupt my entire household. She's too incorrigible to make a decent slave." Suddenly his face lit up. "I have it! I will give her to the lowest-ranking man residing within the *Kasbah*. She will become his slave, submissive to his every need. Is that not a clever solution, Jamal? If I recall, the Negro blacksmith is a huge giant of a man. He will do nicely for Zara.

"As long as Zara is kept alive, her father will cease his raiding," Ishmail continued. "Yet her defiance will be rewarded by having to submit to a man far beneath her in rank. I will make it known that Youssef's daughter is my captive, that her continued good health will depend upon Youssef's willingness to abide by my laws. All raids must cease immediately."

"You would give Princess Zara to Abdul?" Jamal asked, aghast. He knew the man well; he was an animal. A strong-willed woman like Zara wouldn't last a week with him.

"A perfect match, wouldn't you agree?" Ishmail said complacently.

"Slay me now," Zara cried. She had remained mute as long as she could. "I will become no man's slave!"

"Silence, lady, or you'll get your wish. Take her away and present her to Abdul with my good wishes," Ishmail told the guards.

"Wait!" Jamal demanded. "I have a better solution. Give the Berber wench to me. I have need of another slave."

Ishmail frowned as he mulled over Jamal's request. "Why do you wish to burden yourself with such a troublesome slave? Let Abdul tame her. Abdul is a better master than Youssef's daughter deserves."

"Youssef will demand proof that his daughter is not being mistreated before he agrees to stop his raids. Can you be certain Abdul won't kill Zara after she cuts him to pieces with her sharp tongue?" He shook his head. "Nay, I think not. Youssef has spies everywhere. He will know what is taking place."

"The princess has a magnificent body," Ishmail allowed. "Perhaps you can find some use for her. I can't be bothered with reluctant maidens, but you are young and vigorous and might enjoy the fight. Still . . . I will give her to you only if you promise to make her pay for defiling me with her spittle."

"Slay me and be done with it!" Zara spat.

Jamal sincerely wished he could gag Zara. Her mouth would be her undoing if she didn't shut up. "I will endeavor to teach Princess Zara humility, my lord, and administer discipline when necessary. As my slave, she will obey or suffer the consequences. For her affront to your person, she will toil in the stables for an indefinite period. She will rake dung alongside the stable slaves, sleep on straw and share their crude meals."

The sultan smiled. "That's a start, Jamal. Your haughty princess will soon learn who is master and who is slave. Once she is taught submission, she may prove useful in your bed, but I don't envy you that task."

"Then she is mine?" Jamal asked, concealing his pleasure. The sultan was a cruel and perverse man; one never knew where one stood with him.

"You were promised a reward for your service, Jamal. Consider the woman your prize. If you'd rather have gold, speak now and I will give the woman to Abdul."

Jamal had a niggling feeling that one day he might wish he'd taken gold instead of Zara, but some internal demon demanded that he not abandon the courageous princess. He knew he was biting off more than he could chew, that Zara was a troublesome female, but he looked forward with relish to the confrontation. Zara was a beauty worth taming and he was just the man to tame her.

"I would have the woman, my lord," Jamal said, sending Zara a look that warned her to silence.

"She's yours," Ishmail decreed. "Take her from

my sight, she offends me. If keeping her alive will prevent her father from plaguing me, then I am happy you are the one who must deal with her."

Caught between the restraining grip of Ishmail's guards, Zara sent Jamal a scathing look that spoke volumes about her feelings. Stable slave, indeed. Well, she'd prefer to muck camel dung than to let Jamal use her body. Besides, once her father learned of her fate, he'd not let her languish long in Jamal's stables. Youssef was resourceful; he'd find a way to free her from her onerous role as slave, and soon she'd be riding at his side, where she belonged.

Jamal snatched Zara's robe and shirt from the floor and wrapped them around her. "We're leaving immediately for Paradise," he said, hustling her from the hall.

"Paradise, ha!" Zara sneered. "Hades, you mean."

Before she could say anything further, Jamal scooped her into his arms and carried her away from the glowering sultan.

Chapter Three

Jamal carried Zara from the Hall of the Sulanate and into a nearby alcove, where they were hidden from the curious stares of guards, supplicants, merchants and servants milling about in the outer ward. Zara struggled to hold her robes about her as Jamal set her on her feet.

"Turn around while I get dressed," she demanded.

Jamal stared at her with smoldering eyes. "I've already seen your breasts and tested their firmness. They are exquisite."

Excitement shuddered through him as he recalled how smooth and pliant they had felt against his palms. He stared at her chest, his eyes glazed with lust. He felt himself harden when he saw a plump nipple peep out from between her spread fingers, but he knew this was neither the time nor place to explore his unaccountable need for the Berber vixen. Soon, he vowed to himself, he would know every luscious inch of Zara, daughter of Youssef.

"Get dressed," Jamal ordered in a voice made harsh with desire.

Realizing Jamal had no intention of turning his eyes from her, Zara presented her back and quickly pulled on her shirt, then her *djellaba*.

The elegant curve of her back was as sensually enticing as her breasts, Jamal mused as he made a visual exploration of the smooth expanse of her silken flesh. He couldn't wait to have her writhing beneath him, giving him untold pleasure. But he would give her pleasure, too. More pleasure than she had received from her Berber lover.

Once her body was decently covered, Jamal found he could breathe normally and think clearly again. He was surprised that the sight of Zara's nude body had such a profound effect on him. He was no stranger to a woman's body. He used his own concubines frequently and with great zeal. When he was sailing the high seas he put into ports often enough to slake his lust with prostitutes. Yet Zara excited him as few women had in more years than he cared to count.

He wanted her.

Zara read Jamal's mind as effectively as though he had spoken aloud. His expressive dark eyes were a mirror into his soul. Had they met under different circumstances, she might have been attracted to him. Whereas most Arab men wore thick, black beards, Jamal's face was smooth and golden rather than swarthy. His nose was straight, his forehead high, his chin square and determined. He was a man to make any girl's heart beat faster . . . any girl but her.

Jamal noted Zara's preoccupation with his face and grasped her arms, bringing her hard against him. "Do you like what you see, vixen? Without your betrothed to pleasure you, you'll be needing a man soon. Perhaps I shall make you wait," he said with typical male conceit. "Our joining will be all the sweeter for it. But if you find waiting is painful, you have but to tell me and I'll ease your suffering."

"Braying ass. Conceited dog," Zara hissed. "You are the last man I want in my bed."

"We shall see," Jamal said complacently. He stared at her lips, lush and red and enticing, so close he could see little drops of moisture clinging to their surface. He battled against the need to taste their sweet fullness, goaded by the heat that had been simmering inside him from the moment his hand had closed upon her soft breast. The battle was lost before it had even begun.

Zara realized a moment too late what Jamal intended. Grasping her head between his large hands, he held her steady as his mouth came down hard on hers. She opened her mouth to voice a protest and found it filled with the bold thrust of his tongue. She tensed, hands pressed against his shoulders. A strangled sob caught in her throat, suppressed by the fierceness of his kiss.

Driven by some insatiable need, Jamal cupped the twin moons of her buttocks, molding her against him. The rise of his manhood stirred against her and suddenly he needed more. Holding her with one hand, he pushed inside her clothing with the other to caress her breast, testing the fullness of it, palm rubbing over the nipple.

He shook with a desire so potent it convulsed the length of his body. He wanted her naked beneath him, open to him in all ways. He wanted to teach her all the erotic subtleties of loving he'd learned from his travels abroad. He wanted her as his love slave, obedient to his every whim.

He wanted her.

Suddenly aware of Zara's pounding fists against his chest, Jamal finally returned to his senses. He set her firmly from him. He would have the Berber wench but on his own terms. She needed to be taught submission; she had to learn to obey her master.

Jamal's kiss had shaken Zara more than she cared to admit. His hands upon her made her want things that could never be. She cursed herself for a fool. Poor Sayed was not yet cold in his grave and here she was allowing the enemy to take liberties she had never allowed her betrothed. What manner of man was Jamal to confuse her senses so? For a brief moment, while his tongue was plundering her mouth and his hands caressing her flesh, she had wondered what it would feel like to take this man inside her body, to let him plumb her most secret places.

Pure bliss, a perverse devil inside her whispered.

The thought was sobering.

"We're wasting time here," Jamal said harshly. How had the little vixen gotten under his skin so quickly? he wondered. Allah forbid if she ever found out how susceptible he was to her willowy charms. He must need a woman desperately to get so worked up over a viper-tongued seductress. His concubines would soon cure him of his obsession with Zara, he thought, eagerly looking forwared to his homecoming.

"My home lies two leagues west of Meknes," he told Zara. "We will leave immediately."

Zara was given a mount of her own, a pure white mare with a black star on her forehead. After riding camels most of her life, she found the gait of a horse less jarring and more restful. She was happy to leave the sultan's fortress behind but couldn't help worrying about her fate as Jamal's slave. She wouldn't mind working in the stables, if that was to be her lot. It was far better than having Jamal use her body for his pleasure. But after his amorous display in the palace, she was not so foolish as to believe he wouldn't take her whenever it pleased him. Her worst fear was that her unprincipled body would respond.

Sheik Jamal was far more experienced than she, and judging from her reaction to his kiss, he would wring a response from her whether she was willing or not.

They rode for nearly an hour before the sere brown landscape slowly gave way to palm and fig trees. A profusion of flowers and lush vegetation grew in abundance. Zara blinked, certain she was seeing a mirage when a huge body of water appeared ahead of her. But as they entered the vast oasis, Zara realized that the sparkling blue lake was no mirage. She gazed about in wonder. The oasis was huge, with a cluster of dwellings hugging the north shore of the lake. Jamal's palace was built on the south shore, sitting like a sparkling jewel amid verdant green vegetation. High, whitewashed walls surrounded the compound, and a bulb-shaped marble tower rose majestically from the center of the palace.

They passed through the *gate* into the compound itself. Beyond the tiled front courtyard Zara noted several other buildings. There were barracks to shelter Jamal's soldiers, a grainary, stables, servants' quarters and a separate kitchen.

Lush gardens of gardenias, camellias and Damascus roses sent perfumed scents wafting through the air. Beyond the house was an orchard that stretched to the edge of the oasis. A vineyard grew on one side of the stunning white marble palace.

"Welcome to Paradise," Jamal said as two stable slaves hurried forward to take their horses.

Zara merely sniffed, unwilling to admit her fascination with Jamal's grand home.

Haroun, Jamal's lieutenant, approached from the barracks, his face wreathed in a broad smile of welcome. He saluted and said, "Did all go well in Meknes? Your message told me little of the mission you were undertaking for the sultan. I should have been riding at your side."

"I had Ishmail's army at my disposal," Jamal said. "The sultan ordered me to capture the Berber *cadi* responsible for the raids upon his caravans. We set a trap, but the Berbers scattered into the hills when we appeared. Unfortunately, Youssef escaped."

Haroun's gaze settled disconcertingly on Zara. His eyes narrowed and his thick black brows rose upward in silent query. "Have you brought back a new slave? He doesn't look strong enough to be of much use."

Jamal laughed. "You're wrong, my fine friend, this particular slave is perfectly suited for what I have in mind." Then he surprised Haroun by ripping off Zara's turban and tossing it to the ground. Pale blond hair spilled out, framing her face in a halo of molten gold. "What think you now of my slave?"

"Allah and the Prophet!" Haroun said, bug-eyed with shock. "If the rest of her is as lovely as her face, she will outshine the loveliest pearl in your harem. Who is she?"

"I am Zara, daughter of Youssef, you gaping ass," Zara said imperiously.

The insult brought forth a burst of laughter from Jamal. "Zara has a sharp tongue, my friend. Watch lest she cut you to ribbons with it."

Haroun didn't think it at all amusing. "Why would you want such an ill-tempered woman when you have Leila, Saha and Amar, docile jewels all, waiting to give you pleasure?"

"I wish I knew," Jamal muttered beneath his breath, but it was loud enough for Haroun to hear and wonder. "I suppose I couldn't bear to see her beautiful head separated from her body. Zara had the audacity to offend the sultan. I talked him out of beheading her. Then he threatened to give her to Abdul, his blacksmith. I may yet live to regret my rashness, but I asked Ishmail to give her to me instead."

"I had no idea you wished to enlarge your harem. Shall I take Zara to the women's quarters?"

"I am *Princess* Zara," Zara corrected in a haughty tone. If Jamal intended to break her spirit, he was wasting his time.

"No longer a princess but a lowly slave," Jamal pointed out. "Ranking below all my other slaves." He turned to Haroun. "Zara is to work in the stables. Tell Ahmed she is to rake dung from the stalls."

Haroun appeared puzzled by Jamal's words. Women as beautiful as Zara did not rake dung. They served their masters in bed, giving and receiving pleasure. "Are you sure, my lord? Perhaps she would better serve you in your bed."

" 'Tis the sultan's wish that Zara be taught humility and obedience. He insisted that she be punished for insulting him. She spat at him. Had I not promised to obey his wishes in the matter, Zara would have become Abdul's slave. He would have killed her the first time she insulted him. I convinced Ishmail that Zara should live, that his cause would be better served if she was held as a hostage to insure her father's compliance."

"I would have preferred death," Zara loudly proclaimed.

"You will do as you're told," Jamal warned ominously. He turned to Haroun and shrugged. "See what I mean? She is incorrigible. She is to remain in the stables, working alongside the other slaves until she learns obedience. Instruct the guards that she is not to be allowed outside the palace walls."

"I understand, my lord. Come along, wench. Ahmed will be glad for the extra pair of hands. Jamal's stables are vast, surpassed only by the sultan's."

As he watched Zara walk off with Haroun, Jamal decided that Zara would be his stable's finest addition to date. The green-eyed, fair-haired Berber vixen was more difficult than his feistiest mare . . . and infinitely more enticing.

Head held high, Zara accompanied Haroun to the stables, determined to survive the meanest task without complaint. But despite Jamal and the sultan, she would never become a docile slave. She was a Berber warrior, too proud to be tamed.

Haroun placed Zara into Ahmed's keeping with little ado, saying only that it was Sheik Jamal's wish that the woman work in the stables alongside the other slaves, and that she was to be given no special treatment. Within minutes of Haroun's departure a rake was placed in Zara's hands and she was shoved into a stall that was ankle deep in dung.

Four slaves worked in the stables. Zara met them when they gathered around a small brazier to cook their evening meal. Rice, meat and vegetables were provided by Jamal's kitchens, along with tea leaves and fruit. The evening meal was simple but ample, and Zara was pleased to note that Jamal didn't starve his slaves.

Jamal had purchased Ahmed, Nails, Mustafa and Abdullah in slave markets in various cities.

All were young and randy. From the moment Zara appeared, there began a rivalry among them that Jamal had never anticipated.

Jamal took his evening meal alone, brooding over the events that had brought Zara into his life. He had yet to greet his own women and yet he could not get Zara out of his mind. He had deliberately avoided the stables today. He didn't like casting Zara in the role of stable slave, but she had brought it on herself. He was determined to break her spirit, and softening toward her wasn't the way to go about it.

Jamal was so engrossed in his thoughts that he didn't hear Hammet, the head eunuch in charge of his household, sidle up beside him.

"May I have a word with you, my lord?"

Startled, Jamal's head shot up. Dressed in a wide sleeved brocade robe edged in silver thread, Hammet was middle-aged, short and plump, with a kind disposition. Jamal depended on Hammet to keep his house in order and his women in line.

"What is it, Hammet? Is there a problem?"

"Your women sent me to tell you they are lonely, my lord. They eagerly await a visit from you. They beg most humbly that you attend them tonight."

Jamal's brow quirked upward. "Shall I pleasure all three at once, Hammet?"

"That is their wish, my lord. They promise you a night of a thousand delights."

Jamal had frolicked with all three women at once before, but for some reason the idea didn't hold the same appeal as it once did. Perhaps he was getting old.

"Tell them I will attend them in an hour, Hammet. If I am to please all three, perhaps you should prepare a vial of restorative. I've had a long, exhausting day."

Hammet bowed himself out of the room, leaving Jamal to anticipate the many delights to be had with his concubines. All three women were young, lush and ripe. He had chosen them expressly for their experience in the arts of love. But it wasn't Leila, Saha or Amar he wanted to make love to, it was a tall Berber vixen with the supple curves of an *houri*.

Zara stretched out on her bed of straw and groaned. Every bone in her body ached. She was filthy, smelled of dung, and felt exhausted beyond endurance. But those were the least of her problems. Even in the dark she could feel the avid dark eyes of her companions upon her, and despite the warm night, she shivered. Though she had spoken but briefly to the other stable slaves, Zara knew what they were thinking. She was fair game. Earlier she had heard them arguing over who would have her first, and she had hidden a pitchfork beside her in the straw before making her bed.

Despite her fear, Zara must have fallen asleep for she awoke abruptly to the sound of footsteps shuffling across the floor. She braced herself and reached for the pitchfork, somewhat comforted when her hand closed over the handle. Suddenly a body fell on top of her and she cried out. She might as well have remained mute for all the help it brought her.

"Quiet, woman," a voice rasped into her ear. "Our master sent you here to pleasure us, and since I am the strongest I will have you first."

It was Mustafa, a huge man with the strength of a bull. She had seen him lift an anvil today without breaking out in a sweat.

"Get off me, you stinking piece of camel dung! I was sent here to work, not to pleasure the sheik's stable slaves. Touch me and I will tell your master."

Her commanding voice captured his attention, but not for long. He groped her breasts, trying to rip her clothes aside to get to her bare skin. "Hold still, woman! Once I impale you with my mighty lance you will beg for more. I am as big as a horse. Whatever you did to displease our master is our gain."

He found the sash holding up Zara's pantaloons and released it, crying out in triumph when his hand encountered flesh as soft as silk. "Aiyee, tonight I will taste heaven. Open yourself for me, woman."

Digging into the straw, Zara's hand closed upon the pitchfork. Grasping it close to the shank, she brought it upward, thrusting it against Mustafa's chest.

"Release me, foul beast," Zara said with quiet menace. "Never touch me again. Tell your companions they will suffer horribly if they do not leave me alone. I will emasculate them in their sleep. I will cut off their testicles and feed them to the pigs. Believe me, I do not lie. I am Princess

Zara, daughter of the great *cadi* Youssef. Consider yourself lucky that I do not kill you."

Mustafa sprang away, impressed by Zara's bravery yet at the same time angry that a mere woman should talk to him so. "You are but one small woman against many. I have but to call my companions to hold you down while I take my pleasure."

Holding the pitchfork protectively aloft, Zara warned, "Try it and tomorrow your master will have your heads separated from your bodies."

Her words gave Mustafa pause. What if the master had put the woman to work in the stables as punishment for some minor infraction? To use her as Mustafa wanted might enrage the master, and then what would become of him? Sheik Jamal was a kind master and Mustafa would rather remain in his household than be sold, or possibly killed.

He rose slowly. The moment his weight was gone from her, Zara leaped to her feet. "Get out of my way!"

"Where do you go, lady?"

"To find a bed not infected with vermin like you."

Pitching aside her makeshift weapon, she held her pantaloons about her slim waist with one hand and ran from the stables, not daring to look back. Her knees were knocking together and she was trembling. Had Jamal truly sent her to the stables to pleasure his slaves?

Zara had no idea where she was going, except away from the stables. She'd rather sleep with pigs than be ravished by humans more foul than pigs. Unfortunately, Zara was trapped within the compound. The gates surrounding Paradise were guarded by Jamal's men-at-arms and too high to scale. She followed a moonlit path to the inner courtyard. Slipping through the arched entrance, Zara stared in awe at the lush gardens within the enclosure, and the sparkling pool fed by a fountain at its center.

Jamal's marble palace was built around the tiled courtyard, with all its rooms opening onto it. A covered walkway marched along all four sides of the square, held up by marble columns. Zara visualized Jamal's concubines walking, laughing and talking in the jewel-like setting, like fluttering birds amid the colorful blossoms.

But it was the pool that drew Zara. The night was warm, and she was filthy and sweaty beneath her clothing. Her own stench offended her. Glancing about, she saw no movement within the palace. She supposed Jamal was frolicking in the harem with his concubines and not likely to leave any time soon. She gazed longingly at the pool. It proved too inviting to resist.

Creeping to the edge of the pool, Zara removed her *djellaba*, shirt and pantaloons and eased into the water. Though the water only reached her knees, it felt like heaven. In the center of the fountain a fat cherub knelt on a pedestal, holding an ewer from which a steady stream of cool, clear water spewed forth.

Zara waded to the fountain, raised her face to the moon and let the water spill down upon her. She lamented the lack of soap and scent to rub upon her skin, but the cool water was enough to restore her.

Unbeknownst to Zara, Jamal was watching from the double doors opening into his chamber. He had pulled aside the silken curtains wafting in the gentle breeze and was going to take the short walk across the courtyard to the harem when he'd seen her. He stepped out into the star-studded night, lured by the object of his erotic fantasies, her nude body a pale column of gold beneath the bright moonlight.

Moving behind a marble pillar, he watched her enter the shallow pool and wade to the fountain. He lost the ability to breathe when she turned toward him, lifting her face to the sky as water from the cherub's ewer spilled down upon her golden head.

She was a goddess, created by Allah to tempt the holiest of men, and Allah knew he had never aspired to the state of holiness. His erection rose full and hard. Release was but steps away in his harem, yet he couldn't turn away from the tempting *houri* bathing in his pool.

Her arms were raised, fanning her hair to catch the spray from the cherub's ewer. The simple motion pushed her breasts upward and out, providing a feast for his hungry gaze. Her nipples were distended, and he ached to lap the drops of water clinging to their coral tips. Jamal blessed the brightness of the moon as his gaze slid downward, past Zara's narrow hips, across her flat stomach to her smooth mound. She was plump and pink there, and he longed to part her pale thighs and sip of her sweet nectar.

When Zara turned her back to him, he admired the supple curve of her spine, the perfect twin moons of her buttocks, the long, elegant length of her legs. He wondered if the backs of her knees were sensitive and wanted to press kisses there and on the tender flesh between her pale thighs.

Zara would have liked to remain in the pool longer but she feared discovery. A household this size was bound to have servants wandering about, but still she lingered. Suddenly she shivered, and the hairs at the back of her neck prickled. She glanced around, feeling eyes on her that she could not see.

Probing the shadows beneath the walkway, Zara sensed but did not see him. Yet his presence was so strong, every nerve ending in her body tingled with awareness. What would he do if he found her in his pool?

Jamal knew the instant Zara sensed his presence. She became watchful; her body tensed. He heard her gasp aloud when he stepped out from behind the pillar.

"Do not let me interrupt your bath."

Zara stared at him, seeing him for the first time without his turban. His hair was dark, wavy, and clubbed at his neck with cord. He wore a silk caftan, belted at his narrow waist.

"I was just leaving."

"I insist that you stay."

She was surprised to hear him summon his servant. "Hammet, bring soap and fragrant oils. My new slave wishes to bathe."

Chapter Four

Zara truly did try to turn her gaze away as Jamal released the sash on his caftan and let it slide down his body. But the mesmerizing beauty of his muscular, fully aroused form fascinated her. His chest was broad and lightly furred. A narrow band of hair reached down to his groin and was lost in the dark forest between his legs. She stared at his manhood, rising full and heavy against his stomach, and suspected he was much larger than most men. Tearing her gaze away from his groin, she glanced down the long length of his legs, which like his chest were covered with fine dark hair.

Her gaze returned to his erection, and this time she did look away.

Jamal chuckled, aware of where her eyes had taken her. With consummate grace he sat down at the edge of the pool, dangling his legs in the water. A moment later Hammet appeared at his side, bearing a jar of soap, a vial of perfumed oil and a stack of linen drying cloths.

Jamal's gaze never left Zara as he said, "Thank you, Hammet, you're dismissed. I will have no further need of you tonight. And take these with you," he added, handing the eunuch Zara's filthy clothing.

Hammet held Zara's clothing between thumb and forefinger, as if offended by its stench, then left as silently as he had appeared.

"Come here," Jamal commanded.

Zara shook her head and edged away from him, her eyes wild with panic. Where could she go? What could she do? Her clothes were gone, she couldn't run about naked, not with animals like Mustafa around.

"Come here, I said," Jamal repeated more harshly. "You can't wash properly without soap."

"I'm clean enough," Zara insisted. "I want my clothes back."

"In good time," Jamal said. He offered his hand to her.

Since no other choice was open to her, Zara approached Jamal warily. She halted just out of his reach. "What do you want?"

He glanced down at his massive erection and laughed. "Isn't it obvious?"

"I'm not your love slave. You have concubines to ease your lust. The silly girls are probably pining for your attention."

"So they are." He lunged for her, grabbing her by the hair and dragging her between his spread thighs, facing him. "Now behave while I bathe you."

He dipped his fingers into the jar of soap and, starting at her shoulders, spread jasmine-scented lather over her torso. His hands paused on her breasts, molding them against his palms, gently squeezing the nipples between his thumb and forefinger until they became swollen and distended. He searched her face as his hands explored her body, smiling smugly when she tilted her head back and groaned.

Zara was on fire. Her breasts felt heavy and engorged and her nipples were aroused. If Jamal didn't stop she would die. Then she felt his hands moving down to her stomach, rubbing around her navel, pressing places on her abdomen that added a new dimension to her torment.

Jamal was entranced. Zara's smooth, hairless body was perfection. Unlike his concubines, who sat around eating and preening all day, it was obvious Zara spent long hours in strenuous activity. Her stomach was flat, not an ounce of superfluous fat marred her torso, and her legs were taut and lightly muscled.

Jamal's hand cupped her silken mound, spreading soap over her loins, then dipped down between her thighs, and up again into her tender cleft. Zara cried out, struggling to escape his invasion of her body, but his strong legs held her like a vise.

He worked his fingers against her flesh, seeking and finding the tiny pearl of her femininity. Zara's body spasmed as fire licked along her nerve endings. She pushed against his chest to make him stop, but he merely laughed at her.

"Do you like that, Princess?" he whispered against her ear. "Spread your legs and let me pleasure you." He slid two fingers inside her and Zara's knees buckled.

"No, stop! Send me back to the stables but don't use me like this!"

Jamal went still. He seemed angry. "I'm not using you. I want to give you pleasure. We will pleasure one another."

"That's not at all what I want. Berber women are free to choose their own lovers. We are men's equals."

Schooled in the ways of Islam and the teachings of Allah, Jamal was surprised at the concept of women being men's equals. Even in his mother's country women were possessions. They could not own property or enter into contracts. They had to obey their husbands and submit to their wishes.

"You are a slave, and slaves have no rights," Jamal pointed out. "I can take you here, beside the pool, if I so desire."

"I will not submit easily."

Jamal stared at her. Her beauty was mesmerizing. Allah help him, for he *did* want her, but force did not appeal to him. Force had never been necessary in his dealings with women. *I will have her willing and submissive*, he vowed to himself, *without the use of force*. Seduction was a game Jamal played well. Zara was his possession, and he was determined to have her in his bed. He wanted her for his love slave, eager and submissive to his needs.

"I will strike a deal with you, sweet vixen. Here's my wager. Within four weeks you will invite me inside your body. If you do not, I will set you free."

Zara couldn't believe what she was hearing. Jamal had just offered to free her if he couldn't seduce her within four weeks. Allah was indeed kind to her. She would never willingly place herself in Jamal's bed. He was her enemy. Sayed was dead, and it was Jamal's fault.

"Is that all there is to the wager, my lord?" Zara asked suspiciously. She did not trust him.

"If you lose, if you take my manhood inside you," Jamal continued evenly, "you will reside in my harem and come to me when I want you."

Zara thought his proposition over carefully. Clearly Sheik Jamal had an inflated ego.

"I agree. But I can only lose the bet if I take your manhood inside me willingly. If you take me by force, or without my permission, you lose the bet. Am I correct?"

"So be it."

"Will you answer a question for me?"

"What is it you wish to know?"

"Did you send me to the stables to pleasure your stable slaves?"

"What ever gave you that idea? You went to the stables because the sultan wanted you punished for your brazen behavior." His brows came together in a black scowl as comprehension dawned. "Which of my slaves accosted you? Is that why you left the stables tonight?"

"You can't blame them for thinking I was meant for their pleasure. Nothing was said to disabuse them of the notion that I was theirs for the taking."

"What did they do to you?" Jamal asked fiercely. If they had touched her he would have their heads.

"Nothing . . . yet. Mustafa found a pitchfork in his face when he tried to force me. I told him you would punish him if he touched me."

"And so I would have. You'll sleep in my harem from now on. You'll be safe there."

"Safe?" she hooted. "It will be a simple matter for you to seduce me if I sleep in the harem. Nay, I will return to the stables with the other slaves, but you must tell them I am not to be touched."

"Zara, my fierce Berber warrior," Jamal said softly. "You are too proud for your own good. I will tame you yet, my fiery pearl."

He stared at her mouth, lush and moist, and decided his seduction would start tonight. "Turn around, let me soap your back." When she appeared reluctant to obey, he gently turned her and closed his legs around her so she couldn't escape.

Dipping another glob of soap from the jar, he spread it over the elegant curve of her back, massaging the knobs of her spine with the pads of his fingers until she moaned; the pressure was wonderfully soothing after her hard day's labor. Then she felt him squeezing her buttocks, his fingers slipping into the separation between the perfect halves, sliding between her thighs to tease the sensitive nub there, probing her opening.

Abruptly his hands fell away and he pushed her down into the water. "Rinse off." She came up sputtering. Jamal grasped her beneath the arms and hauled her out of the water. She stood there shivering in the night air as he dried her with a soft linen cloth.

"I can do that myself," Zara declared. When Jamal touched her, her body behaved strangely. She felt weightless, without substance. Her flesh tingled and burned; his touch set fires inside her. In order to win her freedom she had to gird herself against him, to remember that he was the enemy, else she'd end up in his bed.

"Allow me," Jamal insisted. "Your skin is like silk. I wonder, do you taste as delicious as you look?"

Fearing he intended to find out, she backed away from him. But Jamal was not ready to let her go. Scooping her up in his arms, he carried her through the open double doors into his chamber, placing her on his sleeping couch. His dark eyes glowed as he stared down at her. Light from the hanging oil lamp bathed her in gold dust and magic. Jamal trembled with desire.

"Don't move," Jamal whispered. "I'll be right back."

Spellbound, Zara couldn't have moved had she tried. In any event, she wouldn't have gotten far. Jamal returned almost instantly with the vial of scented oil he had left beside the pool. She watched in trepidation as he poured a generous amount into his hands and sat down on the couch beside her.

"What are you going to do?"

"You'll find out, just turn on your stomach and lie still."

She turned with great reluctance on her stomach. Then she felt his hands on her. The heat of his skin had warmed the oil, and he spread it over her back, buttocks and legs, gently massaging her sore muscles. The relief was so intense, Zara could not stifle her groan of pleasure. Working in the stables had taken a toll upon her.

"Turn over," Jamal whispered huskily.

"I don't think—"

"Don't think, just feel," he said as he easily flipped her to her back. Then his hands worked the same kind of magic over her breasts, stomach and the front of her legs.

When he dipped his oiled fingers between her thighs, Zara stirred and murmured a weak protest. She was thoroughly enjoying the massage until his blatant sexual overture spoiled her pleasure.

Zara squealed in surprise when Jamal bent his head and kissed her breasts, first one then the other. He kneaded them, lifting them to his hungry mouth to suckle and lick. She whimpered when he bit gently upon a tender crest. Immediately he soothed it with the moist warmth of his tongue.

She shivered. The pleasure was sharp, almost unbearable, and dangerous. Losing the wager meant permanent captivity.

"Stop!"

"I haven't done anything yet," Jamal whispered. Then he drew one nipple deep into his mouth, sucking vigorously as his hands stroked the length of her slick body.

"I won't let you seduce me!" Zara cried, nearly mindless with pleasure. What she and Sayed had done together was child's play compared to what Jamal was doing to her now.

Leaving the sweet enticement of her breasts, his mouth fastened onto hers, his tongue delving deeply, tasting of her. Nectar of the gods, he thought as he nibbled and sucked on her lips. But it was another set of pouting lips that drew his mouth downward. She shuddered uncontrollably as he traced a path to the glistening cleft between her legs.

"You taste of jasmine," he said, referring to the scent he had used to massage her body.

Her hips rose off the couch, pleasure stabbing her as he tongued the tiny jewel between her legs. Suddenly he thrust two fingers into her inner wetness. She climaxed violently as his fingers thrust in and out of her.

While she lay recovering from the violent climax, Jamal rose above her. His sex was painfully distended, the tip wet with his juices. When he flexed his hips, Zara came to her senses, realizing her danger. She pushed against him so hard he landed on his rump on the floor. She leaped to her feet before he gained his wits, backing away from him, her green eyes blazing.

Jamal matched her anger as he picked himself off the floor and returned her glare.

"What made you think I'd let you seduce me so easily?" Zara asked. "I want my freedom."

"I gave you pleasure," Jamal said. "You let me

put my tongue and fingers inside you."

"Did you give me a choice?"

"I could take you now if I wanted to. You are my slave. Slaves obey their masters."

"Then you would lose the wager, my lord," she said sweetly. "You are a man of your word, are you not?"

"I am a *man*. I can only be pushed so far. I'm obsessed with you, Zara. I've made no secret of the fact that I want you. Four weeks, my fiery warrior. Count the days, for you will be mine long before that."

He rose abruptly and pulled on his caftan. His erection was still full and heavy, his lust unassuaged. This kind of sexual frustration was foreign to him. When he wanted a woman all he had to do was ask and one would be available. His manhood had never known the kind of deprivation he was now experiencing.

Moving away from Jamal, Zara felt unspeakably vulnerable without her clothes. In the short time since their meeting, Jamal had learned her body more intimately than she knew it herself. It was humiliating.

"Give me back my clothes so I can to return to the stables."

"You are unlike any woman I've ever known," Jamal said sourly. Never had he met a more contrary female. Why wouldn't she give herself to him? It wasn't as if she were a shy virgin. She had enjoyed his loving, as far as it went. Did she still mourn her Berber lover? Not one to give up easily, Jamal renewed his vow to have Zara in his bed soon. He swore he would make it happen.

Zara hugged herself and shivered as Jamal rummaged through a chest containing an assortment of clothing. He found what he was looking for, handing her a white shirt, pantaloons and *djellaba* that must have belonged to him. She donned them quickly, rolling up the sleeves of the shirt and tightening the sash around her slim waist to hold up the trousers. Then she slipped the *djellaba* over her head.

"Come along," Jamal said as he picked up the oil lamp and held it aloft.

"Where are we going?"

"I'm escorting you back to the stables. Your companions will be told in no uncertain terms that you're not to be touched by them."

He grasped her arm and pulled her into the courtyard and out the gate. Zara dug in her heels. "I need a weapon. The pitchfork is too unwieldy to use effectively."

"You want me to give you a weapon?" Jamal asked with amusement. "I'm not stupid, Zara."

"What if I promise to use it only to protect myself? Do none of your slaves carry weapons?"

It was a logical question. Many of his slaves carried weapons, but only those loyal to him. Some even served as men-at-arms. "Only those I trust."

She gave him a guileless smile. "I'm a helpless woman. What harm can I do?"

Jamal gave a shout of laughter. "There's no denying you're a woman, sweet vixen, but helpless is not a word I would use to describe you. I told you I would speak with the slaves. After I finish with them, they will not dare to accost you."

Gripping her wrist firmly with one hand and the lamp with the other, he pulled her along with him to the stables. Once inside, he came upon one of the slaves sleeping in the straw and nudged him awake with his foot.

Abdul came up in a crouch, ready to defend himself. When he saw Jamal, he blanched and fell to his knees. "What is it, master, what have I done?"

"Rouse the others," Jamal ordered.

Within minutes all four slaves stood before him, glancing warily from Jamal to Zara. Ahmed, the stable master, stepped forward. "What have we done, master?"

Jamal pushed Zara forward. "Listen well, for I will say this but one time. Zara is to work, eat and sleep in the stables; she is *not* here for your pleasure. Abuse her at your own risk, is that clear?"

A look of silent communication passed among the slaves before Ahmed spoke for all of them. "We understand, master. Your new slave is safe with us."

Jamal nodded curtly, turned on his heel and strode from the stables. He should have gone directly to the harem to relieve his frustrations with his concubines, but he was no longer in the mood. For the first time in his memory he sought his bed without first easing himself with a woman, despite the fact that he needed one desperately. His sex ached and his lust was unappeased, but the woman he wanted was sleeping by choice on a bed of straw in the stables instead of reclining on a soft couch in the women's quarters.

Jamal had never met a woman quite like Zara. Her flesh was sweet and soft, her face lovelier than the moon and the stars, yet she insisted upon being treated as a man's equal. He had tasted her passion tonight and it had but whetted his appetite for more. Since he had no intention of freeing her any time soon, he was determined to seduce her and enjoy every minute of it.

Zara crawled into her bed of straw, still wary despite Jamal's warning to the stable slaves. Quiet settled over the dark stables. It was very late, and she was exhausted. She closed her eyes, ready to drop off to sleep, when she heard a noise and then a voice whispering into her ear.

"You are a slave like the rest of us, Berber wench. You may have opened your thighs for our master tonight, but he still brought you back to the stables to sleep. If you had pleased him you would be in the woman's quarters now, sleeping upon a soft bed."

Zara did not recognize the voice; it could be any one of the stable slaves. "Who are you?" The air around her did not stir; her tormentor was gone.

The next day Zara was given the foulest of chores. Ankle deep in dung, she raked and swept and mucked out the stalls. That night she fell asleep over her dinner, too exhausted to finish her meal. The next day was the same, and the day after that. Fearing the consequences of running into Jamal, she stayed away from the courtyard pool, using water from the well to wash the day's grime from her face and hands.

Zara did not like the way Mustafa continued to stare at her, as if she were a sweetmeat and he a starving man. At the end of the third day of back-breaking toil, a stroke of luck placed a weapon in her hand. She was at the well and found a knife someone had left in a basket of fruit. No one was nearby as she quickly snatched it up and hid it within the folds of her *djellaba*. The next day she had reason to be grateful for her good luck.

Mustafa had been goading her for days, some-how making sure that she was given the hardest and dirtiest chores. When he told her he would take over her work load as well as his own if she would lie with him, she spit in his face. Being shamed by a woman enraged Mustafa. He retal-iated instinctively. He backhanded her with his hamlike hand, sending her flying against a stall. Regaining her feet in a crouch, Zara pulled her knife and flew at Mustafa, though he was three times her size.

Their struggle brought the others running, ap palled that Mustafa had deliberately disobeyed Jamal's orders. Ahmed tried to break up the fight, receiving a cut on his hand for his efforts. Over and over the combatants rolled on the ground. Despite being smaller than Mustafa and a frac-tion of his weight, Zara was holding her own. Mustafa got in one or two good punches, but Zara wielded her knife with dexterity. Mustafa was bleeding from several small cuts, and Zara's right cheekbone was swollen and purple.

Zara did not hear the sound of running footsteps, or the commanding voice issuing crisp orders. She had no idea Jamal was nearby until Mustafa was pulled off her.

"Master," Mustafa said, bowing low. "Forgive me."

Zara looked up at Jamal from her position on the floor and recoiled in fear. His face was twisted into a mask of rage, terrible to behold. Haroun, his lieutenant, stood beside him, awaiting orders.

"Take Mustafa to the slave market in Meknes and sell him, Haroun," Jamal said with quiet menace. "Take him away now, before I kill him myself."

"Please, master," Mustafa begged, "it won't happen again."

"You're right, Mustafa, it *won't* happen again." He turned his back on the slave as Haroun dragged him away. Then he dropped to his knees beside Zara. "Are you all right?"

Still winded from her fight, Zara merely nodded.

"What was that all about? It seems I can't trust you out of my sight."

"I'm surprised you need to ask," Zara said bitterly. She tried to rise but was too shaky. It was then that Jamal saw the bloody knife in her hand.

"Where in Allah's name did you get that? Give it to me!"

Zara handed it to him; it had served its purpose. He helped her to her feet, grimacing when he saw the fresh bruises on her face. The bruises from the sultan's blows had just begun to fade. Rage welled up in him. Some men enjoyed striking women, but he wasn't one of them. Seeing

Zara bruised and battered made him want to kill. Zara might be rash and foolish but she was not lacking in bravery. How much simpler his life would be if she but acted like a woman, taking her ease in the harem and sharing his couch at night.

"You can't stay here," Jamal said, coming to a decision. The sultan be damned. Zara could not remain in the stables. She was his slave and she would obey him.

Zara merely stared at him. What could she say? She didn't want to stay in the stables either, but she didn't like the alternative.

"Come with me. You stink of dung and sweat."

"Where are you taking me?"

Jamal noticed that the stable slaves were listening with avid interest. "Go back to your chores," he told them.

He waited until they were alone before answering Zara's question. "You know where I want you. Beneath me, in my bed."

"You can't force me."

Jamal gave her an amused grin. "I can. But I'd rather have you lie with me willingly."

Zara faced him squarely. "I'll never agree to that."

His voice was low and evocative. "We'll see, sweet vixen. Meanwhile, you can join my household staff. But first we have to rid you of the stink of the stables. I'll take you to the *hammam*, where you can bathe."

Taking her hand, Jamal led her away. They had reached the courtyard before Zara realized where he was taking her.

"You're taking me to the harem!"

"Aye, to the women's quarters. Nafisa will take care of you. She'll see that you're given proper clothing and a bed. Hammet can inform you of your duties tomorrow. Come along, Zara. Even you must realize there is a limit to your obstinateness."

After three backbreaking days in the stables, Zara was ready to give Jamal that small point. She didn't want to go back to the stables and she wanted a bath. Jamal had said she wouldn't be a part of his harem of women. She'd be a house slave, not a concubine.

"I will not fight you on this, my lord. Take me to the *hammam* so that I may rid myself of the stench of the stables. Allah forbid that I offend your delicate senses." Her words were shrouded in sarcasm that was not lost on Jamal.

"You do not offend me, Zara, I am quite taken with you. But I can wait to have you."

"So can I, my lord. Wait to be free, that is. Have you forgotten our wager?"

"I have not forgotten. And I rarely lose a wager."

Jamal led her to a pair of richly carved and painted double doors at the far end of the courtyard. "The harem lies behind these doors," Jamal pointed out. "You are standing in the courtyard of the concubines. My women come and go as they please, with certain restrictions. They visit the village, the *souk*, and even, upon occasion, go to Meknes accompanied by Hammet and several men-at-arms. But you, sweet vixen, are a slave. You are not allowed those privileges. You will be confined to the house, the courtyard, and the gardens within the walls."

After that rather lengthy speech, he opened the doors and pulled Zara inside the harem.

Chapter Five

Zara felt as if she'd stepped into another world. A world far removed from the black tents and sun-baked villages constructed of mud bricks where her people lived, loved and died. The room was not overly large but was memorable for its ornate furnishings, silk wall hangings and rich carpets upon the floor. Satin, velvet and brocade-covered couches, piled high with thick cushions, were scattered about the room. Polished ebony tables, inlaid with mother of pearl and holding baskets of fruit and sweetmeats, were placed before the couches. Three women occupied the room, taking their ease upon the couches.

"Jamal!" squealed a plump brunette with cherry red lips and melting brown eyes. "You do us great honor by coming to us in the middle of the day." She batted her long lashes at him. "How may we serve you, my lord?"

A petite redhead with extraordinary breasts preened for Jamal's benefit. "Aye, my lord, what can we do for you?"

A second brunette, lovelier than the first, if that were possible, gave him a smile that was so sexually charged, Zara had to look away. "Look, ladies! Our lord has brought a new eunuch to wait upon us."

Three pairs of eyes turned to stare at Zara.

Zara studied each concubine in turn. All three wore short vests that barely covered their breasts, silken pantaloons and transparent caftans. Soft pointed slippers adorned their feet, and their fingers were laden with rings. Each wore a silk veil that could be pulled across their face and fastened.

The redhead wrinkled her nose distastefully. "Where did you find so pitiful a slave, Jamal? His stench offends me."

Jamal bit back a smile. "The new slave is a woman, Saha. She will serve you, Leila and Amar in the harem and perform minor household duties."

Leila sent Zara a condescending look. "What a pathetic excuse for a woman."

Zara would have flown at Leila had not Jamal placed a restraining hand on her shoulder. "Where is Nafisa?"

"I am here, my lord." A stout elderly woman entered from another room, huffing from her exertions. "What do you wish of me?" Suddenly her gaze fell on Zara and a frown wrinkled her brow. "Is that a woman, my lord?"

"Aye, Zara is indeed a woman, Nafisa. I'm counting on you to make her look like one. The sultan has presented me with this new slave."

"Slave, my lord?" Nafisa repeated. "Is she to serve you in no other way?"

"Nafisa, Jamal knows what he wants and obviously it isn't a filthy beggar who's probably riddled with disease," Amar said sharply.

"Riddled with disease!" Zara cried, shrugging off Jamal's restraining hand as she leaped at Amar. The lovely concubine fell beneath Zara's surprise attack before Jamal could pull her away.

"That's enough!" Jamal said, giving Zara a shake. "You will behave or return to the stables."

"I'm not diseased," Zara muttered angrily.

"She's vicious," Amar said, picking herself off the floor and setting her silk veil back in place. "She will not make a good slave, my lord. She needs a beating."

Jamal agreed wholeheartedly. "Zara, these are my concubines, Saha, Leila and Amar. Your duties include serving them in the harem. Saha has a temper to match her red hair. Leila is like a playful kitten, but beware of her claws. And Amar can be fractious if stroked the wrong way."

"Why is Zara so filthy, my lord?" Nafisa asked, unable to contain her curiosity.

"Oh, yes, I almost forgot to introduce Nafisa, mistress of the harem," Jamal told Zara. "Zara is filthy because she has been serving as a stable slave," he explained.

"A stable slave!" Saha gasped.

"Zara must have displeased you greatly, my lord," Amar said with a smirk.

A hint of compassion crossed old Nafisa's wrinkled face. "Come along, Zara, I'll soon rid you of the stench of dung and horses."

Zara followed, as eager to escape Jamal's sniping concubines as she was to have a bath. As she passed through an arched doorway, she glanced over her shoulder and saw Jamal stretched out on a couch, his women crowded around him like a litter of puppies, eager to please and be pleased. Her face flamed, recalling all those arousing things Jamal had done to her that night beside the pool, wondering if he meant to bed his women while she was in the next room.

The *hammam* was hot and steamy, and Zara couldn't wait to immerse herself in the sparkling water. The pool dominated the large room, whose floors were inlaid with white and blue tiles. Benches lined the walls around the pool.

"Allow me to remove those filthy robes, Zara," Nafisa said kindly. "Why are you dressed like a man?"

"This is how I always dress," Zara explained. "Normally I wear the blue robes of my people."

"Blue robes? Allah help us. Are you one of the Blue Men? How can that be when you are a woman?"

"My father is Youssef, *cadi* of the Berbers who live in the Rif mountains. I ride at his side."

Nafisa stared at her. "You ride with bandits?"

"We do not think of ourselves as bandits. We are free people, fighting for equality. We raid the sultan's caravans because we are driven to it by high taxes."

"I know nothing of politics." Nafisa shrugged as she pulled off Zara's shirt and helped her out of her pantaloons. The old woman wasn't prepared for the sight that met her eyes, and a shocked gasp left her throat. "Blessed Allah, you are lovely. That hair, that skin, you are like a rare butterfly emerging from its cocoon. If the sheik saw you like this he'd—"

"The sheik has already seen her like this," Jamal said from the doorway, "and was as awestruck as you are, my good Nafisa."

"What are you doing here?" Zara cried, trying to hide behind the ample Nafisa.

"This is my home, I go wherever I please."

"Am I not allowed to bathe in privacy?"

"You are my slave. I am your master. I will decide what you are allowed and not allowed." He ambled into the *hammam* and dropped down onto one of the benches, stretching his long legs in front of him. "You may continue, Nafisa."

Zara bit her lip to keep from flinging back a sharp retort, noting that Nafisa seemed not at all disturbed by Jamal's presence. Did he regularly watch his concubines bathe? she wondered.

"Why aren't you with your women?" Zara dared to ask.

Why, indeed? Jamal thought but did not say. Instead of easing the lust Zara had created inside him with one of his women, he was torturing himself by watching her bathe. He was already hard and growing harder.

"I sent them to the village with Hammet," Jamal said. " 'Tis market day and they love to browse in the *souk*."

" 'Tis the master's right to be here," Nafisa said with a hint of censure. "Lie on the bench, Zara, so that I may tend you properly. You have neglected your body most shamefully."

Jamal watched with growing excitement as Nafisa swiftly and efficiently rid Zara of all her body hair. When she had finished, Zara's skin was once again as smooth and soft as satin. His eyes feasted on her plump pink mound, recalling how moist and hot her tight sheath had been when he'd aroused her with his mouth and fingers. His loins grew heavy, his manroot rose, hard and engorged. This seduction was going much too slowly, he thought. Tonight he would escalate his efforts to bring Zara to his bed. But for now he had suffered enough torment. Rising abruptly, he called Nafisa to his side, spoke briefly to her, then left the *hammam*.

Zara noted Jamal's absence when she rose to enter the pool. Her relief was immediate and heartfelt. The knowledge that Jamal was watching her while she bathed had excited her. Her nipples had puckered into taut buds, and she wondered if Nafisa had noticed. Allah take Jamal, she thought grumpily. Why should this arrogant sheik, enemy of her people, be the only man to fully arouse her womanly passions?

She had loved Sayed, but her feelings for him were tepid compared to the exhilaration she felt when Jamal touched her. It shouldn't be like that, she thought, disgruntled. He was too sure of himself, too powerfully male, too arrogant. He wanted her in his bed, and she didn't know how long she could resist the compelling appeal of his seduction.

Nafisa washed Zara's body and hair with jasmine-scented soap, then rinsed her several times with warm water that had been heated on a brazier. When Zara had finished bathing, Nafisa wrapped her in a large square of linen cloth and rubbed her body dry. Then she bade Zara lie down on the bench so that she could massage oil of jasmine into her skin. It felt wonderfully relaxing, but had the hands upon her been Jamal's, Zara reflected, the massage would have been erotic and arousing. Praise Allah that it was Nafisa administering to her and not Jamal.

The clothing Nafisa brought for Zara to wear was not fit for a slave. Zara gazed with distaste at the short, sleeveless blouse fashioned of rich turquoise brocade, thinking that it would barely cover her breasts. The silken pantaloons were a pale ivory color and embarrassingly transparent. They belled out from the waist and hugged her slim ankles. But they were so sheer her skin tones were clearly visible. Then Nafisa handed her a veil to cover her face.

"I cannot wear these clothes," Zara protested. "They're not proper attire for a Berber princess."

"I am but following Sheik Jamal's orders," Nafisa said with a shrug. "Now be a good girl and get dressed. Your master left orders that you are to serve him tonight. After you finish dressing, I'll show you to your room. It is tiny, but more than adequate for a slave. There is even a small walled garden for your enjoyment." She gave Zara an assessing look. " 'Tis unusual for Sheik Jamal to bring home a female slave. Male slaves and eunuchs perform the day-to-day tasks at Paradise. The only women in the palace are myself and his concubines."

"Do you expect me to be grateful for such an honor?" Zara asked bitterly. "I didn't ask to be a slave. I vow I will not remain one long. My father will come for me soon."

"We'll see," Nafisa said sagely. "Hurry, now. There will be time for a nap before your duties begin."

Since no other clothing was forthcoming, Zara quickly donned the revealing costume, but drew the line at the veil. "Berber women do not hide their faces," she declared haughtily.

"You are in an Arab harem," Nafisa said, not unkindly. "You will obey your master. Come along, I'll take you to your room."

Zara entered a small chamber scarcely bigger than a large closet. There were a sleeping couch, a chest for her clothing and a low table. A pile of cushions was stacked against one wall. A double door opened into a small walled garden. It was indeed adequate for her needs, Zara decided, for she wouldn't be remaining long. At the end of four weeks, if her father didn't come before then, she would be free. Jamal was a man of his word, and when he failed to seduce her, he would have no choice but to free her.

"Rest, Zara," Nafisa said as she left her charge. "Someone will come for you when it is time to serve your master."

"How am I to serve the sheik?" Zara asked warily.

"You will bring his food from the kitchen and serve him."

Relief shuddered through Zara. She knew Jamal could order her to his bed and she would have no say in the matter. She almost wished he would, for then he would lose his wager and she would be free. Lying with the enemy was repugnant to her, but it would almost be worth her freedom. Almost . . .

Since there was little to explore in her room, Zara lay down on the couch and promptly fell asleep. What seemed like scant minutes later, someone arrived to awaken her. She opened her eyes and met the gaze of a young man about her own age. He had a long, sad face, expressive brown eyes and skin as smooth and flawless as her own. She knew instinctively that he was a eunuch, for no other males were allowed in the harem.

"I am called Hakim. I bring your supper." He motioned to a tray of food he had placed on the table. "You must eat quickly. When you finish I'm to take you to the master."

"Thank you, Hakim. The food smells delicious," Zara said, walking to the table. She saw that Hakim had placed a cushion before the table and she sat down cross-legged upon it.

"I'll return for you shortly," Hakim said as he quietly let himself out of the room.

Zara ate ravenously, thoroughly enjoying the rice with tiny bits of capon breast in it, creamy yogurt with peeled grapes, a dish of figs, warm flat bread and fresh apples and oranges. She was just finishing her meal when Saha barged into her room, her eyes blazing furiously.

"I understand you are to serve Jamal tonight. Since he brought you home, we have been sorely neglected." Her fiery gaze slid over Zara's face and body. "You are not half as beautiful as I. Even Leila and Amar are lovelier than you. Have you bewitched Jamal?"

"I am no witch, and I do not serve Sheik Jamal in bed," Zara declared hotly. "I am not a love slave. You are more than welcome to him."

"I am not stupid. Our master wants you. And what Jamal wants, Jamal gets. Why were you sent to work in the stables?"

" 'Tis a long story, one that will bore you. 'Tis not my aim to challenge you for Jamal's affections."

"Are you ready, Zara?" Hakim had sidled into the room, hoping to rescue Zara from Saha's vicious tongue.

"I am ready, Hakim," Zara said, rising quickly. "Please excuse me, Saha. Unlike you, I have duties to perform."

"I hope those duties will not be performed on your back," Saha muttered to herself.

"Hurry, Zara," Hakim said as they passed through the harem door into a long hallway. "Fasten your veil; it isn't seemly for the guards to look upon your face."

"Nay, Berber women do not hide behind veils."

Hakim looked uncomfortable but said nothing more. It wasn't his place. He took her directly to

Jamal's chamber and opened the door. "Go, the sheik is waiting for you."

"Come in, Zara," Jamal said curtly.

Zara looked past the doorway into the room. She saw Jamal seated upon a cushion before a low table. An old man was seated nearby, preparing mint tea with great ceremony over a brazier. Hammet stood by the door with his arms folded over his ample chest.

" 'Tis my wish that you serve my meal tonight, Zara," Jamal said imperiously. "Hammet will take you to the kitchen."

"Yes, master," Zara said. Her sarcasm brought an involuntary smile to his face. "Shall I make my obeisance?"

"That would be refreshing." His eyebrows shot upward in surprise when Zara bowed low with negligent grace, sending him a searing look that singed the air around him.

"You may rise," Jamal said. His gaze slid over her slender form, settling on her breasts. "Your choice of costume pleases me."

"I had no choice in the matter."

"Why are you unveiled?"

"I hide my face from no one, man or woman."

"You will in the future," Jamal said as he summoned Hammet with a wave of his hand. "Take the slave to the kitchens, Hammet."

Zara was more than happy to escape Jamal's daunting presence. She returned a short time later bearing a tray laden with an array of tempting dishes. Jamal was alone. The old man brewing the tea had packed up his paraphernalia and left.

"You may go, Hammet," Jamal said, waving the eunuch away. "Zara will see to my needs tonight."

Zara set the tray on a side table and began placing separate dishes before Jamal. When she finished she stood back and waited to be dismissed.

"You may pour my tea," Jamal said, motioning toward the silver teapot resting upon the brazier. Zara bit her lip to keep from flinging out a scathing insult. What she really wanted to do was drown Jamal's smug smile in hot tea.

Jamal watched her every move, admiring the way her hips swayed beneath the transparent pantaloons. If he stared hard enough he could see her plump pink mound through the silken material. Beneath his caftan he felt his erection engorge with blood and thicken.

"Have you eaten?" Jamal asked as he sampled the succulent melon.

"I have eaten, thank you. May I leave now?"

"Nay, you may not. Sit here." He patted the cushion beside him.

She eyed him warily. "Why?"

"I do not like to eat alone." When Zara made no move to join him, Jamal grasped her wrist and pulled her down beside him. "There, that's better."

"Saha would love to join you. So would Leila or Amar."

"Perhaps later. It's you I want now. Is your room satisfactory?" he asked conversationally.

"It will do."

Suddenly he pushed the food away and leaned over to kiss her shoulder. "I find I'm no longer hungry."

"Shall I return the dishes to the kitchen?"

"I had no idea you'd be such an obedient slave, princess. What do you have up your sleeve?"

"Nothing, my lord," she said sweetly. "I'm not even wearing sleeves."

His black eyes glittered wickedly. "So I noticed." His hand traveled the length of her bare arm and back, sending ripples skittering over her sensitive flesh. Two tiny pearl buttons held the edges of her abbreviated vest together, and before Zara could protest, Jamal had released them. Her breasts literally popped into his hands. His sudden intake of breath told her how much he enjoyed the view.

"What are you doing?"

"Trying to seduce you, what else?" He pushed her back against the cushions and lowered his head to lick at her nipples. "You know I want you."

"Take me against my will and you lose the wager," she challenged, gritting her teeth against the sudden jolt of pleasure he had caused with his tongue.

"I never should have made that wager," Jamal muttered sourly. He raised his head to stare at her mouth. It was adorably lush and red and he wanted to kiss her senseless. But most of all he wanted to sheath himself inside her, to feel her heat contract around him, to taste her passion, to give her pleasure.

"Feel how much I want you," Jamal said, grasping her small hand and placing it upon his erection.

Zara inhaled sharply. His caftan provided a

scant barrier between her hand and the hot, pulsating length of him. Her fingers tightened involuntarily and she heard him groan. In seconds he had removed her hand and stretched out full length on top of her.

"You want me," he said triumphantly.

"Nay, I do not."

Her answer seemed to amuse him and he chuckled. "Open to me, Zara. Take me inside you. I promise you won't be sorry."

She sighed raggedly. "Nay, I cannot."

His eyes turned dark with desire as his mouth crushed down on hers, kissing her fiercely, willing her to respond as he molded her breasts with his palms. His lips left her mouth and followed the graceful line of her throat to her breasts. He kissed and licked the perfumed flesh, the scent of jasmine heightening his desire for her. His mouth closed over an erect nipple, sucking hard on it, then biting down lightly, and she cried out softly.

"Yield to me, sweet *houri*," Jamal whispered hoarsely.

"I cannot lose the wager," Zara replied in a strangled voice. She was aroused, painfully so, but losing the wager and remaining Jamal's slave was abhorrent to her.

"Forget the wager," he said fiercely. "You are my possession. Give to me. Let me taste your passion."

"You are demanding more than I can give. You're asking for my soul," Zara declared passionately.

"Nay, I want only your body," Jamal denied.

His words sounded flat and without substance.

In truth he wanted much more from the Berber princess. He wanted her body, her soul, her joys, her sorrows. He wanted to possess her very essence, to give her his in return. When he thrust into her tight sheath he wanted her to forget any past lovers and cling to him in sweet passion.

Allah help him. He wanted her so desperately his concubines held no appeal for him.

That terrifying thought made him pull away and stare at her. What had Zara done to him? She had turned him into a eunuch; he wanted only one woman. Zara. What in the blessed name of Allah was he going to do? He could force her and lose his wager. *And lose her forever.* Or he could continue his seduction, which seemed to be failing.

"You have bewitched me," he said harshly. "Leave me! Return to the harem. I need to think."

Zara scrambled to her feet and stumbled toward the door.

"On second thought," Jamal said thickly, "send Saha to me. Perhaps she can quench the fire you have started."

Zara turned and raced from the room, her cheeks burning. Let him vent his lust with Saha, she thought dully. Let the redhead pleasure him all night long; she didn't care. But for some obscure reason, she did care.

"Sheik Jamal is an extraordinary lover," Saha told Leila and Amar as they sat beside the pool in the small garden outside the harem. "He was tireless last night," she lied. It wouldn't do to tell her companions that Jamal had dismissed her, telling her he was too tired to do either of them justice. "There was no end to his loving. I was quite exhausted when he sent me back to my room."

Leila and Amar sighed dreamily, wishing it were they who had spent the night in Jamal's arms.

"Do you not think our sheik is a magnificent lover, Zara?" Saha baited.

Zara, who was serving refreshments to Jamal's concubines, paused, sending Saha a withering smile. "I do not know, Lady Saha."

"You have spent many hours alone with Jamal," Leila contended. "He must have found you unworthy of his attention if he did not let you pleasure him."

"Jamal does not like blondes," Amar said smugly. "Zara is not beautiful as we are, and she is far too skinny and tall to attract a man such as our master."

"I do not like mint tea, Zara," Saha said. "Fetch me something cool to drink. Perhaps a fruit sherbet."

"These apples are bruised, Zara, bring fresh ones," Amar ordered.

"I need a wet cloth to wipe my face, Zara," Leila said. "Be sure it is scented with my special fragrance."

Zara had taken just about all she could from Jamal's spoiled women. They were indolent, pampered creatures with mush for brains. They didn't have a thought in their heads that wasn't of a sexual nature.

"I'm busy," she said, deriving great pleasure

from the shocked silence that followed her words. "Do it yourselves."

"I said I wanted something cool to drink," Saha repeated, thrusting her cup of tepid tea at Zara. "Take this away."

A sly smile turned up the corners of Zara's lips as she took the cup and deliberately emptied it into Saha's lap. Saha leaped to her feet, her eyes brilliant with hatred as Zara gave her a wicked smile.

"I've never seen you move so fast, Saha," she taunted.

"Berber bitch! How dare you treat me with disrespect? Wait until I tell Jamal. Then we'll see who has the last laugh." She charged across the garden, and ran headlong into Jamal.

"Oh, my lord, praise Allah you're here."

Jamal's knowing gaze traveled over Saha's drenched caftan, and he knew without being told that Zara was the cause of her vexation. "What has upset you, Saha?"

Saha pointed an accusing finger at Zara. "Your Berber slave has insulted me. Look what she did to me!" She held out her damp caftan with thumb and forefinger. "The witch threw tea in my lap."

Jamal wanted to laugh but knew it would only make matters worse. Zara would never learn obedience if he made light of her escapades, though in truth they amused him.

"What do you suggest I do, Saha?"

Saha's smile was not pleasant. "The bastinado, my lord. Ten strokes on the soles of her feet should be sufficient."

Jamal blanched, stunned by Saha's viciousness. Ten strokes of the wooden rod upon the soles of Zara's tender feet would cripple her. "Aren't you being a bit harsh?"

"Zara deserves it, my lord," Leila contended. "She refused to serve me when I bade her bring me a wet cloth to bathe my face."

"She would not fetch me a fresh apple," Amar added. "Zara is a slave, is she not? She has been disobedient and sullen. After she is severely punished, you'd be wise to sell her."

Jamal turned his dark gaze on Zara, who didn't seem at all repentant. "You have displeased my women, Zara," he said sternly. "What do you have to say for yourself?"

Zara gave him a contemptuous smile. "I have no desire to please your women. You do that well enough without my help."

Jamal nearly burst, trying to contain his laughter. Attempting to sound stern, he said, "Sarcasm does not become you, Zara."

"Zara is stubborn and fractious," Leila said sulkily. "Send her away."

"Aye, my lord," Zara agreed sweetly. "Send me away. Your wager is all but lost, and I will be free shortly anyway."

"What wager?" Saha wanted to know.

"Enough of this bickering," Jamal ordered. He preferred not to divulge the terms of the wager he'd made with Zara. He was having such dismal luck seducing her that he'd rather it didn't become common knowledge.

"You *are* going to punish Zara, aren't you?" Saha asked, clinging to Jamal as she stared meltingly into his eyes.

"Aye, Zara will be punished according to her infraction," Jamal intoned grimly. "Come with me, Zara."

Zara wondered if she had gone too far. She didn't relish being punished, but the look on Saha's face when she'd dumped tea in her lap was almost worth it.

Chapter Six

How angry *was* Jamal? Zara wondered as she followed him to his chambers. Angry enough to use the bastinado on her? She shuddered. Would she be able to withstand the excruciating pain of being beaten upon the soles of her feet? Allah help her.

Once inside his chamber, Jamal rounded on her. Zara's fear escalated when she noted the fierce expression on Jamal's face.

"What are you going to do?"

"The bastinado seems an appropriate punishment for your insolent behavior toward my women, don't you agree?"

Zara swallowed visibly. She had seen the damage done by a bastinado and it wasn't pretty. "No, I do not agree. 'Tis much too harsh for my minor offense. Your women are a lazy lot whose brains are situated between their legs."

Jamal couldn't help it. He burst into laughter. Zara's canny assessment of his women was accurate. His new slave was truthful to a fault. Unfortunately, she must be punished for her disobedience. He couldn't have her upsetting his household with her disruptive behavior.

"Perhaps you're right," Jamal agreed, "but 'tis not your place to judge my women. I did not acquire them for their intelligence."

"That's obvious, my lord," she said sweetly. "You think on the same level as they do, only *your* brains are in that appendage between your legs."

Jamal's expression turned from amusement to anger in the blink of an eye. "You go too far, slave! If you do not curb your tongue I will have it cut out. 'Tis back to the stables with you. Obviously, you would rather wallow in dung than take your ease in comfortable quarters."

Through some kind of silent communication, Hammet appeared at Jamal's elbow.

"Fetch Zara clothing that is more appropriate for work in the stables, Hammet. She is to resume her chores there until she has learned humility. Take her away; she offends me."

Back to the stables, Zara thought dismally as Hammet escorted her from Jamal's chambers. She supposed she deserved it. Her sharp tongue had pricked Jamal's anger and she must pay the consequences. But at least she'd been spared the bastinado. She tried to convince herself that the stables were better suited to her tastes than the harem, but it didn't work.

Hammet plucked a set of rough clothing from a nail just inside the stables and thrust it at her. "You can change in an empty horse stall while I find Ahmed and tell him you're back. Be quick about it."

Zara stumbled into an empty stall and quickly donned the shirt, baggy pantaloons and *djellaba*, feeling more at ease in the familiar robes that all but obscured her figure than in the fancy harem clothing that displayed far too much skin. She had just pulled the *djellaba* over her head when Hammet pulled open the stall door.

"I have spoken with Ahmed. Your duties will begin immediately. They are the same as before." He handed her a rake. "I personally don't think this is woman's work, but the master isn't a man to be crossed. You have a vicious tongue, Zara. Learn to curb it and you can become our sheik's favorite. You have more brains than Saha, Leila and Amar put together."

Having had his say, Hammet turned on his heel and left her to contemplate her dismal future as a stable slave.

None of the stable slaves bothered Zara that night. Or the next. Or the night after that. Zara assumed they feared reprisal from Jamal and was grateful for that much at least. But stable work was backbreaking toil, and as each day passed, Zara had cause to regret her disrespect toward Jamal's concubines. When would she learn to curb her sharp tongue? she wondered grumpily. Never, she supposed. Though she missed her soft bed in the harem, she was too proud to ask for it back.

Zara had claimed an empty stall for herself and forked fresh straw in it for her bed. It provided the only bit of privacy she had enjoyed since being assigned to the stables three days before. She had just eaten her supper, washed her hands and face, hung a lantern from a hook and was preparing to bed down for the night when she sensed someone staring at her over the low wall of the stall.

"Are you ready yet to admit defeat and act like a lady?" Jamal asked. His eyes glowed like polished ebony in the lamplight.

Zara glared disdainfully at Jamal. "Youssef's daughter will never admit to defeat. As long as I do my work, you have nothing to complain about. Two weeks have already elapsed since we struck our bargain. Soon you will be forced to free me."

Jamal spit out an oath. That cursed wager again! He'd never encountered a more provoking female. He didn't want Zara sleeping on a bed of straw in the stables. He wanted her in his bed, in his arms, her body sated with his loving.

Jamal unlatched the gate and stepped into the stall. "Yield to me, vixen. I will swathe you in fine silks and brocades and give you jewels that match your green eyes."

He pulled her against him so that she could feel the hard ridge of his need against her soft belly. "Can you not feel how much I want you?"

"I suggest that you visit your harem," Zara countered. She hated the way her body betrayed her each time Jamal touched her, and she tried to pull away from him. He would not allow it.

" 'Tis you I want, Zara. I have already tried to

108

assuage my need for you with my concubines, but they failed to quench the fire inside me." His arm curved around her waist. "Come, I will teach you delights beyond those you achieved with your bandit lover." His piercing gaze held her suspended. "Have you ever had tiny silver balls slipped inside you? When you move, or even breathe, they hit against one another, creating an erotic clamor that will bring you sublime rapture beyond anything you have ever known."

Zara shuddered, aroused by Jamal's seductive words and the tone of his voice. They were more arousing than the most intimate of caresses. If she didn't put a stop to it soon, she'd be begging him to show her all the delights of which he spoke.

"Save them for your concubines," Zara countered freeing herself from his grasp. "I am extremely happy where I am. You can take those little silver balls and—"

"Enough! You are a willful vixen with the heart and soul of a Berber warrior. I will leave you for now, Zara, but mark my words, you *will* be mine, in every way possible for a man to have a woman. When I place those silver balls inside you, you will beg for release that only I can give you. Good night, sweet vixen. Pleasant dreams." Her shocked expression amused him. He hoped her dreams tonight were erotic ones.

"Cur! Camel dung!" Zara flung at him. No man had ever spoken to her of such things. Were there really erotic toys such as silver balls? Just thinking about them moving against one another inside her made her feminine parts tingle and weep.

"Why? Why do you want me when there are willing women within your household?" Zara wanted to know.

Suddenly he grew serious, his expression grim. "I wish I knew. Perhaps Allah in his wisdom will reveal the answer to me one day." He turned on his heel and left.

Sleep that night was a long time coming for Zara.

Jamal was having even greater difficulty finding sleep. He summoned Leila to his bed and then dismissed her when he found she did not appeal to him. He considered calling Amar or Saha but realized it wasn't his concubines he wanted. Only Zara would satisfy him, and he had no stomach for forcing a woman to his bed. The Berber vixen had turned him into a cursed eunuch!

Having finally found sleep, Zara wasn't prepared to be awakened a short time later. A hand came down over her mouth, and she felt a warm breath next to her ear.

"Awaken, Princess. I bring a message from your father."

Full awareness came swiftly at the mention of her father.

"I will remove my hand if you promise not to cry out."

Zara nodded vigorously and the hand came away. "Who are you?"

His words were a mere whisper of sound against her ear. "I am Rachid the camel trader, one of your father's spies. I heard a rumor that you were a stable slave but didn't want to believe it. The sheik is a fiend to force you to perform such menial work."

"From whom did you hear the rumor?"

"The sheik's concubines spoke of you when they visited the *souk* yesterday. But I heard it from other sources, too. I promptly relayed the news to Youssef. He is camped in the mountains just beyond the oasis. His reply came today. He wants you to be prepared for a rescue attempt tomorrow night. The Blue Men will come in the darkest hours before dawn."

"How will it be accomplished?" Zara wanted to know. She was literally shaking with excitement.

"Youssef and his men will scale the walls. Be prepared."

"What can I do to help? They must be careful; guards are everywhere."

Her words were met with silence. The messenger was gone.

The next day passed far too slowly for Zara's liking. She tried to keep busy but found herself staring at the high walls surrounding Paradise far too often. Where was her father now? she wondered. Her heart leaped into her throat when Jamal appeared and asked to have his horse saddled. He and Haroun were going hunting in the mountains.

Zara's first thought was that they would find her father. Then she chided herself for thinking such a thing possible. Youssef was too smart to be caught. He knew the mountains well and was as wily as a fox. Jamal would never find him.

Tonight she would be with her people and never have to see Jamal again. Somehow that thought was not as comforting as she'd expected.

Jamal's mind wasn't on hunting. His thoughts were consumed by the stubborn Berber vixen who fought tooth and nail to stay out of his bed. Was he so repulsive then? His concubines didn't think so.

"If your mind isn't on hunting, Jamal, we are wasting our time out here," Haroun commented dryly.

"I needed to get away, my friend," Jamal said testily. "As you have noticed, I've not been in the best of moods of late."

"Force the witch to your bed, Jamal," Haroun advised. "You have been patient longer than most men in your place would be. Once you've feasted on Zara's sweet flesh, you can turn your mind to more important matters. It isn't like you to neglect your concubines. Had I a woman like Saha to pleasure me, I might never leave my bed."

Jamal grew thoughtful. "You covet Saha, my friend?"

"Forgive me, my lord, I meant no disrespect. It is wrong of me to desire that which is not mine. I accept whatever punishment you deem proper."

"We have been together a long time, Haroun. I would not dream of punishing you for so minor an offense. Saha is a troublesome baggage who needs a firmer hand than mine to control her."

Haroun grinned. "I would tame her with gentle but unyielding patience were she mine."

"Why have you never married, Haroun?" Jamal asked curiously.

Haroun flushed and looked away. He didn't dare tell Jamal he could not marry as long as he coveted Saha so fiercely. "I have yet to meet a woman I wish to marry," he said at length.

Jamal let the subject drop. "Perhaps you're right, I'm not in the mood for hunting. Let us return."

Suddenly Haroun reined his mount to a halt. "My lord, look! The remains of a campfire, a recent one. Who do you suppose travels this way?"

"Caravans usually don't stray so far off their normal paths," Jamal mused as he dismounted to study the tracks visible in the sandy soil, "yet there are camel tracks. What do you make of it, Haroun?"

"The camels were not carrying heavy burdens, my lord," Haroun said, kneeling for a closer look at the tracks. "The hoof prints are smaller than those of the camels normally used to carry heavy burdens.

"Racing camels," Haroun and Jamal said, coming to the same conclusion at the same time.

"Berber racing camels," Jamal clarified. "And they are much too close to Paradise for comfort."

"Do you suppose Youssef comes for his daughter?"

" 'Tis my thought exactly. There have been no raids upon the sultan's caravans since Zara's capture. I received a missive from Ishmail just yesterday, thanking me for convincing him to spare the life of the *cadi's* daughter. He is pleased with Youssef's restraint since his daughter's capture."

"We must prepare for a rescue attempt by Youssef. I will alert the guards and put out extra watches."

"Capturing Youssef will certainly please the sultan," Jamal said. Yet even as he spoke the words, he imagined Zara's devastation should her father end up as the sultan's prisoner.

"I suggest you move Zara back to the harem," Haroun said. "You don't want to make it easy for Youssef to find her."

Jamal gave the suggestion considerable thought before rejecting it. "Zara will remain in the stables. Moving her now might alert Youssef to the fact that we know of his scheme. Youssef will find a welcome party waiting for him when he attempts a rescue. We have plans to make, my friend. Plans that must be kept secret from Zara. The stable slaves need to be warned to keep out of sight tonight no matter what happens."

Zara noted Jamal's return with apprehension. He and Haroun had bagged no game, which seemed unusual in an area abounding with wild animals. Nothing seemed amiss, so she assumed that her father had remained safely hidden during the sheik's foray into the mountains. She saw Jamal and Haroun speaking quietly to Ahmed and chafed with curiosity. There was no reason, however, for them to suspect a rescue attempt by her father tonight.

Night came too slowly, but when it finally arrived, Zara's excitement escalated. So as not to raise suspicion, she crept into her stall at her usual time and feigned sleep. Fearing to close her eyes lest she fall asleep, she stared into the darkness, anticipating a sweet reunion with her father.

Zara did not hear the soft whisper of nearly silent footsteps as Jamal and Haroun entered the stables and melted into the shadows. Guards were stationed beneath the walls, at various sites near the gate and outside the stables. These precautions were to be observed nightly, until Youssef appeared. Jamal had a gut feeling it would be tonight.

The Blue Men slipped over the walls as silent as wraiths, nearly invisible in the blue-black darkness of night. Jamal watched from the shadows as they hit the ground and crept toward the stables. He counted six of them. Obviously they meant to slip in and out of the compound without creating a disturbance. It was a daring rescue attempt, albeit one doomed to failure.

"They're coming," Haroun whispered into Jamal's ear. "Give the signal and my men will make short work of them."

"Nay, we do not yet know which is Youssef. If he is among them, I want him alive."

Jamal and Haroun sank deeper into the shadows as one shadowy figure crept into the stables. The other Blue Men remained watchful just outside the entrance, unaware that they were under surveillance.

Zara heard a whisper of sound and sprang to her feet. "Father, is that you?"

"Aye, daughter, 'tis I. We must leave quickly."

Youssef pulled a blue robe from beneath his clothing and handed it to her. "Put this on. You'll be less conspicuous in the moonlight."

When the blue robe was in place, Youssef said, "Take my hand, we will leave together."

Zara placed her trembling hand trustingly in her father's.

"That foul beast hasn't hurt you, has he? My spy said you appeared well."

"I'm unharmed," Zara assured him. "I'll be better once I leave this accursed place. We must go quietly; there are others sleeping in the stables."

They moved toward the door, guided by a sliver of moonlight. Zara's hopes soared. Freedom was within sight. They were going to make it! They had but to negotiate the short distance to the wall and use the ropes that had been lowered to hoist themselves up and over to the other side.

A voice echoed in the darkness, issuing a crisp order. "Now!" Immediately a dozen armed men rushed from their hiding places to challenge the Blue Men, cutting off their escape.

"Nay!" Zara cried. "We've been betrayed!"

" 'Tis no betrayal, sweet vixen," Jamal said, stepping out of the shadows.

Youssef sheltered Zara behind him, facing Jamal squarely. "Let my daughter go, Sheik Jamal. You have me. You no longer need Zara."

"You are wrong, Youssef, I *do* need Zara. You can't imagine how desperately I need her. As for you, my fine bandit, the sultan has plans for you. Your fate is in his hands now."

"Nay!" Zara cried, stepping out from behind

her father. "Would you have my father's death upon your conscience?"

"Youssef has broken the law, Zara. Now he must pay."

"All the Blue Men have been rounded up, my lord," Haroun reported. "Do you want them executed immediately?"

Zara gave a strangled cry and clung to her father.

"Nay," Jamal said, "lock them in an empty storage room until I decide what's to be done with them. 'Tis the sultan's right to dictate punishment."

"Move," Haroun said, prodding Youssef with the tip of his scimitar.

Zara's chin rose stubbornly. "I will go with them."

"Nay, you will not," Jamal said with quiet authority. When Zara ignored him and tried to follow her father, Jamal grasped her arm, pulling her toward the house. "You, my lovely Berber warrior, will stay where I can keep an eye on you."

He dragged her through the inner courtyard and into his chamber.

"Is all well, my lord?" Hammet emerged from the shadows holding an oil lamp that he had just lit in anticipation of Jamal's return. He set it down on the table and turned his gaze to Zara.

"Extremely well, Hammet. Youssef has been captured."

"Shall I take this . . . er . . . rather smelly person to the harem, master?"

"I'm sorry the smell of horse dung offends you,

Hammet," Zara said sweetly, "but I find the scent far more pleasing than the stench of your master's chamber."

"Shall I fetch the bastinado?" Hammet asked, startled by Zara's defiance.

"Not just yet, Hammet," Jamal said, sending Zara a smile that did not quite reach his eyes. "Tonight Zara will share my bath and my bed. You may seek your own bed."

"Are you sure you won't need my help?" Hammet asked, reluctant to leave his master at the mercy of the Berber vixen.

"I can manage, thank you. It will take more than a razor-tongued female to do me harm."

Hammet left reluctantly. Once he was gone, Zara rounded on Jamal. "What are you going to do to my father?"

"Your father is a bandit. The sultan, not I, will be his executioner." That said, he pushed her toward a slatted partition at the far end of the room. "Come along, you are long overdue for a bath."

Jamal pushed her behind the partition and Zara found herself in a *hammam* no less elegant but on a smaller scale than the one in the harem. The huge sunken tub was surrounded by cushions and couches and gleaming white tiles.

"Take off your clothes. You must bathe if you are to sleep in my bed."

"I'd prefer to sleep on the floor," Zara argued. "We have struck a bargain, remember?"

Jamal gave her a smile that was far from comforting. "Things have changed. Your father is my prisoner now."

"Nothing has changed!" Zara charged.

"We'll discuss it later. Do as I say. Undress and get into the bath. There's soap in the jar next to the tub."

Muttering to herself, Zara undressed quickly and sank into the tub. The water was warm and felt delicious against her skin as she immersed herself to her neck. She closed her eyes and laid her head back against the rim, unable to restrain the sigh that slipped past her lips.

She sensed him watching her, felt his burning gaze upon her. The piercing heat seared her every place it touched. He made no move toward her, just stood there watching.

She opened her eyes and stared back at him, startled by the intensity of his desire. "Must you watch?"

He did not answer as he turned abruptly and returned to his bed chamber. He was back seconds later with a caftan. "When you've finished your bath, put this on and come to bed. You're safe with me tonight, or what's left of it. Neither of us would enjoy the experience. You're too worried about your father."

The charged atmosphere quickly cooled after Jamal left her to enjoy her bath in private. As Zara soaped and rinsed her body, then tackled her hair, her thoughts grew dark and dismal. What would become of her father? Would he be put to death by the sultan? What could she do to keep Jamal from releasing her father into the sultan's custody? Was there nothing she could offer Jamal to keep her father safe?

The answer came to her, clear and concise and definitely unwelcome. She had only one thing to offer Jamal . . . herself. She could surrender to his seduction and remain his slave forever. Even though permanent captivity would likely kill her, she'd do it for her father and all the people who depended upon him. Without Youssef to lead them, the Berbers would lose their fight against unfair taxation and might never regain their lost lands.

Her solution to the problem was not a simple matter and could not be decided upon without considerable thought. First she had to appeal to Jamal to grant her time alone with her father. She had to know how to best serve Youssef without endangering his life. If she must sacrifice her innocence to save her father's life, then so be it. Jamal wanted her. And to be perfectly honest, she'd just as soon let Jamal be the man to give her that first taste of pleasure.

Jamal was waiting for Zara when she returned to the bed chamber. He was lying in bed, gazing absently out the window at the star-studded sky. He smiled at her and held out his hand.

"Come, you must be exhausted."

"How did you know my father would come for me tonight?" Zara asked as she perched gingerly on the side of the bed. "Who betrayed him?" She needed answers before she could sleep.

"No one betrayed Youssef. I discovered the remains of a camp while hunting yesterday and put two and two together. Caravans never come this close to Paradise. It's off the beaten path. I knew Youssef would come for you sooner or later and decided to keep watch every night until he showed up."

"Let him go."

"Are you mad? I'm not anxious to commit suicide. And that's what it would be if I betrayed Moulay Ishmail. The sultan wants Youssef. Go to sleep, Zara. I'm too tired to do battle with you."

"Do you want me, Jamal?"

He sighed and closed his eyes. "More than you can imagine. But when I take you it won't be a quick coupling in the middle of the night."

"I wish to speak with my father. Will you allow it?"

"Ask me tomorrow. I may be more inclined to allow it then."

His answer instilled little confidence in Zara. She had to speak to her father before he was sent to Meknes. She took a deep, steadying breath and said, "I am willing to bargain for the privilege of seeing my father."

She finally had Jamal's attention. His eyes opened slowly and he searched her face through narrowed lids. "You have very little to bargain with, sweet vixen."

His voice was low and provocative, sending a shiver down Zara's spine. "I have something you covet, my lord."

"What I covet can be taken without your permission."

Her chin rose fractionally. "By force, my lord. Is that how you would have me?"

"Nay, sweet vixen. I want you hot and willing. We will strike a bargain, you and I. One we can both live with."

Chapter Seven

Surrounded by the warmth of Jamal's body, Zara awoke slowly the following morning. The moment she opened her eyes she became aware of many things at once. His large hand cupped her breast and his body was curved around hers. She hadn't fallen asleep until dawn, lying stiffly at Jamal's side, waiting for him to reach for her. But he did not. His gentle snoring had finally lulled her to sleep.

"You're awake." His breath was warm against her ear. "Did you sleep well, sweet vixen?"

"Nay. I do not like your hands on my body." Could he tell she was lying?

He pushed himself to his elbow and turned her to face him. "I like the feel of my hands on you. Your breasts are magnificent. Full and firm but not overly large. Your nipples stand out like ripe

122

cherries, my favorite fruits. I intend to feast on them until I am sated."

Zara pushed his hands away. "We have a bargain to strike," she reminded him. "When can I see my father?"

His eyes narrowed. "Aye, a bargain. Very well, sweet vixen, we shall strike another bargain. State your terms and I'll state mine."

"You want me, my lord. You may have me as a willing participant in your bed until you tire of me. In return, I ask only that you set my father free."

Jamal gave a derisive snort. "Nay, Zara. I cannot free your father and you know it. Here are my terms. You may visit your father daily until he is sent to Meknes. In return, you will come to my bed willingly whenever I want you."

"That is not acceptable, my lord."

"You forget," Jamal reminded her, "that you are my slave. I have no need to bargain with you when I own you body and soul. The reason I do so now is because I prefer not to force you to my bed. But you have made a shambles of my patience. You have no rights, sweet vixen. Accept my terms or your father will suffer the consequences."

Zara bit the soft underside of her lip, her mind working furiously. Had she driven Jamal too far? Most men would not have put up with her defiance. They would have bedded her whether she wished it or not.

"You said I might visit my father while he is here."

"That is true."

"Then grant me one small boon. Do not send Father to Meknes right away. You will find me most appreciative if you hold him prisoner here instead of sending him to the sultan."

"Sooner or later Youssef must go to Meknes," Jamal contended.

"Make it later," Zara pleaded. "The sultan doesn't know Father is here yet, and as long as his caravans are no longer threatened, he will not care."

"He will care. Ishmail wants Youssef's head. But I will grant you this boon, my sweet. For the time being, Youssef and his followers will remain my prisoners. Do not ask more of me than that."

Zara felt a surge of joy. As long as Youssef remained, she knew she could find a way to free him. Obtaining her father's freedom would be worth the loss of her innocence. She had retained it longer than most women; thirteen was considered the ideal age for brides and concubines.

"Very well, I agree to your terms."

Jamal gave her a slow, provocative smile. "Allah be praised. My patience is about to be rewarded. In my arms, sweet vixen, you may be as wild as you like."

"I wish to see my father," Zara said, refusing to return his smile. Her decision gave her little joy.

"I will arrange it. You have this day to prepare yourself for me. After your visit with your father, Hammet will take you to the harem. Nafisa will take care of you."

The moment Jamal spoke his name, Hammet entered the chamber. "Are you ready to break your fast, my lord?"

"Aye, bring enough for two. Zara will share my repast."

When Hammet left, Jamal rose naked from the bed. The sight of him took Zara's breath away. His legs were long and strongly made; his torso rippled with muscles and tendons beneath smooth golden skin. His entire body bespoke power and supple grace. Hands on hips, legs spread apart, he faced the open window and drew in several deep breaths before glancing at Zara.

"Come, we will bathe together before our food arrives." He held out his hand. "Come."

Zara placed her hand in his and followed him into the *hammam*. Fresh soap and drying cloths had been laid out and the tub sparkled with fresh, clean water. Hammet's doing, she supposed. Jamal removed Zara's caftan and led her into the water. Then he reached for the soap.

"You have a lovely body," Jamal said as he rubbed jasmine-scented soap over her torso. "Tonight I will explore you thoroughly. Before night's end you will know my body as intimately as I will know yours."

His hands slid provocatively over her breasts, stomach and hips, and then he turned her around to soap her back and buttocks. "Sit on the edge of the tub," he requested.

Zara dared not disobey, lest he change his mind about her father. When she was seated on the lip of the tub, he reached down for her right foot. Lifting it from the water, he soaped her foot and leg, his hand straying into the damp tunnel between her legs. Zara gasped and squirmed. Jamal seemed not to notice as he finished with one leg and reached for the other. By the time he was done, Zara was trembling.

"Now you may bathe me," Jamal said, "but not with jasmine-scented soap. I prefer something less feminine." He handed her a jar that smelled of pine and spices.

Zara wanted to throw the soap in his face but thought better of it. As long as her father was Jamal's prisoner, she was vulnerable and totally under Jamal's control. He knew she would do anything to keep Youssef safe. Dipping into the soap, she began to spread it over his body. She was surprised to find that she enjoyed the feel of his flesh beneath her fingertips, so smooth and firm, so hard beneath the velvety surface of his skin. She was startled when his muscles jumped in reaction to her touch. Did her hands on his body give him the same kind of pleasure as his hands on her body gave her? she wondered dimly.

Zara skirted around Jamal's half-aroused manhood as she spread soap down his legs. When she finished she stepped back and said, "I am done, my lord."

Jamal was puzzled by her shyness. Had she never touched her bandit lover's body? "Soon, sweet vixen, you will be as comfortable with my body as you are with your own. You have much to learn despite your experience. Unfortunately, there is no time now to teach you. Come, let us break our fast together."

Hammet had their meal set out when they returned to the bed chamber. Zara ate quickly of the boiled eggs, flatbread, fresh fruit and yogurt. She couldn't wait to see her father.

"I'm finished," Zara said, setting down her fork.

"I have just begun my meal," Jamal complained. "I know you're anxious to see your father so I'll have Hammet take you."

Once again Hammet appeared as if by magic. Did he read his master's mind? Zara wondered. She watched carefully as Jamal removed a brass key from a small casket sitting atop an ebony table inlaid with mother-of-pearl.

"Slip my *djellaba* on over your caftan," Jamal told her as he handed Hammet the key. "You must dress modestly in public, Zara."

Zara did not object. Indeed, she was grateful for the encompassing garment. Without proper undergarments, the caftan was fit only for the harem.

Hammet led Zara through the courtyard to a row of one-story buildings built against the south wall of the compound. He stopped before the first squat building and fit the key into the lock. The door opened and Zara stepped inside.

The single window high in the wall admitted a dim beam of light. Zara spied her father immediately. He sat cross-legged on the dirt floor, his back resting against a bench that also served as a bed. Before him on a low table were the remnants of a meal and a jug of water.

"Father!"

Youssef rose to his feet and held his arms out to his daughter. Zara rushed into them, hugging him fiercely.

"I'm sorry, daughter. Things didn't work out as

127

planned. Now we are both Sheik Jamal's prisoners. I cannot think who could have betrayed us."

"No one betrayed us, Father. Jamal saw camel tracks and signs of a recent campsite while in the hills hunting. Caravans rarely come this way. He suspected that you and the Blue Men were in the vicinity. There could be only one reason for you to be here, to rescue me. He set a trap for you."

"I have failed you, Zara. I am as good as dead. The sultan wants my head and will likely have it once I'm sent to Meknes."

"You're not going to Meknes, Father," Zara said, lowering her voice. She knew Hammet was just outside the door and didn't want him carrying tales back to Jamal.

"How can that be?"

"I've persuaded Jamal to keep you here for the time being. That will give me time to find a way to free both of us."

Youssef was no fool. "You *persuaded* Sheik Jamal?"

"I struck a bargain with him."

Youssef frowned. "You have no bargaining power, daughter."

"You're wrong, Father." She flushed and looked away. "I have something Jamal wants."

"You mean he hasn't already taken what he wants from you?"

"Nay, he has taken nothing from me. I was not willing, and he would not force me."

Youssef appeared confused. "You are his slave, are you not? He has the right to do with you as he pleases."

"You don't know Jamal, Father. He is . . . not

128

like most men. Perhaps his English mother influenced him, but he is not a man who enjoys taking a woman by force."

"You can't sacrifice yourself for me," Youssef argued, appalled. "I won't let you."

"You can't stop me. Jamal won't hurt me, I'm certain of that. I know I can find a way to free us once I earn his trust."

"It's too dangerous. You must not do this. Have you forgotten your betrothed so soon?"

"Nay, I've not forgotten. But I won't let you lose your head without doing everything within my power to prevent it."

Suddenly the door opened and Jamal stepped inside. He sensed the tension between father and daughter but did not remark upon it. "As you can see, Zara, your father is well. He has been neither starved nor beaten. Go with Hammet; he will take you to the harem."

Zara wanted to protest but dared not. For her plan to work, Jamal must learn to trust her. "I will return tomorrow, Father."

Jamal's gaze followed Zara out the door. Then he turned his attention to Youssef. "Your daughter has pleaded for your life."

"I thought my fate was up to the sultan."

"So it is, but it pleases me to grant Zara's wish, at least for the time being. You are to remain here as my prisoner until such time that I decide you are no longer of use to me."

"By that I take it to mean that you will keep me alive for as long as my daughter pleases you in bed. When you tire of her, you will send me to

Meknes. What will become of my daughter then, Sheik Jamal?"

Jamal frowned. Youssef's accusation came too close to the truth for his liking. "What did Zara tell you?"

"That you have not harmed her, and that she has struck a bargain with you. Zara is a beautiful woman, and few men would leave her untouched. I thank you for that. But 'tis not my wish that she sacrifice herself for me."

" 'Tis no sacrifice, Youssef. What Zara and I do will be for our mutual pleasure. Count yourself lucky to have such a caring daughter. Whatever happens, Zara will not be made to suffer for your sins. She and I have struck a bargain. I am a man of my word."

"You are a man who wants a woman and will go to any lengths to get her," Youssef charged. "I cannot like what Zara is doing. Take her to wife if you want her that badly."

"*Wife?*" Jamal nearly strangled on the word. "Zara is my slave, nothing more. I have three concubines. I do not need a wife. I am at sea for long periods at a time, and a wife would be a hindrance. Besides, your daughter has already had a lover. She knows a man wants a wife who's had no others before him."

Youssef nearly choked on his anger. Jamal deemed it expedient to leave and did so while Youssef was still raving over Jamal's unjust accusation.

Zara wondered what Jamal and her father were talking about as she followed Hammet into the courtyard where the three concubines were taking their ease. Leila sat at the edge of the pool, dangling her feet in the water. Saha sprawled on her stomach on a nearby bench, popping sweetmeats into her mouth while Amar sat at her feet, strumming a stringed instrument. When Zara appeared, all activity came to a halt.

"The Berber witch is back," Saha said disparagingly. "Why does Jamal subject us to such a violent person?"

"She has bewitched our master," Leila said.

"What is that offensive slave doing here, Hammet?"

"I but follow my master's orders," Hammet said, shoving Zara before him. "I'm to take Zara to Nafisa. Zara is to entertain Jamal tonight in his chamber."

"What!" Saha cried, eyes blazing. "How can Jamal want someone like her when he can have us? You must have heard wrong, Hammet."

"My hearing is perfect, Lady Saha. It is not your place to tell our master whom to bed."

"Why would Jamal prefer a bad tempered stable slave when we are all eager to please him?" Leila asked with a pout. " 'Tis as I said, Saha, the Berber slave has bewitched Jamal."

"I am no witch!" Zara denied hotly.

"Inside with you," Hammet said, pushing Zara through the door into the harem. "Pay them no heed. They are jealous because Sheik Jamal has been sorely neglecting them since you arrived. I will leave you to Nafisa but will return later to escort you to the sheik's chambers.

"Make Zara presentable, Nafisa," Hammet said

to the old woman, who met them at the door. "She is to entertain the sheik tonight."

Nafisa's weathered face broke into a knowing grin. "So Jamal will finally have you. I wondered how long you would hold out. He is brave and handsome and an extraordinary lover, I am told. You have caused much contention among Jamal's concubines. He summoned Leila to his bed chamber then sent her away without giving her a chance to pleasure him. They blame you for his lack of interest."

" 'Tis not my fault," Zara claimed. "I would rather mate with a camel."

Nafisa's eyes widened. "I know Jamal. He would not force an unwilling woman, slave or no. He has his mother's kind heart."

Zara's chin rose slightly as she began to refute Nafisa's words, but she couldn't. Jamal wasn't forcing her. She had been the one to suggest the bargain they had eventually struck and now she must pay the price. And do so willingly.

"You are right, Nafisa. I go to Jamal willingly. You must help me to prepare myself for him. I"—she nearly choked on the words—"wish to please him." *At least until I have gained his trust and freed my father*, she thought.

"I knew you would come around," Nafisa cackled. "Our master is a persuasive man, and according to Saha, Leila and Amar, an experienced and unselfish lover. You are fortunate, Zara, that Jamal has been so patient with you. Come, I will prepare you for our master's bed."

The day passed swiftly as Zara was stripped of all bodily hair, bathed, massaged, pummeled, oiled and pumiced. Her long blond tresses were washed and rubbed to a brilliant shine with a silken cloth, and her fingernails and toenails were painted with red enamel. During the grueling session, Saha, Leila and Amar wandered into the *hammam* to watch.

"She is too skinny to please Jamal," Leila declared.

"She has big feet," Amar added snidely.

"I'll wager she has had so many men, her sheath is as large as that of a she-camel," Saha snickered. "After one night with Zara, Jamal will send her back to the stables."

"Leave us," Nafisa severely admonished. "Your remarks are uncalled for and unbefitting a lady."

One by one the three concubines disappeared into their rooms, leaving behind a heavy cloud of enmity. "They hate me," Zara said, not really caring. Soon she'd be gone, and Jamal and his harem could go to the devil for all she cared. But tonight was a different story. In order to keep her father safe from the sultan's wrath, she *had* to please Jamal. Unfortunately, she had no idea how to go about it.

"You may rest in your room until Hammet comes for you," Nafisa said. "He will bring appropriate clothing for you to wear."

When Zara hesitated, Nafisa asked, "Is something bothering you, child? You have nothing to fear from Jamal. He will not harm you."

"You are wise, Nafisa. I would ask your counsel."

Nafisa's brow puckered. "In what way?"

"I . . . I don't know what to do tonight. What will Jamal expect of me?"

Nafisa stared at Zara, disbelief etched upon her wrinkled features. *"You don't know what to do? I don't understand, child."*

Since they were alone, Zara spoke freely. "I am still a virgin. I know what men and women do together, but how can I please Jamal if I do not know how to go about it?"

Stunned, Nafisa stared at Zara. "You have never taken a man inside your body?"

"Nay."

"Does Jamal know?"

Zara shook her head. "He thinks Sayed was my lover. Sayed was my betrothed," she explained. "He was slain the day I was taken captive by Jamal. I never bothered to correct Jamal."

"Perhaps I should prepare an aphrodisiac for you," Nafisa suggested. "Though you profess to be willing, you seem somewhat reluctant."

"Nay, I need no drug. Just tell me how to act."

Nafisa chuckled. "You don't need me to tell you how to act. Jamal is an expert in the art of arousing a woman, and you will undoubtedly respond. He will introduce you to erotic pleasures that might shock you, but he will do nothing to harm you. Remember that and all will be well."

Zara mulled over Nafisa's words as she rested in her chamber later that afternoon. There was no question in her mind that Jamal was an expert at arousing a woman, for she'd had more than one sample of what his talented hands and mouth could do. He had kissed her and touched her intimately, and his erotic descriptions of the things he would do to her had left her breathless and wanting.

Should she tell Jamal she was a virgin? she wondered. She decided to wait until later to make a decision.

A knock on the door brought her thoughts to a halt. Moments later Hammet entered. He held a goblet in one hand and something sheer and lovely draped over his arm.

"Nafisa prepared sweet almond milk for you. She said it will help calm you. These are the clothes you're to wear tonight," he said, placing a silken garment on the bed. "Sheik Jamal requested that you share his meal tonight. The milk will stave off hunger until you sup."

Zara accepted the milk and took a sip. "It's delicious," she said, "thank you."

Hammet waited until she finished every drop, then took the empty glass and departed.

Zara turned her attention to the clothing she'd been given to wear. She gasped in dismay when she discovered the "clothing" consisted of a single sheer veil made of contrasting shades of iridescent blue silk. Feeling much like a lamb going to the slaughter, Zara draped herself in the veil and sat down to await Jamal's summons.

By the time Hammet returned, she was shaking like a leaf from nervousness. It didn't help any when the eunuch presented her with a gift from Jamal. The huge emerald that slid from the small velvet pouch into her palm was perfect in every respect. It hung from a slim gold chain, which Zara placed over her head. The emerald felt cold and intrusive between her breasts, and Zara wanted to tear it off and fling it away. The golden chain reminded her of her captivity, and that she was about to become the kind of woman she despised, a submissive love slave. No fetters or chains could have been more demeaning than Jamal's gift. Swallowing her pride, she followed Hammet to Jamal's chambers.

Zara stood still as a statue after Hammet pushed her inside and closed the door behind her. Her eyes darted about, trying to look anywhere but at the sleeping couch resting upon a raised dais. The cloying scent of incense wrapped itself around her, drawing her into Jamal's world of erotic fantasy.

"I've waited a long time for this night, Princess," Jamal said, rising to greet her. His hungry gaze slid over her slender, ill-concealed figure, then back to her face. "Are you wearing my gift?"

She nodded awkwardly.

He closed the distance between them, pulling the emerald from between her breasts. "It's warm from your skin. I chose it because it matches your eyes." His gaze drifted downward. "The veil becomes you. Later I will remove it so that I may feast upon every inch of your sweet flesh."

"I'll try to please you, Jamal. If you wish to please me, you will get this over quickly so that I may return to my room."

Jamal gave her a smile that melted her bones, though she'd die before admitting it.

"Ah, sweet vixen, you must think little of me if you believe I'll take my pleasure and dismiss you quickly. Nay, when dawn colors the sky you will still be with me. Before this night ends you will swoon from the splendor of my loving. Resign yourself, my warrior princess, for you are mine now, and I am a vigorous lover."

"Keep my father safe and I'll willingly submit to your every desire, my lord." The words nearly choked her.

Jamal gave a hoot of laughter. "Have I finally tamed you, my pet? I think not. I'm not stupid. I know why you have suddenly become obedient. I want you hot and passionate, not acting like a martyr on the altar of my lust. I vow before this night is over you'll wonder why you resisted me so long." He took her hand. "Come sit beside me, and we will share a light meal."

Zara wanted to claw the smile from his face and fought desperately to hold both her temper and her tongue. Jamal was the most egotistical, arrogant man she'd ever met. She had promised to go to him willingly but she'd never said she'd enjoy it.

Servants moved about silently, serving a dish called *harina*, a hearty soup with tomatoes and peppers. There were also olives and flatbread, and at the end of the meal, honey cakes and fruit, with mint tea to wash it down. Jamal ate sparingly, taking small sips of tea as he watched Zara pick at her food. At length he motioned for the meal to be taken away. The servants cleared away the remnants of the meal and disappeared.

By that time Zara began to feel lightheaded and tingly all over. The odd sensation reached deep into her innards, causing a sensation that made it difficult to concentrate on anything but the way her body was behaving.

Jamal noted her distress and gave her a sharp look. "Did Nafisa prepare almond milk for you before you arrived?" he asked conversationally.

Zara looked at him curiously. "Aye."

Jamal spit out an oath. "I wish she hadn't."

"Does it matter?"

Jamal shrugged. "Not really." But his eyes told her otherwise. His gaze, sharp and intense, searched her face, watching, waiting, for something . . . something . . .

Zara squirmed on the cushion beside him, assailed by a peculiar sensation that traveled through her veins like wildfire, creating a wanting inside her that frightened her. What was happening to her? Her hands clenched and unclenched nervously in her lap as she tried to sort out the weird things going on inside her body.

She gave a small cry of surprise when Jamal scooped her into his arms and set her on her feet. "I want to taste you," he said, pulling her into his arms. His mouth came down on hers, savoring her taste, exploring the softness of her ripe lips. "You taste like honey," he whispered against her mouth.

His tongue flicked out to lick hungrily at her lips, then slipped between her teeth to sip more fully of her sweetness. Zara groaned. She was hot, so hot. Burning. Her blood was on fire. Her nipples ached, and she ground her hips against Jamal's erection to obtain relief from the scalding heat of her arousal, but there was no relief, only more fire.

Jamal thrust his leg between hers, aware of her

distress and the cause of it. Allah take Nafisa. He didn't want Zara like this. He hadn't ordered the aphrodisiac that Zara was given in the almond milk. He needed no help in arousing his princess.

Zara moaned again, riding his leg and pressing her breasts against his chest. Her nipples were so sensitive they ached. Something was happening to her! She wanted Jamal's hands on her; she wanted him inside her.

"Ride me, sweet princess," Jamal whispered hoarsely. "Take the edge off your hunger. Later I will arouse you again, when the effects of the drug have warn off."

"You gave me a drug?" Zara gasped, nearly beyond coherent thought. If she didn't get relief soon she'd explode.

"Shhh, don't talk. You're nearly there."

Suddenly she screamed, her climax so intense she blacked out for a moment. When she came to herself she was lying on the bed, and Jamal was holding a wet cloth to her head.

"What happened?"

"I'm sorry, Zara. Nafisa acted on her own. The drug will wear off in a short time, and then I will prove that I need no help from aphrodisiacs to bring you to ecstasy."

Zara groaned. Allah help her.

Chapter Eight

Captivated by the blond temptress dozing in his bed, Jamal watched the steady rise and fall of Zara's breasts. The lust rampant within him was incredible. Piercing and powerful, it rose like a ravening beast inside him.

Still, he preferred to make love to Zara while she was in full control of her emotions. It wasn't enough that her body craved him. That could be blamed on the drug she'd been given. Nay, he wanted her to need him with her heart and mind, and not because she'd ingested an aphrodisiac.

Zara had fallen asleep a short time before, and Jamal decided to let her sleep off the effects of the drug. The night was young. When she awakened she'd be in full control of her emotions; that was when the real seduction would begin.

When Zara stirred and made a small sound, Jamal could not resist drawing her onto her back and viewing the soft, sleeping form of his slave. Tangled hair the color of ripe wheat. Pale skin as flawless as alabaster. She was sweetly curved with narrow waist and magnificent breasts. A powerful drive stronger than his own life force made him raise her veil, baring her body to his greedy gaze. Her beauty was mesmerizing. He groaned as his hands sought her breasts.

He cupped them gently, weighing them within his large palms and then bringing each to his mouth to suckle gently upon the dusky ripe peaks. Zara stirred beneath his tender touch and he smiled.

Zara awakened to erotic sensations that were incredibly arousing. She arched up, her body soaring with sweet pleasure that was terrifying and exhilarating at the same time. The feeling was succulent and delicious and she almost purred in contentment.

A hand moved down her body in a heated caress and Zara's eyes popped open. She was momentarily distracted by the wet tug on her nipple of a very talented mouth. Though the room was lit by a single lamp, she recognized Jamal's dark head bent over her, laving her breasts with the moist heat of his mouth.

Suddenly Jamal's head rose and he smiled at her. "You're awake. Good. How do you feel?"

She tried to rise but his hard body pinned her against the bed. "I feel somewhat . . . strange. What happened? The last thing I remember was—" The truth finally dawned on her and she stared in horror at Jamal. He was smiling; a predatory smile that made her want to hit him. "Allah help me! You drugged me."

"Nay, not I," Jamal denied. "Blame Nafisa if you must, but do not judge her harshly. She meant you no harm. It was a light dose and has already worn off. When you respond to me next, it will be a true response and not drug-induced. You will receive pleasure, sweet vixen, never doubt it."

Zara did not doubt Jamal's ability to arouse her. She stared at his mouth, at his strong white teeth, soft, mobile lips and clever tongue and knew she was lost.

"Raise your shoulders," Jamal said. "The veil is becoming but I prefer you naked."

His deep voice wrapped itself warmly about her and she obeyed without question. She watched in rapt fascination as the gauzy cloth was lifted from her body and floated across the room, settling in a brilliant puddle on the carpeted floor. The arousing scent of incense filled the air, creating an atmosphere ripe with promise. Her mouth went dry and she swallowed reflexively.

"Are you thirsty?" Jamal asked as he offered her a goblet that had been resting on a tray with sweetmeats and other tempting morsels.

Zara glanced warily at the goblet, then at Jamal.

" 'Tis just fruit juice, I swear it." To prove his words, he took a healthy sip before handing the goblet to her.

Zara accepted, drinking thirstily before handing it back to him. Jamal set the goblet on the tray and leaned down to lick the remaining drops from her lips. Her lips must have proven too heady to resist, for his mouth opened and slanted across hers. He kissed her passionately, forcefully, a hot, heady taste of sin and seduction.

The need to resist this arrogant sheik was strong within her but she forced it down, aware that resistance would not bode well for her father. Jamal wanted a submissive vessel for his lust, and she'd promised to indulge him. Her father's freedom meant more to her than her innocence. If appeasing Jamal's lust would gain his trust, then she'd hand him her virginity on a silver platter. The sooner she gained his trust, the sooner she could free her father.

Jamal's hands slid down her body, finding sensitive places that made her tingle and burn. His mouth followed in the wake of his hands, searing a path to her breasts, where he feasted hungrily upon her nipples. She felt her nipples harden under his touch, felt incredible pleasure as he stroked them, and she felt that pleasure settle between her legs. All pretense fled as Zara let out a low, agonized groan. What she felt was very real.

Difficult as it was, Jamal forced himself to practice constraint. He wanted to bring Zara to the brink of madness before releasing her. And then he wanted to do it again and again. His breath quickened as her nipples hardened beneath his fingertips. Then he took one swollen bud between his teeth and caressed it with his tongue. When his lips left her breasts and traveled down to her navel, he heard her swift intake of breath.

"Jamal . . . Blessed Allah, have mercy."

"Allah can't help you, sweet vixen. Only I am

capable of giving you the release you crave."

The heel of his palm rested lightly on the smooth pink mound at the apex of her legs, massaging in erotic circles. With his other hand he pressed upon a place down low on her stomach, and the unexpected burst of pleasure caused her to cry out.

"What did you do?" she asked, gasping.

"I know many ways to give you pleasure." His hand moved between her thighs, apparently pleased by what he found there for he smiled and took her hand, bringing it between her legs. "Your love juices are flowing for me, my sweet. Can you feel them?"

She pulled her hand free. It came away wet, and her face flooded with color. Then he introduced a new torment when he gently probed her with his fingers. Zara stiffened and jerked upward, forcing his fingers deeper. A flash of panic seized her. If she was going to tell him she was a virgin, now was the time.

"Jamal, there is something—"

Her words ended in a squawk of surprise as Jamal lowered his head and kissed her there, his face burrowing between her legs as he feasted on her succulent flesh.

He raised his head and gave her a long, poignant look. "I'm going to bring you to pleasure with my mouth first. You are so sensitive there." His fingers played upon slick moist flesh as he parted her and returned to his banquet. His tongue was like living flame as it delved inside her, teasing, taunting, sending tiny bursts of fire through her body.

She felt herself thickening and swelling, and then it began. The heady rise of blood, the explosion of passion. He sensed her rush toward ecstasy and thrust his finger inside her. The results were immediate and rewarding as Zara screamed.

Zara heard her own moaning, keening sounds as breaking waves of indescribable rapture washed over her. Her body was still vibrating with it when Jamal stripped off his pantaloons and knelt between her legs.

"It's just beginning, sweet vixen," he whispered in a voice that sounded as tightly drawn as a bow.

She looked down at his body, her eyes glazed with fright when she saw his fully aroused erection. He was huge. She'd seen him aroused before but not like this. Then he was pressing himself inside her, stretching her, pushing deeper, harder, hurting her.

"Stop!" She struggled beneath him, trying to escape the pain.

At first Jamal didn't want to believe Zara was a virgin, but the truth hit him forcefully when his manhood butted against the unquestionable proof of her innocence. He went still, searching her face, seeing her anguish for himself and finally believing.

"Why didn't you tell me?" he asked harshly.

"Would you have believed me?"

He was shaking all over, his body demanding release. "It doesn't matter. It's too late now. I've waited too long for this moment. 'Tis your duty as a slave to please your master," he added harshly.

Zara clenched her teeth against the pain. "Allah take you!" Her anger was incandescent, fueled by Jamal's arrogance in thinking she'd submit willingly to slavery. "Your *slave* is willing to grant your every wish, *master*."

Her scathing sarcasm was not lost on Jamal. It fired his own anger until they were both caught in the heat of it. Resentment, raw emotions and unbridled passion brought a new dimension to their joining. Jamal's face darkened. Unspeakable lust for the Berber princess was sharp and unrelenting.

"Give me your mouth, *slave*," he ordered harshly. "The taking of a virgin must be done with finesse. I will try not to hurt you, but your sharp tongue has sorely tried my patience."

Zara stared at him a moment, then lifted her mouth. Though she knew she had pricked his anger, she didn't regret lashing him with the sharp edge of her tongue. She didn't want to accept pleasure from him. She wanted to keep her rage and resentment alive. She feared the consequences should he make her crave his body, his touch, the passion he wrung from her.

Jamal's mouth came down hard on hers, his anger slowly eroding into something he could control . . . passion. At least he'd been able to control his passion in the past, until he'd acquired a certain Berber slave. Then all thought fled as he flexed his hips and thrust through Zara's maidenhead.

Zara screamed into his mouth, her body going rigid as he pushed his entire length inside her. He was killing her.

"Relax," he whispered against her mouth. "Every woman since the beginning of time has borne the pain. I promised you pleasure and so you shall have it."

He was tearing her apart. Zara's breath caught in her throat; she was afraid to breathe lest she shatter. But Jamal seemed to know what he was doing, caressing her until the pain receded and she was ready to respond.

"Now the pleasure begins," he said when he felt her soften and her resistance ebb. "You're tight, Zara, so very tight, but that makes the pleasure all the sweeter. Move with me, open to me, come with me."

The delicious pressure of his sex inside her released a primitive instinct as she rotated her hips against his powerful body. Jamal responded to her tentative movements, thrusting and withdrawing, manipulating her body in delightful ways that took away all conscious thought.

He lowered his head and kissed her mouth again, tenderly, deeply, murmuring erotic words of encouragement. He moved within her and she welcomed his thrusting heat by wrapping her arms around the breadth of his back and pressing against him restively. Instinctively he pulled her more tightly against him and delved deeper into the honeyed sweetness of her, again and again, moving in and out with increasing vigor.

Waves of heat rippled across her skin and gathered in great pools of fire deep within her. She grasped his shoulders and clung to him as his thick manhood pressed deeper and his powerful muscles bunched and shifted beneath her fingertips. His buttocks flexed, surged, thrusting her higher and higher, into a world of white-hot splendor. Huge, consuming swells of pure sensation crested and grew, sweeping her upward into mindless bliss. She cried out his name as she shattered.

Jamal felt her ecstasy swell and burst within her, heard her cry out his name, and rejoiced in the knowledge that he had given her pleasure. Then his own culmination was upon him and he stiffened, spewing his seed into her. He shouted his pleasure, thrusting deeply until there was nothing left for him to give. For a moment he lost all sense of time and place as he spiraled downward from euphoria into the arms of perfect contentment.

It was true, Jamal thought as he drifted in a mist of serenity: no woman had ever made him feel the way he felt now. He was a hedonist who craved sensual pleasure and delighted in finding new and diverse ways to obtain it. Beautiful women, erotic play and sexual excitement were as necessary to him as eating and breathing, and he usually indulged his appetite to the fullest. He was considered a master at love play and had spent a considerable part of his adult life refining his skills.

His concubines and lovers had not been innocents and thus were able to please him in diverse ways. Yet Jamal thought it more than passing strange that a complete innocent had fulfilled him as he'd never been fulfilled before. He glanced down at Zara and realized she was watching him, her expression puzzled and a tiny bit frightened.

"Did you enjoy that?" Jamal asked. An arrogant half-smile curved his lips. He knew well and good that she had.

"What did you do to me? I've never lost control like that." Zara compared the feeling to that of being possessed. The sensation, while pleasurable in the extreme, was like losing her soul, and she wasn't ready to give that to any man.

"I wasn't expecting a virgin, Zara. You still have a lot to learn, but I will take great pleasure in teaching you the joys of erotic love play."

"May I go back to my room now?" Zara didn't think she could handle any more pleasure tonight.

Jamal chuckled and stroked her breast. "The night is young, sweet vixen. Together we will explore some of the fascinating positions available to lovers."

"You've exhausted me," Zara complained. She feared she'd not survive another passionate encounter with Jamal. The man was insatiable.

"We'll rest a moment," Jamal said. He turned and reached for a pitcher of warm water that had been placed within reach on a nightstand beside a stack of fine white linen cloth. He poured water into the bowl and wet one of the cloths. "Part your legs for me, Zara, so I can cleanse my seed from you with scented water."

Zara's legs shifted apart and he touched the cloth to her. The scent of jasmine floated up to her as he carefully removed all traces of blood and sperm. When she was clean and sweet-smelling, he wet another cloth and washed himself. When he turned back to her, he had a small vial in his hands.

Zara saw it and stiffened, wondering what he intended next.

"Relax, Zara, I won't hurt you. When I enter you again it will not hurt. This is merely fragrant oil," he said, showing her the vial. "I will massage it into your skin and it will relax you. Turn on your stomach."

She obeyed without comment, knowing that it would do her no good to protest. Then she felt the soothing heat of his hands as he spread the oil over her skin, lavishing it on her back, her shoulders, her buttocks, the backs of her legs. It felt so wonderful she almost fell asleep beneath his sensual massage. By the time he'd finished, having turned her over to spread oil on her breasts, belly and more intimate parts, Zara's blood was pounding through her veins and her love juices were flowing.

"You're ready for me again, sweet vixen," Jamal whispered into her ear. He lifted her atop him. "Take me inside you."

She opened her legs and straddled him, gasping as he slid effortlessly into her wet passage. She felt herself stretching but it did not hurt. He gripped her hard and bucked his hips, and then she was riding him shamelessly, unable to resist the promise of pleasure. Anger at Jamal for using his sexual prowess to turn her into an obedient slave honed her passion to a sharp edge, and when she reached that ultimate peak, passion and anger combined to create a burst of incredible sensation. She climaxed violently. Jamal shouted with the pure joy of it and tumbled into a whirlpool of incandescent bliss.

Zara was asleep before Jamal plucked her off him and laid her down beside him. Then something remarkable happened. As he watched her sleep, renewed desire clutched hotly at his groin. If he hadn't just taken Zara twice he would have understood it, but this was something totally new and utterly incomprehensible to him. He wanted to take Zara again and again, to fill her with his body, to make her desire him as fiercely as he desired her. But he knew she'd be sore if he took her again so he was content to lie beside her while he attempted to come to grips with what had just happened between them. No other woman had ever made him feel the things Zara did.

Jamal had already left when Zara awoke the next morning. She was surprised to find herself still in his bed. Golden sunshine streamed through the open door, and the room was redolent with incense. In the light of day the fragrance seemed heavy and cloying, whereas last night it had created an aura of sensuality. Allah help her. She hadn't realized how Jamal's lovemaking would affect her when she'd agreed to become his love slave. She'd be fortunate to escape with her soul intact. As for her heart, she didn't dare think about that.

Zara stretched, groaning when her muscles protested. She ached in all those intimate places Jamal had spent hours exploring last night. The thought of soaking in a warm bath brought a smile to her lips. It was fortunate Jamal had a private *hammam*, for the thought of sharing a bath with Jamal's concubines filled her with dread. She knew she couldn't compete sexually with the skillful concubines and preferred to keep to herself rather than be questioned about her night with Jamal.

The bath was as soothing as Zara had known it would be. Someone, Hammet no doubt, had left jasmine soap and a stack of drying cloths for her use, and she lay back in the scented water and closed her eyes.

"You stayed with him all night!"

Zara's eyes flew open. She groaned aloud when she saw Saha advancing toward her, her face contorted with rage. Zara scooted down in the water as Saha stood at the edge of the tub, staring at her with hatred.

"What are you doing in Jamal's bath?"

"What are you doing in Jamal's chambers?" Zara shot back.

"I go where I wish. I am not Jamal's slave, you are. No woman has ever spent the entire night in Jamal's bed. You bewitched him," Saha charged.

Zara's lips thinned. "Leave me, Lady Saha. I wish to bathe in private."

"You put on pretty airs for a slave, Zara. Jamal will soon tire of you and return to the loving arms of his concubines."

"You are welcome to Jamal if you think you can please him," Zara taunted. "When was the last time you or the others shared his bed?"

Saha gave her a dangerous half-smile. "Be wary, *slave*, for you may not live much longer to please our lord." She turned and stalked away.

Zara tried to ignore the concubine's jealousy as she finished her bath. She was just reaching for the drying cloth when Jamal strode into the *hammam*. He squatted beside the tub and smiled at her. "I'm glad you availed yourself of my bath." He reached down and lifted her from the water.

Zara reached for the drying cloth but Jamal brushed her hands aside and took up the task himself. "Are you sore?" he asked when he drew the cloth between her legs and saw her wince.

"A little," she admitted.

"I was pleased with you last night. I wasn't expecting a virgin. Tonight I'll show you how silver balls can be used to give pleasure."

Zara swallowed convulsively, his words conjuring up erotic fantasies. "Tonight? Perhaps one of your other women—"

Jamal grimaced. "They do not appeal to me. Nay, Zara, you will come to me tonight. Hammet will escort you. Now, are you hungry? Hammet has brought food to break your fast. I ate earlier but will take tea with you."

"I have nothing to wear." Her words were curt, her manner abrupt. Allah, she wanted to hate him for what he'd made of her. He had given her incredible pleasure, but it had cost her her pride.

"Hammet has brought a caftan for you to wear. You'll find it in my bed chamber."

After donning the caftan, Zara ate heartily of tart yogurt, fresh melon, figs and sweet honey cakes. Jamal watched her eat, his gaze fastened hungrily on her lips. When she finished, she dabbed at her lips with her napkin and said, "I would like to see my father now."

"I assumed you would. I gave Hammet the key. He'll escort you. I have business in the village and won't see you again until you join me tonight."

He cupped her cheek, his sultry gaze dark with promise. "I can hardly wait, sweet vixen. Wear nothing but a cloak over your nakedness when you come to me tonight." Then he leaned forward, licked the seam of her lips with the tip of his tongue and pressed a kiss to her mouth. "And wear the emerald. I love the contrast of vivid green against the white flesh of your breasts."

Zara could think of nothing to say as Jamal strode from the chamber. She was still collecting her wits when Hammet entered, bowed low and said, "I will take you to your father, lady."

Zara scrambled to her feet, wincing at the unexpected soreness between her thighs. "I am ready, Hammet."

Youssef stared at Zara when she entered his prison, seeking signs that would reveal her state of well-being. Had she succumbed to the handsome sheik? he wondered. Had he hurt her? Allah, he felt so helpless.

"Father!" Zara fell into Youssef's arms, hating to see him cooped up in an airless room barely large enough to turn around in. The longer she took to form an escape plan, the more her father would suffer. She could do it, she knew she could. But at what cost to her emotions? she wondered. How long could she control her feelings with a vigorous lover like Jamal tempting her, making her feel sinful things she didn't understand?

"Are you all right, daughter?" Youssef asked. "You look pale. Did that devil hurt you? Or did you give up on that dangerous plan you were bent upon?"

Zara didn't have the courage to look her father in the eye. "I'm not hurt, Father, truly. Jamal was . . . gentle. But all that doesn't matter," she went on in a rush. "It won't be long before I have his trust. And when I do I will use that trust to gain our freedom. I will be no man's slave."

Youssef's strong, hawk-nosed features turned fierce. "You are a good daughter, Zara. I do not deserve your sacrifice. I will kill Lord Jamal for what he has done to you. Once I am free, I will not rest until he is punished."

"Forget Jamal, Father. He will return to the sea and pirating soon. It is the sultan we must battle for our freedom. Our raids must continue upon Ishmail's caravans, only next time we'll be more careful. We'll use the sultan's money to pay the taxes he levies against our people."

Youssef smiled. "You are a true zealot, Zara. Were all Berbers as fiercely loyal as you, we would be free men today, in control of our own cities."

" 'Tis time to leave, lady," Hammet said, appearing in the doorway. "I am to return you to the harem."

Zara did not relish the thought of returning to the harem. She had much more to say to her father, but Hammet was adamant.

"I'll see you tomorrow, Father," she assured

him as Hammet closed and locked the door behind her.

To Zara's chagrin, all three concubines were lounging in the main room when she entered. She tried to ignore them but Leila invited her to take refreshments with them. Not wishing to gain their ill-will, she acquiesced, albeit reluctantly.

"Is not Jamal a magnificent lover?" Amar asked with sly innuendo. "Did he enjoy you? Jamal rarely enjoys virgins. They are so unskilled they're pathetic. Virginity is unusual in a woman of your advanced age."

Zara gasped, surprised that her state of virginity was fodder for gossip. "Who told you?"

"We have ways," Saha said smugly. "Nothing is private in a household this size. What does Jamal intend to do with you now that he's had you?"

"Perhaps he'll sell her," Amar suggested hopefully.

Suddenly Nafisa bustled into the room. "Ah, Zara, here you are. Come with me. If you are to attend Jamal again tonight, you must be properly groomed."

Three pairs of eyes narrowed on Zara, their dismay obvious.

"It cannot be!" Saha protested.

Nafisa nodded sagely. "Hammet would not lie."

Saha's pouting red lips curved downward. "Zara is not Jamal's type. She is scrawny and not at all womanly."

Zara had had just about all she could take of Jamal's women. "Jamal must have found something he liked about me," she taunted. "Now if you will excuse me, I'm going to rest. I had little sleep last night."

Saha screamed out in rage, and it was obvious that neither Leila nor Amar was pleased with Zara's words.

Zara walked away, head high, chin raised. She might be a slave now but she wouldn't be one for long. If all went according to plan, she would be gone soon and Jamal's women would be welcome to him. It wasn't as if she had deliberately set out to entice the sheik. Submitting to him had been difficult, given her independent nature and fierce temperament. Once returned to her own people, she intended to forget Sheik Jamal and the ecstasy she'd found in his arms.

Chapter Nine

Zara awoke from a long nap hungry and thirsty. A tall glass of fruit juice and a bowl of yogurt that someone had thoughtfully left on the table for her beckoned, and she drank greedily of the refreshing liquid. Then she ate the yogurt, relishing the sweet/tart taste.

"Ah, you're awake," Nafisa said as she bustled into the chamber. "It grows late. There is much to be done before you go to Jamal."

To Zara's chagrin, Jamal's concubines watched closely as she bathed and made herself ready for Jamal. She couldn't help thinking they were looking for flaws, so intently did they stare at her. Let them stare, Zara thought, ignoring them. If they only knew how desperate she was to leave this place, they wouldn't be harassing her.

The sun was slowly sinking when Hammet

came for her. This time she didn't go to Jamal naked as he had requested. Instead she donned a gold and turquoise caftan that enhanced the golden tones of her skin. Though it wasn't Zara's nature to be submissive to a man, she wanted to appear attractive to Jamal for her father's sake. Her father's freedom was more important than her pride. One day Jamal would be made to pay for enslaving her and she hoped it would be soon. Before she lost more than her pride.

Jamal could barely stand the waiting. He paced his chamber restlessly, waiting for the door to open to admit Zara. He had possessed her just as he'd set out to do, but he felt as if he'd been the one possessed. After partaking freely of Zara's passion, he no longer desired his concubines. His need for Zara was almost obsessive and he was frightened by it.

Jamal was already hard by the time Zara stepped into the chamber, illuminating the room with her incandescent spirit and haunting beauty. Suddenly he had no appetite for the tempting food placed upon the table for his enjoyment; he wanted to feast solely upon Zara's succulent flesh, sate himself with her sweet body. His smile was almost feral as he beckoned her forward. His gaze followed her undulating body, admiring the way her lush charms were displayed beneath the turquoise and gold caftan. He wanted her and he wanted her now. Food and drink could wait.

Zara felt the heat of Jamal's gaze upon her and found it difficult to breathe. Just setting one foot in front of the other proved a chore. The look in his eyes held her in thrall. She hated the way he made her feel, despised pretending to be submissive to his wants, even though she was beginning to crave those very same delights she abhorred. She had to leave soon, before her mind accepted her role in Jamal's life and her body hungered for his caresses. She was a Berber princess, not a slave dependent upon the will of her master.

"You're beautiful," Jamal said. His dark eyes glowed with appreciation as he grasped her hand and drew her down beside him on a mound of cushions. "You have bewitched me, sweet vixen."

"That was not my intention, my lord," Zara said, though in truth that was exactly what she had set out to do.

"It wasn't my intention to become besotted with you," Jamal admitted candidly. "Food and drink pale in comparison to my need for you."

His words were more powerfully arousing than the drug she had been given the first time she'd lain with Jamal. Zara tried to ignore them but Jamal's hands upon her body were forceful reminders. When she tried to passively accept his kisses, Jamal sensed her withdrawal and would not allow it. In a very short time he had stripped her naked, driving her wild with his talented mouth, tongue and hands. He couldn't wait. He had to have her now.

He entered her swiftly, unable to prolong their joining a moment longer. He felt like an eager boy with his first woman.

"I'm sorry, my love, for being impatient. You tempt me beyond reason," he murmured as he thrust full and deep inside her. "But the night is young and we will taste ecstasy many times before the sun rises."

Zara arched sharply upward, meeting Jamal's deep thrusts with a cry of gladness despite her vow to remain unmoved by his loving. Grasping his hips, she undulated beneath him, with him, against him, until her soul left her body and she exploded violently. Moaning and gasping, Jamal climaxed in a frenzy of intense feeling, then collapsed upon Zara, burying his head against her neck as his heartbeat slowed to a steady pounding.

Once he regained his strength, Jamal reared up and stared at her, clearly baffled by the depth of his feelings for his slave. There was no explanation for the way Zara had burrowed beneath his skin to touch his heart. There were no answers to why he had allowed such a thing to happen. He harbored no special tenderness for his concubines. Only Zara, his slave, had reached him on a level that went deeper than sexual gratification.

"I don't know what you've done to me, sweet vixen, but I suddenly find myself wanting more of you than you're willing to give. Surrender to me, Zara. Give yourself wholly into my keeping. Admit it, you want me as desperately as I want you."

"I cannot help the way my body responds, Jamal. You are an expert, whereas I am a novice. But know this, my lord, my heart and mind utterly reject what I've become."

Jamal was silent a long time. When he finally spoke, his words shocked Zara.

Connie Mason

"Would you yield all to me if I made you my wife?"

"Your wife! Nay! You cannot mean it." She felt as if she were suffocating. To be Jamal's wife would compromise her beliefs, her very existence. She could not bear the burden. "You would not be happy with me. I cannot compete with your concubines."

"Perhaps you're right," Jamal allowed. "But I've always found it difficult to resist a challenge. And you, sweet vixen, are a challenge worth pursuing."

"Jamal, I—" Words stuck in her throat.

"We will speak of it later." His eyes glowed darkly, promising untold delights. "If you are rested we will explore more fully the erotic love play I spoke of before. Are you ready to learn the secret of the silver balls?"

Zara stared at him. "I don't think—"

"You're not supposed to think, only to feel." He slid down her body, pressing her legs apart with the palms of his hands. Using tepid water and soft cloths left for that purpose, he cleansed his seed from her body and his. Then he bent his head and kissed her smooth mound, finding her joy spot with the tip of his tongue.

He caressed and loved her with his mouth, savoring the taste and scent of her. After several minutes in which they were both distracted, he reached for a small velvet pouch he had placed nearby. Zara watched warily as he pulled the drawstring and released two round silver objects into his palm.

"There is nothing to fear," Jamal said, holding

up two smooth, perfectly symmetrical balls for her inspection. "I promise you will like them and even ask to be pleasured with them in the future."

Zara doubted it. Despite the years during which she'd ridden with her father and associated with men, she was basically innocent. Until Jamal had shown her, she'd been ignorant of the many and diverse erotic pleasures possible.

"Open for me, love," Jamal said, his voice husky as he stared at the dewy pink flesh between her legs. "Relax," he whispered as he slid one small silver ball into her moist passage and waited for her to adjust to the strangeness. Then he spread her with his thumbs and inserted the second silver ball.

The two balls bounced against one another and Zara jerked violently as intense pleasure spiraled through her. "What's happening?"

"Tell me how you feel."

"I feel . . . Allah help me . . . I feel as if my insides are on fire." She shifted positions and the tiny balls bounced against one another, sending shards of pure rapture radiating through her veins. The powerful climax that resulted was a volatile combination of agony and ecstasy. She writhed and cried out. "Blessed Allah, the pleasure! I cannot bear the pleasure."

"Bear it, sweet vixen, bear it and remember." Grasping her hips, he tilted them to the right, causing Zara to gasp and cry out again. Then he tipped her hips to the left and Zara rushed headlong to another fierce orgasm. Overcome by delirium, she lost all sense of reality.

"No more, please, no more," she begged weakly. "You're killing me."

A wicked smile turned up the corners of his sensuous lips. "I told you you'd enjoy it." Carefully he removed both silver balls and slipped them back into their pouch.

Zara breathed a sigh of relief. Any more pleasure and she would die from it. "May I return to my chamber?" she asked hopefully.

"The night is still young and I can't bear to part with you. Rest, love. Then we will eat and go where the night takes us."

Where the night took them was beyond anything Zara had ever dreamed or imagined. The silver balls remained in their pouch, but Jamal found other ways to give and receive pleasure.

Though the precise words were never spoken, Zara felt confident of Jamal's intense feelings for her. It was the kind of power she had wanted. Intuition told her that she would never find a better time to plan her escape, that Jamal's trust was as strong as it would ever be. Tomorrow she would ask Jamal's permission to visit the village.

Zara awoke early the following morning. Jamal was still sleeping soundly beside her as she rose and took advantage of his bathing room. When she returned, Jamal was sitting up in bed waiting for her.

"I missed you."

"I'm here, my lord."

"Looking lovelier than the moon and the stars. If I didn't have to go to Meknes today I would keep you in my bed and make love to you the rest of the day."

"Meknes?" Fear lanced through her. "Does your visit have anything to do with my father?"

"Not this time, sweet vixen. The sultan is pleased that the raids upon his caravans have ceased. To my knowledge he has not learned that Youssef is my prisoner. He thinks the attacks have ceased because Youssef fears you'll be harmed if he continues them. My visit concerns my pirate ship. Ishmail is greedy for more plunder and wants me to return to pirating."

"How long will you be gone?"

Jamal looked pleased. "Will you miss me?"

Zara shrugged.

"I shall return by nightfall. Hammet has orders to bring you to my chamber when I return."

"Will you grant me a favor, Jamal?"

Jamal sent her a brilliant smile. "Since you pleased me so well last night, I am in an expansive mood. What is it you wish, Zara?"

"I wish to visit the village. I've been cooped up in your palace too long. I'm bored. I'm accustomed to vigorous exercise in the sun and the wind."

Jamal's dark brows rose. "Isn't what we've been doing nightly exercise enough? Perhaps I'll request your presence in my bed in the afternoons as well as the nights. Will that satisfy your craving for exercise?"

Zara retained her temper through sheer grit. Did Jamal think of nothing but coupling? "That's not what I meant and you know it."

"Tell me what you need and I'll buy it for you,"

Jamal said, skirting the issuc. "Silks, satins, jewels? Do you like rubies?"

"I want to walk to the village and visit the *souk* myself. Send a guard along, if you wish, but do not deny me the pleasure of walking through the *souk*." If her plan to free her father was to work, she needed the freedom to seek help in the village.

Jamal wavered uncertainly. Since Zara had submitted to him she had changed. She seemed more at peace with her captivity. Though she hadn't agreed to become his wife, she hadn't refused outright. His own feelings were contradictory and confusing. Asking Zara to marry him had shocked even himself. The offer had been rash, but he couldn't bring himself to regret it. When had he become so obsessed with Zara? he wondered. Did he trust her enough to allow her more freedom?

"Please, Jamal," Zara said, hating the way he made her beg for so small a privilege. "Your concubines are allowed to go where they please."

"They are not slaves," Jamal reminded her.

Green fire ignited in the centers of Zara's eyes. Being reminded of her lowly station was a stunning blow to her pride. She bit her bottom lip to keep from venting her spleen. Yet anger wasn't the only emotion warring within her. She had feelings for Jamal she didn't dare explore. When she was in his arms, experiencing the enchantment of his unique loving, she felt as if she belonged there.

Jamal wasn't cruel like the sultan. He didn't treat his women badly. As his slave she had suffered nothing but the erotic pleasure of his loving. And in a moment of weakness he had asked her to marry him. Which, of course, was out of the question. It was important that she banish all tenderness for the handsome sheik from her mind and heart and concentrate on escape. Her father's life depended on her ability to remain unmoved by Jamal's sensual assault. She could not allow herself to fall in love with him. All she wanted from Jamal was his trust.

"Are you going to refuse my request?" Zara asked shortly.

"I'm going to humor you. You may visit the *souk*. Haroun will assign two men-at-arms to guard you. Ask Hammet for a *djellaba* and veil your face well."

Elated, Zara bowed her head in acquiescence to Jamal's conditions. "Thank you, my lord. If it pleases you, I will visit my father now."

Jamal frowned. He was surprised that word hadn't already reached the sultan concerning Youssef's presence at Paradise. Soon he must place Youssef into Ishmail's keeping whether Zara liked it or not.

"Aye, visit your father. I must prepare for my journey to Meknes. But first—"

Pulling her down beside him on the bed, he rolled her beneath him, spread her legs and thrust inside her. He smiled, pleased to find her as ready for him as he was for her. She was moist and soft and yielded sweetly to the deep penetration of his rock-hard erection. If he lived to be one hundred he'd never understand his consuming need for Zara. But right now he didn't care.

His thoughts were focused entircly on the woman beneath him and giving her pleasure.

Zara moved with Jamal, her loins thrusting up against him, wanting, needing everything he could give her. She'd been surprised to find her body ready to receive him even though she'd been given no warning of his intention. There was no dryness, no pain at his abrupt entrance. Only pleasure. Rocked by jolts of ecstasy spiraling through her, she wondered how she would live the rest of her life without Jamal.

Much later, after they were both dressed and ready to leave, Jamal opened a small casket sitting on a lacquered chest and removed a large brass key. He called Hammet, who appeared instantly, handed him the key and told him to escort Zara to her father. It wasn't the first time Zara had seen Jamal remove or replace the key in the casket, but she was happy to learn that it was still kept there.

Zara was shocked by Youssef's appearance. He was pale and wan and looked as if he'd lost considerable weight. He was a man accustomed to living with the elements, racing his camel over mountains and through valleys with the sun and wind in his face. If she didn't free him soon, she feared he would waste away in his dark prison, deprived of sunshine and fresh air.

"Are you well, daughter?" Youssef asked with concern. He hated the thought of Zara being used by Jamal. He knew she had offered herself to the sheik but he could not like it. If Jamal wanted her, he should marry her. She had been an innocent until Jamal violated her.

"I am well, Father. We must speak quietly; Hammet waits outside the door. I think I've finally gained Jamal's trust. He's give me permission to visit the *souk*. I have a plan, Father. Remember the man who came to me in the stables and told me you were coming to rescue me?"

Youssef nodded. "His name is Rachid. He's a camel trader who spies for me in the village."

"My plan depends on Rachid's willingness to help us."

"The danger to you is too great. Should Jamal learn of your betrayal, he will punish you. I hear his temper is fearsome when roused to anger. 'Tis said he's fair and just until he's crossed. I fear for you, daughter."

"I can handle Jamal," Zara said with more bravado than she felt. "Where can I find Rachid?"

"You'll find him in the village, Zara. He is the only camel trader in the *souk* who sells and trades racing camels. Quickly, tell me your plan."

When Zara left her father a short time later, she was more determined than ever to free him. He was barely existing in Jamal's foul prison. With firm resolve she prepared for her walk to the village. Hammet provided her with a black *djellaba*, which she donned over her caftan, fastening the veil over the lower part of her face so nothing but her eyes showed. Jamal had already left for Meknes with Haroun, but two men-at-arms were waiting for her when Hammet escorted her to the gate. They were given a bag of coins to pay for Zara's purchases.

The walk to the village was hot and dusty, but Zara relished each step, for it took her closer to freedom.

The *souk* was crowded with people, some haggling over prices, some trading and others hawking their wares. Her passage warranted only a passing glance, for the villagers were accustomed to seeing Sheik Jamal's concubines strolling though the *souk* with their guards in attendance. Zara made a great show of examining merchandise for sale and purchasing geegaws she had no use for. When she finally approached the open grassy area where the camel traders did their business, her gaze settled on the man buying and selling racing camels. It had to be Rachid.

"I would like to speak with the camel trader," Zara told her vigilant guards. "Racing camels are of great interest to me. My people find them perfect for their needs and ride them exclusively."

The guards exchanged glances. They saw no harm in Zara's speaking with vendors since no orders had been issued disallowing it. Still, they hesitated.

"Please," Zara said prettily. "I wish only to discuss his animals. They are sleek and look swift of foot, do they not?"

"I prefer horses," the first guard grumbled.

"They are mean-spirited animals," the second guard added. "Go then, speak to him if you must, but do not linger."

Bouyed by her success, Zara approached the small, bearded camel trader. She introduced herself quickly. "I am Zara, daughter of Youssef. Are you Rachid?" The man nodded. "Listen carefully, for I have little time," Zara continued. "Pretend we are discussing your camels."

Rashid nodded his understanding. "How is your father? I am sorry things worked out as they did. What can I do to help?"

"I need a sleeping draught. Something strong but not so strong as to kill. Can you get it for me? And if so, how soon?"

Rachid pretended interest in the camel nearest to him. "It is possible for me to obtain what you need." He pulled at his beard. "Give me an hour. Continue your stroll through the *souk*. I will find you."

Zara thanked him and left, aware that the guards were watching her intently. She didn't want to arouse suspicion when she was so close to her goal. She spent a long time browsing through vendor stalls, purchasing small items, inspecting and rejecting others and lingering over an array of vibrant silks. After a while she began to despair that Rachid had failed to obtain what she needed. Then she felt a jolt and something was thrust into her hand. Her palm curled around a small packet and she quickly thrust it into her pocket. When she looked around she saw no one but the usual crowd of people going about their business.

Zara left the *souk* soon afterward. Her guards seemed relieved as they escorted her back to the harem. She thanked them for their escort and hurried inside.

"Did you enjoy your outing?" Nafisa asked as Zara passed through the main room.

"It was good to be outside the palace walls,"

Zara replied, eager to return to her room.

"You must rest now, Zara. You want to be fresh and rested when you go to Jamal tonight, don't you?"

Zara merely nodded as she continued on her way. Once in her chamber she removed the packet from her pocket, shed her *djellaba* and sank down on the bed. Then she opened her palm, unfolded the packet and studied the powder inside, wondering how much it would take to make Jamal sleep deeply without doing him harm.

Suddenly Saha appeared in the doorway and Zara closed her fingers over the packet. "I've brought you something cool to drink," Saha said, offering Zara a tall glass of sparkling red liquid. "I know how hot and dusty the *souk* can be on a day like this."

Zara eyed Saha suspiciously. Her act of kindness was unexpected and totally out of character. But if Saha meant to offer friendship, Zara certainly didn't want to discourage her. "Thank you, Saha, how thoughtful of you. Have you changed your mind about me?"

Saha gave a delicate shrug. "You seem to please Jamal and it has occurred to me that I should try to be more tolerant of you. I do not wish to incur Jamal's wrath for treating you badly. One day he will tire of you and turn to his concubines for comfort. So drink, Zara, and consider my offering an act of friendship."

"Why not?" Zara replied, aware that she wouldn't be in the harem long enough to develop a friendship with Saha even if she was inclined to do so. Saha was the last person with whom she'd share her plans.

Zara accepted the glass from Saha and lifted it to her lips. The cool liquid had just barely touched her lips when Nafisa rushed into the room and slapped the glass from Zara's hands. Zara watched in dismay as the glass shattered on the floor, creating a splash of red against the pale peach-colored carpet.

"What have you done, Saha?" Nafisa cried, rounding on the frightened concubine, who was cowering in a corner. "Jamal will kill you for this."

Zara was slow to react. When it finally dawned on her what Saha had tried to do to her, she began shaking.

"Please, Nafisa," Saha begged, "do not tell Jamal. No harm was done."

"No harm?" Nafisa cried. "You tried to poison Zara. What if I hadn't heard Amar and Leila talking about your plans? What if I hadn't arrived in time to prevent such a tragedy? Jamal must be told."

"You meant to poison me!" Zara cried, finally finding her voice. "Why can't you realize I'm no threat to you?"

"Jamal asked you to marry him," Saha charged.

The breath caught in Zara's throat. "How did you know?"

"Everyone knows," Saha claimed. "There are no secrets here."

"Get out!" Zara ordered. "The sight of you sickens me."

Realizing the gravity of her sin, Saha felt real fear. "Will you tell Jamal?"

"I will tell him," Nafisa said, answering for Zara. "Now get out of here. Go to your chamber and await word from Jamal."

Turning on her heel, Saha fled, sobbing loudly.

"What will happen to her?" Zara wondered.

"That's for Jamal to decide. What she tried to do cannot be dismissed."

Zara didn't want to feel compassion for the misguided concubine but she couldn't help it. Since Zara's arrival at Paradise, Jamal had all but ignored his women.

"Fear not, Zara, I will see that nothing like this happens again."

Exhausted from her trip to the village and lack of sleep the previous night, Zara decided a nap was in order. She hid the packet containing the sleeping powder beneath her mattress, then lay down and drifted off to sleep. Hours later she was awakened by the sound of angry voices and loud wailing. Within moments Jamal burst into her chamber.

"Are you all right? Nafisa sent word to me the moment I arrived home." Dropping down beside her, he dragged her into his arms and hugged her tightly. "How dare Saha try to poison you! I'll never let you out of my sight again."

"I'm fine, Jamal, truly. Nafisa arrived in time to prevent me from drinking the poison."

"I shudder to think what would have happened if Nafisa hadn't learned of Saha's plan to do away with you." He grasped her hand. "Come with me."

She followed him into the main room where

Saha, Amar and Leila huddled together on a couch, sobbing quietly. One look at Jamal's stern visage sent them into a fresh paroxysm of tears.

"Quiet!" Jamal ordered harshly. "What you have done is wrong and must be punished. Since Saha is the perpetrator, she will be dealt with first." He crooked a finger at Saha. "Come with me." He strode through the harem, taking both Zara and Saha with him.

Once beyond the harem doors, Zara noted with surprise that Haroun awaited them. Haroun had eyes for no one but Saha. His lust for the beautiful concubine was evidenced by the burning look he bestowed on her.

"What are you going to do to me?" Saha asked fearfully. "I could not bear being whipped, my lord. And the bastinado would kill me. Forgive me, Jamal, I beg you."

"I can't forgive you, Saha, but neither can I inflict pain upon a woman. Though you deserve to be beaten, it will not be by my hand."

Hope flared in Saha's eyes, but Jamal was quick to extinguish it. "I am giving you to Haroun. May Allah have pity on him."

Haroun looked thunderstruck. Jamal's generosity humbled him. He had long lusted after Lady Saha. He knew what Saha had tried to do to Zara, but still he wanted her. He was strong. He would tame Saha and keep her in line. He would see to it that she never bothered Jamal or Zara again.

"I am truly grateful, my lord," Haroun said, finally finding his voice. "You will not regret your generosity."

"So be it," Jamal said. "Take her away; the sight

of her sickens me. Keep her in the village, tie her to the bed, beat her if you wish, but keep her out of my sight. Choose two worthy men from among my men-at-arms and I will present Amar and Leila to them."

Afraid that Jamal would change his mind, Haroun sent Saha for her *djellaba*. When she returned, he literally dragged her away. Jamal watched them go without visible regret.

"All three, Jamal?" Zara asked, stunned by his swift and decisive justice. "You will give away all three of your women?"

Jamal sent her a smoldering look that spoke eloquently of his desire. "I have said it before and I will say it again, Zara. I need no other woman but you."

Chapter Ten

A week had passed since Zara's first visit to the village. Just today she had returned to the *souk*, with Jamal's permission, and arranged with Rachid to have racing camels waiting at the back gate during the darkest hours of night. Zara had discovered the gate during her explorations and learned that it was little used and normally left unguarded except for one sentry, who made rounds every hour or so.

Zara dressed carefully for her visit to Jamal that night, choosing a sunny yellow caftan with a deep pocket. She knew what must be done but not how to accomplish it, except that Jamal had to ingest the sleeping draught before he took off her clothing. Without her caftan she would have no access to the sleeping draught in her pocket. The escape had to be accomplished tonight. All the arrangements were made; she had to make it happen.

Zara was ready when Hammet came for her. Her footsteps echoed hollowly as she walked through the empty harem. All three concubines were gone now. Jamal's justice had been swift and relentless. Amar and Leila had been given to two deserving soldiers, who found houses for them in the village. The soldiers looked decent enough to Zara, but the concubines would never again have the luxuries they had enjoyed in Jamal's household.

Jamal drew Zara into his arms when she entered his chamber. He never tired of seeing her, of holding her in his arms, of making love to her. It still frightened him when he recalled how close he had come to losing her. Saha had gotten off easy; he could have put her to death had he been of a mind to do so. Had Zara actually consumed the poison, his retribution would have been harsh and swift.

"There is something I must tell you tonight," Jamal said, drawing Zara down with him on a couch. "I have thought upon it during this past week, since my last visit with the sultan."

Zara lost the ability to breathe. "It's about my father, isn't it?"

"In a way. 'Tis time I returned to pirating. The sultan is a greedy man. He is ever eager to add to his depleted coffers, and my pirate ship brings him substantial riches. Your father cannot stay here in my absence. I have no choice, Zara. Youssef must be turned over to Moulay Ishmail."

Zara blanched. Praise Allah that her escape plans had been set into motion.

Her stricken expression must have convinced Jamal that she was devastated by his decision, for he said, "I've kept Youssef here as long as I dared. I have fulfilled my part of our bargain."

"Why can't I see to my father's care in your absence?" Zara asked. "We both know the sultan will kill him."

Jamal hardened himself against Zara's pleas. His decision was final—Youssef must be sent to Meknes. "You won't be here to care for your father. I'm taking you with me."

Zara's eyes widened in shock. Obviously her plan to bind Jamal to her had worked beyond her wildest expectations. Her mouth went dry. Jamal cared for her, cared enough that he wanted her with him. Allah forgive her for what she was about to do. No matter how desperately she wanted to be with Jamal, she could not bear being his slave, nor could she endure the thought of her father's death. Escape was the only answer.

"I . . . have never been on a ship. Perhaps I will not like it."

Jamal pulled her against him. "I want you with me, Zara. I am not ready yet to part with you. The sultan hinted that I should return you to his harem. He's decided he wants to tame you himself, but I cannot bear the thought of Ishmail's hands upon your sweet flesh."

When Jamal started to remove her caftan, Zara demurred, saying, " 'Tis difficult to accept the fact that my father will soon die, my lord. How can you expect me to respond to you when you are sending my father to his death?"

"I would keep Youssef here if I could, Zara."

"I need time to come to grips with my grief. Let me get something cool to drink. I do not feel too kindly disposed toward you right now."

"Very well," Jamal agreed. "There is food and a pitcher of apricot nectar on the table. Choose whatever you desire."

Zara walked slowly to the table and poured two glasses of nectar. Turning her back to Jamal, she poured the contents of the packet into one of the glasses and stuffed the empty paper back into her pocket. Then she returned to Jamal's side and handed him the doctored drink. Her face was devoid of all emotion as she watched him take a huge gulp of the juice. She sipped at hers, not really thirsty or hungry.

"I will speak in Youssef's behalf," Jamal promised in an effort to placate her. "I'm not hungry for his blood."

"Is that your last word?"

"Aye, my decision is made."

"Then I am no longer obliged to honor our bargain. I wish to return to the harem."

Jamal drained his glass and set it down with a bang. The glass shattered but he paid it no heed. "Nay! I will not be denied. You are still my slave and I will have you whether or not you are willing."

Didn't Zara realize he cared for her? Jamal wondered. He'd never felt this way about another woman. His feelings were so strong he couldn't endure a long sea voyage without Zara. His decision to take her with him had not been lightly made.

Zara stiffened with indignation. She'd acted the meek love slave long enough. She'd held her temper, bit her tongue and forced herself to submit to Jamal's sensual nature. Against her will he'd taught her to crave his touch and enjoy his lovemaking, but captivity was not a way of life she would ever choose. With Allah's help she would not be a slave much longer. Jamal had drunk all the draught and would soon succumb to sleep.

"Slave I may be but I do not wish to accommodate you. Our bargain is over." She started to rise.

Jamal grasped her wrist, refusing to let her leave. "Forget that ill-conceived bargain. I will have you, sweet vixen. I should have known your submission was but an act. Do you feel nothing for me?"

Feel nothing for him? Her body was aching for his touch, but to admit it would compromise what remained of her pride. "I honored our bargain; you have no complaints."

His eyes blazed with fury. "Have you played me for a fool? Did you deliberately seek to capture my heart?"

He whipped her caftan over her head and tossed it aside. Anger and desire combined to make him hard as stone.

"Nay! I never wanted your heart, only your trust." Allah, what was she saying? She must not arouse his suspicions. Jamal didn't look the least bit sleepy yet. In fact, he looked wide awake as he stripped off his own caftan and flung it aside.

Jamal pushed her back against the cushions and pinned her there with the hard length of his body. His lips flattened against his teeth, giving him a feral look. "Tell me you don't want me. Say the words and I'll send you back to the harem."

Zara stared into his eyes, stunned by the intense longing within their dark depths, and the ability to speak left her.

"Say the words, sweet vixen," Jamal repeated. Silence. Zara still hadn't found her tongue. "That's what I thought," he said smugly. "You can't say it because it would be a lie."

His smile turned predatory as his mouth burned a path to her breasts. Her erect nipples became the objects of his attention as he kissed and sucked the tender buds, then nipped them between his strong white teeth. Zara arched and cried out, wanting this yet denying her need for the handsome sheik with her whole heart.

"Shall I get the silver balls?" he asked huskily. "You seemed to enjoy them the last time."

"Nay!" Zara choked out. Allah help her.

Jamal shrugged and lowered his head to resume his assault upon her succulent nipples. When his lips traveled downward to her smooth mound, Zara finally found the courage to say the words he had demanded of her.

"I do not want you! Pray stop!"

Jamal raised his head and gave her an amused smile. "Too late, sweet vixen. You had your chance. Now you must pay the consequences. Come, Zara, yield to me."

His head lowered and his tongue parted her, finding the tiny jewel at the top of her thighs. He spent several breathless moments tormenting her before sucking the erect bud into his mouth. Zara screamed, stiffened and then went limp.

Jamal shifted upward between her outstretched legs, flexed his hips and prepared to thrust into her. Suddenly his eyes grew murky and a confused look passed over his face. Then his eyes rolled upward and he dropped heavily on top of her. The sleeping potion had finally worked!

Zara poked Jamal and called his name. He did not budge. She let out a sigh of relief. For a time she had feared the powder wouldn't work. Now she realized that Jamal had such a vigorous constitution that it had taken longer than usual to take effect. She squirmed from beneath him, breathing hard from the effort, and stared at him. He was so still it frightened her.

She felt his neck for a pulse and found it beating strongly. She nearly collapsed with relief. She had no idea how long he would sleep, but at least she was assured that he *would* wake up. She was shaking when she pulled a light blanket over him and backed away.

Zara found her caftan and donned it quickly. Then she rummaged in Jamal's chest until she located a black *djellaba* and pulled it on over her caftan. Next she opened the casket holding the key to her father's jail and removed it, replacing it with the emerald Jamal had given her. Then she sat down to wait. According to her calculations,

Rachid wouldn't arrive with the camels for several hours yet.

She watched Jamal sleep, unable to turn her gaze from his handsome features. He was so strong, so virile, so absolutely captivating that it was going to be difficult to forget him. Perhaps it would be easier to forget him if she thought of him as the man responsible for Sayed's death, not as her lover.

She breathed in a shaky sigh and stared into the dark courtyard, noting that the moon had slipped behind a cloud and the shadows had deepened. Still she waited. Finally it was time. She gave Jamal's sleeping form one last, lingering look and slipped out into the courtyard. She made as little noise as possible, aware that Hammet slept on a pallet outside Jamal's door.

Zara was nearly invisible in her black *djellaba* as she crept through the darkness. She watched in silence as the sentry walked past her father's prison and disappeared around the corner. A sigh of relief slipped past her lips when he failed to see her. She was shaking like a leaf when she fitted the key into the locked door and turned it. The door swung open on noiseless hinges, and she whispered her father's name.

"I am here, Zara," Youssef said, appearing in the opening. "Where's the sentry?"

"He passed by a moment ago. We must hurry and release the others before he returns."

Youssef stepped into the night shadows, closed the door to his prison and locked it. Then he tossed the key into the bushes. The other Berbers had been imprisoned in a common hut not far from Youssef's tiny prison. The door had no lock but was barred from the outside with a stout board. Youssef lifted the bar and gave a hushed command. One by one the men crept out of their prison, merging into the shadows to keep from being seen.

"Instruct the men to follow the wall to the back gate, Father," Zara whispered. "I'm right behind you." She was thankful that the Berbers' blue robes blended into the darkness so well.

Hugging the gate, Youssef and Zara made their way to the back gate, keeping their eyes peeled for the sentry. He passed them without incident as they crouched behind a fig tree. Once the guard had continued on his way, they crept along the wall to the back gate. Luck was with them. They found the gate unguarded. Unfortunately, it was locked.

"Climb over," Youssef hissed. "I'll give you a boost."

Moments later Zara was scrambling up and over the gate, followed closely by her father. At first they didn't see Rachid, and Zara panicked. Then she spotted him, leading a string of camels from a grove of olive trees.

"Thank you, my friend," Youssef said, clapping his tribesman on the shoulder. "You will receive payment for your camels."

"I ask no payment, Youssef. It is the least I can do. Your daughter is a brave woman. She's the one who deserves praise. Allah be with you."

"We must leave," Youssef said, taking swift charge, "before we are discovered." They mounted quickly and rode off into the night, leaving the oasis and Sheik Jamal far behind.

Jamal's dream was not a pleasant one. He tried to rouse himself from the throes of a deep, troubled sleep but could not. He fought, but his arms would not move. Something was wrong, terribly wrong, but he was powerless to check the panic racing through his drugged mind. Then he felt hands upon him, shaking him, and he concentrated on the words being shouted into his ear.

"Master, wake up!" The shaking continued, more vigorously now. "Master, please, what has happened to you?"

Jamal's brow furrowed. With tremendous effort he raised one lid at a time. His eyes were gritty and unfocused, and several minutes passed before he recognized Hammet.

"Hammet? What is the meaning of this?" What had happened to his voice? It sounded hoarse and distorted.

"Allah be praised," Hammet said with a sigh. "You must try to rouse yourself, my lord. I fear you will not like the tidings I bring you."

"Water," Jamal said as he tried to push himself into a sitting position. He succeeded only with Hammet's help, gulping down the goblet of water the eunuch held to his lips. "What happened? Am I ill?"

"I've sent for your physician; he will be here shortly. Meanwhile, I fear I am the bearer of disturbing news."

"Disturbing news?" Jamal repeated, finding it difficult to concentrate.

Before Hammet could explain, a short, intense man sporting a beard and wearing a black skullcap upon his head bustled into the room.

"I will explain later," Hammet said, backing away to allow the physician room to attend his patient.

David ben Israel was a Jewish physician of some renown. He'd been Jamal's personal healer since Jamal's birth; had brought him into the world, in fact. He was an old man, but a wise one. His status was one of semi-retirement, for his duties at Paradise were light.

"Have you been ill, my lord?" David asked as he lifted Jamal's lids to examine his pupils.

"I am never ill," Jamal said.

"Stick out your tongue."

Jamal dutifully presented his tongue, wondering what it meant when David hummed in response to his examination.

"What is the last thing you remember?" David asked, rocking back on his heels.

Jamal closed his eyes and tried to recall last evening's events. He smiled when he remembered making love to Zara. Suddenly his smile dissolved into a frown. Zara. What had happened to her? Had she returned to the harem?

"Well?" the doctor said impatiently. "I can tell by your smile that you recall something."

"Aye. I was with Zara. I recall making love to her before everything went blank."

"Did you eat or drink anything?"

"Nay . . . oh, aye, I drank a glass of apricot nectar."

187

The humming sound grew louder as David searched the room for Jamal's glass.

Suddenly it dawned on Jamal what the physician was hinting at. "You think I was poisoned?"

"Not poison, my lord. Ah, here it is," he said, gathering splintered pieces of glass from the table and floor. He held a large piece up to the light. Then he tasted a tiny sample of the residue left on the surface. "I can't be sure, but I think tests will prove that you've been drugged, my lord."

"What! By whom? Who would do such a thing?"

"That I do not know, my lord. The drug wasn't strong enough to do you permanent harm, but to be safe I'll mix you up something to purge the remaining potion from your system. You have slept off the worst of it."

The fuzziness began to clear from Jamal's brain and his thinking process returned as a horrible thought struck him. Had Zara been given a similar drug? Was she even now sleeping off the effects? Was she ill? Then he recalled that when Hammet had awakened him, he had mentioned something about disturbing news. He trembled with unexplained fear. There was more here than met the eye and he intended to get to the bottom of it.

"Hammet!" His summons brought the eunuch instantly to his master's bedside.

"I am here, my lord."

"My trusted physician seems to think I was given a drug to make me sleep. What do you know about it?"

"I know nothing about the drug, my lord. I have failed you. Forgive me."

"I do not hold you responsible. Have you seen Zara?" Jamal asked sharply. "I will send David to attend her. If she was fed the same drug, she could be ill. Her system isn't as robust as mine."

"Zara isn't in the harem." Hammet's expression was sad but wary. His master's temper was going to be formidable when he learned the full extent of his slave's treachery. "Nafisa came to me early this morning, wanting to know if Zara was still with you. She wasn't. I knew she had not left though the door, for I was sleeping on a pallet outside your chamber and would have heard her. She must have left through the courtyard."

"Perhaps she's in the *hammam*," Jamal suggested hopefully. Hammet shook his head. "Did you check every room?"

"The entire palace, my lord."

"The courtyard? The palace grounds?"

"Zara is gone, my lord. So is her father and all the Berber prisoners."

Jamal reared up from bed and strode to the casket where he kept the key to Youssef's prison. His swift intake of breath was the only indication of his rage. Inside the casket, resting on a bed of satin, was the emerald he had given Zara. It was damning evidence and all the proof he needed. He felt raw and betrayed. He'd been deceived by a Berber vixen who whored for her father. Those were harsh words, but Jamal could think of no other explanation for what Zara had done.

It hurt to realize that Zara had deliberately deceived him. She had used his obsession for her, building his trust to the point that he was blinded to her devious intent. What a fool he'd been. What an utter, sentimental fool.

"I need a bath to wash the scent of that insidious little witch from my body," Jamal ground out. "Summon Haroun. I will speak with him after I've bathed."

"I will leave you, my lord," David said as Hammet hurried to do Jamal's bidding. "I can see that you no longer have need of me. The effects of the drug are all but gone from your system." He bowed himself out of the chamber, leaving Jamal in a fine rage.

An hour later Jamal and Haroun were inspecting the small airless room that had once held Youssef. Jamal didn't expect to find anything and wasn't surprised when he caught a whiff of Zara's special scent. He would recognize the fragrance anywhere. Jasmine. He'd had the scent specially formulated for Zara and had instructed Nafisa to use it exclusively on his beautiful slave. The memory of kissing, tasting and caressing Zara's jasmine-scented flesh brought a fresh onslaught of pain. How could she have betrayed him like this? He would have married her; given her the world had she asked.

Nothing of value was learned from the sentry on duty the previous night, yet all the Berbers were gone. The man guarding the front gate swore no one had gone in or out after the gates were closed for the night. That left only the back gate. It was still locked but could be easily scaled.

A key was produced and Jamal stepped through the opening.

"Camel tracks, my lord," Haroun said, calling Jamal's attention to the large hoof prints on the ground beyond the gate. "Our men do not ride camels, and caravans do not come this close to the walls even if they did venture into the oasis. This is a well-planned and executed escape, my lord."

"Aye," Jamal mused thoughtfully. "Had I not been so obsessed with Zara I would have taken precautions. I was willing to lie to Ishmail for the Berber witch. Never again, Haroun, my friend. When I find Zara I will not play the besotted fool again. I refuse to become a victim to her feminine wiles."

"Do you intend to go after her?" Haroun asked, surprised by Jamal's obsession with Zara. What was one woman when there were so many?

"Wild horses couldn't stop me," Jamal said tautly. "Zara betrayed me and must pay the consequences. Selling her to the slave trader would be a fitting punishment for a traitor such as she."

The words were spoken in haste. Despite the blow to his pride, Jamal would never send Zara to the slave market.

"Shall I provision the men for a long search, my lord? The Blue Men are wily foe. No doubt Youssef has already left his village for the mountains. Berbers can move their black tents from place to place faster than we can ferret them out."

"We will find them, Haroun. Zara will learn she cannot play me for a fool. She yielded her body sweetly, but her mind and heart remained unfettered by any emotion save dedication to the Berber cause. If I hadn't been so besotted, I would have seen through her. Zara deceived and tricked me into believing she could be trusted."

What Jamal didn't say was that he had come to care for Zara more than he had ever cared for another woman save his dear mother.

"When do we leave, my lord? We are short on supplies, but that can be remedied within a day or two."

"Be prepared to ride in three days, Haroun. As much as it shames me, the sultan must be informed about what has taken place here. He is not going to be happy."

"Will you tell Ishmail the truth?" Haroun asked.

"Aye, I must. I have kept Ishmail in the dark about Youssef for Zara's sake, but now there is no longer reason to do so."

"Ishmail will be angry."

"I will placate him with promises of future plunder from my pirating ventures. Go now, Haroun, do what must be done to prepare my men-at-arms."

Jamal was still fuming when he returned to his chamber. He shooed away the servants who were cleaning his room and began to pace, still too upset to prepare for his departure. Everything in the room reminded him of Zara. Her jasmine scent filled his nostrils. He gazed at the cushions arranged upon his couch and visualized her as she had been the night before, her naked body writhing upon them, her tight sheath wet and eager for the attentions of his hands, mouth, tongue and manhood.

How could he have been so trusting? How could Zara have fooled him so completely? Because he had been too besotted to see the truth, he told himself. Allah help him, he'd even fancied himself in love with the Berber vixen. He would recapture her, he vowed, and when he did he would never indulge her again. She would become just another slave in his household, to be used or discarded as he willed. If he wanted her sexually, he'd take her. No one made a fool of Jamal abd Thabit twice.

Youssef, the Blue Men and Zara were given a jubilant welcome upon their return to their village. A great celebration was planned but quickly squelched when Youssef explained their need to leave the village and hide in the mountains. Men, women and children spent the next day packing provisions and belongings onto the backs of sturdy camels. The mountains offered the kind of safe haven that the village could not. Living in tents had its advantages. They could be dismantled and erected at a moment's notice.

Zara joined the exodus the following day, riding upon the back of her racing camel as the slower beasts of burden followed behind. Zara rode like the wind, free at last, relishing the hot breeze and the sun against her face, wearing the clothing she preferred, the blue robes of her people. But Zara was not at peace. Her heart was troubled.

Jamal.

He had taught her the joys of loving and being loved. She didn't have to be experienced to know that Jamal was not a selfish lover. He always made sure she received pleasure before taking his own.

He had asked her to marry him, and she had betrayed him.

Allah forgive her. How could she marry the enemy? Yet the thought of living the rest of her life without Jamal was excessively painful. No matter how hard she tried to hate the handsome sheik, she always arrived at the same conclusion.

She could never hate Jamal.

She might even . . .

Love him.

Chapter Eleven

Zara walked with dragging steps to her father's tent. Her shoulders were slumped, her eyes dull from lack of sleep. The deep purple smudges beneath her lids attested to the turmoil raging within her. Her mind told her that deceiving Jamal had been the right thing to do, yet her heart wept. She had done a despicable thing to Jamal, but she'd had no choice. Her father had faced death, she'd been enslaved, and to add to her misery, she had had to fight a growing attraction to her avowed enemy.

A week had passed since she had drugged Jamal and escaped with her father and the Blue Men. A week during which she felt like a stranger among her own people. She was sure that everyone knew she had bargained for Youssef's freedom with her body. Though her sacrifice wasn't mentioned openly, Zara sensed her people's pity and did not want it.

Jamal had made her his in the most basic way, taken her body and given unstintingly of his own. He had given her a glimpse of rapture and surprised her by suggesting she become his wife. He had admitted to being besotted with her and wanting to take her with him aboard his ship. She had repaid his high regard for her by drugging him. How he must hate her.

But the true cause of her sleepless nights was the inescapable knowledge that she had become too fond of the dangerous, sensual Sheik Jamal. He had but to touch her and she turned to ash, burning hotter, brighter than the most torrid fire.

Youssef greeted Zara exuberantly when she slipped through the tent flap. "Ah, daughter, I'm glad you've come. Did you see Mohammed ride into camp a short time ago?"

Zara nodded. Mohammed's presence in their camp was the reason for her visit to her father's tent. She knew Mohammed was their spy in Meknes.

"Rumor has it that the richest caravan in recent years is en route from Marrakech to Meknes," Youssef continued. "The cargo is comprised of tribute and taxes from the south, intended for the sultan's coffers."

Zara's spirits rose. "Are we to raid again, Father?" Taking part in a raid was exactly what she needed to banish thoughts of the man who had made her his love slave and stolen her heart.

"Aye, daughter, as soon as the caravan is located. It was supposed to have left Marrakech two days ago. Since we need to pinpoint its precise location, I'm riding out at dawn tomorrow to follow the caravan route until I locate it."

"I'll go with you," Zara said, eager to do something, anything, to keep her mind and body occupied.

"Not this time, Zara. I've already picked a dozen men to accompany me. Rest assured you'll be at my side when we attack, but I prefer that you remain in camp this time. You will act as leader in my absence. You are as fierce and loyal as any of my men."

Puffed up by Youssef's words, Zara said, "I will not fail you, Father. Do you truly think danger exists?"

Youssef searched her face. "Aye. You have humiliated the sheik, Zara. He is not a man to trifle with. You've hurt his pride. I fear he will not rest until he finds us, and I pray he is not successful. His vengeance will be swift and violent."

"We are constantly on the move," Zara contended. "I think you exaggerate the danger from Jamal."

Youssef's dark eyes grew pained. " 'Tis no secret Jamal wants you, Zara. Drugging him and then fleeing was an insult he will not tolerate. He will search for us, but I feel reasonably certain we are safe for the time being. After we've relieved the sultan's caravan of its riches, we will move deeper into the mountains."

"How long will you be gone, Father?"

Youssef shrugged. "I'm not sure. Perhaps a week, certainly no longer. Once we locate the caravan we will know when and where to attack. 'Tis important that we know how many guards are assigned to the caravan."

"Do you have any instructions for me?"

"I have faith in your ability to lead the men should the need arise, daughter."

"That means a great deal to me," Zara said. She turned to leave but Youssef's hand upon her arm stopped her.

"Let us speak frankly, Zara. I can see you are unhappy. Is it because of Jamal? I know that having to submit to him was demeaning for you and I blame myself for your sacrifice, but I did not demand it of you. If you wish it, I will find and kill him."

"Nay, Father!" Zara cried, horrified at the notion of Jamal's death. "My sacrifice was for our people." Though in truth it was no sacrifice, she wanted to add. "Jamal did not harm me," she admitted. "He was gentle even though I repeatedly tested his temper."

"One day," Youssef predicted, "there will be a confrontation between me and Jamal, and I cannot promise the outcome will be to your liking." His eyes narrowed. "What has the foul beast done to earn your regard, daughter? How can you harbor a fondness for the man responsible for the death of your betrothed? The man ravished you!"

Zara flushed. "I despise Jamal, Father," she lied. "I just wish I hadn't had to resort to subterfuge to gain our freedom."

"Very well. Go then, daughter, and see to the security of the camp. I will leave tomorrow at first light."

*   *   *

Jamal and his men-at-arms found no trace of Youssef and the Blue Men despite having scoured the mountains and foothills for several days.

"It is hopeless, Jamal," Haroun said, giving his shaggy head a weary shake. "The mountains are too vast, the hiding places too many. We'll never find Youssef."

"I'll find him," Jamal said with grim determination. "I promised Ishmail Youssef's head and, Allah willing, I'll bring it to him."

"Admit it, my lord, you're more interested in Youssef's daughter than you are in Youssef."

"Zara played me for a fool, Haroun. I was besotted with her and she deceived me. Aye, admittedly I want her, but only to punish her and for naught else. 'Tis the first time a woman has humiliated me, and it does not sit well with me."

Haroun recalled what Jamal had said about sending Zara to the slave market and vowed to see it done if he ever got his hands on the feckless Berber bitch. "You were fortunate to escape punishment when the sultan learned you had Youssef and let him escape. Ishmail is not an easy man to placate."

"I promised him all the plunder from my next pirating expedition instead of a percentage," Jamal said, recalling the sultan's violent outburst when he'd been told of Youssef's escape.

"How soon will we sail?" Haroun asked, thinking of Saha and how he'd hate leaving her behind. It hadn't taken long for the concubine to learn that he was a strict and demanding master, that he would not tolerate disobedience. She was quick to realize that she was now the property of a simple soldier. After a beating or two he couldn't have asked for a more passionate mistress. He was nearly as besotted with Saha as Jamal was with his Berber princess.

" 'Tis only a matter of time before we return to sea," Jamal said with a shrug. "How soon depends on when we find Youssef and his wily daughter."

"It grows dark, shall we make camp?"

"See to it, Haroun. I'm going to ride ahead to see what lies beyond the next rise. Youssef's camp has to be somewhere in these mountains, and the longer it takes to find it, the angrier the sultan becomes."

Zara gave the order that no campfires be lit in her father's absence. Meals were to be cooked over small braziers that did not light up the night.

Youssef had been gone two days and thus far all had been quiet. Two blue-robed men walked the perimeter of the camp, guarding against a surprise attack, though Zara doubted Jamal was anywhere in the vicinity. There had been no attacks upon the sultan's caravans since she and her father had escaped, and she hoped the sultan had been gulled into thinking that no more raids would take place.

Zara retired to her tent, satisfied that all was well. Unfortunately, sleep was a luxury that had been denied her of late. The moment she closed her eyes, her vivid memory returned her to those erotic nights spent in Jamal's arms. Drenched in sweat, she tossed and turned and flung off the blankets, growing wet in all those places Jamal had caressed and kissed. Her body ached for his touch; she trembled with the disturbing need to know his loving again.

Zara tried to shut down her thinking process but failed miserably. Jamal had taught her body to want him and she had proved an apt pupil. How he must hate her, she reflected. He must feel humiliated and hurt. If she ever fell into his hands again, he would make her life miserable. A proud man like Jamal would surely retaliate for being made a fool of. She trembled at the thought of Jamal's swift justice and implored Allah to keep her out of the sheik's hands.

Standing on a ridge above the Berber camp, Jamal held his hand over his horse's muzzle and peered down. He'd been surprised when he stumbled upon the camp a short time ago.

Jamal watched for perhaps thirty minutes before he had all the information he needed to launch a pre-dawn surprise attack. He and his men would surround the Berber stronghold, silence the two sentries and capture the entire tribe while they slept. Allah was good. Soon he'd have the cunning Berber vixen back in his possession where she belonged.

Zara slept fitfully. She awoke in the wee hours before dawn, her body tense, her senses tingling with foreboding. All was quiet. Nothing seemed amiss. The night was dark and moonless; not a shadow was visible in the murky blackness. She shifted upon her pallet of furs and tried to explain her disquiet. There was nothing to fear, she told herself. The black tents were all but invisible against a backdrop of black sky and dark mountains, and Zara chided herself for being fanciful. The sentries were reliable and no alarm had been given.

A camel snorted and Zara stiffened. When the sound wasn't repeated, she allowed herself to relax. She was being foolish, she told herself, feeling fear where there was nothing to fear. As it was still too early to rise, she closed her eyes and forced herself to doze.

Outside in the yawning darkness, Jamal and his men surrounded the black tents. The guards had been easily dispatched and were left unconscious and bound by the camel pen, where four of Jamal's men were endeavoring to keep the camels quiet. Jamal remained watchful as his men silently crept into all the tents save one, which Jamal had saved for himself. In a bloodless, silent coup, Jamal's men had subdued the sleeping Berbers and herded them together inside a large tent.

Jamal gazed at the untouched tent, aware that it was the one in which Zara slept. He knew because he had questioned one of the sentries before knocking him unconscious.

"The camp is secure, Jamal," Haroun reported. "The sentry was right. Youssef is not here. Half the male members of the tribe are gone. We captured mostly women and children."

"I do not make war upon women and children," Jamal said, furious at having missed Youssef. "Guard them well, my friend. After my business with Zara is concluded, I will issue further orders." He glanced toward Zara's tent. "See that I am not disturbed."

Zara sat up amid the rumpled bedclothes, her breath hammering in her chest. Something was wrong, she knew it. The eerie silence was not normal. She started violently when she felt a hard hand on her shoulder. Whipping her head around, she saw a shadowy figure hovering over her. She reached for the knife beside her pillow, but the intruder was too fast for her. He kicked it away before she could grasp it.

Her voice rose on a note of panic. "Who are you? What do you want?" She tried to rise.

A light flared and Jamal's hand tightened upon Zara's narrow shoulder, sending her a silent warning. She winced but did not cry out; pain was not new to her. Then, in the flickering light of the lamp she saw his face and knew real fear.

Jamal hauled Zara to her feet, bringing them nose to nose. "It is I, sweet vixen, your worst nightmare come to life."

"Jamal! Allah help me. How did you—"

"Beseech Allah all you want, Zara, He will not help you."

"I have but to scream to bring men to my aid."

Jamal laughed. The sound was far from comforting. "Your men are my prisoners. *My* men are in control."

"The sentries—"

"Have been taken care of. My one regret is that Youssef is not here. But fear not, he cannot remain at large forever. The sultan has placed a hefty price upon his head."

Zara searched his face, visible now in the awakening dawn. His eyes were cold and emotionless, his face hard and relentlessly unforgiving. Her chin rose slightly. No matter what he had planned for her, she would not beg for mercy. She had betrayed him, and for that he meant to punish her. He would never know that she had not escaped unscathed. During her weeks of captivity she had discovered hidden depths of emotion for her handsome captor. He had ignited fires inside her that still burned hotly.

"You will never capture Father. He is too smart for you."

Jamal smiled without mirth. "But I have his daughter. You brought him to me once and will do so again." His gaze slid the length of her with insulting intensity. "Take off your clothes, Zara."

"What!"

"Now, sweet vixen. Haroun will make certain we're not interrupted."

"If this is your way of punishing me—"

"Punish you?" He laughed harshly. "You think bedding me is punishment? Is that how you felt each time you lay with me? Was it such a chore? You are an accomplished actress, sweet vixen. I could have sworn you swooned from ecstasy in my arms. You even learned to enjoy the silver balls and the special kind of pleasure they gave you. You cannot lie to me, Zara."

Zara wanted to deny everything but couldn't. She hated to be reminded of her wild, responsive nature where Jamal was concerned. It nettled her to recall how she'd begged him to come inside her, to take her to Paradise. She had pretended nothing. Everything she'd felt had been very real.

"It was all pretense," Zara lied. "Hate me if you must, but I did what I had to do for my father and my people."

"You whored for your father!" Jamal charged angrily. How dare she deny all those feelings they'd shared? How dare she renounce the emotional involvement that made their loving so special?

Zara tried not to cringe beneath his implacable rage. "It wasn't like that. I'm not a whore."

"You are now. You're my whore. Are you going to remove your clothing or must I do it for you?"

Zara glanced toward the closed tent flap. "Don't even think it, sweet vixen. My men are everywhere." He tore off his *djellaba* and then reached for her. His hands were swift and sure as he ripped apart the fine linen shirt she wore and tossed it aside. In the dim light of early morning her breasts gleamed like pale alabaster. Next he attacked her baggy pantaloons, tearing them to shreds in his eagerness to see her naked.

When she was completely nude, he stepped back in silent admiration, his anger slowly dissipating. "Allah knows I want to hate you," he told her. "You beguiled me with your sweet body in order to gain my trust. Your punishment must be as painful as your deceit."

"I'm sure it will be," Zara said, licking moisture onto her dry lips. "But I don't regret my actions. My father's life is more important than my own."

"Whore," Jamal said, attacking his own clothing with impatience. His shirt flew across the tent. "I want you, Zara. I want you to remember how my hands feel upon your sweet flesh, how my mouth tastes, the feel of my lips caressing all those places that drive you wild."

Zara closed her eyes. As if she needed to be reminded her of the way he'd made her feel. From the moment she'd left Jamal, she'd thought of little else. Why couldn't their lives be less complicated? Why weren't they able to love freely, without guilt? Why did they have to be on opposite sides?

"You hate me. Why do you want me?" Zara asked as he pulled her against him.

"The line between hate and love is frequently too finely drawn to distinguish one from the other," he said cryptically. "Be thankful I'm merely bedding you instead of demanding your life."

With lithe, pantherlike grace he eased her down on the pallet of fur. A dangerous half-smile curled his lips as he reared up and looked at her. His expression was one of unswerving masculinity, unrelenting determination. His gaze raked over her. The lush length of her body held him enthralled. Her breasts were soft and full, her nipples dark cherry temptations. The plump pink mound of her womanhood was already weeping for him.

His gaze unsettled her. She recognized the fierce glitter in his eyes only too well. How could he do this to her again? How could he make her want him by merely looking at her?

Sparks of rebellion burst inside her. "Allah take your soul! Do not touch me!"

"Ah, but I will do more than touch you, sweet

vixen. Before I am through with you, you will call me master."

"Nay!" she cried. "I am no man's slave."

"Are you not? You are my slave and my whore."

He brought her hard against him, crushing her breasts against the solid wall of his chest. His shaft prodded against her stomach. His mouth came down hard on hers and the world spun away.

His mouth never left hers as he stripped off his boots and pantaloons. Then he drove his hands through the heavy mass of her blond hair, holding her head steady as he continued to ravage her with soul-destroying kisses. The sound coming from her throat seemed more like a moan than a protest as his tongue thrust between her teeth. He kissed her roughly, fiercely.

Suddenly his mouth parted from hers and he stared at her, his eyes burning into her soul. "I could kill you and no one would stop me."

She sifted through his words in a haze of desire. "Do it then, Jamal. Kill me and be done with it."

"Allah help me, I cannot." His voice was husky with emotion. "But I will never trust you again."

Gathering her courage, Zara said, "You feel something for me, Jamal, I know you do." It was a mistake.

His features turned to stone. "You will cease telling me what I feel and don't feel. You will obey me. All I want from you is your body and the pleasure it gives me. You will spread your legs when I ask it of you and surrender willingly. When you begin to bore me I will send you to the slave market and let a new master deal with you."

Zara's mouth fell open. Was that to be her fate? Would she be displayed upon a slave block like a piece of meat and sold to the highest bidder? She did not think Jamal could be so cruel.

Zara could think of no answer. In fact, her mind went blank as Jamal pushed her breasts together and rubbed his face in the cleft, then thrust between them with his tongue. His mouth found a ripe nipple. He rolled it between his teeth, sucked it into his mouth and drew deeply upon it. Little mewling sounds escaped her mouth as her hands moved unbidden over the hard, taut muscles of his back and buttocks.

"Once again you seduce me with your soft, sweet body and greedy mouth and hands," Jamal whispered against her lips. "You're dangerous, sweet vixen."

Her skin was flushed and damp, her mouth looked swollen and pillaged from his kisses. He stared into the vivid green pools of her eyes and felt as if he were drowning. Though he knew he must be dreaming, he imagined that her eyes held the soft, dreamy look of love. He blinked, banishing the image. He was nothing but a besotted fool who hadn't learned his lesson. Zara didn't love him. She had used his obsession with her to deceive him. She cared nothing for him. The only truth was lust. There was no pretense in the way her body responded to him. She craved what he could give her, and that was no lie.

"You forced me to act as I did," Zara said. "Becoming your love slave was never my intention. I rebuffed your every attempt to bed me until my

Thrill to the most sensual, adventure-filled Historical Romances on the market today...

FROM ![logo] *LEISURE BOOKS*

As a home subscriber to Leisure Romance Book Club, you'll enjoy the best in today's BRAND-NEW Historical Romance fiction. For over twenty-five years, Leisure Books has brought you the award-winning, high-quality authors you know and love to read. Each Leisure Historical Romance will sweep you away to a world of high adventure...and intimate romance. Discover for yourself all the passion and excitement millions of readers thrill to each and every month.

Save $5.⁰⁰ Each Time You Buy!

Each month, the Leisure Romance Book Club brings you four brand-new titles from Leisure Books, America's foremost publisher of Historical Romances. EACH PACKAGE WILL SAVE YOU $5.00 FROM THE BOOKSTORE PRICE! And you'll never miss a new title with our convenient home delivery service.

Here's how we do it. Each package will carry a FREE 10-DAY EXAMINATION privilege. At the end of that time, if you decide to keep your books, simply pay the low invoice price of $16.96, no shipping or handling charges added. HOME DELIVERY IS ALWAYS FREE. With today's top Historical Romance novels selling for $5.99 and higher, our price SAVES YOU $5.00 with each shipment.

AND YOUR FIRST FOUR-BOOK SHIPMENT IS TOTALLY FREE
IT'S A BARGAIN YOU CAN'T BEAT! A Super $21.96 Value!

![logo] *LEISURE BOOKS* A Division of Dorchester Publishing Co., Inc.

Get Four Books Totally FREE – A $21.96 Value!

▼ Tear Here and Mail Your FREE Book Card Today! ▼

PLEASE RUSH
MY FOUR FREE
BOOKS TO ME
RIGHT AWAY!

Leisure Romance Book Club
P.O. Box 6613
Edison, NJ 08818-6613

AFFIX
STAMP
HERE

father became your captive. I did what I had to do in order to free him."

"Deceitful vixen," Jamal whispered against her lips. "Your wishes no longer matter to me. 'Tis my needs you'll cater to from now on. Spread your legs and receive your master."

She heaved against him with such force that he was nearly bucked off her. "Son of a goat! Cur! You were never my master."

She raised her hand to strike him but he seized her wrists, holding them together with one hand and pulling them above her head. He covered her bucking body with his, subduing her with his sheer strength.

"Not true, sweet vixen. I mastered you the first time you took me inside you."

Their bodies were meshed together, legs entwined, her breasts flattened against his chest. His staff was hard and heavy and painfully engorged. She could lie all she wanted about not craving him, but he knew different. To prove his point, he spread her thighs with his knees and thrust deep, embedding himself to the hilt. He groaned as the scorching heat of her surrounded him, welcomed him. He was so ready he could have climaxed immediately. But a perverse demon inside him refused to allow that.

Satisfying Zara had always been a large part of his own pleasure. He had intended to take her roughly, quickly, without any consideration for her pleasure, but the moment he slid inside her he realized he wanted Zara to feel the same sublime rapture he did. No matter what she had done to him, cruelty was not an option where Zara was concerned. He flexed his hips and began to move slowly, penetrating deeply, bringing a surprised gasp from her parted lips as he brought his hands and mouth into play.

His long, talented fingers stroked and caressed her buttocks as his mouth sucked and licked her nipples. His breathing turned harsh and rasping and his hips jerked harder, faster, taking Zara along with him into a world of bursting stars and exploding planets.

"Come, sweet vixen," Jamal panted into her ear. "Come for me now."

Abruptly he turned her, bringing her on top of him, forcing a deeper penetration. Zara screamed as Jamal touched the tiny jewel between her legs, hurtling her over the edge, into a swirling pool of raw sensation. Jamal shouted his pleasure and followed her to a rapturous climax.

He stayed in her a long time. Until he'd grown completely soft. Until his heartbeat slowed to a steady thunder and his lungs began to take in air once again. Until the scattered pieces of his body returned to normal.

"Do you still deny that I am your master?" Jamal asked with lazy amusement. "Your body obeys my every command without question."

She gave him a look of wounded outrage, then turned her face away. "Unhand me. You have done your worst. Now leave me alone."

"Done my worst?" Jamal repeated with a snarl. "Nay, sweet vixen, I've done my best. I had meant to take you swiftly, without giving you pleasure, but I am too soft-hearted to leave you wanting. It may not always be this way, so enjoy it while you can."

He was growing hard again; he could feel himself swelling inside her. She must have felt it too, for she tried to roll off him. His arms came around her like a vise, holding her captive against him.

"Nay, not again," Zara cried, her eyes growing wide with alarm. It wasn't unusual for him to take her more than once a night, but he generally rested between each bout of loving.

"Aye, again, sweet vixen." He grasped her hips and placed her beside him on her stomach. Before she could move he was over her, lifting her to her knees so he could enter her feminine passage from behind. "This way leaves my hands free to fondle you." His breath was hot upon her neck, his hands molding her breasts, his fingers teasing her nipples. Then he thrust inside her.

Zara arched her back, thinking with the last rational bit of her brain that Jamal was right. He had mastered her body even as her mind rejected what he was doing to her. With wretched awareness she realized that no man but Jamal had the power to bend her to his will. It was a frightening thought. She wanted to be more than a slave to him, but fate and circumstances were working against her. Jamal would never entertain tender feelings for her. He hated her.

Her thinking process broke down when Jamal's thrusting grew frenzied. They raced unheedingly toward the stars and reached them simultaneously.

Throughout that long morning Jamal loved her

yet another time before calling for food. Then he loved her again. Afterward he ordered Zara to dress, then he flung open the tent flap and called for Haroun. While he waited for his lieutenant, he pulled on his own clothing. Zara was fully dressed and awaiting her fate when Haroun entered the tent a short time later.

"Take the prisoners to the slave market in Fez," Jamal ordered shortly.

"The women and children, too?"

"Nay. Leave them. They're too much trouble." He hated the thought of mothers and children being separated, which was bound to happen if they were put on the block. "Take half the men-at-arms and leave the rest here with me. I'm going after Youssef. I probably won't catch the wily bastard but I have to try. After you have delivered the prisoners, return to Paradise. I will join you as soon as I can."

Haroun's eyes slid to Zara. "What about *her*, Jamal? What do you want done with the Berber witch?"

Jamal's eyes darkened with an emotion he was hard pressed to explain, so he didn't even try. "Take her from my sight. I gave her my trust and she betrayed me."

Without further ado, Haroun grasped Zara's arm and pulled her from the tent. In Haroun's opinion Jamal couldn't have made his wishes clearer. He recalled the day Jamal had spoken of sending Zara to the slave market. As far as Haroun knew, Jamal hadn't changed his mind. It never dawned on Haroun that Jamal wanted Zara taken to Paradise, to await his return. It was Haroun's personal opinion that Jamal was better off without the Berber bitch. Haroun hoped Zara would be sold to a man who would beat her into submission. Jamal was too good a man to suffer betrayal at the hands of a woman. With Allah's help, Haroun intended to see justice done.

"Where are you taking me?" Zara asked when she was hoisted upon a horse.

" 'Tis Jamal's wish that you be taken to the slave market and sold."

"Nay, Jamal would not—"

But he would, Zara thought, swallowing the rest of her sentence. Jamal hated her. By his standards her fate was a just one.

Chapter Twelve

Zara glanced around her opulent surroundings with a sinking heart. She was one of several women being held in Kadeem el Haka's harem, awaiting the slave auction, which was to be held on the next market day. Haroun had wasted little time in delivering her and the other prisoners to the slave master in Fez. A deal was quickly struck, and Haroun accepted the money in Jamal's name and hastened to Paradise to await Jamal's return.

Zara and other women in the harem had been fed, bathed, pampered and dressed in rich silks and brocades. Obviously these women were intended for their masters' beds, to be indulged and spoiled and treated like possessions. Was that the fate Jamal intended for her? Zara wondered. Allah help her should another man lay hands on her. She would fight tooth and nail and gladly suffer the consequences.

With nothing to do but eat and sleep, Zara had too much time to think. She recalled Jamal's anger when he'd sent her away with Haroun. His smile had been cold and dangerous and did not reach his dark, glittering eyes. And it broke her heart. He had made love to her with such overwhelming tenderness, such caring, she hadn't wanted to believe that his intention all along had been to sell her.

Zara listened to snippets of conversation around her and was amused at how her thoughts differed from those of her lovely companions. While she longed for open spaces and mountains, they dreamed of pleasing a rich master, one who would indulge their every whim and shower them with gifts. They aspired no higher than to become a love slave, but she abhorred being treated as an object, letting men rule her life.

Blondes, brunettes, redheads. Plump, thin, fat. The women prattled on while Zara closed her mind to all but her own misery. Had Jamal found her father? she wondered. Somehow she doubted it. Youssef was a wily desert fighter who knew how to avoid capture.

Suddenly the curtains to the harem parted and Kadeem stepped through. The chattering women fell silent, staring at the man who held their fate in his hands. Kadeem was short, obese and richly dressed in colorful robes of silk and satin. He wore a ring on each thick finger and several gold chains around his fat neck. His dense black beard covered a weak chin, and his eyes looked too small for his round face. He smiled with pleasure and rubbed his palms together as he surveyed his harem of lovelies.

"I hope you're enjoying your stay, ladies," he said obsequiously. "Soon you will all have new masters." His words were met with titters. "My customers are all rich and powerful men, so you can be assured of masters who will keep you in luxury."

Zara gave an unladylike snort. Camel driver or potentate, all men were vile pigs interested in their own pleasure. She had thought Jamal was different, but ultimately he'd proved her wrong. He'd used her and then discarded her with careless disregard. Why couldn't he understand why she had acted as she had? Had he been *her* prisoner, he'd have done everything in his power to escape.

Zara looked up to find Kadeem standing over her, hands on hips, a scowl darkening his swarthy features. "You laughed, lady. Do you not wish for a rich master?"

"I want no master," Zara proclaimed. "Slavery does not appeal to me."

Kadeem sneered. "Now I know why your former master sold you so cheaply, Berber wench. You have a sharp tongue. I will encourage your new master to use the bastinado on you. If he does not, I fear he will end up cutting out your tongue. When you are on the slave block you will curb your insolence or suffer the consequences, do you understand?"

Zara didn't think she'd ever understand the

need for women to submit meekly to men, but she wisely held her tongue. When the time came, she'd show her new master that she was not easily tamed, nor would she submit willingly.

When Zara did not reply, Kadeem seemed satisfied. Purposely ignoring Zara, whom he considered too troublesome, he chose a plump redhead to warm his bed that night. The woman went along submissively, though her expression denied her willingness. Unfortunately, she had no choice. Zara thanked Allah that Kadeem did not favor her.

Four days in Kadeem's harem seemed like an eternity. To Zara's vast relief, Kadeem passed over her each time he returned to the harem to choose his companion for the night. A time or two he seemed on the verge of selecting her, but her mutinous expression must have changed his mind.

Finally it was time for the auction. All the women were bathed, massaged, dressed in diaphanous garments, perfumed and groomed to perfection. Though Zara did not accept her fate, she decided to bide her time and plan an escape when her situation improved. She had escaped from Jamal, hadn't she?

Jamal returned to Paradise in the worst of moods. He hadn't been able to run down Youssef. The man was craftier than a fox. He seemed to know every hiding place in the Rif mountains and used them to his advantage. After three days of combing arid land and towering mountains, Jamal decided to return to Paradise.

To Jamal's chagrin, it was the promise of Zara's sweet body that lured him back home. At least he hoped it was merely her body he wanted. He must not forget that Zara had used him. She was deceitful and sly. But Allah help him, he still wanted her.

Haroun hurried to meet Jamal when he spied the sheik riding through the gates. "Welcome home, Jamal. Was Allah kind to you? Did you find Youssef?"

Jamal gave a snort of disgust. "The man is like a chameleon; he changes colors to blend into his surroundings. Once again he has escaped me."

Haroun frowned. "The sultan will not be pleased. Have you reported to him yet?"

"Nay, I was anxious to return home. Did you follow my orders concerning the prisoners?"

"Aye, they will be sold at the next slave auction. Kadeem el Haka was well pleased. Healthy males are in high demand. As for the woman—"

Jamal went still, his mind refusing to accept the implication of Haroun's words. "What woman? You were ordered to leave the women and children behind."

Haroun's dark face assumed a puzzled look. Was Jamal toying with him? A thought that did not bear entertaining entered his mind. "The women and children *were* left behind, my lord. All but one."

Haroun watched the color drain from Jamal's swarthy features and he stepped back in alarm. Allah help him! What had he done?

"Zara! Where is Zara?" Jamal's voice held a note of terror. And something else. Something that sent fear racing through Haroun.

"Forgive me if I have done wrong, my lord. You said to take Zara away and I did as you asked. Zara and the Blue Men were sold to the slave master in Fez."

"Allah curse you!" Jamal cried, shaking his fist at Haroun. "It was never my intention to sell Zara. You were to bring her here to await my return."

Haroun fell to his knees, his arms raised in supplication. He'd never borne the brunt of Jamal's temper but had witnessed the punishment of those who displeased him. "You spoke of selling Zara. I assumed it was what you wished. The Berber wench deserved to be punished for drugging you, and I thought you wanted to be rid of her. I had no way of knowing you jested, that you still wanted her. Forgive me, my lord."

Jamal stared at Haroun, his anger fearsome to behold. Zara was gone. Her sweet body and lush lips were no longer his to kiss and caress. A new master would own her, a man who would never appreciate her passion as he did. He had nurtured that passion, cultivated and sustained it by giving her unparalleled rapture.

Struggling for control, Jamal asked, "When is the auction to be held? For your sake, I pray it hasn't already taken place."

Haroun swallowed convulsively. "Tomorrow, my lord. The slave auction is held on market day, which is Thursday."

Jamal spit out a curse. "That doesn't leave me much time to reach Fez. Go to the village and purchase a racing camel from the camel trader.

Camels have more stamina than any of my Arabian horses. They can endure a fast pace for prolonged periods and require less water. Hurry, Haroun. I wish to leave within the hour."

Haroun rushed to follow Jamal's orders. His horse was nearby and he leaped into the saddle and galloped through the gate toward the village. He found Rashid the camel trader with little difficulty.

"Quickly, I wish to purchase your fastest racing camel for Sheik Jamal," Haroun said, pulling a bag of money from his belt. "Name your price."

"Does the sheik intend a long journey?" Rashid asked shrewdly. He knew that Jamal had gone in search of Zara and Youssef and returned empty-handed. His spies had brought word of Jamal's return even as Jamal was speaking with his lieutenant.

"You ask too many questions. Just choose the camel and name the price."

"If a long journey is intended, then this camel will do," Rashid said, pointing to a rangy animal resting nearby. "But if 'tis speed the sheik requires, then I would recommend a different type animal."

"Speed, man, speed. The sheik needs to reach Fez as swiftly as possible. I have done a terrible thing. I took his favorite to the slave market and now he wants her back."

"Ah, you speak of the slave Zara, do you not?"

Realizing he had spoken out of turn, Haroun said, " 'tis of no consequence. Which camel do you recommend?"

"This one for speed." Rashid picked up the

leading reins of a sleek, dun-colored animal and handed it to Haroun, naming an outrageous price.

Haroun muttered to himself as he counted out the money. "You drive a hard bargain. If I wasn't in a hurry I would haggle, but Jamal is waiting and I have already incurred his anger."

Haroun mounted his horse and rode off with the camel in tow. Rashid waited until he was gone before calling to his assistant to take over. Then he selected another camel, an animal every bit as fast as the one he'd sold to Haroun, and sped away from the oasis.

Jamal rode like the wind. He traveled alone, racing toward Fez as if the Devil were chasing him. He rode until darkness and the mountainous terrain made it too dangerous to continue. He stopped and lay down beside the camel, snatching a few hours' sleep, till the light of dawn allowed him to carry on. Fez was still a long way off, and he beseeched Allah to let him reach Zara in time.

Zara wasn't the first slave to be led to the slave block. Kadeem was saving her for last. She had been bathed and dressed in provocative clothing. Transparent pantaloons hugged her hips, then flared out and clasped her ankles with jeweled bands. The short silk jacket barely covered her breasts, baring her entire midriff. Her nipples had been rouged and were clearly visible beneath the thin material. More of her anatomy was revealed than concealed, and she trembled with fury at being made the object of men's lust.

Zara watched from a holding area as the men were led out and sold first. Then it was the women's turn to be offered for sale. With growing horror Zara saw prospective buyers come forward to inspect the women intimately, stroking their breasts, testing the texture and smoothness of their flesh, touching them in places that brought raucous laughter from the men and titters from the women. The physical inspection was embarrassing and utterly demeaning.

Most of the women were ordered to remove their clothing, to pose nude before their would-be masters. Some didn't seem to mind, turning their bodies in ways that showed them to the best advantage. Those women were quickly sold amid brisk bidding and carted off by their new masters. A fair crowd still remained when Zara was finally brought forth.

Murmurs of appreciation rippled through the crowd as Zara took her place on the slave block. Her blank expression gave no hint of her terror as she stared straight ahead, making eye contact with no one.

"Show us her breasts!" a man in the front of the crowd demanded.

Kadeem stepped in front of Zara, ready to snatch away the meager scrap of material covering her breasts. But the fierce look in her eyes momentarily stayed his hand. He did not note the direction of Zara's gaze.

Zara was staring at the curved knife Kadeem wore at his waist. As the slave master stepped in front of her, blocking her from view, she acted instinctively, without regard for the consequences. Her hand moved so quickly, Kadeem didn't realize she had freed his blade until he felt it pressing against his groin. He froze, his eyes locking with Zara's, and guessed from her determined expression that the fierce Berber wouldn't hesitate to emasculate him.

His worst fears were confirmed when Zara snarled, "Touch me, Arab pig, and I'll slice off your balls and stuff them in your mouth."

Kadeem began to sweat profusely. "What do you hope to accomplish by this? Cut me and my men will slay you where you stand."

"I will have the satisfaction of knowing that you will never use that foul thing between your legs again." The blade pricked him through his clothing and Kadeem squealed.

"What are you waiting for, Kadeem?" the man in front shouted. "Bare her breasts for us."

"Decide fast, Kadeem," Zara hissed. "Leave my clothing intact or suffer the bite of the knife where it will hurt you the most. I refuse to be humiliated before these foul pigs who call themselves men."

Kadeem decided to back off. Making a scene now would cost him dearly, both in profit and pride. Should she humiliate him before his best customers, she would never bring the price he expected.

"I will leave your clothing intact if you will remove the blade and slip it back in its rightful place. I swear this on Allah's grave."

Zara hesitated but a moment before replacing Kadeem's knife. She didn't want to die, and she surely would if she harmed Kadeem. Once the blade rode comfortably at his waist, Kadeem turned to the crowd and said, "It is best to leave something to the imagination. It will serve to whet your appetites for the tempestuous Zara. Look at her, men. Is she not delectable? Her breasts are high and full. Her nipples are like ripe cherries. If you look closely you can see her mound through her pantaloons. I guarantee that it is plump, pink and will sheath the mightiest sword."

Zara kept her eyes focused on the cloudless sky as the men strained forward to catch a glimpse of the various body parts Kadeem had described. Kadeem had truly captured their fancy. Zara hissed as Kadeem turned her around and patted her bottom.

Kadeem ignored her. "Are these not sweet? Like perfect twin moons, round and succulent." He squeezed with both hands.

Zara made a strangled sound deep in her throat and Kadeem's hands fell away. "Who will start the bidding?"

"Is she a virgin?" asked an obese bearded man dressed in flowing white robes and turban.

"Zara is not a virgin, my friend, but something better. Her previous owner trained her himself. She is proficient in all manner of love play and guaranteed to satisfy the most jaded of men. You will not be disappointed."

His words set off a round of bidding that was fierce and competitive. The price doubled and re-doubled, until only three men in the crowd were rich enough to participate in the lively auction.

Then the white-robed man in the back made a bid so outrageously high that it shut out the remaining two bidders.

"The prize goes to Sheik Sidi Bennaur," Kadeem announced grandly. "The price was high, but I'm sure he will find the beauteous Zara well worth it."

Sidi Bennaur came forward with mincing steps. A half-grown boy with the face of an angel trotted behind him. He waved a plump hand in Kadeem's face. "You know my preferences, Kadeem, and it's not for women with lush curves." Absently he patted the boy's blond head. "Boys like Azzi are more to my tastes. Once in a while I'll attempt a woman, but she must be as slim and sleek as a boy for me to enjoy her."

Zara stared at Sidi Bennaur with distaste. Not only was he perverted but freely admitted it. She pitied the poor children forced to submit to his depraved tastes.

"The woman is a gift for a friend who has done me a great service. Ali ben Baha has an enormous appetite for women, but unfortunately he tires of them quickly. Pray Allah my gift pleases him, for she has cost me a small fortune. Are you sure she is experienced in bed sport, Kadeem? I would hate to send my friend inferior goods."

"I was told that her previous master taught her to both give and receive erotic pleasure. Your friend will thank you for the gift."

Zara fumed in impotent rage. They were speaking over and through her as if she were mute and blind.

"Should she displease him, Sheik Ali ben Baha

will give her to his stable master, a man known for his perverse appetites."

A commotion caught Zara's attention and she watched in dismay as a man rode through the marketplace, scattering people and beasts of burden who dared to get in his way. Unerringly he headed toward the slave block. Zara swayed with shock when she recognized Jamal, racing toward her atop a sleek camel.

Jamal spied Zara immediately. She wasn't hard to spot in the nearly empty slave market. She was lovelier than the moon and stars, and he feasted upon the sight of her. Then he realized the implication of the empty slave market and his heart sank. He was too late. Allah help him! He skidded to a halt before the slave block, threw his leg over the saddle and slid to the ground, bracing himself for the jolt when his feet hit the dirt.

"Am I too late for the auction?" Jamal asked, though he already knew the answer. With a knowing glance he sized up Sidi Bennaur, marking him as a man who did not enjoy women.

"The auction is over, my friend," Kadeem said. "Zara was the last to be sold. She is now the property of Sheik Sidi Bennaur."

Jamal forced himself to speak calmly despite his racing heart. "I will double the bid."

Kadeem recognized an opportunity to increase his profit when he saw one. He was acquainted with Sheik Jamal from previous dealings. Haroun had told him that Zara had been Jamal's slave. "It is up to Sidi Bennaur whether or not to sell her to you. If he chooses to give her up, I, of course, will take a broker's share for the resale."

Jamal turned his dark scrutiny on Sidi Bennaur. Jamal's hands were clenched into tight fists at his sides, the only outward sign of his inner turmoil. "Of what use is the woman to you, Sidi Bennaur? I understand young boys are more to your taste."

Zara inhaled sharply, still in a state of shock over Jamal's unexpected appearance. Why would Jamal wish to buy her when she had been sent to the slave market by his order? Nothing made sense.

Sidi Bennaur waved a fat beringed hand in the air, dismissing Jamal's words with a scowl. " 'Tis no concern of yours what I do with the slave. She is mine now. I do not wish to sell her."

"I find this strange, my lord," Kadeem said. "Why did you instruct your man Haroun to sell the woman if you still wanted her?"

Jamal turned his gaze to Zara. His eyes were dark and unreadable, but something within those unfathomable depths spoke to her of strong emotions. She blinked, fearing her eyes were deceiving her. When she looked again into Jamal's eyes they had turned murky.

His voice was fierce as he explained, "Selling Zara was a mistake. Haroun misunderstood my orders. Zara was to be taken to my palace to await my return. It was the Blue Men who were to be sold."

"What say you, Sidi Bennaur? Will you sell the woman to Sheik Jamal and make both of us a tidy profit?" Kadeem asked. His eyes glittered with anticipation, so great was his greed.

Sidi Bennaur made a pretense of considering

227

Kadeem's offer as he stroked his chin with one hand and caressed the young boy standing meekly at his side with the other hand. At length he said, "I have not changed my mind. My great good friend, Ali ben Baha, is a connoisseur of women and ever eager for new female flesh. He makes his home at the edge of the desert near Er Rachidia. The beauteous Zara will be outfitted like a queen and sent by caravan to Ali."

"I will pay three times what you paid for Zara." Jamal's voice was brash and demanding.

He did not intimidate the effeminate Sidi Bennaur in the least. Bennaur was a cruel and perverse man. He would have denied Jamal's request no matter what Jamal offered, simply because it pleased him to do so.

"I refuse your offer, Sheik Jamal," Sidi Bennaur said with a sniff. He motioned to Zara. "Come along, lady, you will stay at my home until I can arrange for a caravan to take you to your new master."

"Ali ben Baha will find me to be a difficult slave," Zara declared, finally finding her voice. "I am defiant and disobedient. I am proud and haughty and refuse to submit willingly to a man not of my own choosing. I am Zara, daughter of Youssef, the Berber *cadi*. The first time Ali touches me I will slit his gullet."

Sidi Bennaur gathered his robes around him, recoiling in shock. He glared at Jamal. "I understand now why you sold the woman. I hope you had her beaten regularly. Ali ben Baha is just the man to teach her obedience. He is not a patient

228

man. If she refuses to curb her tongue he will cut it out."

Sidi Bennaur clapped his hands and two burly men appeared at his side. "Seize the woman!" Bennaur ordered. "Take her to my home and guard her well."

Jamal wanted to launch himself at Bennaur's men and tear Zara away from them, but he knew he had no legal right. Bennaur had purchased and paid for her, and there was nothing he could do as long as the man refused to give her up. He forced himself to pretend indifference. Zara was truly lost to him.

"I wish Ali ben Baha joy of the Berber vixen," Jamal said with forced joviality. "I've grown rather fond of my throat. Having it slit while I am sleeping does not appeal to me. I realize now that selling the slave was a wise move on my part." Zara had no idea he spoke out of despair and resignation.

"Most prudent," Kadeem agreed, recalling how Zara had threatened the most delicate part of his anatomy with his own blade.

Zara sent Jamal a look of pure frustration. His appearance here just didn't make sense. Why had he traveled all this way to buy her back if he felt that way about her? Had sending her to the slave market truly been a mistake?

Jamal read the bewilderment on Zara's face but could do nothing about it. He had lost her. Soon she would belong to another, warming to his caresses, begging for his kisses. Jamal had no choice but to return home and forget that Zara had ever existed. He turned to leave, seeing no point in remaining. He had done a terrible thing to Zara, though the fault did not lie entirely with him. Losing her cut deeply into the part of his heart he'd always kept free of involvement.

"How could you, Jamal?" Zara cried as Bennaur's men dragged her away.

Jamal turned to look at her, his dark eyes bleak with despair. Their gazes locked, and he felt a terrible jolt in the vicinity of his heart. The look they shared was one of pain.

Of betrayal.

Of heartbreak.

Chapter Thirteen

Jamal paced the carpeted floors of his chamber, his mood as foul as his temper. He'd returned home from Fez immediately after Zara was taken away by Sidi Bennaur's men. Three days had passed. Three days in which the emptiness of the palace and silent women's quarters produced a kind of loneliness Jamal had never experienced before. During those three endless days and nights Jamal wavered between riding to Zara's rescue and forgetting her.

Then, in a sudden jolt of insight, Jamal made up his mind. He pulled open his chamber door and roared for Hammet. The eunuch rushed into the chamber a few minutes later, his robes flying behind him.

"I am here, my lord."

"Summon Haroun." Jamal's words were sharp,

demanding immediate obedience. Hammet didn't wait around for further orders.

Jamal continued pacing until Haroun stood before him, salaaming respectfully. "You wished to see me, my lord?"

"How many men can you provision and have ready to ride by dawn?" Jamal asked without preamble.

"Twenty," Haroun said without hesitation. "More if you wait until they can be recruited from the village."

"Twenty will do."

"What enemy do we fight?" Haroun asked, though he already suspected what Jamal had in mind.

"Perhaps none. It depends on how willing Sidi Bennaur's men are to relinquish Zara without a fight."

"Ah," was all Haroun said. No other words were necessary.

"You may go, Haroun. We have a long, hard ride ahead of us. The caravan has a head start, but it shouldn't be difficult to intercept the slow-moving camel train before it reaches Er Rachidia."

Haroun turned to leave. "I will prepare the men. I am convinced you won't be happy until you have the woman back in your bed."

Jamal hated to admit it, but Haroun was right.

Zara cursed the slow-moving, clumsy camel upon whose back she rode. Had she been riding a racing camel, she would feel more at ease. But no, Sidi Bennaur had insisted that she ride in a *howdah*, a basketlike chair with curtained sides and canvas top to protect her from the relentless sun, and wear a *djellaba*, which covered everything but her eyes.

The heat inside the enclosure was nearly suffocating, forcing Zara to pull aside the curtain to allow air to circulate. The journey to Ali ben Baha's desert home near Er Rachidia was a long one. They had already left the mountains and were now traveling along the edge of the desert, over a flat, stony plain, broken by reddish sand buttes and strips of green date palms bordering thin rivers. Monotonous little red-brown villages literally built from the earth were strung along the parched land. Water holes were infrequent, known only to men familiar with the desert. Zara was warned to drink sparingly from her water bag, for there were long stretches where water was not available.

Despite the blistering days, nights were bitter cold. Zara slept alone in a large white tent with carpets on the floor and braziers to keep her warm. Though she traveled in luxury, she could not be happy about it. How could she when she was on her way to a master she did not know, to be enslaved in a harem and used to satisfy her master's lust? Few Berbers could afford the kind of luxury she'd enjoy in Ali ben Baha's harem, but she couldn't forget that among her people she had been a free woman. Berber women lived unrestricted lives compared to their Arab sisters.

Zara wondered where her father was now. Was he worried about her? Did he know about her misfortune? Youssef would be enraged to know that Jamal had sold her at the slave market.

Jamal.

Until now she'd avoided thinking about the darkly handsome sheik. It was too painful. She recalled the look she and Jamal had exchanged as Sidi Bennaur's men dragged her away. Had that been longing and regret and, yes, anguish she'd seen deep within the dark, mesmerizing depths of his eyes? Zara had no idea why Jamal had appeared in the slave market to reclaim her when she had been sent away at his order. No matter the reason, she'd never forgive him for abandoning her to such a fate. Nor, she supposed, would he forgive her for betraying his trust and fleeing with her father.

With regret Zara realized that Jamal held no strong feelings for her. She had been but a sacrifice on the altar of his lust. Her own feelings for the arrogant sheik were more complicated. She didn't hate him, though she should after the callous way he'd banished her from his life. She knew she wasn't altogether blameless. Drugging him had been a despicable thing to do. But desperate situations called for desperate measures, and she had done what had to be done.

Zara shaded her eyes against the scalding rays of the midday sun and stared into the distant horizon. A cloud of dust appeared over the crest of a butte, and Zara prayed it wasn't a sandstorm hurtling toward them. As the cloud of swirling dust and sand grew closer, others in the caravan took notice. Suddenly a cry went up and Zara saw a dozen or more blue-robed men mounted on racing camels appear from within the swirling core of sand and dust.

"Father!" Her cry was lost amidst the shouts of camel drivers and guards as they ran hither and yon in confusion.

The Blue Men were widely feared throughout the land. Their reputation as bandits and fierce fighters was legendary. Neither the guards nor camel drivers wanted to defend the caravan against these ferocious warriors. To Zara's surprise, the guards laid down their weapons as the Blue Men surrounded the caravan.

Youssef brought his racing camel to a halt beside Zara's lumbering beast. His camel knelt and he slid from the saddle; then he ordered the camel driver to bring Zara's mount to its knees. A moment later he pulled Zara from the *howdah* and hugged her tightly.

"Praise Allah you're safe," Youssef said with heartfelt relief.

"How did you know where to find me?"

"From Rashid. Haroun went to the village to buy a racing camel for Jamal. Haroun let slip that you had been sent to the slave market by mistake. Jamal wanted the fastest racing camel available so that he might reach Fez in time to stop the sale. Rashid set out to find me the moment he learned what had happened.

"Unfortunately, he didn't find me before the sale took place. But I learned that Sidi Bennaur was sending you by caravan to Ali ben Baha, who resided in Er Rachidia. I recruited men from other tribes and set out to intercept the caravan."

"Jamal arrived in Fez too late to stop the auction. He said it was a mistake, that he never intended to sell me. He tried to buy me from Sidi Bennaur but his offer was refused."

"Forget Sheik Jamal, daughter. I will find a mate for you from among our own tribe members. Together we will continue to raid Moulay Ishmail's caravans. It will be a rare caravan that makes it through to Meknes with its cargo intact. Come, daughter, 'tis time to leave. Everything of value is being stripped from the caravan. The cargo will be sold and the money used to buy weapons and food for our people."

Jamal rode with his small army through endless stretches of shifting sand, which seemed to reach to the horizon, creating a vast, ever changing panorama. The caravan route was a winding, rutted road worn down by the hundreds of camels and men that traveled the same path year after year, century after century.

Jamal's sharp eyes spied the cloud of dust ahead and he experienced a surge of joy. At last. He'd soon have Zara back in his arms where she belonged.

Haroun rode up beside Jamal, pointing to the caravan in the distance. "Jamal, look! What do you make of it?"

Squinting against the glare of the sun, Jamal saw what Haroun was referring to. The caravan appeared to be traveling toward them, not away from them. It was returning to Fez! It couldn't have reached the home of Ali ben Baha and returned so soon. Digging his heels into the sweat-slick flanks of his Arabian stallion, Jamal broke away from his men and raced ahead to meet the caravan.

Reining his stallion to a dancing halt, Jamal demanded that the caravan be halted. The head camel driver complied without question. Soon ten camels and twice as many men waited to see what this new confrontation would bring.

"I am Sheik Jamal abd Thabit." His anxious gaze searched for Zara among the travelers. He spied the *howdah* perched atop one of the camels and wondered why Zara wasn't peeking through the curtains. "Release Princess Zara to me and no one will be hurt."

One man stepped forward, a lieutenant in charge of the guards sent to protect the princess. "She is not here, my lord."

Rage exploded through Jamal. "Not here! What in Allah's name have you done with her?"

"Nothing, my lord. Blue Men attacked the caravan two days ago. They relieved us of our cargo and took the princess with them. We are returning to Fez. It would be foolish to continue on to our destination with nothing to present to Ali ben Baha."

"Youssef!" Jamal spat. "How in Allah's name did the Berber *cadi* know where to find Zara?"

"The wily bandit seems to know everything," Haroun said with a shrug. "What do we do now?"

What, indeed? Jamal wondered. Of late he had done nothing but chase an exasperating, utterly bewitching female across the width and breadth of Morocco. Had he lost all semblance of pride? he wondered. Zara had turned him into a witless, besotted fool and he'd allowed it. Because of his obsession with Zara, he had failed the sultan. Youssef had escaped. It was no wonder Moulay Ishmail was angry with him. The sultan was a cruel man who enjoyed torturing his slaves and punishing those who failed him, and if Jamal wasn't careful, he would be next.

"Jamal? What are your orders, my lord?" Haroun repeated. "Do you want us to give chase to Youssef and his Blue Men?"

There was no decision possible but the one Jamal made. "Nay, Haroun, the men are weary. We will return home."

Haroun searched Jamal's face, recognized his anguish and wisely decided not to ask the question burning on the tip of his tongue. Jamal didn't need to be reminded of Zara when she was all but lost to him. Shaking his head in commiseration, Haroun vowed to find a way to ease his master's heartache.

Jamal's oasis kingdom shimmered like a brilliant jewel amidst a sea of brown. From a distance, the lake at its center sparkled with the radiance of a million blue sapphires. It was always good to return to his peaceful existence in his white marble palace, Jamal thought as he rode through the gate.

Unfortunately, his sojourn ashore was limited. It was no secret that he no longer basked in the sultan's high regard. For his own continued health he thought it expedient to return to sea to fulfill his promise to the sultan. He hoped to return with enough wealth to appease the disgruntled Ismail.

Despite the pleasure Jamal experienced when he entered his home, his homecoming wasn't quite the same this time. There was no female laughter echoing through the halls, no voluptuous women occupying his harem.

No Zara.

Nothing but the silent comings and goings of his servants and the ever present, ever loyal Hammet. And of course, Nafisa, the lone occupant and keeper of his empty harem.

Raids upon the sultan's caravans began almost immediately. It was a rare occurrence when a caravan reached its destination intact. The sultan was at the end of his patience. His losses were enormous, thwarting his plans to build great mosques in his honor and to bring his nation under one rule . . . his. He blamed his misfortune on one man. Youssef. Youssef and his blue-robed bandits were systematically depriving him of tribute and taxes, then using the profits to feed and arm the Berber hordes.

The sultan held Sheik Jamal abd Thabit solely responsible for the renewed assault upon his caravans. If the sheik hadn't wanted Youssef's daughter in his bed, none of this would have happened. Youssef's capture should have ended the raids once and for all. Without their leader, the Berbers would have been without direction. Had Jamal brought Youssef to Meknes instead of allowing him to escape, Ishmail's caravans would now be safe from attack.

Ishmail considered ordering Jamal's death, but in the end decided against it. At least for the time being. Jamal was responsible for this situation, and Ishmail decided to allow the sheik one final chance to redeem himself. If he failed this time, heads would roll. Ishmail had been lenient because Jamal's father had died fighting Berbers, but his good will would last only so long.

Jamal returned to Paradise after a day of hunting with his favorite peregrine falcon. He enjoyed the sport and usually bagged enough small game to feed his entire household, but this time his favorite pastime had done nothing to lift his mood.

Haroun met him at the stables, a wide smile splitting his bearded face. "Did you have a good day, Jamal?"

Jamal tossed the game bag at Haroun's feet. "Aye, send my catch around to the cook." He glared at Haroun. "Why are you looking so pleased with yourself?"

"You'll see," he said cryptically. "Hammet is waiting for you in the *hammam*. You must be hot and tired after a long day of hunting. A bath will ease your aching muscles." Still grinning from ear to ear, he slung the sack of game over his shoulder and walked away.

Jamal stared after him in consternation. What in Allah's name was his lieutenant up to? Shrugging away Haroun's odd behavior, Jamal entered the house and went directly to his chamber. Through the lattice wall separating his room from the *hammam*, he saw Hammet fussing with a stack of clean drying cloths. Pulling off his dusty white robes, he entered the *hammam* and greeted his head eunuch with little enthusiasm.

240

Hammet didn't seem to mind Jamal's shortness, for his grin was every bit as foolish as Haroun's had been. Was there some kind of conspiracy going on? Jamal wondered sourly.

"You may leave, Hammet," Jamal said. "I'm quite capable of bathing myself."

His grin firmly in place, Hammet bowed his way out the door.

Jamal threw off the rest of his clothing and lowered himself into the bath. The water was soothing and he closed his eyes. It was a mistake. The incredible vision of a beautiful, naked Zara, taking him inside her body, writhing beneath him, her golden skin flushed, her face aglow, her blond hair dancing around her flushed face, her breasts rosy from his kisses, sent blood rushing to his groin.

He muttered a curse, trying to ignore his body's immediate and violent response to the image generated by his need for the Berber vixen. He was hard as stone, and no one but the delectable Zara could ease his tormented flesh. He clenched his jaw and ground his teeth, wishing he'd never met the Berber Princess who had altered his life forever. He forced himself to remember exactly who she was and what she had done. It didn't help. Forgetting Zara was not going to be easy.

The soft whisper of footsteps on the tile floor captured Jamal's attention. Assuming Hammet had returned, he said, "I didn't call, Hammet. Return to what you were doing."

His eyes flew open when his words were answered by feminine titters. Swiveling his head around, he was shocked to see Saha, Leila and

Amar standing naked beside the *hammam*. He had forgotten how lovely they were. Then unbidden came the thought of how incredibly skillful his sensuous former concubines were at giving pleasure.

"Are you not happy to see us?" Saha asked as she lowered herself into the water.

"We are very glad to see *you*," Leila murmured shyly as she and Amar entered the pool together.

Saha urged a thoroughly confused Jamal to sit on the edge of the pool as she dipped her fingers into a pot of scented soap and rubbed it into Jamal's skin. She exchanged a knowing smile with Leila and Amar when she noted that Jamal was fully aroused. Her hand strayed momentarily to his erection and then quickly moved away as Leila and Amar used spatula-like scrapers to remove soap, sweat and dirt from his body. When he was scraped clean, Saha rinsed him with clean water from a ewer and urged him back into the water. The three concubines fussed over him excessively, their hands everywhere at once.

"Why are you here?" Jamal asked in a muffled voice. With Saha's breasts pressed against his face it was difficult to speak.

"We're here to make you happy, my lord," Saha said, batting her long lashes at him.

"You are no longer mine. You have new masters now."

"Haroun said you had need of us," Saha said with a coy smile. "Leila and Amar's masters agreed that they should try to cheer you. We will remain as long as you as you need us."

Jamal frowned. "Haroun had no right to make

such a decision. Go back to your masters. Tell them I appreciate their concern but I am content the way I am."

Saha's gaze lingered on Jamal's groin, not at all convinced that Jamal was content. He was still swollen, his juices running hot within him.

"Come, my lord, let us dry you. Once you return to your chamber, you can send us away if you truly have no need of us."

The three women helped Jamal from the *hammam*, sighing when they saw the size of his rod. Each recalled with fondness the long, satisfying hours spent in Jamal's bed. Jamal was an insatiable lover, and his appetite for erotic love play had brought them great pleasure. In all their years with Jamal he had never left them wanting.

Teased by three pairs of hands, Jamal was drawn as tight as a bowstring. His body begged for release. His former concubines were eager to please him. He knew their bodies intimately, knew which places to touch to bring them the most enjoyment. If Haroun had meant for them to sweeten his disposition, he just might have picked the right way to do it. Jamal couldn't argue the point that he needed a woman. What he did question was whether these three women could ease the ache of Zara's loss.

Lying on his back on his bed, Jamal allowed the three women to have their way as he stared at the ceiling, wondering why he was only marginally aroused by them. Just thinking about Zara did more to arouse him than anything the three concubines had done thus far.

His mind wandered, remembering the velvety

texture and golden luster of Zara's sweet flesh, and her enthusiastic response to his loving. She had been an innocent until he relieved her of her virginity, but her response had been anything but innocent. She had more natural passion in her little finger than Saha, Leila and Amar combined, with their vast experience and practiced caresses.

Saha and her companions were growing frustrated by Jamal's apparent lack of interest. His body was responding but his mind was far away. He just wasn't cooperating. Growing desperate, Saha rummaged through a drawer in the bedside table and found the small velvet pouch she had been looking for.

"Hold out your hand, Jamal," she whispered into his ear. Only half aware, Jamal presented his palm, surprised when he found it filled with two small silver balls. "Which one of us will you pleasure first, my lord?"

Jamal frowned, then shrugged. "You first, Saha."

Saha squealed with delight as she stretched out on the couch beside Jamal and spread her legs. Jamal warmed the balls in his hand, then carefully inserted them in Saha's slippery sheath. Leila and Amar stood beside the couch, whispering words of encouragement as Jamal rotated her hips. Saha peaked quickly, arching sharply upward and screaming her release.

Leila was next. She cleansed the balls in a basin of water and handed them to Jamal. He obliged her, placing the balls inside her with great care. When she deliberately held back in order to keep the pleasure from ending too soon, Jamal would not allow it. In a matter of minutes his expert manipulation cast her into the throes of ecstasy.

Once again the silver balls were cleansed and then it was Amar's turn. Her orgasm came quickly and violently. She had become painfully aroused just watching her companions attain rapture and could not hold back when it was her turn.

"Now it is your turn, Jamal," Saha said. "How may we pleasure you? Do you wish me to take you in my mouth? Perhaps you'd like to use us as a man would use a boy lover. What is your pleasure, Jamal?"

"Watching you attain ecstasy was my pleasure," Jamal said. "Go back to your masters now and tell them you have pleased me."

"But that would be a lie!" Amar gasped, shocked by Jamal's dismissal. Though cloaked in polite words, it was a dismissal nonetheless. "We gave you no pleasure. Do not send us away, my lord. Our masters will be angry with us."

"Haroun beats me when I displease him," Saha admitted. "He is a stallion in bed but he demands obedience."

"My new master cannot afford the luxuries we enjoyed in your harem," Leila complained. Her full lips were pursed into a pout and her large oval eyes held a hint of tears. "Let us stay."

"Have you forgotten the reason I gave you away?" Jamal asked harshly. "The three of you tried to poison a woman who meant you no harm."

"It was Saha's idea," Leila claimed.

"I did not encourage it," Amar declared.

245

"You are all liars," Saha said with a hint of disgust.

"Go!" Jamal ordered. "You may remain temporarily in the harem but do not expect more of me than I am willing to give."

"What has that Berber witch done to you?" Saha wailed. "How can you feel anything but hatred for Zara? I heard she drugged you and escaped with her father. What she did to you is no less a crime than what we tried to do to her."

"I'm still alive," Jamal said curtly. "Zara did not want my death, but you, ladies, would have killed Zara with your vile potion. All she did was put me to sleep. Leave me, now. Make the most of your temporary stay, for I suspect your new masters will soon miss you and want you back in their beds."

Retrieving their discarded caftans, the disgruntled women dressed quickly and filed out of the chamber. Hammet watched them leave with unbridled curiosity. He'd never seen a woman leave his master's chamber with anything but a smile on her face. Judging from the sour expressions on the faces of Saha, Leila and Amar, he'd venture to guess they had been less than pleased with Jamal's performance. Jamal's shout brought Hammet's speculation to a halt and he hastened to attend his master.

"You summoned me, master?"

"I ought to have you and Haroun drawn and quartered!" Jamal shouted. Hammet seemed unperturbed by his master's display of temper. "Whatever possessed you to bring those women back into my home?"

"We wished to please you. You have not had a woman since . . . well, for a very long time. If you do not favor those three harpies, let me go to the slave market and purchase a trio of submissive virgins for you to train to your specific needs."

Jamal frowned. "I do not want submissive virgins. I want . . ." His words trailed off. What he wanted was a hot-blooded, sharp-tongued hellion with a face like an angel and the disposition of a wildcat. A warrior woman as fierce a fighter as any man he'd ever known.

"If you will tell me what you want, master, I will endeavor to find it for you," Hammet said, concerned over Jamal's well-being. He'd never seen his master so obsessed with a woman before. Women were of little account to most Arabs. They had scant value beyond the pleasure gained from their bodies and their ability to bear children.

"I'm weary, Hammet. Leave me in peace."

Hammet shuffled backward toward the door.

"Wait. Summon Haroun to my chamber."

Jamal donned a caftan, located quill, ink and parchment in his chest and wrote out a message. Haroun arrived just as Jamal brushed off the sand he had used to dry the ink.

"What can I do for you, Jamal? Hammet said the women did not please you. I will beat Saha if she offended you."

"Forget the women, Haroun, they're not the reason for my summons. 'Tis time I returned to sea. I can feel Ishmail breathing down my neck. Find a trusted man to deliver a message to Captain Brahim in Tangier." He rolled up the parchment and handed it to Haroun. "He is to have my ship provisioned and made ready to sail the moment I arrive in Tangier. It might take Captain Brahim a few days to round up my crew, but I trust him to follow orders."

"Are you sure this is what you want, Jamal? We've been friends a long time and I can't see you abandoning a cause. I know you, Jamal. The Berber princess is the first woman you've gone to such lengths to keep with you. You displayed little remorse when you got rid of your concubines, but the loss of Zara is tearing you apart."

"I did not ask for your advice, my friend. You are neither my conscience nor my father. Zara has made her choice and it definitely isn't me. 'Tis time I regained my pride and let her go. Her father and her people are her life. She doesn't want me.

"Zara is like the desert wind, blowing hot and wild. She can neither be tamed nor made into something she is not. She is part of the land, a brave free spirit whose love cannot be harnessed."

"By Allah's beard, you love the woman!" Haroun cried, aghast. "I never thought I'd live to see the day Sheik Jamal abd Thabit succumbed to love. With all the women available, why did you pick someone totally unacceptable to a man of your rank and presence? Zara is doomed, you know. The sultan will not allow Youssef and his daughter to live. You are wise to forget her."

Jamal agonized over Haroun's words long after his lieutenant left. Had he arrived in time to rescue Zara before her father snatched her away, things would have been different. He truly wanted to forgive Zara for betraying his trust, and in time he would have. Perhaps he already had. He could picture her now, sharing his bed, clinging to him sweetly as he bound her to him with his passion. He would have planted his child in her and made her his favorite concubine.

Regrettably, Youssef had reached her first. Perhaps it was for the best.

Jamal made preparations for his journey to Tangier. He had quite forgotten about Saha, Leila and Amar, who were still happily ensconced in his harem. Their new masters had not yet asked for their return, assuming that Jamal was satisfied with the temporary arrangement and unwilling to displease him.

Preparations were progressing according to Jamal's expectations when armed soldiers from the sultan's royal guard arrived from Meknes. Moulay Ishmail demanded Jamal's immediate presence at the royal palace and had sent his personal guard to assure Jamal's compliance. When questioned about Ishmail's orders, all the captain of the guard would say was that Youssef had resumed the raids upon the sultan's caravans.

Aware of the sultan's vindictive nature and his penchant for cruelty, Jamal suspected that he'd been summoned by Ishmail to receive his death sentence. Ishmail's anger over Youssef's escape from Paradise had been festering a long time, and Jamal supposed the sultan wanted revenge.

Chapter Fourteen

As usual the royal palace was teeming with supplicants and subjects seeking audience with the sultan. Jamal was hurried past the Hall of the Sultanate, where Moulay Ishmail held court seated upon his ornate throne. Jamal caught a brief glimpse of the scarlet-robed monarch as he passed by the huge gilded doors inlaid with gold. If Ishmail saw him, he gave no indication.

The room Jamal was taken to was stark in its simplicity, nothing like the opulent quarters he'd occupied during his previous visits to the royal palace. In addition to a narrow couch, there was a low lacquered table surrounded by cushions, and a plain chest for clothing. A bowl of fruit and a tea service gracing the table saved the room from austerity. Through a lattice partition Jamal saw a private *hammam*, beyond which was a small walled garden. Jamal felt somewhat cheered by it, until he realized the wall was unusually high and had no outside outlet.

He was a prisoner.

The door had been locked behind him, and the garden walls were too high to scale. There was no escape. He could taste death, and it did not appeal to him.

Suddenly the door opened and a young slave girl dressed in revealing harem pants and skimpy vest stepped inside. She was small and dark with sultry black eyes that promised untold delights. "My name is Zinab. I bring towels for your bath, my lord. Allow me to assist you."

"Who sent you?" Jamal demanded to know.

"The sultan, my lord. He said you would be dirty after your journey to Meknes and should avail yourself of the *hammam*." She gave him a coy smile. "He said I was to serve you in any capacity you desire."

Jamal gave a bark of laughter. "So, the condemned man is to be indulged before he goes to his death."

Zinab appeared puzzled by his words. "I do not understand. I am here merely to serve you."

"Come, then, Zinab, the *hammam* awaits. You can bathe me, and while I rest my weary bones I will consider the ways in which you can serve me."

Zinab's smile was genuine. She greatly admired the tall, dark sheik and preferred him to the short, stout sultan, who used her vilely most of the time. She was elated to serve a handsome, virile man like Jamal.

Zinab's efforts were wasted on Jamal. He appeared only mildly interested in her, though she tried her best to arouse him as she slipped off her clothing and followed him into the *hammam*.

Jamal had scant time to think about Zinab's curvaceous little body as she attended him in his bath. He was too busy trying to figure out what was in Moulay Ishmail's perverse mind. Despite the fact that his chamber had few amenities, the sultan had not confined him to the dungeon. He had a private *hammam* and his own walled garden. And a beautiful woman to ease his body. The more he thought about it, the less sense it made.

Jamal had seen the results of some of Moulay Ishmail's more depraved acts and witnessed others firsthand. The sultan seemed to enjoy using torture as a means of punishment, but thus far Jamal couldn't describe his treatment as torture. More of the sultan's perversity?

Then suddenly the answer came to Jamal. He hadn't been summoned to Meknes to receive a death sentence. The sultan was using the alluring Zinab as an inducement. The talented love slave was a tidbit offered to him as a reward for his compliance, Jamal surmised. And he would bet his considerable fortune that the sultan had some distasteful task in mind for him, something that concerned Youssef and his lovely daughter.

When Jamal returned from the *hammam*, he found a fresh set of clothing laid out on his bed. He started to pull the clothes on when Zinab laid a hand on his arm. "How else may I serve you, my lord?" Her arms crept around his neck as she pressed her full breasts against his chest and ground her pelvis into his groin.

He was a young, virile male, and Jamal's flesh hardened automatically. He groaned and gently removed her arms. If he succumbed to Zinab, he would be playing right into the sultan's hands.

Zinab smiled up at him through long, feathery lashes as dark as sin. "Do you not find me pleasing, my lord? I have been trained to give pleasure in every manner known to man. I can take you in any orifice you prefer. If you enjoy watching me receive pleasure, I have silver balls for your use. I do not mind being tied with silken bonds and spanked, if that is what it takes to arouse you. Tell me, my lord Jamal, tell me what you want."

Her speech momentarily distracted Jamal. Zinab could hardly be more than fifteen, yet she already possessed the knowledge of an experienced *houri*. As a love slave she would doubtless be beyond compare, capable of providing many delightful hours of erotic entertainment. It surprised him that he did not want her.

"You are like a delicate blossom, Zinab, and I'm sure some man will find you a delightful diversion. Regrettably, I am not that man."

Zinab's mouth fell open. This had never happened to her before. "You do not want me?" Her mouth trembled and her eyes shimmered with unshed tears. Then to Jamal's utter surprise, she fell to her knees before him. "Do not tell the sultan, my lord. I will be most severely punished."

Jamal lifted her to her feet, drying her tears with the end of his shirt. "What happened or did not happen in this room will remain a secret between us. Now put on your clothes and return to the harem. If the sultan asks, I will tell him that you pleased me."

"Why won't you let me pleasure you?" Zinab asked curiously. "Do you not enjoy women? If you prefer boys—"

"For the love of Allah, do not accuse me of that depravity! Since we have shared one secret, I feel safe in revealing another. There is only one woman I want and she is unavailable. I suspect the sultan is trying to lure me into doing his bidding by presenting me with you. Softening me, so to speak."

Zinab gave him a watery smile, no longer the seductress but a young girl who looked and acted older than her years. "Your lady is lucky. I envy her."

"Go now, Zinab. If the sultan asks, tell him I was well pleased with you."

Zinab slipped from the chamber and Jamal heard a click as the door was locked behind her. Though it rankled to be placed at the sultan's mercy, he supposed he'd find out shortly what Ishmail had in mind for him and sat down to wait.

Jamal had just finished his evening meal when the head eunuch appeared with a summons from the sultan. The corridors were empty now; so was the Hall of the Sultanate. Supplicants and subjects had returned to their homes, and the royal court had adjourned for the day. Jamal was led past guards standing at attention, past the cavernous reception hall to the sultan's private chambers. A tall Nubian slave opened the door to the sultan's outer chambers, invited Jamal inside and promptly left.

The room was empty. Jamal was left to cool his heels a good thirty minutes before Moulay Ishmail appeared from his inner chamber and seated himself with great pomp upon an ornate brocaded couch. Jamal dropped to his knees and made his obeisance.

"You may rise, Jamal," Ishmail said imperiously. He did not invite Jamal to sit or to drink mint tea with him as he had on previous occasions, a sure sign of his anger. "I understand you enjoyed my gift. I trained Zinab myself; she is incomparable."

"I found no fault with little Zinab, my lord sultan." If Ishmail expected more from Jamal, he wasn't going to get it.

The sultan's hard eyes narrowed on Jamal, pinning him with his cruel glare. "You disappoint me, Jamal. I thought you were the one man I could trust. It never occurred to me that you would become so besotted with the Berber witch that you would forget to whom you owe allegiance. It was remiss of me to pardon you for letting Youssef escape. I've reconsidered my rash decision concerning your dereliction of duty. You should have brought Youssef to Meknes instead of keeping him at Paradise.

"Your promise of pirate loot blinded me to my duty, and I showed mercy where none was due. Now the raids continue and I am being beggared by Youssef and his warrior daughter. I have considered many courses of action, Jamal. One was to order your death for defying my commands.

Another was to employ torture to appease my anger. But since I am a magnanimous fellow, I have decided to give you one last opportunity to redeem yourself."

Jamal nearly laughed in the sultan's face. Ishmail was famous for his cruelty; there was nothing magnanimous about him. "You are most gracious, great sultan."

Ishmail smiled. "I am, aren't I? But my mercy does not come without a price. This is the last time I will indulge you. Fail me and you will pay with your head. Succeed and little Zinab will be yours. You've already had a taste of her sweet flesh. 'Tis but a sample of what she is capable of. She is sweet and submissive, nothing like your fierce warrior woman."

"Tell me what I can do to put myself back in your good graces, Excellency."

Ishmail's expression turned ugly. "Bring Youssef and his daughter to me dead or alive. Do not return until you have flushed the bandits from the mountains. I cannot afford to lose another caravan. You are no fool, Jamal; you know I do not countenance failure. There will be no leniency for the girl this time. She is too much like her father. I've ordered Captain Hasdai to place one hundred seasoned soldiers at your disposal. Your mission is to find and destroy the enemy."

"What if I refuse?" Jamal dared to ask. How could he hunt down and destroy a woman he cared about? The woman he . . .

Loved.

Ishmail's smile did little to encourage confidence. "You will not refuse. You value your neck too well. You will be released from your chamber at dawn. I will be on hand to watch you lead my army to victory. You may go."

Jamal knew better than to protest his curt dismissal. One did not gainsay the sultan and live to tell about it. He salaamed. As he backed out of the chamber, Ishmail said, "Dream of little Zinab tonight, Jamal, and how well she pleasured you today. Perhaps your lusty dreams will make you eager to return to her."

The door to Jamal's chamber opened at the precise moment a glorious pink dawn appeared in the eastern sky. Jamal had already performed the ritual cleansing ceremony required of all Muslims, faced Mecca when the *muezzin* called the faithful to prayer and consumed a light repast. Captain Hasdai was waiting for him when he stepped into the corridor.

"Allah be with you, my lord Jamal. One hundred hand-picked soldiers are waiting in the outer courtyard. They are all eager to bring the Berber bandits to their knees for the honor and glory of our sultan."

"Allah be with you, Captain Hasdai," Jamal returned shortly. He was in no mood for small talk. His thoughts were bleak as he reached the huge outer courtyard where the sultan's elite army was gathered.

"Your men-at-arms arrived from Paradise an hour ago. Do you wish them to join us?"

Jamal's mood lightened perceptibly when he saw Haroun standing beside his prancing stallion. Jamal hurried over to speak to Haroun while

Hasdai saw to the pack camels that would accompany the army into the Rif mountains.

They clasped arms. "I thought you could use your own men around you," Haroun said. "No one at Paradise knew what the sultan had in store for you, but we wanted to be nearby in case you needed us. Hasdai explained the situation to me, and I made hasty preparations for our men to join the sultan's army. You have no choice, Jamal. If you value your life, you must obey the sultan. He wants Youssef and Zara. There is nothing you can do to save them this time."

Jamal did not reply. One hundred men, all eager to ride to battle, were waiting for orders. He mounted Kacem and rode to the head of the column. Before he gave the signal to ride, he happened to glance up and saw the sultan standing on his balcony, watching their departure. Ishmail's expression was one of sadistic pleasure and vicious expectation. It didn't take a wizard to know that Ishmail was eagerly anticipating the torture and death of Youssef and Zara. That Jamal might fail did not bear considering.

Zara watched with trepidation as Rachid rode into camp. His racing camel came to a dusty halt, and Rachid sought out Youssef the moment he had slid from the saddle of his kneeling animal. Zara hurried to her father's side to hear the news Rachid had brought.

They entered Youssef's tent and Zara made mint tea while Rachid imparted his news.

"Sheik Jamal was escorted to Meknes by a company of the sultan's soldiers. Haroun followed a day later with Jamal's men-at-arms. I thought it expedient to follow."

"You did well," Youssef praised. "What did you learn?"

"I heard many rumors. Unfortunately, most of them seem to be true. Sheik Jamal has been given command of more than one hundred men from Ishmail's elite army. His orders are to bring you and Zara in dead or alive."

Zara inhaled sharply. "Are you sure, Rachid?"

Rachid nodded. "I watched them ride out at dawn three days ago. They were joined by Jamal's men-at-arms."

"Allah spare us," Zara said quietly. "I did not think Jamal would—" Words failed her. She and Jamal had shared an intimate relationship. Admittedly, it wasn't concluded amicably, but it hurt to think that after all they had shared he wanted her dead.

"Few men refuse an order from the sultan and live to tell about it," Youssef said cryptically.

Youssef was an astute man. By now he realized that Zara was more than fond of the handsome sheik and that she had been unhappy since she'd fled his palace. Youssef realized that nothing was likely to come of those tender feelings, and it hurt him to see Zara suffer from unrequited love.

"What are we going to do?" Zara asked. There was a catch in her voice that she couldn't hide. "We're being hunted down like animals."

"We'll move south, into the Atlas Mountains," Youssef said. "If necessary, we'll take refuge in the desert beyond the Atlas." Suddenly he smiled. "We'll lead your Jamal a merry chase, daughter."

A pain shot through Zara. "He's not *my* Jamal, Father. He is the enemy."

Within hours they were charting a course for the High Atlas.

"They were here," Haroun said, stooping to examine the hard, rocky ground.

"How long ago?" Jamal asked.

"It's hard to tell. Two days, two weeks, who knows?"

Jamal was secretly pleased that Youssef and his bandits had managed to stay one step ahead of the sultan's men. Jamal had no idea what he would do if they actually found the Berbers. His greatest fear was that Zara would be killed in battle or become the sultan's captive. It was up to him to see that Zara was kept safe. Traipsing through mountains and desert gave him plenty of time to think . . . and plan.

"They're headed for the High Atlas," Hasdai said when the trail led them out of the Rif mountains. "Youssef is clever. He might even attempt to lose us amid the dunes and buttes of the Sahara."

"Perhaps we should turn back and report to the sultan," Jamal suggested. Anything to lead them away from Zara.

Hasdai looked at Jamal as if he had lost his mind. "The sultan's orders were to search until Youssef is found. I value my life, even if you do not. Ishmail warned me to be watchful, that you couldn't be trusted where the Berber princess is concerned. The sultan said you had captured Youssef once and allowed him to escape."

"I did not *allow* Youssef to escape. 'Tis a long story, Captain, one I won't bore you with. Shall we continue?"

That conversation was the first inkling Jamal had that he was being closely monitored by Ishmail's men. Obviously he would have to be very careful in the future. If Jamal was confident of only one thing in this life, it was the certainty that he would never knowingly endanger Zara's life.

The chase continued.

One week, two weeks, three weeks passed with no sign of the Blue Men. Jamal and the sultan's army skirted the edge of the desert now, descending the slopes of the High Atlas to the lowlands that extended into the Sahara. They traveled over forested slopes, through steppe grasslands and drought-resistant scrub vegetation. They crossed streams that drained from the Atlas into the Sahara and they rested at date-palm oases where they replenished their supply of precious water.

They camped one night on a thickly forested plain on the edge of the desert. While camp was being set up, Hasdai sent out a night patrol to scout the area. Jamal was with Hasdai when the patrol returned. Their excitement sent Jamal's heart plummeting to his toes. They had found Youssef's camp just beyond the crest of the next mountain. The Blue Men had pitched their tents beside a narrow stream in a stand of tall evergreen trees.

Hasdai smiled grimly. "We will attack at dawn, when they least expect it." He called his second in command, issuing orders to be relayed to the troops. "Are you in agreement, my lord?" he asked Jamal as his lieutenant hurried away.

Jamal's heart was lodged in his throat but he managed to say, "In perfect agreement, Captain. If you will excuse me, I should see to my own weapons and men."

Haroun stood nearby. When Jamal entered his tent, Haroun followed. "What are your orders, my lord?"

"I must warn Zara."

"That's treason."

Jamal's eyes were the windows into his soul, revealing a man tormented by conflicting emotions. He could follow Ishmail's orders and watch Zara be destroyed, or he could warn her and commit treason. Either choice was painful, but Jamal let his heart make the decision for him.

"I know Moulay Ishmail well, my friend. He is a master of cruelty. Watching the brutal torture of Youssef and Zara will give him great pleasure. I cannot allow that to happen. I do not expect you to compromise your honor, Haroun, so I release you from your service to me."

Haroun looked aggrieved. "I am your man, Jamal. I have no great love for our sultan. Tell me what to do."

"Nothing at the moment. As soon as the men have settled down for the night, I'm going to sneak into Youssef's camp. I will decide what to do once I get there."

"I will go with you. You'll need a man to keep watch."

"There is no need—"

"It is settled," Haroun said. "I will return to

your tent after the camp has settled down. Pray Allah for a dark night."

Jamal paced restlessly as he waited for Haroun to return. Perhaps his nightmares would stop now, he reflected. Since he'd become an unwilling participant in this venture, his sleep had been plagued by terrifying nightmares involving Zara. In his dreams she was the sultan's prisoner, a victim of his depraved nature. Her screams of pain were so real they ripped him apart.

Jamal stopped pacing when Haroun slipped inside the tent. "It is time, Jamal. Hasdai has retired to his tent and the men have all made their beds on the ground. I passed the word around to our men to remain vigilant."

Jamal nodded, grateful to have a man like Haroun at his side. Together they stepped out into the darkness. The night was cold but Jamal's black woolen *djellaba* protected him from the bitter wind blowing from the desert. Allah must have answered his prayers, for there was no moon visible in the cloudy skies.

"We will separate and make our way to the horses," Jamal whispered. "Try to avoid the sentries."

Jamal slipped past the sentry without being seen, and when no cry of alarm was given, he assumed Haroun was as successful as he in avoiding detection.

Haroun had reached the horses first. Without a word they saddled their mounts and led them through a tangle of underbrush, around cedar, evergreen and oak trees. A safe distance from camp they mounted and went in search of Youssef's hideout. Some time later they halted on a ledge overlooking a grassy slope.

Jamal's sharp gaze scanned the valley below, noting a break in the trees where a narrow river gouged a course out of the rock.

"There they are, Haroun, below us," Jamal pointed out. "Do you see the tents amid the trees?"

Haroun studied the slope below and finally saw the outline of several tents.

"I see them."

"I'm going down."

Jamal started down the slope. Haroun followed close behind. Youssef's camp was so well hidden, Jamal was surprised the patrol had found it. But Ishmail's highly trained Negro soldiers were famous for their tenacity and cunning. Jamal reined in at the edge of the campsite, in a thick grove of fir trees. He dismounted and handed his reins to Haroun.

"I'm going the rest of the way on foot. Keep the horses quiet."

Jamal crept through the trees until he could see the entire camp spread out along the bank of the river. The campsite was so well concealed that only one sentry had been posted, and he was dozing against a tree.

Jamal studied the alignment of tents, trying to figure out which one belonged to Zara. He noted one tent set apart from the others, and it was that dwelling on which Jamal concentrated. The night was still ink black, and it would be easy to slip into the tent without being seen.

Then Allah rewarded him.

The tent flap opened and Zara stepped outside. She had removed her turban, and her golden hair spilled down her back in glorious disarray. Jamal saw her walk the short distance to the narrow river and kneel down to wash her hands, face and neck. He smiled grimly and crept forward toward her tent. He glanced at the sentry, saw he was still dozing and slipped through the open flap.

Zara finished her ablutions and retraced her steps to her tent. The night was peaceful. Too peaceful, she thought, but could find no reason for her disquiet. Families were sleeping together in their black tents and the single men were sprawled on the ground, wrapped in their blankets, their heads resting on their saddles. Her tent had been pitched a short distance away from the others, to afford her a modicum of privacy, and she approached it now with a strange foreboding. Since she saw nothing to cause her edginess, Zara ducked into her tent, secured the flap . . . and froze.

She wasn't alone.

She sensed his presence moments before his hand covered her mouth and he hissed into her ear, "Do not struggle, sweet vixen. I mean you no harm."

Jamal! Despite his reassurance, she grappled with him, but was soon subdued by his superior strength. Fear raced through her. They had been found! Jamal would take her to Meknes, where she and Youssef would be punished in the most horrible way imaginable.

"I'll remove my hand if you promise not to

scream. Heed me, Zara, I mean you no harm. I've come to help. Shall I remove my hand?"

Zara nodded vigorously, though she didn't believe his promise not to hurt her. But she would listen to him before calling for help. She wouldn't accept death easily. She had more to protect now than her own life.

Jamal removed his hand from her mouth. Then he turned her into his arms and brought her against him, resting his forehead against hers. "Praise Allah I found you before Captain Hasdai launches his attack. You have scant time to spare; they'll be here at dawn. Gather your belongings. I'm taking you away from here now."

It was too dark in the tent for Jamal to see the obstinate expression on Zara's face, but he could tell by her tone of voice that she wasn't going to be convinced easily.

"I'm not leaving." She tried to pull away from him. "I have to warn Father."

"I'll take you by force if I must," Jamal warned, tightening his grip.

"Call off the attack," Zara pleaded. "If you can't do that, then at least let me warn Father and our people. There are women and children in the camp. Have you no heart?"

When her words seemed to make no impression on Jamal, she began to pound on his chest with her fists. In desperation she opened her mouth to scream. Jamal must have sensed her intention, for his mouth slammed down on hers, sucking the breath from her in a deep, drugging kiss that boldly proclaimed his need for her.

A strangled sound escaped her throat as her

pounding fists opened and slid around his neck, pressing closer to the heat of his mouth, losing herself in his kiss. These long, empty weeks without Jamal's touch had been pure torture. She'd told herself time and again that she hated him, but her heart wouldn't be convinced. When his tongue nudged her lips apart and plunged inside, she caught fire. Suddenly there was no tomorrow or yesterday. There was only today, this man, this hour, this minute.

There was only desperate need.

Chapter Fifteen

Zara felt a wild, uncontrollable longing to be with Jamal again, to have him inside her. She kissed him back, clinging to him, branding him with the hot pressure of her body.

Jamal's physical reaction was immediate and overwhelming. He wanted to press her down upon her pallet and thrust his rock-hard erection inside her. He wanted to devour her with his kisses; the glorious scent of her intoxicated him. Everything about her was purely female and wholly captivating.

Nothing had changed, Zara thought in a brief lucid moment. Jamal had only to touch her and she came violently alive. The ache between her legs deepened and intensified, her nipples hardened, her breasts became heavy and sensitive to the slightest caress. She moaned and opened her mouth to the sweet entrance of his tongue.

"Zara, sweet vixen," Jamal groaned against her mouth as he pulled her down with him to her pallet.

His mouth was fused to hers as he released the sash holding up her baggy trousers and pulled them down around her ankles. With a sweeping motion he hiked her shirt up to her neck. His mouth moved down to lick her nipples as he raised himself slightly and shed his own trousers, too impatient to remove his boots and pull them all the way off.

"I can't wait," he whispered hoarsely.

"Nor I. Hurry!" She arched upward, crying out as Jamal flexed his hips and thrust into her soft, wet center. She was hot, so very hot.

He took her quickly, roughly, right there on the pallet, his passion white-hot and explosive. Zara writhed beneath him, rising up to meet his thrusts with blinding ardor, her hands roaming his flesh and her mouth returning his kisses. She met every swift, hard plunge of his hips and thrust of his tongue. She heard her own keening, moaning sounds as her body whirled out of control. He kissed her wildly, violently, as if he couldn't get enough of her and wanted to absorb every sound of her pleasure into his body.

He plunged and retreated, then plunged again . . . and again . . . and again. "Come, sweet vixen! Now! I can wait no longer."

Zara came in a mindless rush of molten heat, consumed by fierce, aching ripples of pleasure that crested and grew and swept her into a place of blinding ecstasy. Her scream was muffled by Jamal's mouth, just as Jamal's hoarse shout was muffled by hers. His body stiffened as he pumped his wet seed into her.

Long minutes passed before Jamal eased away and struggled to his feet. "I didn't mean for that to happen. Allah help me, for I have no control where you're concerned." With an efficiency of motion he pulled up his trousers and fastened the sash. Then he reached down to help Zara. "Time is running out."

Still dazed from the violence of their loving, Zara allowed Jamal to help her to her feet and fasten the sash at her waist.

"Come, we must leave quickly."

Zara finally found her voice. "I meant it when I said I'm not going anywhere with you. I can't leave my father. He needs me."

"You won't do him any good if you're dead," Jamal said harshly. He wanted to shock her into compliance. "The sultan has nefarious plans for you and Youssef that will make you wish you were dead."

"My father—"

"Even if he escapes now, Youssef won't be able to help you. 'Tis only a matter of time before he's caught. The sultan would like nothing better than to decorate his wall with Youssef's head."

"Are you trying to frighten me?"

"I'm being brutally honest. Put on your *djellaba*; we must leave immediately." When she made no move to obey, he felt around in the darkness until he found her robe folded at the foot of the pallet and pulled it over her. Then he grasped her hand

and dragged her toward the tent opening.

Zara dug in her heels. "Father must be warned. There's still time to get our people to safety."

Jamal deplored the use of violence and had no stomach for it, but Zara gave him no choice. Since she steadfastly refused to leave of her own free will, he was forced to take matters into his own hands. He hoped she would forgive him.

"Zara," he said, turning her to face him. "This isn't the way I wanted it, but I will do anything to protect you. I cannot leave you here. The danger is too great."

"You can't—"

She never completed her sentence. With a cry of remorse, Jamal brought his fist forward and delivered a fast, solid clip to her jaw. The blow wasn't hard enough to cause permanent damage; just a sharp tap that would keep her quiet for an hour or two. He caught her in his arms before she hit the ground.

"Forgive me, sweet vixen," he whispered as he released the flap and peered into the darkness.

Nothing had changed. Less than an hour had passed since he'd entered Zara's tent, though it seemed an eternity. The black, moonless night was his ally now. The sentry was still dozing against a tree. There were no campfires to give him away as he crept from the tent with Zara in his arms. He returned the way he had come, slipping into the thick cover of trees where Haroun waited.

"Praise Allah, you're back," Haroun said with a sigh of relief. "Another minute and I would have come charging in after you."

"Praise Allah that you didn't."

"I assume that's Lady Zara in your arms. What's wrong with her?"

"She's unconscious. I had to use force."

Haroun frowned. It was unlike Jamal to hurt a woman. "If you have a plan, perhaps it's time you shared it with me."

"That's precisely what I intend, my friend." He shifted Zara in his arms. "I'm placing Zara in your care. You're to take her to Paradise and await me there. Mount up and I'll hand her up to you. You can ride double to the nearest village. I have coin on me, enough to purchase a mount for Zara and see you safely to Paradise."

The widening of Haroun's eyes betrayed his shock. "What are you going to do?"

"You don't want to know." He placed a kiss on Zara's lips and handed her up to his trusted lieutenant. "Take care, my friend. You hold my life in your arms." Then he reached beneath his robes for the sack of gold coins he'd stuck in his pocket and handed it to Haroun.

"You ask a great deal of me, Jamal. Lady Zara isn't going to be happy about this when she awakens. She's a warrior woman, as fierce as any man I've ever faced."

"Do what you must to keep her from returning to her father."

"How will you explain my absence to Captain Hasdai?"

"I'll think of something. You must be ever vigilant, my friend. Zara is crafty. Guard her with your life. Tell Nafisa and Hammet to keep her confined to the harem. I'll make things right with Zara when I return."

"Good luck," Haroun said with amusement. "I won't question your sanity, Jamal, though I know you must be mad to betray the sultan. Ishmail isn't a man to accept failure. He wants Youssef and Zara."

"I can handle Ishmail, Haroun. Go now. Go quickly. Allah be with you."

"Allah be with you, my friend," Haroun returned as he kneed his horse forward.

Jamal watched him ride into the dark night, and then he turned back toward Youssef's camp. He knew things would never be right between him and Zara if he allowed her father and the Blue Men to be slaughtered by the sultan's army. He was trying to decide how best to approach Youssef when the sentry suddenly awakened, saw him, and cried out a warning. Jamal made no effort to escape as men poured out of the tents and surrounded him. A few minutes later Youssef pushed his way through to Jamal.

"By Allah's beard, how did you get here? Are you alone?"

"I must speak with you privately, Youssef," Jamal said earnestly.

Youssef felt a frisson of fear and glanced at Zara's tent. Was she still sleeping? "Very well, follow me. It must be urgent for you to walk into my camp without an army at your back. You were an instant away from having your head separated from your body."

Jamal said nothing as he followed Youssef into his tent. The *cadi* struck a light to an oil lamp and turned to face Jamal. "Explain yourself."

"I came to warn you. The sultan's army is camped nearby. They know you're here and plan to attack at dawn. Without my warning you'd all be slaughtered in your beds."

Youssef's eyes narrowed. "Why should I believe you? You are Ishmail's man."

"I am my own man. I do this for Zara's sake. I plan to make Zara my wife, and I do not want your death to mar our future happiness."

"Your wife!" Youssef sputtered. "You seem sure of yourself, Sheik. Perhaps we should get Zara in here and ask her how she feels about becoming your wife. My daughter has a mind of her own and cannot be coerced into marriage."

"Heed me well, Youssef, you have little time left in which to flee the sultan's soldiers. I urge you to break camp now. You have women and children to protect. Ishmail wants your head. You will be pursued relentlessly, until you are caught. You may be resigned to your fate, but I won't let that happen to Zara. I'm taking her with me."

"Zara will never leave of her own free will," Youssef declared. He recognized the wisdom of Jamal's words, but knew it would take more than words to convince Zara.

Jamal took a deep breath and said, "Zara is no longer here. She departed with my lieutenant over an hour ago. I will join her at Paradise as soon as I am able."

Enraged, Youssef reached for his scimitar, but then let his hand fall to his side. "Did Zara leave of her own accord?"

Jamal shook his head. "I wish it were so but it

is not. Zara refused to leave so I took matters into my own hands. Zara means everything to me, though she believes otherwise. Until I can convince her of my love, she is in a safe place."

Youssef's expression softened. "I could kill you, Jamal, but it wouldn't bring my daughter back. Regrettably, you speak the truth. I am a hunted man. One day I'll be caught, and I do not wish for Zara to share my fate. Do you truly love her?"

Jamal smiled. "The woman vexes me to distraction. She adds zest to my life yet drives me crazy with her fierce pride. She is contrary, disobedient, fierce and obstinate. I have never in my life loved a woman until Zara. I will protect her with my life."

Youssef's lips twitched. That was quite a speech for a man who could have any woman in the kingdom and beyond. "You appear to know my daughter well. If you recall, I once pleaded with you to marry Zara instead of making her your concubine."

"At the time I could not see past my lust. But we waste time talking. I must return before I am missed. The penalty for treason is death. Where will you go?"

Youssef rubbed his bearded chin as he considered the possibilities.

"I have a suggestion," Jamal said. "How well do you know the Western Sahara?"

Youssef smiled. "Well enough not to die of thirst or hunger. We are nomads, Sheik. We go where the winds take us."

"My advice is to flee into the Sahara. When Captain Hasdai comes with his men, he'll find tracks leading into the desert. I doubt they'll follow where death awaits them. Only one familiar with the Sahara would venture into it. After a time you can return to your walled village in the Rif mountains and tend your sheep. If you wish to live in peace, I'd advise you to stop your raids upon the sultan's caravans."

"I know your advice is well meant, Sheik, but I am a patriot and must do as my heart directs. The only promise I can make is that we will remain in our walled city for the duration of the winter. Farewell, Jamal, take good care of my daughter. She is well loved by me."

They clasped arms and Jamal left quickly. He had accomplished what he'd set out to do but he was filled with a bone-deep foreboding. He reached Hasdai's camp just as the soldiers sleeping upon the ground began stirring. When he tried to slip inside his tent, however, two soldiers emerged from the waning darkness and challenged him with drawn scimitars.

"What's the meaning of this?" Jamal blustered. "Where is Captain Hasdai?"

"I am here," Hasdai said, stepping from behind the men. "Where have you been?"

"To relieve myself," Jamal said, thinking fast.

"You have been gone all night, my lord."

"Are you questioning my loyalty, Hasdai?"

"The sentry saw you and your lieutenant leave, but thought nothing of it until you failed to return in a reasonable time. I was about to order a patrol out to find you when you returned. Where have you been, and where is Haroun?"

"I was restless. I decided to ride out and look

over the enemy camp. Haroun insisted upon accompanying me."

"Where is Haroun now?"

"I sent him on an important errand. My ship's captain is expecting me in Tangier to take the *Plunderer* out on another voyage. I didn't have time to send word to him when I was so hastily summoned to Meknes. Haroun is to inform Captain Brahim of my delay." It was a lame excuse but Jamal could think of no other.

"I will give you the benefit of the doubt, my lord, but you will be under close surveillance during the attack. Ready your men. We ride out immediately. If Allah is with us, we will find the Berber rebels still abed."

Jamal's men-at-arms rallied around his tent awaiting orders. When Hasdai was out of earshot, Jamal told them that he had sent Haroun to Paradise on an important mission and that they were to slip away and follow without informing Captain Hasdai of their departure. He also told them to inform Haroun that he was to take the Princess Zara to his ship in Tangier and send her without delay to his mother in England. If the men were curious, they made no mention of it, for they were unquestioningly faithful to Jamal. As Jamal and the soldiers rode out to subdue the enemy, Jamal looked back and saw his men-at-arms drifting away from the main group and riding in the opposite direction.

The enemy was gone. The hasty departure of the Blue Men was evidenced by the numerous personal effects left behind. They were traveling light, and their tracks led directly into the desert beyond the forested slopes and grassy plains.

Captain Hasdai spit out an oath and sent a blistering look at Jamal. "The enemy was warned in advance of our attack. Youssef knows we dare not follow him too deeply into the desert, for we are not desert fighters. The Blue Men are familiar with all the water holes and oases, but we know them not."

He pinned Jamal with his dark, implacable gaze. "You are under arrest for treason, Sheik Jamal."

"Are you mad?" Jamal sputtered.

"Seize him!" Hasdai ordered. Jamal was instantly surrounded.

Suddenly Hasdai noticed that Jamal's men-at-arms were missing. "Where are your men?" Comprehension dawned. "You were wise to send them away, for they would share your fate. You betrayed us. You warned Youssef of our impending attack," Hasdai accused. "You are under arrest. When we return to Meknes, the sultan will decide your fate. It grieves me to do this, my lord, but you've given me no choice."

Resigned for the moment to his fate, Jamal asked, "Are we to return to Meknes immediately?"

Hasdai shook his head. "The sultan would be most displeased if I didn't follow the fleeing Berbers. You will be returned to camp and remain under guard until my return. If Allah is with us, we can catch Youssef before he goes too deeply into the desert."

"Your horses are no match for the Berbers' superior racing camels, born and bred in these harsh desert climes."

"Enough!" Hasdai ordered. He was well aware of his chances of finding Youssef, but his loyalty to the sultan was unshakable. He issued crisp orders to his second in command, and soon Jamal was securely bound with leather strips, hoisted upon his horse and escorted to the campsite by a half-dozen burly Negro soldiers, who were to remain behind to guard him.

Zara regained her senses slowly, aware of the thick arms holding her securely to the saddle and the fast clip of the horse's gait over the rocky plain. The hard chest supporting her was not Jamal's—she knew that intuitively. The hand binding her was large and meaty, with thick fingers and blunt nails. Nothing like Jamal's strong, aristocratic hands, which could be as gentle or as rough as the situation demanded.

"You are awake, lady. Good," Haroun said when he felt Zara stir against him.

Zara turned her head to look at Haroun, and pain exploded in her jaw. She felt betrayed. "He hit me! Jamal struck me. Why, Haroun?"

"Jamal wanted to protect you. Since you wouldn't leave of your own accord, he took matters into his own hands."

"Where is he? Where are you taking me?"

"Jamal is still with the soldiers. I'm taking you to Paradise, where you will be safe."

"My father is in danger! Jamal is going to attack my people." She turned in the saddle, pounding

Haroun's chest with her fists. "We must go back. I have to warn them."

"I gave my word to see you safely to Paradise. Rest easy, lady, Jamal will see that no harm comes to your father."

Zara went still. "He told you this?"

"No, he didn't have to. I have known Jamal most of his life. I know how his mind works. He cares for you, lady, and would not want Youssef's death to stand between you. He returned to your camp after placing you in my care. My guess is that he went to warn your father."

"Can you be absolutely certain that is what Jamal did?"

"One can never be certain of anything save death, lady."

"Then we must go back."

"It is too late. We are nearing the village of Tinerhir. Jamal instructed me to purchase a horse for you. We can also buy food in the *souk* for the journey over the High Atlas."

Zara said nothing but her mind worked furiously. Haroun was but one man and she was a clever woman. She wasn't going anywhere until she knew the fate of her people. Besides, what Jamal had done to her was unforgivable. He didn't seem the kind of man to strike a woman, yet he had done precisely that.

By the time they entered Tinerhir through the high, arched gate, Haroun had been lulled into complacency. Zara seemed subdued, and Haroun assumed he had convinced her that going to Paradise was in her best interests.

* * *

Jamal was released from his bonds to eat and relieve himself, and then he was promptly rebound. The six men Hasdai had left behind to guard him were aware of their responsibility and took no chances. If they let Sheik Jamal escape, the sultan would have their heads, but only after long and painful torture.

It seemed like forever, but in truth only seven days passed before a haggard Hasdai and his exhausted men returned to the campsite. They had followed Youssef as far as they dared. When they'd run out of water and food, they were forced to return. They had lost several horses due to dehydration, and half his men were suffering from heat stroke.

Hasdai rarely failed his sultan and was furious with Jamal. "I never thought you a traitor, my lord. Unlike you, I will never allow a woman to lead me around by my balls. Princess Zara must truly be amazing in bed for you to betray our master. Make no mistake, my lord, you will not escape punishment. Moulay Ishmail will know the full measure of your betrayal, and you will suffer for it."

"I doubt it not, Hasdai," Jamal said grimly.

Zara found the ideal opportunity to escape Haroun and seized it. Haroun was sleeping. He was rolled up in his blanket on the ground, his head resting on his saddle. He had bound Zara's wrist to his with a length of leather cord and had fallen into a deep sleep. If she so much as moved he would feel the tug and awaken. The ritual was always the same. Each night Haroun bound Zara to him with the cord. Though Zara appeared docile, he'd learned that most women were devious creatures and he was taking no chances.

Zara had doubled her fist when Haroun fastened the thong around it that night. Once the thong was in place, she relaxed her fist and was gratified to find the thong was now loose enough to manipulate around her slim wrist. While Haroun slept she worked on the knot, until she could slip her hand through.

She arose cautiously and crept to where her horse was tethered. Haroun had purchased a blooded Arabian mare for her in Tinerhir, and Zara was well pleased with the beautiful animal. Not bothering with the saddle, Zara led the mare through the darkness, away from the snoring Haroun. When she was several yards away, she leaped upon the mare's bare back and sped off into the night.

Haroun awakened at dawn, saw that Zara had slipped her bonds and flew into a rage. He recalled his promise to Jamal and knew he had to go after her. He knew where Zara planned to go and had only to follow.

Jamal's hands were tied, forcing him to control his stallion with his knees, no mean feat when traversing mountainous terrain. But Hasdai was no fool. Jamal was not left unbound for more than a few minutes at a time. They had left the campsite and were traveling on a heavily forested pass through the High Atlas now. It was cold, and patches of snow appeared in the crevices high above them. Escape seemed unlikely, but Jamal remained alert nevertheless. It was a long way to Meknes.

Zara crouched behind a tree on a slope high above the retreating army. She had heard the pounding hooves and seen the trail of dust and thought it prudent to seek concealment. The route was routinely used by caravans, but she thought the riders were moving much too fast for a caravan. Her caution paid off when she saw the sultan's soldiers retreating over the mountains. Then she saw Jamal and froze. His hands were bound behind him and he was surrounded by soldiers. Jamal was a prisoner! Her mouth opened in silent protest.

Her sharp mind sorted through the facts and quickly found the answer. Haroun hadn't lied when he'd said Jamal had warned Youssef about the impending attack. Jamal's absence from camp must have been noted, and now he was in serious trouble. Jamal had committed treason, an act that might very well mean his death.

Zara was so engrossed in the passing army, she failed to hear the almost silent footsteps behind her. She started violently as a hand clamped solidly over her mouth.

" 'Tis the sultan's army. Do not cry out."

Haroun! How had he caught up with her so quickly? Zara nodded her head in vigorous agreement, and Haroun's hand fell away. "Do you see what has happened, Haroun? Jamal is Hasdai's prisoner. What does it mean?"

Haroun's expression turned grim. "Captain Hasdai must have found out that Jamal warned

Youssef. My guess is that he's being taken back to Meknes for execution."

Zara stifled a cry. "No! Please, Allah, no! Is there nothing we can do? Where are Jamal's men-at-arms?"

"Knowing Jamal as I do, I'd say he found some excuse to send them away before he was arrested. There are only two of us and more than a hundred of them, Zara," he said dryly. "There isn't much we can do to help him."

Zara flushed. Of course Haroun was right. The odds were against them. Unless . . . Her mind worked furiously. "We must find my father. He will help us to save Jamal."

"By now Youssef and his followers are deep in the Sahara. It's the only place they could go where Hasdai wouldn't follow."

"If Captain Hasdai is returning to Meknes, I doubt Father will remain long in the desert," Zara mused thoughtfully.

"Where else can he go?"

"Back to our walled village in the Rif mountains. Ishmail won't think to look for him there. The women and children grow weary of wandering from place to place and long for their homes. Winter is approaching. The village can easily be defended against attack should Ishmail send his army back into the Rif mountains, though I doubt he will. We must ride like the wind, Haroun. If Allah wills, Father will help us save Jamal."

Three weeks later, after crossing the High Atlas and bypassing Meknes, Zara and Haroun arrived at the Berber village where Zara was born. Youssef had beat them there by one day.

284

Chapter Sixteen

Youssef was stunned when he saw Zara enter the village. He had resigned himself to her loss and now here she was, pleading for his help to rescue the man who had enslaved her. Though Youssef believed that Jamal cared for Zara, he was reluctant to go to the sheik's aid. Attempting to rescue a man who was likely to lose his head seemed like a lost cause.

"Please, Father," Zara begged. "We owe our lives to Jamal. I don't know precisely how Captain Hasdai learned of Jamal's treasonous act, but somehow he did and it's up to us to save Jamal."

Youssef regarded his daughter's earnest face. Despite his misgivings, he could not deny her request. But there were certain things he needed to know before committing his men to Jamal's cause.

"Do you love the sheik, Zara? Is there no man in our tribe you would have?"

"I care deeply for Jamal, though Allah knows he doesn't care for me in the same way. He is very possessive of me, but he is like that with everything he considers his." She flushed and looked away. "There is no other man I want, Father."

"Allah knows the match is an unlikely one," Youssef said with a sigh. "Nevertheless, he risked his life and reputation to warn us and will pay a steep price for his betrayal."

Zara's chin rose stubbornly. "Not if I can help it. Will you help, Father? Haroun is waiting for your answer."

"Just tell me one thing, daughter. If we succeed, you know Jamal must flee Morocco. There is nowhere in this country he can hide to escape the sultan's wrath. Jamal knew the danger he faced when he came to warn us. My question is this: Will you go with Jamal when he leaves Morocco?"

Zara flushed and gently touched her stomach. She was certain she carried Jamal's child, a child she already loved. She wanted it even if Jamal did not. "It would be difficult to leave you, Father. Besides, what makes you think Jamal wants me with him?"

"Jamal will not leave without you, of that I am certain." When Zara started to protest, Youssef quickly added, "I strongly urge you to go with him. I want you out of harm's way. I wouldn't say that if I didn't believe that Jamal loves you."

"Jamal has loved many women," Zara scoffed. She wasn't as certain of Jamal's love as her father appeared to be. "I'll make that decision when the time comes. First we have to rescue Jamal while his head is still attached to his body."

"Then let us make plans. Call Haroun to join us."

Jamal saw the cone-shaped spires of the royal palace rising high above the city of Meknes and felt a curious kind of relief. After many weeks the arduous journey was ended, and he'd finally learn his fate. He wasn't afraid to die. What he truly hated was dying before being granted one last glimpse of Zara's beautiful face. At least she was safe, he thought gratefully. In all their years together Haroun had never failed him. Haroun would see that Zara reached his mother in England safely.

The narrow, winding streets of the *medina* were teeming with people, all staring with curiosity at the large contingent of armed soldiers riding toward the palace. Pressed against the walls to keep from being crushed by the horses, people speculated openly about the prisoner being escorted to the palace. Those who recognized Jamal were stunned, and the buzz on the street preceded Jamal all the way to the royal palace.

They rode through the gate, past the granary, the lush gardens and the barracks, finally entering the palace grounds. Weariness etched the faces of the soldiers as Hasdai dismissed them and they hurried toward the barracks. Not a man among them envied Hasdai the chore of informing the sultan that Youssef had escaped yet again.

"Dismount, Sheik," Hasdai ordered. "The sultan was informed the moment we entered the city and will summon us directly. There is little Ishmail doesn't know. His network of spies is extensive."

Jamal threw his leg over his horse and slid to the ground. He turned around and pushed his arms toward Hasdai. "Unbind me. I cannot escape now even if I wanted to."

Hasdai wasn't so certain. Jamal was as sly as a fox. After giving Jamal's request careful thought, he unsheathed his knife and cut through the bindings.

The resulting pain was so intense, Jamal bit his tongue to keep from crying out. Blood rushed to his hands, and several minutes passed before he could speak. "Thank you."

Hasdai's reply, if any, was forestalled by the approach of a palace guard. The man halted before Hasdai, gave Jamal a cursory glance, and said, "The sultan is waiting for your report in the Hall of the Sultanate."

Hasdai squared his shoulders and nudged Jamal forward. Hasdai wasn't looking forward to this audience. Moulay Ishmail's mood changes made him difficult to predict. If he become angry enough, he wouldn't hesitate to order Hasdai's death along with Jamal's. Death he could face; it was the torture he feared.

The Hall of the Sultanate was packed with people. Evidently Jamal's humiliation was to be made public. Few spectators dared to look Jamal in the eye for fear of earning Ishmail's displeasure. Jamal strode forward, aware of his soiled clothing and disheveled appearance. He was exhausted, dirty and worried about Zara. By now she should be close to Tangier, where his ship awaited to carry her to safety.

Jamal dropped to his knees beside Hasdai and made his obeisance to the sultan.

"Where are my enemies?" Ishmail thundered. "Since you have returned without them, am I to assume you let them escape? You may rise and explain."

Hasdai looked uncomfortable as he shifted from foot to foot. He'd seen the sultan in a rage before and knew what to expect. He glanced at Jamal and wished there was some way to avoid this. He'd always respected and admired the sheik, but he owed his loyalty to the sultan.

"I will explain, Hasdai," Jamal said, taking pity on the man. He addressed the sultan directly. "Do not blame Captain Hasdai, great Ishmail. I am solely to blame for this failure."

Ishmail's beady black eyes settled disconcertingly on Jamal. "I eagerly await your explanation, Sheik Jamal. Was I wrong to trust you again? How have you betrayed me?"

Jamal dragged in a deep, steadying breath. "Call it what you will, but I confess to warning Youssef of the planned attack, thus allowing him time to flee."

Ishmail leaped to his feet, his face mottled with rage. "Treason!" he bellowed, pointing a thick, beringed finger at Jamal. "Why did you betray me?" Jamal opened his mouth to speak but Ishmail jumped into the void. "Nay, do not say it. I already know. 'Tis the Berber princess. She has bewitched you. You're a foolish man, Jamal. No woman alive is worth a man's life." He gave Jamal a truly evil smile. "Your punishment must be equal to the crime. Torture first, I think, then a slow death. When the pain becomes unbearable, think of the fleeting pleasure the Berber wench gave you and curse her for bewitching you."

"Let me remind you, great sultan, of how greatly you benefited from my pirating ventures. My loyalty never wavered, not once in all the years I served you. My only excuse is that I could not bear the thought of Zara's death. I am guilty of loving too much. If nothing short of my death will appease you, then so be it."

"You are guilty of loving unwisely," Ishmail charged harshly. "You will die for your mistake. Nothing less will satisfy me, and well you know it." He rubbed his bearded chin in a thoughtful manner. "But you are right. In the past you have served me faithfully and enriched my coffers, and for that I will grant you a boon. Before your torture begins, I will allow you two nights in which to make your peace with Allah. On the second night you may experience pleasure one last time with a woman. You seemed to enjoy my little Zinab. I will send her to you. After your death, all your property, including your ship and monies in your treasury, will be confiscated in my name."

Two nights. He was to have but two nights in which to dream of Zara and what might have been. As for his property and wealth, it meant little to him. What mattered was Zara's safety. Allah willing, she was well on her way to England.

Jamal was surprised to find himself incarcerated in the same small room in which he'd been held the last time he'd been summoned under guard to the palace. He had access to the *hammam* and the small walled garden, neither of which offered any hope of escape. The walls were still too high to scale, and jagged pieces of glass imbedded in the top were an additional deterrent.

Jamal stared at the wall a very long time, wondering if he could fashion a rope of bedding long enough and strong enough to hold his weight. But there was no way to anchor the rope on either side of the wall. There were no trees in the garden, only flowers and shrubbery, and no trees on the other side of the wall. He sighed and returned to the room. At least it wasn't the dungeon, Jamal thought as he stretched out on the narrow couch. He was tired. So very tired . . .

Jamal slept the entire night through. When he awakened the following morning he realized this would be his last day on earth.

Zara mingled with a group of women slaves at the fountain, listening to their chatter. She had arrived in Meknes with her father and Haroun just yesterday. Her eavesdropping was rewarded when she learned the women were from the royal palace. They all seemed eager to discuss Jamal's torture and execution, scheduled for the following day.

"It's so romantic," sighed a small veiled woman with soft brown eyes. " 'Tis said the sheik betrayed the sultan for a woman."

"Were I that woman I would swoon with pleasure, Talia," a second woman declared.

"You've been with him, Zinab. What is Sheik Jamal like?"

"He is very handsome," Zinab said on a sigh, "and gallant. But he loves another. The sultan has ordered me to pleasure him on this, his last night on earth."

"I would gladly trade places with you," Talia sighed.

"Come, 'tis time to return," Zinab said. "I must prepare myself for Jamal. 'Tis my wish that he will die a happy man."

That produced titters among the women as they picked up their pitchers of water and turned away from the fountain. Zara followed, eavesdropping as the conversation continued.

"Will you pleasure the sheik in the dungeon, Zinab?" Talia asked, giving a delicate shudder. She'd never seen the dungeon, but she'd heard it was a horrible place.

"Sheik Jamal is not confined in the dungeon. He's been given a small room in the palace. You know the one, it lies at the end of the east wing. The room has a *hammam* and opens into a small walled garden. The walls are too high to scale, and the room so small and sparcely furnished that 'tis little better than a dungeon."

Zara had all the information she needed as she hurried away to tell her father where to have the horses waiting. The rest was up to her. She must not fail.

A few hours later Zara passed through the palace gate, pretending to be a slave carrying a jug of water. Her body concealed by a *djellaba*, her face hidden behind a veil, she walked unchallenged into the palace through the women's entrance.

Zara was well aware of the danger she faced but chose to ignore it. When she'd arrived in Meknes yesterday, gossip about the torture and execution of one of the sultan's most trusted men was all the townspeople could talk about. Zara and her father had donned white robes instead of the distinctive blue ones that marked them as Berbers, so they could mingle freely with the townspeople without risk. If everything went as planned, Youssef and Haroun would be waiting with horses shortly after midnight beneath the east wall.

The sun was still high in the sky, but Zara had much to accomplish before dark if she was to save Jamal's life. Success depended upon finding Zinab, the slave girl, and Zinab's willingness to help her. Still carrying the jug of water, Zara found the kitchens.

"Pour the water into the kettle," someone ordered. Zara followed orders, then turned to face a sharp-eyed woman stirring something in a pot over a brazier. "Lend a hand, girl. Turn and baste the lamb on the spit." Zara hurried to do as she was bid.

That chore done, she asked casually, "Have you seen Zinab?"

"Zinab no longer works in the kitchen. You'll find her in the harem. She's been ordered to attend the condemned prisoner tonight." The woman cackled gleefully. "At least he'll die a happy man."

Zara worked silently for a few minutes. When the kitchen slave's back was turned, she slipped out the door. Praying she wouldn't be recognized by Badria, the harem mistress, Zara hurried through the maze of hallways toward the women's quarters. She was grateful that she had learned something of the palace layout during her brief stay as a captive, else she'd be hopelessly lost now.

"Lady, where do you go?"

Zara froze. Being hailed by a guard was the last thing she'd expected. Her eyes were lowered respectfully as she said, "I am new to the palace. I've been instructed to go to the *hammam* to attend the sultan's concubines."

"Go then," the guard said gruffly, "and do not tarry."

Zara scurried off without comment. She entered the harem as unobtrusively as possible. Though it was every bit as opulent as she recalled, Zara did not stop to gawk at the rich carpeting beneath her feet, the sumptuous couches covered in silks and brocades, or the bevy of fluttering, gossiping women dressed in colorful harem clothing. How was she supposed to find Zinab in this throng of beautiful concubines?

Trying to avoid Badria, Zara kept to the outer perimeter of the huge room as she made her way to the *hammam*. The bathing room was a beehive of activity. Zara scanned the room but could not pick Zinab out from any of the other lovely women, for she had been veiled at the fountain. She made a slow circle of the room, listening to snippets of conversation, hoping for a clue to

Zinab's identity. Her perseverance paid off when she heard two women talking about Jamal.

"He is too young and handsome to die," a willowy redhead said.

"I wish I had been chosen to make his last night on earth a memorable one," a sloe-eyed Oriental woman said with a sigh.

"You know our master would not send one of his own concubines or wives to pleasure a traitor," the first woman said haughtily. "Zinab is naught but a slave. Ishmail does the traitor no honor by sending Zinab to him. Look at her." She pointed an elegant finger at a petite brunette. "Slaves shouldn't be pampered and indulged like that."

Zara turned her gaze to the woman in question. Not a woman, Zara decided. Zinab was still a child, albeit a sensual one. Her sultry black eyes held a sexual knowledge far beyond her tender years. A silken curtain of shiny black hair only partially hid full breasts crested with large dusky peaks. Zara's visual inspection ended when Zinab moved to a massage table and lay down.

Since no attendant was nearby, Zara hurried over to the table, her heart pounding excitedly. "Lie still, Zinab," Zara said in a soothing tone as she dipped her fingers into a jar of cream and spread it over Zinab's back and thighs. Then she began to massage the cream into the slave girl's smooth, golden skin.

"You are the envy of all the sultan's women," Zara said in a low voice. "They dream of taking your place in the sheik's bed."

" 'Tis a sad thing," Zinab remarked. "I cannot

believe Sheik Jamal committed treason. He is such an honorable man."

"You know him well?" Zara asked, surprised.

Zinab's eyes grew misty. "Well enough to know he would not commit treason without a good reason. You see," she said, lowering her voice in a confidential manner, "Jamal loves a woman so much he is willing to die for her. 'Tis rumored he committed treason so that his Berber princess and her father could escape the sultan's soldiers. Tonight I hope to give him so much pleasure, he will forget his true love."

As Zara's hands pummeled Zinab's soft flesh, her mind worked furiously. What she intended was dangerous, and she could lose her own life in the bargain, but saving Jamal was worth the risk.

Zara put her mouth close to Zinab's ear. "Listen closely, Zinab. I beg you, do not betray me. I am Zara, the Berber princess whose life Jamal saved."

"You are the woman the sheik loves?" She glanced furtively at the bath mistress and eunuchs serving the concubines, noting with relief that their attention was elsewhere. "You are brave but very foolish to come here like this."

"Jamal risked his life for me. I can do no less for him."

"Why are you here? You're in grave danger."

"I cannot let Jamal die." Zara's answer was simple yet moving.

"You love him," Zinab said.

"More than life itself," Zara admitted.

Zinab's eyes grew round with wonder. "You

must flee immediately and save yourself. There is nothing you can do to help Jamal. It is too late."

"I refuse to accept that." She lowered her voice. "I can save him, with your help. You are young, Zinab, and can't possibly know what it is like to love a man so deeply that you would risk your life for him."

"How I long for a love like that." Zinab sighed wistfully. "But we both know that's impossible. I will die in the palace without ever knowing true love. My body belongs to the sultan and whomever he chooses to give it to, but I will never know fulfillment. I've been here so long I cannot even remember my parents. They were poor and sold me as a slave when I was but a child."

"Will you help me, Zinab? Let me take your place with Jamal. My father and Jamal's lieutenant will attempt a rescue tonight. Jamal must be told about our plans so he will be ready."

"I am to be locked in the room with Jamal tonight. The door won't be opened until noon tomorrow. What will happen to me if Jamal escapes? The sultan will demand my death. I would help if I could, Zara, but I am too young to die."

"You needn't die, Zinab," Zara contended. "Wouldn't you like to be free, to find the love you seek? Let me go to Jamal in your place. You can slip away through the women's gate and go to my father. I will tell you where to find him. He will protect you. Jamal will reward you for your help. You'll have the means to go and do whatever you wish. By helping me you can free yourself from the sultan's vicious moods forever."

"If only it could be so," Zinab said wistfully. "The first obstacle is the women's gate. 'Tis locked at night and I wouldn't be able to get out." Suddenly her eyes lit up. "I know the guard who tends the gate. I think he'd let me out if I agree . . ." Her words fell away and she dropped her gaze.

"Then you'll do it?" Zara asked.

"The sweet taste of freedom makes my mouth water. Once I leave Meknes, I hope to journey far away, where Ishmail cannot find me. I doubt Ishmail will stir himself over the loss of a lowly slave."

Elated, Zara leaned closer and said, "Let us make our plans."

Jamal regarded the high wall surrounding the garden with misgivings. He'd spent the better part of the day examining the structure for toeholds but he'd found only smooth surfaces. Discouraged, he turned away.

Dusk sat heavily upon the earth and Jamal knew it wouldn't be long before Zinab arrived to ease his last moments on earth. The sultan had displayed yet another facet of his depravity when he permitted Jamal to taste ecstasy one last time before suffering a cruel death. It was clear to Jamal that Ishmail's generosity was another example of his sadistic nature.

Jamal thought of the young girl who would soon enter his room. Zinab was sweet but she hadn't Zara's depth or fire. Still, he would have the company of another human being to ease his last hours.

Suddenly the door opened and a woman

stepped into the room. She was dressed in flowing robes, her face heavily veiled. She carried a tray from which arose a tempting aroma. Jamal thought it strange that he could still be hungry with one foot in the grave. He watched with appreciation as Zinab glided into the room and placed the tray of food on the table. A guard stood in the open doorway, admiring the seductive sway of her hips.

"The door will remain locked until the hour of noon tomorrow," the guard said. "Make the most of your last hours, Sheik, for you will take no pleasure in the painful death planned for you." He chuckled at his own wit as he closed and locked the door.

A subtle tension moved over Jamal's tall, solid form as he watched Zinab. He hadn't bothered to light a lamp. Except for a bar of moonlight spilling through the open windows, the room was veiled in shadowy darkness. Jamal sensed a subtle different in Zinab but couldn't put his finger on it. He moved to the lamp and struck a light. A soft golden glow flooded the room, enveloping the quiescent female in a nimbus of mystery and beauty.

"Share my meal, Zinab," Jamal invited, breaking the tense silence.

Zara drifted forward, drinking in the sight of Jamal, her anxious gaze searching for injuries. When she found none she allowed herself to breathe again.

"You are quiet tonight, little one. Remove your veil. I'd like to look upon something lovely to take with me to my death."

Zara didn't move. She could tell by Jamal's tone of voice that he thought highly of Zinab. Had Zinab found ecstasy in Jamal's arms? She and Zinab hadn't spoken of what had passed between them.

"What is it, Zinab? What's wrong? You seem different. I sense—" He could not name what he sensed, for he couldn't bear the disappointment if he was wrong.

"What do you sense, my lord?"

Jamal went still. Hope and fear warred within him. It couldn't be. Yet . . . His hands were shaking when he reached out to whisk away the piece of filmy cloth covering her head and face. Jamal's eyes widened with shock when a curtain of silken blond tresses fell free and Zara's beloved face floated before him in all its golden-skinned beauty.

Cold, raw fear nearly stopped his heart. "Allah, no! It can't be. Am I dreaming? What cruel trick is this? Zara is safe aboard my ship. I could not bear it if it wasn't so."

"You are not dreaming, Jamal. Did you think I'd let you go to your death without a fight? Father is here, too. So is Haroun. We will not let you die."

Zara's sacrifice brought tears to Jamal's eyes. Didn't she know there was no escape for either of them now? They would die together. Their gazes met and clung, and suddenly she was in his arms. He kissed her mouth, her cheeks, her forehead, and returned to her mouth. They did not speak, savoring the intimacy without words. Finally Jamal pulled away.

"You have written your own death warrant, my love. Why did you do it? I could have accepted death knowing you were safe. How did you escape Haroun? What is your father doing in Meknes? If he is recognized . . ."

"You heard the guard, Jamal. The door will remain locked until noon tomorrow. Father and Haroun are even now making plans for our escape. They will bring swift horses to the east wall during the darkest hours tonight."

Jamal shook his head, struck by the irony of it. "The wall can't be scaled. I've already inspected every inch of the structure. It's topped with jagged shards of glass—we'd be cut to pieces even if it could be scaled. It's all for naught, love."

Suddenly Jamal brightened. "Perhaps all is not lost. You will leave this room veiled, just as you arrived. No one but you and I need ever know that the woman with me tonight wasn't Zinab. By the way," he wondered, "what happened to Zinab? How did you get her to agree to this? You have not harmed her, have you?"

A worm of jealousy burrowed beneath Zara's skin. "Zinab is in no danger. You seem inordinately fond of her."

"Zinab is a sweet child."

"A worldly child," Zara corrected.

Jamal grinned despite the gravity of the situation. "Jealous, my love?"

Zara regarded him with exasperation. "This is no time to speak of such things. Just know that I will not leave this room without you. Now, are you prepared to listen?"

"I will listen, but nothing is going to change. The wall can't be scaled."

"Father will find a way to get us out of here. I trust him and Haroun implicitly. They have many hours yet in which to study the situation and arrive at a solution. There is nothing for us to do but while away the hours and await their signal."

"Ah, Zara, your unshakable faith is refreshing. You can't begin to know how much I love you."

Zara went still. "What did you say?"

"I love you, sweet vixen. It may be too late for us, but when you leave here I want you to carry the memory of our last moments together."

He pulled her into his arms and she rested pliantly against him, bemused by his declaration of love. Did he truly mean it or was he merely uttering words he thought she wanted to hear?

"I made you my slave but I was the one enslaved," Jamal whispered against her lips. "Lie with me, sweet vixen. Let me love you. I want to fill myself with your sweet essence. I want to die with the taste of you in my mouth and the scent of you filling my nostrils."

"You're not going to die," Zara said fiercely. "I won't permit it."

Jamal chuckled. "My ferocious warrior woman. If your father and Haroun succeed in their endeavor, I'll never doubt you again. Meanwhile, let us claim this night for ourselves and make it one to remember."

Chapter Seventeen

Jamal dragged Zara against him, raining kisses on her mouth, her eyelids, her cheeks, her chin. Zara moaned as he took her mouth again. Fire raced through her blood, settling low in her belly.

"I'm going to love you, sweet vixen, for all the hours we have left to us. The memories we create tonight will have to last you a lifetime. Should I die tomorrow, I want you to remember that no one will ever love you as I do."

"You're not going to die!" Zara reiterated. "When we leave here, it will be together."

Jamal sent her a wistful smile. "So fierce, my lovely Zara. I love your passion, sweet vixen. Give it to me now."

Scooping her into his arms, he carried her to the narrow couch, setting her on the edge and kneeling at her feet. He lifted each foot in turn and removed her boots. His hands were gentle as he untied her sash and tugged down her trousers. Zara lifted her hips and bottom as Jamal slid the trousers down her legs and tossed them aside. Smiling into her eyes, he began to explore her abdomen, continuing downward to stroke her legs and the insides of her smooth, golden thighs, stopping just short of that soft, smooth triangle.

His touch set her aflame. Liquid fire flowed through her veins. "Jamal, please."

"Spread your legs for me, sweet Zara."

She did it blindly, joyously, desperate for his touch, aching for it. She felt his hand slide upward along her leg, testing the smoothness of her skin. She felt his long, skillful fingers part the petals of her sex and tease her tiny, sensitive jewel. She moaned when he slipped his fingers deep inside her. Searing flames set fire to the flesh that he caressed; her whole being strained toward the ultimate pleasure she knew he would give her.

His fingers moved in and out along the silken crevice as Zara raced toward release. But Jamal was not ready to release her yet from the erotic pleasure he was inflicting. Abruptly he pulled his fingers away. Zara cried out in protest.

"Patience, sweet vixen."

Moving downward, he buried his face between her legs. Zara arched violently into his intimate caress as his mouth closed over her. Then his tongue dipped inside her, gliding in and out of her hot, wet sheath, savoring her sweet nectar. He felt her muscles begin to contract and knew she was on the brink of fulfillment. One last thrust of his tongue brought her to a gut-wrenching climax. Her cries of completion were the sweetest music he had ever heard.

Long moments passed before Zara gained her wits. When she did, she saw that Jamal had shed his clothing and was lying naked beside her, idly stroking her breasts as her tremors subsided. His manhood was still engorged, still pulsing with life, still unappeased. Zara looked askance at him.

"My turn will come," he promised, reading her mind. "We will eat first, then bathe. Come," he said, offering his hand.

Zara would have followed him to the ends of the earth, had he asked. She loved this man with a fierce, enduring passion. That he returned her love was a miracle.

Naked and unashamed, they devoured the food sent for their enjoyment. When the last morsel had disappeared, Jamal swept Zara into his arms and carried her to the *hammam*. He walked into the knee-deep water and let her slide down his body to her feet.

"I will wash you," Zara said, reaching for the jar of scented soap at the edge of the tub. Dipping her fingers inside, she spread soap over his shoulders and torso.

Jamal gave a growl of pleasure as Zara's hands slid over his smooth flesh. She sent him a mischievous smile, dipped her fingers into the jar again and began to lather his hips and legs. When her hands closed around his staff, Jamal gave a hoarse cry and staggered backward. Zara dropped to her knees before him, wrapped her arms around his thighs and opened her mouth to him.

Jamal felt her hot, wet mouth close around him, felt her tongue sliding up and down and around the smooth head, and bit down hard on his bottom lip to keep from ending it too soon. He let Zara have her way until he felt his juices rising and knew he could bear no more.

"Enough, sweet vixen, you're driving me wild. 'Tis your turn. Now I will bathe you."

Zara closed her eyes as Jamal's strong hands traversed her soft body, spreading soap and fire with every stroke, each caress. By the time he finished, Zara was groaning and shuddering. Abruptly he lifted her from the bath and carried her back to the couch. He dried her tenderly with a soft drying cloth and lay down beside her. Then he kissed her, a long, thorough searching of her mouth with his tongue.

She was gasping for breath when he left her mouth and shifted his lips downward, briefly touching the pulse point at the base of her throat with his tongue. His mouth continued its downward path, spreading a trail of fire to her breasts, where he licked and sucked her nipples into erect peaks.

"Had I silver balls, I would intensify your pleasure, sweet vixen," Jamal whispered. "But alas, I have nothing but my hands, lips and mouth with which to pleasure you."

Zara smiled dreamily. "Not true, my love. You have a mighty lance that brings me the greatest pleasure I have ever known. Come inside me now. I am more than ready."

"Praise Allah, for I can wait no longer."

He raised himself to his knees and grasped her buttocks, lifting her hips as he shoved his rigid length into her with one swift, powerful thrust. Zara moaned at the incredible feel of it, trembling all over as he drove in and then out with long, measured strokes. Jamal's hands on her hips were not gentle, nor were the strong, forceful thrusts that drove deep and hard inside her, one pounding thrust after another. But Zara did not want gentleness as wracking spasms shook her slender body and she gave herself up to pleasure.

"More," Jamal urged hoarsely as his hips moved like pistons against hers. "Come to me again. Give me everything, sweet vixen."

Zara couldn't believe it when a second climax rivaling the first shook her. The room tilted and she hurtled into space. Then she felt Jamal go rigid, felt the scalding rush of his seed inside her and heard his shout of ecstasy. He remained inside her a long time, easing his weight on his elbows so as not to crush her. Finally his strength returned and he eased his body off her.

"I can die a happy man now," Jamal said, looking deep into her eyes.

"No one is going to die," Zara claimed. "When father and Haroun come—"

He stopped her words with a kiss. "Promise me one thing, Zara," Jamal said after kissing her into silence.

"If I can," she said warily.

"If we're still in this room when morning comes, you're to leave when the door opens and never look back. Go with Haroun to Tangier. My ship will carry you to safety, to England, where my mother will look after you."

She stared at him. "You ask too much of me."

"What can you promise?"

She gave him a brilliant smile. "To love you till the end of time. Together or apart, I will always love you."

"If you hadn't resisted me, you might have come to that conclusion long ago. Think of all the time we wasted."

"I'm much too proud to endure life as a slave. Or be dominated by a master. I wanted you to treat me as an equal, not as a captive. I'm a Berber princess, my freedom is important to me. I wanted to be free to choose my own mate."

"You are no longer a slave, Zara. In my heart I freed you long ago. Now my words have freed you."

Zara gave him a saucy grin. "Your generosity overwhelms me, my lord. In my heart, I never considered myself a slave."

"Vixen," Jamal said, returning her grin. "There are still many hours left before your father and Haroun arrive."

"Have I convinced you, then, oh skeptical one?"

Jamal shrugged. "Why not? I have nothing to lose by believing I am to be rescued, and much to gain. With you in my arms I can believe anything. Let's not waste a moment of precious time. I'm ready to love you again, Zara."

"Oh, yes, Jamal, please."

He aroused her slowly, lavishing tender nipping kisses over her body, using his hands and mouth to make her body sing. She returned his ardor caress for caress, kiss for kiss, until he was hard as stone and rigid with need.

"Turn over," he urged.

She obeyed blindly. Then he raised her hips and positioned himself behind her. When he finally came inside her feminine passage she thrust back against him, urging him on with small, desperate cries. He leaned over her, his hands free to explore her breasts, to tease her nipples into hard peaks.

Sweat dampened his skin and desire pooled hot and heavy in his loins. The scent of hot female flesh and sexual excitement filled his nostrils as he drove himself harder, deeper, into her slick passage. Then his hands moved lower, finding her swollen jewel and massaging it gently with the pad of his thumb. Muffling her scream with a pillow, Zara began to shake.

"Hang on, sweet vixen. Soon we will soar together."

Zara was already soaring as she felt her soul leave her body and fly upward to meet the moon and the stars. Jamal climaxed violently, then collapsed beside her.

They must have dozed, for Jamal awoke a short time later with the certain knowledge that they were not alone. He pulled a cover over Zara's nude body and sat up, peering into the shadowy corners of the room. A figure cloaked in concealing black robes stepped into the room from the open doors facing the garden and bowed.

"Allah be with you, my lord. Are you and the princess ready to leave?"

Jamal leaped to his feet, unmindful of his naked state. "Haroun? Is that you?"

"Indeed, my lord. Shouldn't you be awakening Lady Zara? I will await you by the wall."

"Allah be praised. How did you get over the wall without the guard seeing you?"

"In good time, Jamal. Youssef and the horses grow impatient. You must hurry. We must be far away from Meknes before the sultan learns you are missing and sends his army after you." Turning abruptly, Haroun disappeared into the dark, shadowy reaches of the garden.

Zara awoke to the sound of voices. Her eyes opened just as a dark shadow passed through the door. "Jamal!" She jerked upright, holding the sheet against her naked breasts. "Where are you?"

"Over here, my love."

She saw him then. He was fully dressed and walking toward her. "I was about to wake you. Haroun was here. He's waiting in the garden for us. You must dress quickly."

Joy suffused her beautiful features as she leaped out of bed. "Now do you believe me, oh doubting one?"

"I'll never doubt you again," Jamal laughed, hugging her tightly. "Hurry, sweet vixen. I don't know how Haroun is going to get us over that wall, but if anyone can do it, he can."

Minutes later they joined Haroun at the wall. Jamal was surprised to see a rope dangling down within reach, held in place at the top by a pronged hook. He gave it a tug and found it surprisingly secure.

"How did you keep from getting cut to pieces

on the broken glass at the top of the wall?" Jamal asked.

Haroun grinned. "Look up."

Jamal gazed up, to the very top of the wall. He could just make out something white spread over a section of the wall. "What is it?"

"A thick sheepskin rug. Is that not clever? It was Youssef's idea. When I reached the top of the wall I reversed the hook so the rope hung down into the garden. Then it was a simple matter to let myself down."

Jamal still was not convinced. "Once we climb to the top of the wall, how are we to descend?"

"That is even more clever. Wait and see. By the way, that was my idea. Youssef insists that Lady Zara go first."

"Can you do it, Zara?" Jamal asked worriedly.

"Easily," Zara replied. "Give me a boost."

Jamal grasped her waist and lifted her until she had a good grip on the rope. Then, bracing her feet against the wall, she slowly climbed toward the top. It was a long way up and she didn't look down. When she reached the top she rested on the sheepskin rug and looked down, wondering how she was going to descend to the other side.

"What is she going to do now?" Jamal wanted to know. "I hope you've got this all figured out, Haroun. If Zara is hurt, I'll never forgive you."

"Just watch," Haroun said complacently.

Jamal's features contorted in dismay as Zara launched herself from the top of the wall and dropped from sight. "Allah help her! What happened?"

"Not now, Jamal. You go next. I will follow and

remove the rope. The sultan will drive himself crazy wondering how you escaped."

Trusting Haroun completely, Jamal grabbed the rope and walked up the side of the wall to the top. He paused a moment at the crest to peer downward into the darkness. He could barely make out the dark-robed figures standing below. Joy bubbled up inside him when he saw a donkey cart piled high with hay.

"Jump!" Zara's voice floated up to him through the darkness and he obeyed instantly, launching himself from the top of the wall. He landed in the hay with a thump. The wind was knocked out of him, but he was otherwise unharmed. Zara scrambled up beside him.

"Are you all right?"

"I'm fine, what about you?"

She rubbed her rump. "I have a bruise or two but nothing serious."

"Out, both of you!" Youssef hissed. "Haroun is already at the top of the wall."

Together they scrambled out of the cart and gazed up at Haroun. The rope came down first and was quickly disposed of. Then Haroun leaped from the wall into the cart, dragging the rug with him.

"Where is the guard who usually patrols this section?" Jamal asked.

"I took care of him," Youssef said. "Come, we must leave while the city still sleeps."

Suddenly a man appeared from the shadows beneath the wall and climbed into the wagon. Without a word he picked up the reins, slapped the donkey's rear and moved the cart down the deserted street. In minutes it had disappeared into the night.

"Come, Zinab waits nearby with the horses."

"Zinab? The slave girl? Are you mad, Youssef? What is she doing here?"

"Zara offered her our protection. Zinab insisted upon accompanying us, and I hadn't the heart to deny her. She isn't safe in the city. Ishmail will scour the area for her once your escape is discovered. He will believe that she was in the room when you disappeared and was the last person to see you. Should Ishmail find her, she'll be severely punished for her part in your escape."

"Escape wouldn't have been possible without Zinab," Zara said. "She is welcome to come with us, isn't she, Jamal?"

"Of course, but we must hurry. 'Tis imperative that we reach Tangier as quickly as possible, before Ishmail confiscates my ship."

They melted away into the shadows, following Youssef through the narrow streets of the *medina*. Zinab was waiting with the horses in an alleyway. Maintaining silence, they mounted and rode away. Youssef signaled a halt a few miles beyond the city.

The skies were still very dark, with no sign of approaching dawn. A sliver of moon hung low in the sky. Zara watched as it slid behind a cloud and disappeared. She knew without being told that the time had come for her father to return to his mountain stronghold. Zara was torn. One part of her wanted to remain with Youssef, to ride at his side as she had always done. But another part of her, a softer part she had just recently discovered, recognized that she was no longer the same woman. She was going to have a child, Jamal's child, and she had to protect that tiny new life growing inside her. But was she prepared to leave the fierce, unforgiving land she loved so dearly? Was she ready to follow Jamal to a strange new place of foreigners and infidels?

Zara's ruminations ceased when Youssef began to speak earnestly to her. " 'Tis time to part, daughter. I must return to the Rif mountains. I will miss you, but it would be selfish of me not to want a better life for you."

Zara felt certain the sound she heard was that of her heart breaking. "I cannot leave you, Father. Jamal will understand. I must stay and fight on."

Jamal nudged his horse closer and grasped the reins from her hands. His voice was hard, unrelenting. "The only thing I understand is that you will come with me. Youssef agrees with me. Leaving Morocco is in your own best interest. You are mine, Zara. I won't let you leave me."

"Protect her well, Jamal," Youssef said, resigned to the loss of his beloved daughter.

"Zara will reside with me in the ancestral home of the Earl of Lanford in Kent County," Jamal said. "Direct your messages to her there."

"Who is the Earl of Lanford?" Zara asked. "You told me your mother resides in England. Is the earl a relative?"

"I am Jamal Brantly, the Earl of Lanford," Jamal admitted. "Before Grandfather died I was merely a marquis. I inherited his title last year in addition to vast estates in Ireland and England and a fortune to go along with it."

Zara was stunned. What other secrets was Jamal hiding? "Do you have wives and concubines in England?"

Jamal chuckled. "England permits a man to have only one wife. Some men keep mistresses, but I've yet to hear of an Englishman with a harem. Fear not, sweet vixen, you are all the woman I need." What he didn't say was that his mother had a young noblewoman all picked out for him to marry. Although he had never agreed to the match, his mother was quite set on it.

"May I have a word alone with Zara?" Youssef asked.

"Of course, but please remember 'tis dangerous to tarry. We'll make a quick stop first at Paradise, then proceed directly to Tangier."

"I will be brief."

Jamal didn't want to drop Zara's reins but reluctantly did so as he moved off to confer with Haroun.

"What is it, Father?" Zara asked. "Have you changed your mind? Do you want me to stay with you?"

"I want you to be happy, Zara. If you cannot abide going to England with Jamal, I won't force you to leave. Are you truly set against becoming Jamal's wife? My heart tells me you love the man."

"I cannot lie to you, Father. I do love Jamal. And I believe he loves me. But England is so far away. It will be like starting life all over in a strange place where nothing is familiar."

"Then you wish to remain in Morocco?"

She dropped her gaze. "I'm carrying Jamal's child."

"Ah, now I understand." He regarded her through slitted eyes, his expression fierce. "Had you told me this before, I would not have allowed you to risk your life in Jamal's behalf."

"That's why I didn't tell you. Jamal doesn't even know yet."

Suddenly Jamal appeared beside them. "We must leave. 'Tis dangerous to dally."

"Jamal is right, daughter. You must go. Your place is with Jamal now." He raised his hand in farewell. "May Allah protect you and the ba—"

"Father!" Zara shook her head. She wanted to be the one to tell Jamal about their child. "Allah guard you and keep you, Father." A sob caught in her throat as Youssef rode off into the night.

Taking no chances, Jamal regained possession of Zara's reins and set both horses into motion. Less than an hour later they reached Paradise. Jamal was so certain his escape wouldn't be discovered until they were well on their way to Tangier that he decided the brief stop was necessary to tie up loose ends.

Awakened from sleep, Hammet stood before his master, wringing his hands as he listened carefully to Jamal's words.

"I don't have long, Hammet. Zara and I must be away before daylight. There is much to be done before the sultan's men arrive to confiscate my home and property. Praise Allah that most of my wealth was transferred to England during my last trip. I intend to take only a small purse of gold coins with me to Tangier. The rest is to be distributed equally among my men-at-arms, the servants, slaves, Nafisa, Dr. David ben Israel, yourself and Haroun. There is enough in my treasury to make all of you wealthy."

Just then Haroun entered the room, followed by everyone who lived and worked in the palace. "Everyone has been awakened, Jamal. They await your orders."

"Some of you may already know," Jamal said, addressing the large group of men and women gathered in his outer chamber, "that I am a wanted man, condemned to death by the sultan. I owe my life to Lady Zara, her father and Haroun. Morocco is no longer safe for me. I plan to leave the country aboard my ship. I must leave here within the hour. Since you are all my responsibility, it is my wish that every slave be set free. Slaves, men-at-arms and servants, all will receive a purse with gold enough for each one of you to pursue a new life." An excited murmur rose up around him.

"Haroun will see to the distribution. I suggest you all leave before Moulay Ishmail's soldiers arrive to confiscate the property."

Dr. David ben Israel stepped forward. "I have always wanted to see England, my lord. Would you have room on your ship for my humble person?"

"And I, my lord," Nafisa contended. "I am an old lady with nowhere to go. I beg you, take me with you. I can be helpful to you and your lady."

"I, too, wish to accompany you, master," Hammet said with great dignity. "No Englishman can take care of you as I can."

"It goes without saying that I will join you, Jamal," Haroun declared. "I have been to England with you many times in the past. I will serve you in England as I served you here."

Jamal was truly touched. "Are you sure, my friends? England is not the sunny country to which you're accustomed. It is cold and damp and dreary."

"It will be a great adventure," David ben Israel proclaimed. "I may be old but certainly not too ancient to enjoy a new adventure."

Nafisa and Hammet nodded their heads in mutual agreement.

"Very well," Jamal allowed. "But a large group traveling to Tangier will arouse suspicion. Here is what I propose. Zara and I will go to Tangier, board my ship and set sail immediately for Mogador, the pirate stronghold on the Atlantic coast. Ishmail won't think to look for us there. Those of you who wish to accompany me to England will meet the *Plunderer* at Mogador. Trust Haroun to lead you there safely."

Haroun frowned. "My place is with you, Jamal."

"Others need you more than I right now, my friend. Fear not, Zara and I will encounter no trouble. Besides, there is much for you to accomplish here before the sultan's men arrive. Distribute the gold and silver according to my wishes. Strip the palace of all valuables and distribute them and the stores of food among the villagers. Better they should have them than the sultan.

"If we reach Mogador first, we will wait for you. If you reach there first, I will look for you at the Pirate's Lair Inn on the waterfront."

"I do not wish to go to England." The crowd parted as Saha stepped forward.

Jamal spit out a curse. He had forgotten about his former concubine. Saha belonged to Haroun now, and Jamal had no say in her fate.

"You will go where I go," Haroun said sharply. "Prepare for our journey, we leave at dawn." He turned to Hammet, Nafisa and the doctor. "Go now and make ready for the journey. Take only what you need, for speed is of the essence."

"One more thing, Haroun," Jamal added. "I am placing Zinab in your care. She wishes to accompany Zara to England and I haven't the heart to deny her."

Though Haroun did not relish the thought of playing nursemaid to a fifteen-year-old seductress, he nodded his head.

After everyone filed out of his outer chamber, Jamal entered his bed chamber, where he had left Zara. He hoped she had gotten some rest in the short time allowed her. He found her sound asleep, her cheek resting on her hands. She looked so appealing, so innocently tantalizing, he had to forcibly prevent himself from tearing off his clothes and joining her. Unfortunately, there was no time now. Once aboard his ship they could indulge themselves to their hearts' content. Perhaps he wouldn't let her out of bed until they reached London. He smiled at the thought of making love to Zara day and night, for all the weeks it would take to reach their destination.

Perching on the edge of the couch, he placed a tender kiss on her forehead. Zara murmured in her sleep and smiled, utterly beguiling Jamal. "Wake up, sleepyhead. It's time to leave."

Zara stirred and opened her eyes. She reached out to him and he gathered her against him. "I'm ready. What time is it?"

"Two hours till dawn. Our horses are waiting. Nafisa has packed clothing for us and the servants have prepared food. You must eat something before we leave."

As if Jamal's words had conjured him up, Hammet entered the bed chamber carrying a tray. "Extra food is being packed for your journey, master. Allah be with you and your lady."

"And with you, Hammet. We will meet again in Mogador."

While Zara ate the rice and lamb and drank mint tea, Jamal explained what had taken place while she slept.

"What if they aren't happy in England?" Zara asked as she bit into an almond cake dripping with honey.

"Then the *Plunderer* will carry them back to Morocco, or anywhere else in the world they wish to settle."

"What if I'm not happy, Jamal?"

Jamal was silent so long, Zara thought he hadn't heard her. Finally he said, "I will make you so happy you'll never wish to leave me, sweet vixen. I will teach you English during the voyage to England, and tell you about all the customs you'll doubtlessly find strange. Trust me, Zara. I

320

love you. I'll never deliberately make you un-happy."

As he sealed his vow with a kiss, Zara prayed it would be so.

Chapter Eighteen

The moon slid out from behind the clouds as Zara and Jamal mounted fresh horses and rode away from Paradise. Hammet and Haroun saw them off, then turned back to the palace to carry out Jamal's orders concerning the disposal of his property.

Overwhelmed by sadness, Jamal did not look back as he rode through the waning night. Losing the home that had been his father's pride and joy was like being separated from an integral part of himself. As long as Moulay Ishmail lived, Jamal knew he would not be able to return to the country he loved, and the thought was devastating. Yet, at the same time, he was filled with a curious excitement.

Jamal had always enjoyed his visits to England. He was an English earl, rich enough to do as he pleased, go wherever he wanted. A whole new life was opening to him, and being of an optimistic nature, he tried to concentrate on all the opportunities England offered him.

Pirating was becoming more dangerous and the pickings slimmer. As much as he had enjoyed the excitement of plundering ships on the high seas, it was time he turned his talents to other pursuits. He had Zara now. She was all the excitement he needed. He could ask for no greater gift than to lie in her arms and make love to her every night for the rest of their lives.

Zara's thoughts were more confusing and less optimistic. Leaving behind her father and everything she had ever known and loved was horribly painful. She knew nothing of England and its people. She couldn't even speak the language. What little Jamal had told her hadn't been reassuring. At least the women weren't required to reside in harems and veil their faces when they walked abroad, she reflected on a happier note.

Zara couldn't help wondering if Jamal would change when they reached England. She had always thought of him as an Arab, but in truth he was half English. How would she compare with the pale English roses she'd heard so much about? She tried not to dwell on England and her reception there, concentrating instead on the babe growing inside her.

Jamal called a halt shortly after daylight to rest and water the horses. Zara was so tired, she had to be lifted from her mount. Jamal placed her beneath a shady olive tree while he led the horses to a stream to drink. When he returned, Zara was fast asleep. He let her sleep for two hours before awakening her.

"We can dally no longer," he said, kissing her awake. "I've laid out some food and filled the water bag. After we've eaten and quenched our thirst, we must resume our journey."

Seven days and seven nights later they reached the amphitheater of hills surrounding the city of Tangier. Strategically located opposite the Strait of Gibraltar, the busy port linked Europe and Africa by sea. The city had just recently been reconquered from the Portuguese by Moulay Ishmail.

Jamal thought it prudent to sell their weary mounts at the city gates and received a good price for the thoroughbred Arabians. They entered the *medina* on foot and wended their way through a maze of streets nearly solid with people. Eventually they would reach the bay, where Jamal's ship was berthed.

"There seem to be more soldiers than usual milling about," Jamal whispered as they passed another pair of soldiers, easily recognizable as the sultan's men by the deep mahogany color of their skin.

As required by Islamic law, Zara's face was veiled and she wore a *djellaba*. But beneath Jamal's white turban, his face was easily recognizable.

"I don't like this," Jamal hissed when two soldiers nudged one another and started in their direction. "It isn't normal to see so many soldiers in Tangier. Follow me. It's too dangerous to remain on the streets during daylight hours."

He ducked through a gate and Zara followed. She was surprised to find herself in a small, lush courtyard. Jamal seemed to know exactly where he was going as he grasped her hand and led her through an ornately carved arched doorway. A woman dressed in transparent harem pants and short vest hurried forward to greet them. Long ebony hair framed exotic, golden-skinned features. Her cat-shaped black eyes were outlined with kohl, and her lips and cheeks were reddened with rouge.

"Welcome to the House of Many Delights, young masters. What is your pleasure today?"

"My wife and I have need of a private room for a few hours, Senobia. You will be paid well for accommodating us. And for your silence in the matter," he added cryptically.

A smile of recognition lit Senobia's eyes. "Sheik Jamal! You have been sorely missed at the House of Many Delights." Senobia's assessing gaze drifted over Zara. "Your request is unusual, but since you are a friend of long standing, I will see that you have all the privacy you need. Follow me."

When Zara realized the kind of house she was in, she remained frozen to the spot. Many delights, indeed. Obviously Jamal was a frequent visitor to this type of establishment and well acquainted with the "many delights" available.

"Come on, Zara," Jamal said, grasping her hand. "We will be safe here until nightfall, when we can go about the streets unnoticed. By then the tide will be in and the *Plunderer* can set sail the moment we board."

Senobia took them to a set of large airy rooms that included a *hammam*, which pleased Zara im-

325

mensely. She was covered with dust and grime and so sweaty she couldn't stand her own smell.

"Have you need of a servant?" Senobia asked.

"If you have one that can be trusted," Jamal said. "We are hungry and need fresh clothing. Send a servant to fetch us clean shirts, trousers and robes." He reached beneath his *djellaba* for the sack of gold coins he'd tied to his sash, removed two shiny gold pieces and handed them to Senobia. "Thank you."

"Are you in trouble, my lord?" Senobia asked.

" 'Tis best you don't know. We will be gone by nightfall. Meanwhile, my wife needs to rest. She is travel weary."

Once again Senobia's sultry gaze probed Zara's slender form, as if she could see through the dense robes to her woman's body beneath. "I will leave you to your privacy," she said. A seductive smile played about the corners of her lush lips. "I will not be far should you need me."

The heady scent of her perfume lingered long after she left the room. Zara whipped aside her veil and glared at Jamal. "You seem to know Senobia well."

"Jealous?" Jamal asked with amusement.

She sat down hard on the sleeping couch and crossed her arms over her chest. "Not at all."

"You shouldn't be. The House of Many Delights is the first stop for many sailors returning from long months at sea. Those who can afford it, that is. Those who can't, visit cribs along the docks that offer less fastidious accommodations. I am a man, sweet vixen. Senobia and her kind are but beautiful distractions to be enjoyed and forgotten. They eased my lust after long months without a woman's comfort."

Zara sent him a mutinous glare, still not mollified. Would Jamal seek other women when she grew large with his child and was unable to accommodate him? Did he think all women were merely objects to be enjoyed? She wanted to be loved beyond simple appreciation of her womanly attributes. She wanted to be his equal in every way.

"Let's not argue about something so trivial. We both need a bath, and you look as if you could sleep standing up. Come. Bath, food, and then sleep."

He helped her to undress, then undressed himself. When he lifted her and carried her to the *hammam*, she rested her head against his chest, listening to the pounding of his heart. The water was warm and soothing. They bathed and rinsed one another, and then Jamal helped her to wash her hair. When they finished bathing, they sat side by side in the water, resting their heads against the rim. Zara was nearly asleep when Jamal finally lifted her out of the tub and dried her. Food and clean clothing were waiting for them when they returned to the bed chamber.

"I'm too tired to eat," Zara said with a sigh.

"You have to eat." He searched her face, not liking what he saw. "Your eyes look bruised and your skin is as fragile as parchment. You don't look well, love. I'm sorry if I've driven you too hard."

There was no better time to tell him about the baby, Zara decided. "It's not that, Jamal, it's . . ."

A disturbance at the door froze the words in her throat.

"Jamal! Soldiers were here looking for you."

Jamal wound a towel around his loins and opened the door. "What are you saying, Senobia?"

"I sent them away. No one knows you're here, but I thought you should know you're being sought. I told them nothing."

"You will be amply rewarded, Senobia, thank you." He closed the door and returned to the couch.

"How could the sultan's men reach Tangier before us?" Zara asked worriedly. "We had many hours' head start and stopped at Paradise but briefly."

"I don't know, but there is nothing we can do about it now. If our luck holds, we can sneak aboard the *Plunderer* without being seen."

"And if we can't?"

"I swear no matter what happens, you will be safe. Nothing will harm you, sweet vixen. You have my word on it. Come, eat something with me. I'm starved."

The *couscous* was cold and swimming in congealed chicken fat. Zara's stomach churned at the sight of the unappetizing mess. She munched on cheese and soft white bread, ate some grapes and figs and drank copious amounts of delicious mint tea. Then Jamal fed her bits of sticky almond cake. He surprised her when his tongue flicked out and licked the honey glaze that lingered on her lips.

That sensual act led to a kiss, several kisses,

and soon Zara was writhing beneath the heat of his caresses, savoring the taste of him on her tongue. Jamal realized where this was leading and gently set her away from him.

With the tips of his fingers he traced the line of her cheekbones, the shape of her mouth, the curve of her brows. "You're too tired, sweet vixen. I've no right to demand a response. Rest, soon we'll be aboard the *Plunderer*, free to indulge our every whim."

"Make love to me," Zara said, pulling his head down to meet her lips. "I'm not that tired. I need you, Jamal."

"I shouldn't listen to you but I'm too weak to deny what we both want."

With one hand he gathered up the silken gold of Zara's hair. With the other he pulled her close. He kissed her again, showing her his need with the bold thrust and withdrawal of his tongue. She clung to him as though to life itself. When he dragged his mouth from hers long enough to look at her, her eyes were half-closed and languid.

"Lie back and let me pleasure you," he whispered against her lips.

She watched in a daze as he lifted the lid from a small casket sitting on the bedside table and removed a little velvet bag. When he pulled the string, two silver balls fell into his palm.

Zara's eyes widened. "How did you know what the casket held?"

He gave her a cryptic smile. "Every room in the House of Many Delights has a chest just like this. Inside are many such items designed to give pleasure. Open your thighs for me, sweet vixen."

Zara's legs fell apart. Jamal shifted his weight between her spread thighs and parted the tender folds of her female passage. Then, one by one, he placed the silver balls inside her and pressed her legs together. As he rocked her gently he leaned over and licked the pointed tips of her breasts into hard little nubs.

Indescribable, gut-wrenching pleasure jolted through her, beginning with her toes and traveling through her to every nerve ending. She began to tremble as if from ague. Her skin glowed with incredible heat. Her moans turned into one long wail as convulsions wracked her body. When she had no more to give, Jamal carefully removed the silver balls and pulled her on top of him. Raising her hips, he impaled her.

Straddling him, she rode him hard as tiny explosions continued to erupt inside her. Then Jamal gave a hoarse shout and stiffened, filling her with his hot seed. Succumbing to exhaustion, Zara flattened herself atop him and fell asleep. Jamal stroked her back and buttocks, murmuring sweet words she could not hear, thanking Allah for giving him a woman like Zara.

Zara was allowed to sleep but a few hours before Jamal awakened her. "Wake up, love, 'tis dark enough to travel through the *medina* now."

Zara stirred, opened her eyes and smiled. "I love awakening in your arms."

He grinned in response. "I'll remember that. Would you like something to eat before we leave?"

Zara shook her head, recalling the greasy food

served to them earlier. "I couldn't eat a bite. I'll be ready in no time. I'm as anxious as you are to reach your ship. Will they be expecting you?"

"I certainly hope so. I sent a message to Captain Brahim some time ago, asking him to provision the ship and gather the crew in anticipation of my arrival. He's probably wondering why I've been delayed."

They dressed quickly by the light of the lamp they had left burning. Noises filtered through the door, and Zara realized that the House of Many Delights would be bursting with customers at this time of night. Before they left the chamber, Jamal placed two more gold coins on the table for Senobia to find.

"This chamber is at the back of the house," Jamal said as he opened the door and peered into the deserted hallway. "There is a rear exit into an alleyway. I've used it a time or two and know the way. Follow me."

Zara thought Jamal knew far too much about this house of pleasure but didn't pursue the subject. As they turned a corner, they had the misfortune to encounter a man and woman in the hallway. Zara pulled her veil across her face and Jamal averted his head as they passed. As luck would have it, the couple paid them little heed, being too engrossed in their own lusty pursuits. Zara breathed a sigh of relief when they reached the alley without mishap.

They kept to the shadows of the narrow, nearly deserted streets. The stalls were closed, so they were able to move swiftly through the *medina*. When they spotted a soldier they turned a corner to escape notice. Though their many detours prolonged their arrival at the docks, avoiding the soldiers seemed the prudent thing to do. At length they reached the docks, where an unwelcome surprise awaited them.

"Duck!" Jamal hissed, pulling Zara down with him behind some barrels of dried fish. "The docks are swarming with the sultan's soldiers."

Grateful for their dark robes, Zara huddled beside Jamal, wondering what they were going to do now. Suddenly two burly soldiers headed in their direction, and Jamal held a finger to his lips, indicating that she should remain silent.

The soldiers walked to within several feet of where Zara and Jamal were crouched behind the barrel. The next sound they heard was that of men urinating against the wall of the building.

"I've needed to relieve myself for the past hour," the first man said with a sigh of relief.

"I'd rather be in my bed with a whore than standing guard tonight," the second man groused.

"So would I, but if we don't capture Sheik Jamal the sultan will have our heads. 'Tis fortunate the sentry squirmed out of his bonds and warned Ismail of Jamal's escape. Otherwise we would have arrived too late to prevent the sheik from leaving Morocco. Look sharp, Mohut, Ishmail is desperate for Jamal's head."

"Aye, we must all keep a sharp eye on the *Plunderer*. Sooner or later Jamal will try to board her."

They walked away, complaining about their lack of sleep and the coolness of the night.

"What are we going to do?" Zara whispered

once the soldiers were out of earshot.

"Can you swim?" Jamal wanted to know.

"Nay, I've had no opportunity to learn. This is the closest I've been to the sea."

"Then I will carry you on my back. The *Plunderer* is anchored just a few yards out. I recognize her by her rigging. 'Tis no great distance. We'll have to slip into the water farther down along the wharf, where the soldiers aren't so thick. The swim will be longer but less dangerous. Once we reach the ship we can climb up the anchor chain. Do you trust me to get you aboard safely?"

Zara swallowed and looked away. "You would have a better chance without me. Go alone, Jamal. Don't worry about me, I can return to my village."

Jamal looked at her as if she had just lost her mind. "You will never convince me to leave you behind. I'm a strong swimmer. I'll have no more talk of leaving you behind."

Zara offered no further argument, since Jamal seemed adamantly opposed to leaving without her. Once Jamal made up his mind, she knew from experience that nothing would change it.

Jamal counted a dozen or more soldiers patrolling the wharf. He studied their movements for several minutes, trying to determine the best place to enter the water. He didn't want to go too far down the wharf, for it would place them a substantial distance from the ship, making for an arduous swim.

Jamal grasped her hand and gave it a squeeze. "We'll stay within the shadows of the warehouses and work our way past the wharfs that line the harbor. Fewer soldiers are patrolling that area."

"Do you think it will work?"

"It will work," Jamal said confidently. "Follow me."

They crept along the wharf, ducking behind barrels and boxes whenever a soldier glanced their way.

"This is far enough," Jamal whispered. "We can enter the water here. Pray Allah we won't be noticed when we leave the shadows. There is nothing between here and the water to shield us. Are you ready?"

Zara swallowed hard and nodded. She had faced danger too many times in the past to cower in fear now. "I'm right behind you."

Boldly Jamal stepped out onto the stretch of beach leading to the water. They were well past the dock area and couldn't depend on seeking shelter beneath the wooden structures.

As they were scrambling down to the water, a voice called out from the dark. "Halt!" Pounding footsteps sounded on the hard sand behind them.

"Run!" Jamal called, swiveling his head to make sure Zara was close on his heels. "We'll be safe once we're in the water."

They almost made it.

Zara tripped on her robe and fell just as Jamal reached the water's edge. She landed hard, knocking the breath from her. She lay still, unable to move as her pursuer skidded to a halt beside her. Reaching down, he hauled her to her feet.

Jamal's heart pounded furiously when he looked back and saw Zara being manhandled by the soldier. He had already discarded his cumbersome robe and was standing in shallow water when he turned back to race to Zara's aid.

"Go, Jamal!" Zara screamed when she realized what he intended. "Save yourself!"

Her words had little impact on Jamal. Without a thought for his own life, Jamal leaped to Zara's defense. He had left his heavy scimitar behind at the House of Many Pleasures, but he did have his knife. He pulled it from his sash and lunged at the soldier.

"Take your hands off her!" Jamal demanded.

The soldier laughed, using Zara as a shield as he sidestepped Jamal's attack. "The sultan's orders are to kill you upon sight, Sheik Jamal." He drew his scimitar and tossed Zara aside like a rag doll.

Jamal spared a brief glance at Zara as he braced himself for the soldier's attack. It came immediately, but Jamal danced agilely aside. The scimitar missed him by scant inches. He continued to dance and spin out of reach, too fast for his opponent. Still, with his shorter, lighter weapon, Jamal was dangerously outclassed. The scimitar was deadly and the soldier was an expert in its use. Twice he drew blood despite Jamal's evasive tactics.

Then suddenly Jamal saw an opening in the soldier's defense and ducked in for the kill. His attack would have worked had the soldier not brought up his scimitar just as Jamal launched himself forward. The scimitar pierced his groin in the same instant that Jamal buried his knife in the man's heart. Both men dropped to the ground. The soldier was dead before he hit the dirt. Jamal was gravely wounded.

Somehow Jamal scrambled to his feet. Footsteps pounded along the wharf and shouts filled the air. Soldiers had heard the disturbance and were racing toward them.

"Into the water," Jamal ordered through clenched teeth.

Zara trembled with fear. Blood was everywhere. Jamal was covered with it. "You're hurt. You can't possibly pull me through the water. Save yourself."

Ignoring her plea, he grasped her hand and pulled her toward the water. "Discard your robe," he gasped as pain lanced through him. He was in shock and bleeding profusely. He had no idea how he would save them both, but leaving Zara behind was unthinkable. Drowning was preferable to what the sultan had in store for them.

Zara pulled off her *djellaba* and left it on the shore. She and Jamal entered the water scant seconds before the soldiers reached them. Fortunately, for them, not one man among them could swim. They stood on the shore shouting and waving their arms as Jamal pulled Zara into the deep water. As they drifted away, Zara heard the captain shouting for a boat.

The moment Zara's feet floated free of the bottom she panicked. She wanted to grasp Jamal around the neck but had enough sense to realize that to do so would doom them both. It was too dark to see the blood-stained water, but Zara didn't have to see it to know that Jamal was losing copious amounts of blood. If they didn't drown in the freezing water, sharks would surely find them.

Zara felt herself start to go under and saw her life pass before her eyes. Then, miraculously, Jamal's arm came around her upper chest, supporting her and pulling her with him through the icy water. She had no idea where he found the strength but blessed Allah for it. Once or twice Jamal faltered and they both went under, but each time he recovered and dragged her with him to the surface.

"Don't give up," he said, choking on a mouthful of salty sea water. "We're almost there. Kick your feet, it will help propel us forward."

Zara wanted to cry out that they wouldn't make it, but as long as he had the courage to try, she had no right to complain. She kicked her feet and was surprised how much it helped. Hours passed, or so it seemed to Zara. In truth it was little more than fifteen minutes before the hull of the *Plunderer* rose up before them.

"The anchor chain, grab the anchor chain," Jamal gasped as the last of his strength drained from his body.

His grip slipped from around her chest just as Zara reached for the anchor chain. She caught it and clung to it like a monkey, searching the dark surface for Jamal. He was nowhere to be seen, and she screamed out his name. Suddenly he popped to the surface a few feet away, and she made a desperate lunge for him with her free hand. She grasped the wet silk of his hair and pulled him toward her.

"Jamal, can you hear me?"

Through a fog of pain, half-drowned and nearly too weak to reply, Jamal heard Zara call to him and rallied enough to grunt in reply.

"Grab the anchor chain. It's right here." She guided his hand to the iron links. "Now hang on while I climb up to summon help."

"The boats—"

"I hear them but I don't see them. Perhaps the soldiers thought we drowned and turned back. Don't give up, my love. Whatever you do, don't let go of the anchor chain."

Even as she spoke, Jamal's arms started to slip away. But Zara wasn't about to let him drown. They had come too far together. Thinking fast, she pulled the sash off her trousers and lashed Jamal to the anchor chain, securing him as tightly as she could with her cold, stiff fingers. Her baggy trousers floated down around her ankles and she kicked them off. Satisfied that he wouldn't drift away, she began a slow ascent up the anchor chain.

Zara had to stop twice and rest before she reached the top. She tried not to think about what this kind of exertion was doing to her baby, and placed herself and her child in Allah's merciful hands. When she finally reached the top railing, she was too weak to pull herself up onto the deck. Filling her lungs with air, she gave a shout loud enough to gain the attention of the watch.

"Who's there?"

"Help! Please, help me. Summon the captain."

The watch grabbed a lamp and went to her aid. He set the lamp down and hauled her onto the deck. "Who are you? What are you doing here?"

"There's no time," Zara said in a gasp. "Sheik Jamal needs help. He's wounded and unable to climb aboard on his own. I tied him to the anchor chain. Quickly, pull him up."

The man stared at Zara as if she were a mermaid who had arisen from the sea. He held the lantern high, his mouth agape as his gaze slid over her dripping form. Her long, streaming hair, the thrust of her breasts against her wet shirt, the curve of her shapely hips, her long bare legs; there was no denying she was a female . . . a lovely one at that.

"What's going on? Who is this woman?"

A man appeared beside the watch. Zara hoped it was the captain. .

"Are you Captain Brahim?"

"How do you know me?"

"There is no time for explanations. The sultan's men are searching for us. I've secured Sheik Jamal to the anchor chain with my sash. He's sorely wounded. You must pull him up before the soldiers find him."

The mention of Jamal brought Captain Brahim to immediate attention. "Jamal is here, you say? Clinging to the anchor chain?"

He snatched the lamp from the watch's hand and held it over the side. What he saw galvanized him into action. "Pull up the anchor!" he shouted. The watch immediately put his back into the task. Two men arrived to help. Within minutes, nearly the entire crew had assembled.

Zara watched in trepidation as the sash securing Jamal to the anchor chain was slit and he was lifted aboard. "How is he?" she asked as they laid him out on the deck.

"Still alive," Captain Brahim said, "but in grave condition."

"He's trying to say something," Zara said, kneeling at Jamal's side and leaning close.

"Mogador," Jamal gasped out. "Raise . . . the sails. No time . . . to . . . lose."

Captain Brahim snapped out an order and the crew leaped into action. Suddenly the deck exploded with activity as the sails caught the wind and the ship inched forward.

"Take the sheik to his cabin," Brahim ordered crisply. "Carefully, now." He turned to Zara. "Who are you, lady?"

Zara swayed, suddenly too weak to stand. No answer was forthcoming as the world spun away, taking her with it.

Brahim caught her before she hit the deck. He carried her into the master cabin and laid her down beside Jamal. Then he shifted his attention to Jamal. He was no doctor, but he knew the look of death upon a man when he saw it.

Zara came to a short time later. The first thing she saw was Brahim's grim expression. "How bad is it?" she asked.

"I've inspected the wound, lady. It is indeed grave. In my humble opinion, not even a skilled doctor can save him."

Chapter Nineteen

"Jamal's personal physician is awaiting the *Plunderer* at Mogador," Zara explained. "He is learned and competent; he won't let Jamal die."

"Even with fair winds 'tis a five-day journey to Mogador." Brahim sent Zara a pitying look. "Jamal's fate is in Allah's hands now."

"He won't die!" Zara said fiercely. "Bring your medicine chest; I will treat him myself. We must keep him alive until we reach Mogador. Pile on the canvas, Captain, and pray for fair winds."

Even though he had no idea who Zara was, the captain obeyed without question. While he was gone, Zara removed Jamal's bloody clothing. Her first look at the gaping wound in his groin sent a spurt of bitter gall into her throat. It was a hideous wound. Fortunately, the bleeding had slowed to a trickle, due, Zara suspected, to the cold salt

341

water. Would the salt also act to disinfect? she wondered as she covered him with a sheet.

Captain Brahim returned with the medicine chest. "You won't find much here except salves and bandages." He set the chest on the desk and lifted the lid.

"Jamal's wound needs stitching; can you do it?" she asked.

Brahim shook his head, turning slightly green. "Jamal always treated the men's wounds himself. I have no skill at doctoring. Can't it wait until we reach Mogador?"

"Nay. The wound must be cleansed and stitched immediately."

Disappointed with the captain's lack of medical skill, Zara set to work, using what little knowledge she possessed. She spent a long time cleaning the wound of blood and gore, marveling at how close the sword had come to making him a eunuch and thanking Allah that it hadn't.

"Fetch me a needle and silk," she said, fighting the waves of nausea that threatened her delicate stomach. The sickening stench of blood, combined with the stifling heat inside the cabin, produced a churning sickness inside her. She swallowed hard, forcing the bitterness to settle back where it belonged.

When her stomach settled down, she took the needle and silk from the captain, threaded the needle and turned back to Jamal. His breathing was shallow, his face so pale she feared he wouldn't last through her crude doctoring. And he was still . . . so very still. Her throat worked convulsively as she took her first stitch.

Sweat dripped into her eyes and she dashed it away. She paid little heed to the fact that she wore only a shirt, and that her legs from thighs to ankles were bare. Only one thing mattered: Jamal had to live.

"Finished," Zara said shakily as she leaned against the bunk for support.

"You did well, lady," Brahim said. He poured a glass of water from a pitcher and handed it to her. "Now, please be so kind as to tell me who you are."

"Zara." Jamal's voice, or a weak imitation of it, brought a cry of gladness to Zara's lips.

"Jamal, you're awake!"

"Where am I?"

"Aboard the *Plunderer*. Captain Brahim has set a course for Mogador. You're going to be fine."

"You lie, sweet vixen. I'm dying. Where is the captain?"

Brahim stepped forward. "Here, my lord."

Jamal grasped Zara's hand. "We wish to be married, Captain. Now. You must perform the ceremony immediately."

"This is no time for—"

Jamal coughed, fought for breath, and said, "This is precisely the right time. Zara must be my wife before I die. 'Tis imperative that Zara becomes the Countess of Lanford before she reaches England. Marry us now and prepare the papers while I am still capable of signing my name."

"Please, Jamal, try not to become agitated," Zara begged. "There is no need for a ceremony now. It can wait."

Connie Mason

Jamal ignored her. "You have your orders, Captain. Bring in the witnesses."

Captain Brahim made a hasty exit.

"I suggest you cover your legs, love," Jamal said. "You'll find clothing in the chest at the foot of the bunk."

There was a smile in his voice, but Zara was not fooled. His pain must have been unbearable, for his face was drained of all color and his words were slurred, as if speaking was a great effort.

Zara found a caftan in the chest and donned it quickly. She was standing beside Jamal when the captain returned with two crewmen.

"Are you sure this is what you want, my lord?" Brahim felt compelled to ask.

"More than my own life," Jamal whispered. "If you haven't met yet, this is Princess Zara, the woman who has captured my heart. Marry us, my friend. Time is growing short."

Jamal could feel his life slipping away. His eyes were dimming and he was standing before a long tunnel. He refused to make the journey to the other side until Zara had the protection of his name.

Captain Brahim performed the short Islamic ceremony uniting Jamal and Zara. With the last of his rapidly waning strength, Jamal signed the papers. Then he sighed and closed his eyes. He was content now. Whatever happened to him, Zara had the protection he'd promised her. His mother would respect his choice of bride and all would be well.

"I will leave you with your bride," Brahim said.

"When a man breathes his last, he should be in the arms of his beloved."

Jamal seemed to rally at the captain's words. "I'm trusting you to bring my friends aboard at Mogador and see Zara safely to England. The ship is yours when I die."

"My lord, I—"

"Leave us," Zara whispered. Jamal sounded as if he had already given up and she wouldn't allow it. He still didn't know about the baby, and she decided there was no better time to tell him than now. Perhaps the knowledge that he was to become a father would impel him to fight harder for his life.

She dropped to her knees beside the bunk and smoothed the hair from his forehead. "Jamal, can you hear me?" No answer. "Please, Jamal, don't leave me. You have so much to live for. I'm going to have your child."

Jamal heard a voice calling to him but was too tired to respond. The entrance to the tunnel yawned before him, and he sensed that a tranquillity he'd never experienced before lay just beyond. Yet something prevented him from taking that first and final step.

"Jamal! I need you. Our child needs you." Her voice rose on a note of despair and anger. How dare he bring her this far only to desert her? "You have no right to leave me like this."

Her anger finally got through to him. Though the mysterious promise of the tunnel still beckoned, it no longer seemed important that he reach the other side. His eyelids fluttered as the voice called him back from the edge of eternity.

Somehow it seemed crucial that he listen and respond.

"Jamal! I'm going to have your baby. Come back, come back to me."

Were his fluttering eyelids a good sign? Zara wondered. She chose to think so as she continued to whisper in his ear, telling him how much she loved him, how desperately she and their child needed him.

I have no child, Jamal thought. Why is Zara tormenting me? He started to drift away again and was suddenly pulled back when he heard an urgent voice pestering him about a child. Inspired by those intriguing words, he deliberately turned his back on the tunnel, drifting toward the voice upon a wave of pain.

Zara sensed the precise moment that Jamal returned to her. His eyelids fluttered open and he stared at her.

"Jamal, can you hear me?"

"Why are you angry with me?" he whispered weakly.

Zara blinked away her tears. Jamal hadn't left her yet, but the knowledge that he still might lingered in the back of her mind. "Have you heard nothing I've said?"

Jamal frowned, trying to recall his strange experience in the tunnel. "I heard . . . a voice. It called me back from the tunnel. I didn't want to return but the voice—was it yours?—accused me of deserting my child. I have no child. What did it mean, Zara?"

Jamal's reference to the tunnel left Zara puzzled, but she didn't dwell on it. He was back with her for the time being and she was grateful for that small miracle.

"I'm carrying your child, my love. I hadn't found the proper time to tell you until now. I thought you'd left me, and it frightened me."

Jamal merely stared at her, unable to comprehend what she was telling him. "I'm so tired."

The door to the cabin opened and Captain Brahim stepped inside, ready to comfort the grieving widow. He was stunned to see Jamal still alive. Not only alive but speaking.

"Are you a witch, my lady? I could have sworn—"

Suddenly Jamal seemed to rally. "My wife has extraordinary powers, Brahim. Powerful enough to snatch me back from death's door. I have much to live for. I'm going to be a father."

He'd heard! Relief shuddered through Zara. "Aye, my love, you do indeed have much to live for."

Even as she spoke, Jamal's eyelids dropped. Brahim leaped forward. "Is he . . . ?"

"Sleeping," Zara said, noting the shallow but steady rise and fall of his chest.

"I don't know what miracle occurred here but I thank Allah for it. Is there anything you need, my lady?"

"Water and broth. Jamal needs nourishment. And something more substantial for me to eat."

Jamal slept off and on the rest of the night and far into the following day. He was still alive but burning with fever, interspersed with bouts of chills. With the help of two crewmen who had volunteered to assist her, Zara bathed Jamal's burning body with cold sea water to bring down the fever. When he shook with chills, she sent the two crewmen away and slipped into bed beside him, sharing her body heat with him. He was still seriously ill but at least he was alive. If the winds held and Allah was kind, they would reach Mogador and Dr. David ben Israel in time to save Jamal. She prayed zealously for a miracle.

Jamal still clung to a thread of life when they dropped anchor at Mogador. Captain Brahim and several crewmen rowed ashore, relieved to find Haroun at the docks waiting for the *Plunderer* to arrive.

"Praise Allah for your timely presence here," Brahim said as he grasped Haroun's arm in greeting. "Where is the rest of your party?"

"Waiting at the inn for word of your arrival. We reached Morador just last night. Where is Jamal?"

"The sheik was mortally wounded by one of the sultan's soldiers. They were patrolling the waterfront when he and the princess arrived in Tangier. Jamal managed to swim to the ship despite his wound."

Haroun grasped the captain's shoulders in a brutal grip. "Do not tell me Jamal is dead, for I refuse to believe it."

"Nay, not dead, but close. 'Tis a miracle he's still alive after the serious wound he suffered. Allah surely was with the sheik, for he managed to get both himself and Lady Zara to the ship. He requires the services of his physician immediately."

"I will get him and the others. I've already hired boats to take us to your ship."

Haroun turned on his heel. The inn was but a scant distance away and he was back with the others a short time later. The boats were summoned, and Jamal's friends piled in with their possessions. Dr. David ben Israel clasped his case of medicines against his chest, entrusting it to no one. He prayed his knowledge of medicine was sufficient to save Jamal.

The doctor hurried to Jamal's bedside the moment his feet touched the deck. Zara watched anxiously as he inspected Jamal's wound, which showed signs of festering.

"Who treated him?" ben Israel asked.

"I did," Zara said, "but I am not skilled. I cleansed and stitched the wound as best I could."

"You did exactly right, my lady. Unfortunately, you did not have the right medicines, and infection rages through his body. The wound must be reopened and the infection flushed out. It won't be a pretty sight, my lady. Perhaps you should leave and let Hammet or Nafisa assist me."

"I will stay," Zara insisted.

Unfortunately, Zara's will was stronger than her stomach. She was exhausted from long days and nights of tending Jamal and pregnant besides. When the small cabin grew pungent with the stench of putrid flesh, she began to sway on her feet. The doctor noted her pallor and ordered her from the room. She started to refuse, but Hammet, who stood nearby in case he was needed, swept her from her feet and carried her onto the deck. The brisk salt air quickly revived her, and Hammet carried her to another cabin to rest.

"Do not worry, lady, my master is in good hands," he told her. "The learned doctor will not let him die. I will send Zinab to you."

Zinab hurried into the cabin a few minutes later. "Oh, my lady, we are all so worried about Sheik Jamal. What a terrible thing to happen. But you are safe now. Captain Brahim says we will sail on the next tide."

"Are you anxious to go to England?" Zara asked.

Zinab shrugged her elegant shoulders. "I have no one in Morocco. If the sultan finds me, I am as good as dead. What else is there for me? I wish only to serve you."

Zara sighed. She wished she could be as optimistic about England as Zinab.

Zara looked so fragile, so exhausted, that Zinab immediately grew concerned. "You must sleep, mistress, you look ill."

"Not ill, Zinab. I'm carrying Jamal's child. But you're right, I need to rest if I am to keep this babe. I've not had an easy time of it." She closed her eyes. Zinab waited until she drifted off and then quietly let herself out of the cabin.

"What did you say?" Saha asked when she heard Zinab telling Nafisa about Zara's condition. They had all gathered in the cabin the three women were to share.

"Lady Zara is carrying Jamal's child," Zinab repeated. "Isn't it wonderful?" She sighed dreamily. "They are so in love."

"Bah, that warrior woman doesn't deserve a man like Jamal. He will tire of her soon, and when he does, I will be here to comfort him."

"You belong to Haroun," Nafisa said, sending Saha a withering glance. "If Jamal had wanted you, he wouldn't have given you away."

"Our master has a hot temper," Saha allowed. "No doubt he already regrets his rash act."

Nafisa gave an inelegant snort. " 'Tis unlikely Jamal will turn to you for comfort any time soon, Lady Saha. Captain Brahim said Jamal and Zara were married aboard the *Plunderer* five days ago. In England a man is allowed but one wife, and they do not keep harems."

"Jamal married the Berber witch?" Saha cried in disbelief. "I cannot believe he would do such a stupid thing." She gave Nafisa a sly smile. "If Zara is indeed with child, Jamal will get scant comfort from her body when she grows large. He will look upon me with new eyes. Should he want me again, Haroun will not stand in his way."

Little Zinab placed her fists on her slender hips and faced Saha squarely. "I do not like you, Saha. You are vain and self-centered. You have been dreadfully spoiled. If you try to hurt Zara, you will have me to answer to."

Zinab's dark eyes were so fierce, Saha drew back in alarm. Nafisa cackled gleefully. "You have met your match in Zinab, Saha."

"That child? She doesn't frighten me." Saha's actions belied her words, though, as she spun on her heel and fled.

Jamal's recovery was almost miraculous. His color was better and he was able to take liquids on his own. The debilitating infection that had raged through his body had been contained, and his death no longer seemed imminent. He continued to sleep a great deal, but the doctor said it was a healing sleep. During his waking hours Jamal wanted Zara with him. Though he spoke little, just having her in the same room seemed to soothe him.

They had been at sea several days when Zara entered Jamal's cabin to find him propped up in bed. He had lost considerable weight, but she was glad to see that the old sparkle was back in his eyes. He held out his hand and she took it, letting him tug her down on the bed beside him.

She gave him a breathtaking smile. "You're better."

"Thanks to you."

"It was the doctor who saved your life."

"My life was saved long before the doctor arrived." He grew pensive. "I almost didn't make it, sweet vixen. I was knocking at death's door when you called me back. I didn't want to return. The pain was too great, the suffering too intense. I was one step away from entering Paradise. The promise of eternal peace and tranquillity was pulling me toward death. Then I heard your voice."

He asked for water and she held the cup to his lips. "I feared you hadn't heard me," Zara said. "I was so frightened."

He searched her face, musing on some private memory. "How long have you known about our child?"

Her gaze dropped to her hands. This was the first time Jamal had mentioned their child since she'd told him. Was he happy about it? "Since before I arrived in Meknes to rescue you."

"By Allah's beard!" Despite his weakness, he had no trouble making his displeasure known. "You risked your life to save mine while you were with child! You could have been caught, or injured, or—" He shivered. He didn't even want to think about how easily he could have lost her.

"I had to! I couldn't let you die. Nothing happened to me. We're both alive, and our baby prospers inside me." She flattened her hand against her stomach. "Are you pleased about the child?"

Jamal placed his hand over hers. "Extremely pleased. You've been through so much. I shudder when I think about you jumping from the wall and running through the *medina* to the docks. And that dreadful swim to the *Plunderer*." He shook his head. " 'Tis a miracle you survived those long hours in the saddle without mishap. Our child is strong, sweet vixen. As strong as his mother."

"Do you remember having the captain marry us, Jamal?"

"Of course. I wanted you to have the protection of my name. I've amassed a considerable fortune and inherited another, most of it safely invested in commerce or deposited in English banks. I wanted it to be yours when . . . *if* I didn't make it to England."

"That's no longer a possibility. Dr. Ben Israel said you're going to recover fully. You were lucky. Had the scimitar entered an inch to the right, you would never have been able to father another child."

"Praise Allah in his infinite mercy," Jamal said on a sigh.

"You're tired. Rest now. I'll go to the galley and get you something to eat."

"No more broth or bland rice," Jamal said, his expression registering his distaste. "I need my strength if I'm going to consummate my marriage."

She gave him a saucy smile. "Judging by my condition, I'd say our marriage has most definitely been consummated." She turned to leave. "I'll be back soon with something substantial for you to eat."

Jamal smiled. For the first time since he'd been wounded, he actually felt as if he would live. He'd been out of touch with reality for many days and had finally awakened clear-headed this morning. He had defied death and owed his return to the living to Zara. Just thinking about his warrior woman made him smile.

"Oh, you're better. Haroun told me you were, but I had to see for myself."

Jamal was surprised to see Saha standing just inside the doorway. "I'm not ready yet to meet my maker. I have too much to live for. Zara carries my child. I'm going to be a father."

Saha's lips turned down into a scowl. "So I heard. That's one of the reasons I wanted to speak privately with you." She approached the bed with mincing steps. "Soon Zara will be too large and ungainly to give you pleasure. I know you, Jamal. You are not a man to forgo your pleasure for very long. When you grow disgusted with Zara's bulk, know that I am most eager to give you what she cannot."

"You belong to Haroun," Jamal contended. "He is your new master. Look to him for your pleasure."

"I was told that England does not recognize slave and master. I will be free to pick and choose my own man. I choose you, my lord."

"Were you not also told that Englishmen are allowed one wife and do not keep harems?"

"They have mistresses," she said smugly. "I will be your mistress." She grasped his hand, placing it on her breast. "My breasts are firm and full." She dragged his hand down to her belly. "Unlike Zara's, my stomach is flat." She took his hand lower, bringing it to rest on her plump mound. "My sheath is hot and tight and my tiny jewel weeping for the touch of your mouth."

"For the love of Allah, leave me, Saha!" It angered him to think that he was too weak to pull his hand from Saha's surprisingly strong grip.

Zara chose that moment to return. She was angered but not surprised by Saha's boldness. Saha stood beside the bed, clasping Jamal's hand between her legs. Zara snorted her approval when she heard Jamal order Saha to leave. Oblivious to Jamal's wishes, Saha spread her legs and pressed his hand more firmly against her. All three occupants of the cabin were unaware of another presence. Haroun stood behind Zara. He'd seen Zara enter the cabin carrying a tray and thought to pay a visit to Jamal while he ate.

"Saha!" he roared. "What is the meaning of this?"

"Control your woman, Haroun," Jamal ordered weakly. "Tie her to the bed if you must, but keep her away from me."

Grasping Saha by her bright hair, he pulled her from the cabin. "I will beat her," Haroun said. "I've been remiss in my duty lately, but I will remedy that at once. I should have left the little witch in Morocco for the sultan's pleasure."

"I didn't invite Saha in here," Jamal said once he and Zara were alone. "I want no woman but you."

Zara set the tray down and fluffed the pillow behind Jamal's head. "Your juices run hot within you, Jamal. There will come a day when I am unable to pleasure you. I suppose Saha was thinking of the future. When I become disgustingly fat, you may want another woman."

Jamal's look told her exactly what he thought of her logic. "Do you think so little of me that I would take another woman when you grow large with my child? That might have been true once, but I am not that same pleasure-seeking man who had never tasted love. Do you think me so self-centered that nothing matters but my own pleasure? You sorely wound me, sweet vixen. I've not made love to another since meeting you and never will. Now that that's settled, show me what you've brought me to eat."

Zara spooned succulent lamb and rice into Jamal's mouth until he was full. When he finished, he urged her to lie down beside him. Nestled against his good side, Zara felt happier than she had ever believed possible. England no longer seemed as frightening as it once had.

* * *

Each day Jamal grew stronger. Zara, Nafisa and Zinab spent long afternoons in his cabin learning the rudiments of English. Saha refused to attend the impromptu lessons, declaring that she wanted nothing to do with the infidels or their language.

The weather turned bitter cold and the ocean churned with winter winds. They dropped anchor at the French coastal city of Brest, and Jamal felt well enough to visit the town to purchase winter clothing for the woman, Haroun and Hammet. Since he always kept a selection of English gentlemen's clothing aboard his ship, including appropriate footwear, he only added a fur-lined cloak and hat to his own wardrobe.

The first time Zara donned her new clothing, she felt as if she were choking. "Did a man who hates women design these restricting garments?" she asked Jamal as she breezed into this cabin. "Given a choice, I'd wear the baggy trousers, shirt and *djellaba* of my people."

Though she cared little for English female attire, Zara thought Jamal looked quite handsome in white linen shirt, satin vest, tight trousers and knee-length boots.

"It always amazed me that English womanhood was willing to endure near torture to appear attractive," Jamal contended. "I prefer you naked any day. I will endeavor to keep you that way as often as I can. Come." He patted the bunk beside him. "Soon we will reach England and we need to talk."

Zara sat down beside him, searching his well-loved face. He still wasn't completely healed but he no longer had that hollow look about his eyes. He was thinner but rapidly regaining both weight and strength.

"What shall we talk about?" Was he already sorry he'd brought her with him?

"You asked me once if I had a wife in England and I said I had no wife."

Zara felt as if the deck had fallen out from beneath her. "You lied! You *do* have a wife."

"Nay, sweet vixen, you are my only wife. But my mother has a woman all picked out for me. I met her on my last trip to England, but she didn't appeal to me. Nevertheless, Mother is set on the match. I know she'll love you once she gets to know you, but I wanted to warn you. My mother is a wonderful woman, warm, kind and generous. Once she realizes that you are the woman I want, she'll accept you with open arms. She'll be ecstatically happy to learn I intend to settle in England, accept Grandfather's title and become a member of the House of Lords."

Zara wasn't so sure about her reception. She gave him a wobbly smile. "You can always divorce me if your mother doesn't approve. 'Tis a simple enough thing to do."

"Not in England. Besides, why would I wish to divorce a woman who holds my heart? The woman who carries my child inside her."

He turned her to face him and began to unbutton her dress. "Now I know why English women retain their virginity until marriage," he quipped as he fumbled clumsily with the tiny buttons. "They can't get their blasted clothes off."

"What are you doing? I can't change here. I left my caftan in my cabin."

"From now on you're going to share my cabin. I'm tired of sleeping alone. And when we get to England, we'll occupy the same room and sleep in the same bed. I don't hold with the English custom of husbands and wives maintaining separate sleeping quarters."

Zara sighed. "Englishmen have strange customs. It will take me a very long time to adjust. Perhaps I never will."

"I don't give a bloody damn, I like you just the way you are."

They had been conversing in English, which Jamal insisted upon now. "Englishmen have strange ways of expressing themselves. Isn't 'bloody' a curse word?"

Jamal smiled. " 'Tis a word a lady would never use in public."

"As long as we're discussing England, what about Haroun, Nafisa and Zinab? And Dr. David ben Israel? Where will they fit into your household?"

"Nafisa can be our child's nursemaid. She and my mother are acquainted from the old days when Father was alive and Mother lived in Morocco. Hammet wishes to be my personal servant, and Zinab can be yours. They will all be paid generously for performing their duties and can come and go as they please. As for the good doctor, he will remain my personal physician and live in my home."

"That still leaves Haroun. It will be more difficult to find a position for him."

"Haroun has visited England many times in the past. He is acquainted with the customs and language. I will employ him in any capacity he wishes. His friendship means a great deal to me, and I want him nearby even if he chooses not to become a part of my household."

"Could he do that? Live separately from you, I mean?"

"Haroun is not a poor man. His portion of the pirate booty throughout the years is not inconsiderable. I advised him to invest his money in English shipping, and he did as I suggested. His profits have been deposited in the Bank of England and his account grows yearly. I did the same and have amassed a fortune. You've married an extremely rich man, sweet vixen."

"That takes care of everyone but Saha," Zara mused. "She is not a happy woman. I get the impression that Haroun is becoming disenchanted with her."

"Saha's fate is in Haroun's hands. Forget them for now. Help me with your dress. I want to love my wife. It's been far too long since I held her in my arms."

"Nay, you can't! You're not well enough. You'll reopen your wound, and the doctor will be angry with me for permitting such strenuous activity so soon."

He gave her a seductive smile. "Fear not, sweet vixen. I will find a way to love you without doing myself injury."

Chapter Twenty

The *Plunderer* anchored in London Pool on a wet, dreary December day. Zara thought it an omen of things to come but tried to shake off her gloomy mood. She couldn't imagine what could go wrong. She and Jamal were more in love than ever and her baby prospered within her, though at nearly four months the babe was hardly more than a small bulge beneath her waist. Her breasts and waist were larger but her stomach was only slightly rounded.

Weather during the six-week voyage to England had kept them mostly confined to their cabins. During the long hours of confinement, everyone but Saha learned to speak enough English to be understood and to express themselves. Jamal's wound was nearly healed and his strength almost fully restored. If Zara had any doubts as to his vigor, she had but to recall the frequency and exuberance of his lovemaking.

"Are you ready to go ashore, love?" Jamal asked as they stood at the railing watching the docking process.

Wrapped to her eyebrows in fur, Zara shivered in the cold wind and stared curiously at the drab buildings lining the wharves and the brisk activity taking place along the waterfront. "It's so different from Tangier. Everything looks gray and dirty here. Where are the sparkling white buildings? The beautiful expanses of green? The mountains?"

"No white buildings here, Zara. Everything is covered in coal dust. If you want green you must go to the country. As for mountains, they exist only in Wales and Scotland. I have many estates scattered throughout England and Scotland. One of them should please you."

"Where do we go from here?"

"To my home in Kent. Mother isn't fond of London. She spends most of her time in the country. Haroun is going to ride ahead to warn them of our arrival. I told him not to tell Mother about our marriage. I want to tell her myself. Haroun is to state that I am arriving with a party of five and that rooms are to be prepared."

"Are you sure that's wise? Not telling your mother about us, I mean?"

"I want her to hear it from my own lips. And I want her to meet you first. Don't worry, she'll love you."

"What do I call your mother?"

"Her name is Eloise, Lady Lanford. Just call

her 'my lady' until she tells you different. You'll get along famously, I know you will."

"How far is it to Kent?"

"Not so far, but I want to take it easy with you. We'll stop on the road the first night. Traveling by coach in winter can be hazardous if roads are icy. Then there are road agents to contend with."

"Road agents?"

"Thieves who stop travelers and rob them. But that won't happen to us. I intend to hire outriders to make the road safe for us."

"The gangplank is in place, my lord," Captain Brahim said as he came up to join them. "Will you and your lady be going ashore now?"

"I'm going ashore first to hire a conveyance to take our party to Lanford Manor, and outriders to protect us. When I return, the entire party will depart for Kent."

"What about the ship? Do you wish her to remain berthed in London Pool?"

"If you're not averse to remaining in London a few weeks, I'll endeavor to find a cargo for you to take back to Morocco. I have decided to give the *Plunderer* to you in payment for your faithful service. I have enough interests here in England to keep me busy, including shipping investments Pirating no longer appeals to me. What you do with the ship is your business."

Brahim appeared stunned. "My lord, you are most generous. The crew is eager to explore London and its environs and will appreciate a few weeks on land. I'll give them the good news."

"I won't be long," Jamal said to Zara after the captain took his leave. "I need to hire a coach large enough to transport our party to Kent and to buy a horse for Haroun. Wait with the others in the cabin where it is warm."

She lifted her lips for his kiss. "Hurry back, my love. I'm most eager to meet your mother and see your home."

Zara watched Jamal stride down the gangplank, thinking him the most handsome man she'd ever seen. She never tired of touching him, of kissing him, of finding ecstasy in his arms. Their lovemaking brought a dimension to her life that had been missing before. Nothing could describe the unspeakable pleasure he gave her. He knew exactly how and where to touch her to produce the most intense bliss she had ever known.

But Zara was not without reservations. England was a strange country. How long would she hold her husband's love? she wondered. Would he find pale English beauties more appealing than she? Would he take a mistress when she grew too large to accommodate him? And what about his mother? Lady Lanford wanted him to take a wealthy English bride, one with a title. In the face of such opposition, could she survive in this cold, dreary country?

Only time would tell.

Jamal arrived back at the ship much later than expected. He'd had a difficult time renting the kind of coach he wanted for his wife and friends and had ended up buying a brand-new coach and four. The coach was roomy enough to seat six and luxuriously appointed with leather seats and squabs and running lanterns. The horses were well-matched and spirited. The equipage had cost a small fortune, but Jamal had decided to splurge. Zara's comfort was important to him. Hiring two brawny men as outriders and an experienced driver had proved less difficult than finding an appropriate conveyance.

"It's very handsome," Zara said admiringly as she climbed into the coach.

The others piled in behind her. Zinab huddled beside Zara, miserable in the damp cold despite Jamal's thoughtfulness in providing fur lap robes to keep them warm.

They made it to Chatham the first night, stopping at an inn that seemed crude and primitive compared to Jamal's palacial home in Morocco with its tiled courtyard, lush gardens and sumptuous baths. They supped on English fare of kidney pie, rare roast beef, boiled potatoes and cabbage. The food was far too heavy and unappetizing for Zara's delicate palate. Since there was no fruit in England at this time of year, she went to bed hungry.

"You'll like Lanford Manor," Jamal said, aware of Zara's misery. "There are hearths in every room to ward off the chill, cheerful gardens and vast orchards that produce delicious fruit in the summer."

He took her in his arms, warming her with the heat of his body. "Barring anything unforeseen, we will reach the village of Maidstone before dark tomorrow. Lanford lies a few kilometers beyond the village. Go to sleep, my love."

Sleep didn't come easily. Grave misgivings plagued Zara. She could neither understand nor explain her disquiet, for Jamal's mother sounded like a caring woman. A loving mother wouldn't hate her son's bride, would she?

The coach sped through Maidstone the following day. The day was cold and bleak, and few people were out and about. Sheets of freezing sleet pelted against the windows of the coach. Having lived in the mountains through many winters, Zara suffered less than Saha and little Zinab, who hadn't experienced bitter winter weather before and hated it.

A gloomy twilight had fallen over the hushed land by the time the coach turned into a long lane guarded on either side by tall oak trees devoid of all their leaves. The outline of a large manor constructed of gray stone came into view, and Zara strained to get a better look.

The house was nothing like the magnificent marble palaces of Morocco with their wide covered walkways and tall arched windows. While homes in her country tended to be built closer to the ground, this imposing structure consisted of three stories and as many turrets. Though Zara couldn't exactly describe it as a castle, nevertheless she thought it monstrously oppressive.

Jamal must have read her mind, for he said, " 'Tisn't nearly as depressing as it looks. The inside is surprisingly cheerful."

Zara gave him a half-hearted smile. "I can't wait to see it."

The coach drove beneath the porte cochere and stopped to discharge its passengers. Jamal hopped down first and helped Zara to alight.

Hammet descended next and helped the other ladies. Suddenly the front door flew open and a serenely beautiful lady of middle years rushed into Jamal's open arms.

"Ah, Jamal, how I prayed for this day. You've always been so adamant about remaining in Morocco that I'd nearly given up hope of having you permanently in England. My fondest wishes have come to pass."

She remembered her manners after a moment and released Jamal. "Welcome. Welcome, everyone," she said, addressing the group who had descended from the coach and stood shivering in the frosty night air. "Come inside where it's warm." She smiled at her son. "I have a surprise for you, Jamal. I hope you'll be pleased."

Lady Lanford led them into the parlor, where the women made directly for the hearth, drawn by the welcome warmth of the cheery fire. Zara was delighted to learn that Jamal hadn't lied when he'd said the inside of the manor wasn't as dreary as the outside. She felt herself warming to the cherrywood furniture, overstuffed chairs and walls brightened with paintings and tapestries.

Though there was nothing here to remind her of the airy, uncluttered Moroccan palaces with their colorful mosaic walls, tile floors and thick carpets, she felt she could be happy here. She came out of her trance when Jamal grasped her hand and pulled her toward his mother.

Zara gripped his hand hard and waited. But before Jamal could perform the introductions, there was a commotion in the hall. Lady Lanford turned away from Jamal and Zara to greet the arrival of an attractive young woman.

"Ah, Caroline, you're just in time. Jamal has finally arrived. Come greet him, my dear. You remember Caroline, don't you, Jamal? She's the surprise I mentioned."

Jamal groaned in dismay. Caroline, Lady Wellsley, was the girl his mother hoped he would marry.

"Wasn't it clever of me to send for Caroline so she could be on hand to greet you?" Lady Lanford said, beaming at her son.

"I hope you don't mind," Caroline said, blushing for Jamal's benefit. "Lady Lanford insisted that I be here when you arrived."

Zara thought Caroline quite attractive with her ash blood hair and porcelain complexion. Her nose was a trifle long and she seemed to have it in the air a lot, but otherwise her face was a nearly perfect oval. She wondered who Caroline was.

"Mother, before this goes too far, I want to present Zara and my friends to you."

Lady Lanford gave the group her friendliest smile, and Zara felt certain all was going to be well.

"I already know Nafisa, Hammet and Dr. David ben Israel, but the other women are unknown to me."

"Saha is Haroun's . . . woman," Jamal said for lack of a better word. His mother would know exactly what he meant. "Zinab"—he indicated the young girl beside Zara—"is Zara's maidservant. And Zara," he said, slipping an arm around Zara's waist, "is my wife."

Lady Lanford gasped in dismay as she sent Caroline a speaking glance.

"I fear we have been premature, Lady Lanford," Caroline said in a brittle voice. "Obviously, your son preferred a heathen to a proper English wife. 'Tis such a shame. A fortune comes with me, you know. Papa will be disappointed. He wanted a duke for me, but an earl would have sufficed." Turning on her heel, she swept past the group and out the door with regal grace.

Lady Lanford stared at Zara, forgetting to close her mouth.

"I'm sorry, Mother, I didn't mean to shock you," Jamal said. "Aren't you going to welcome Zara?"

Finally Lady Lanford remembered her manners. "Forgive me, my dear. Jamal hasn't changed. He does enjoy shocking a poor old lady. Welcome to the family." She gave Zara a half-hearted hug. "Where did Jamal find a beauty like you?"

"I'm a Berber, my lady," Zara said. "My father is Youssef, *cadi* of the Berbers. Have you heard of him?"

Lady Lanford staggered backward as if struck. Color drained from her face and her eyes became two burning coals. "You are Youssef's daughter?" The question came out as a hiss.

"Mother, what's wrong? You look as if you've seen a ghost. You're frightening Zara."

"Zara, Youssef's daughter," Lady Lanford repeated. "Take her away, Jamal! Get her out of my sight!"

Zara recoiled in horror. What had she done?

"Mother, what is it?"

"Don't you know, Jamal? Has no one ever told you?"

"Told me what?"

"You know your father was killed fighting Berbers, don't you?" Jamal nodded. "Obviously, what you don't know is that he was slain by Youssef, Zara's father. I can't look at her without thinking of my poor Ahab."

Zara recoiled in dismay. This couldn't be happening to her. Just when she had everything in life she could ever desire, it was about to be snatched away. How could Jamal love her when his father had died at the hands of Youssef, her own beloved father?

"Mother! I had no idea," Jamal claimed, flying to Zara's defense. "Nevertheless, you can't hold Zara responsible for something her father did."

"I'm sorry," Lady Lanford said, turning away. "Take her away, Jamal. It's going to take a while to become accustomed to having the daughter of your father's killer living in my home. I will see that your friends are settled in their rooms. Meet me in the library later and we'll discuss this in private."

"Mother, I—"

"Nay, son, say nothing. Take your . . . wife and leave me. I need time alone to come to grips with this."

Zara felt as if the earth had dropped out from beneath her. In a daze, she allowed Jamal to draw her with him out of the room and up the curved staircase. Once they reached Jamal's room, he remained thoughtful as he walked to the window and stared moodily into the distance.

"I'm sorry, Jamal. I had no idea," Zara began.

"I did so want your mother to like me."

"Things will work out." The tremor in his voice belied his words. Why hadn't he known the name of the man who had killed his father? Because it had never mattered before, he told himself. Knowing the man's name wouldn't bring his father back. He'd been away at the time and arrived home months after his death.

"No, they won't! How can they?"

He turned to her then, his face softening. "She'll come around. I'll speak to her while you rest. Should I send up something for you to eat?"

Zara shook her head. She couldn't manage a bite. Nor could she pretend that Lady Lanford's shocking disclosure hadn't affected Jamal. She had only to look at him to know he was deeply distressed. Allah help her. Why were there so many obstacles to her happiness?

Jamal left Zara a short time later. He needed to speak to his mother before Zara became more upset than she already was. It wasn't good for the baby. Somehow he had to make his mother understand that Zara was the woman he loved, the only woman he wanted. His father's death had occurred a long time ago. Nothing would bring him back. Blaming Zara for something her father had done was not fair.

Lady Eloise was waiting for Jamal in the library. He could tell she was genuinely disturbed, and he felt her pain keenly.

"Are you all right, Mother?"

"Tell me about Zara, son," Lady Eloise began without preamble. "How did you meet Youssef's daughter?"

"Sit down, Mother, while I explain how Zara came to mean so much to me. When I finish, you will know why I love her as I do."

"I prefer to stand. Begin, son."

Jamal began at the beginning, explaining how he'd met Zara and everything that had taken place since that day. "So you see, Mother," he concluded, "Zara saved my life on more than one occasion."

"Could you find no other way to repay her?" Lady Eloise asked.

While Jamal was speaking with his mother in the library, Zara came to a decision. She needed to be present while Jamal and his mother discussed her future. It was her fate they were deciding, and she wanted to have her say. She needed to let Lady Lanford know how much she loved her son.

With that thought in mind, Zara left the bed chamber and crept down the stairs, meeting no one. She located the library by the drone of voices coming from behind the partially closed door. She intended to knock but froze with her hand raised when she heard her name spoken in anger by Jamal's mother.

"Lady Caroline is twice the lady Zara is," Lady Eloise argued. "She brings a hefty dowry and is a perfect match for you."

"I don't love Lady Caroline, Mother."

"I didn't love your father when he bought me for his harem. Love came later."

"I married Zara; nothing will change that."

"Did you marry her in an Islamic ceremony?"

"Of course."

Lady Eloise smiled smugly. "Then 'tis a simple matter to divorce her and marry Lady Caroline. I can never accept the daughter of the man who killed my beloved Ahab."

Zara didn't wait around to hear Jamal's answer. Turning on her heel, she fled back to her room.

Jamal stared at his mother. He'd never known her to harbor such animosity toward another. "I'm sorry you feel that way, Mother. I understand your feelings, but I don't share them. I loved Father as much as you, but Zara isn't the one who killed him and I don't hold her responsible. If not for Zara I wouldn't be standing here today. She gave me the will to live when I was prepared to die."

Lady Eloise gave Jamal a look filled with sadness and regret. "I know I'm being unreasonable, son, but I can't help it. Obviously you love Zara. Just don't ask *me* to love her."

At a loss for words, Jamal turned away, saddened by his mother's obstinacy where Zara was concerned. "I hope you'll change your mind once you get to know Zara. I'm going upstairs to my wife. She was understandably upset when I left her."

Zara was more than upset, she was devastated. How could she and Jamal expect to find happiness when his mother despised her for being Youssef's daughter? There was no future for her here in England, none at all. Jamal belonged with Lady Caroline, a woman born to be an earl's wife. She should have stayed in Morocco with her father, Zara thought. She was stupid to think she could have any place in Jamal's new life as an earl. She would only be a hindrance to Jamal if she remained his wife.

Her dilemma had but one solution. She must return to Morocco. She would never come between a mother and her son. In time Jamal would come to hate her, and she couldn't bear that.

The door opened, scattering Zara's thoughts. Jamal entered the room, closing the door behind him. "Are you all right, love? Why aren't you resting?"

Zara turned from the window, drinking in the sight of Jamal as if it were the last time she would look upon him. "I was waiting for you. Did you speak with your mother?"

In two steps he was beside her, folding her in his arms. "Forget Mother. She'll come around. Learning that you were Youssef's daughter was a bit of a surprise. Give her time, love. When she learns you're going to give her a grandchild, she'll change her mind."

He kissed her, a slow, lingering kiss that brought tears to Zara's eyes. She loved him so. She'd do anything to make him happy, even leave him. He might not realize it at first, but later he'd come to appreciate what she'd done for him. He deserved an English beauty like Lady Caroline, not a Berber outlaw's daughter for a wife.

Zara returned his kiss, sadly aware that her time with Jamal was limited. One day soon she would make her way back to the *Plunderer* and return to Morocco with Captain Brahim. But for now she wanted to savor the sweetness of Jamal's loving, storing away enough memories to last a lifetime.

When Jamal found himself becoming aroused by Zara's kisses, he reluctantly set her away from him. "You're tired, love. We've the rest of our lives to make love. I don't want to hurt you or our child."

"I don't want to wait, Jamal. Make love to me now. I need you."

Jamal searched her face, concerned for her well-being. Desperation and fear were clearly visible in the green depths of her expressive eyes. Zara had never exhibited fear before, and it alarmed him. She was overwrought, but that was only natural given his mother's reaction to her. Still, if making love to her would offer her comfort, he certainly wasn't going to deny her.

"Ah, sweet vixen, making love to you is my pleasure."

He undressed her slowly, carefully manipulating the buttons on the front of her dress and pulling it down her arms. He kissed her bare shoulders and then her lips, caressing the inside of her mouth with his tongue. He delved deeper and she opened to him, her tongue dancing with his in sweet surrender.

Her dress fell to the floor with the downward sweep of his hands and he lifted her out of the puddle of cloth. She wore no corset. A single tie held her chemise together and when he released it her breasts spilled free. He stared at the full mounds before bending his head and taking a nipple into his mouth.

"I have never tasted anything sweeter," he groaned against the budding crest as he licked and sucked first one then the other into taut little nubs. "Sunlight and warm rain. Soft Moroccan nights and moonlight. Your golden skin reminds me of everything I love."

Zara moaned, inflamed by his words. He had but to touch her and she turned to fire.

Her chemise and petticoats were dispatched with dexterity. Her stockings and shoes followed. When she stood before him naked and glowing, she began pulling at his shirt. Jamal laughed at her eagerness, helping her to remove his clothing. When they were both naked, he lifted her into his arms and took her with him onto the soft feather mattress. He kissed her until she clung to him as though to life itself. After several soul-wrenching kisses he dragged his mouth from hers long enough to look at her.

Her eyes were languid, her expression bemused as his gaze slid from her face, past her flushed breasts to her slightly rounded stomach. He placed a kiss where his child grew, his expression one of rapt adoration.

Zara started to speak but lost the ability when he stroked his hand between her legs. She shivered, raising her hands to his back and caressing his smooth, golden flesh. She touched her lips to his chest.

"You're magnificent," she murmured against his heated skin. "There will never be another man like you."

Jamal's dark brows rose. "Another man? There had better not be."

He kissed her again, then again, the sweet taste and scent of her driving him wild. He wanted to take it easy with her, but urgency drove him. To touch Zara was to want her.

He explored her thoroughly, his hands, mouth and tongue savoring every inch of her golden skin. He licked and suckled her breasts, kissed the fragile curve of her stomach, trailed a wet path to her slick sheath, drawing a quivering cry from her when his tongue delved inside. He spread her legs wider and buried his head between them, savoring the liquid heat of her response. Her fingers dug into his arms as she arched sharply upward, soaring like a bird to a place where splendor awaited.

"Allah help me! I'm dying!"

"Nay, sweet vixen. Death isn't this sweet. Savor the moment. Come, Zara, come now."

The feel of his lips, the thrust of his tongue, the solid weight of his hands guiding her hips unleashed a raw passion she couldn't control as she reached for pleasure and found pure rapture.

Rising up slowly, Jamal lowered his weight upon her and slid inside her. He groaned as the walls of her sheath tightened around him, the pleasure so intense, his control nearly deserted him. Zara shifted her hips to take him deeper. He gave her everything he had, his very soul, as he moved against her, his hips thrusting against hers, his flanks quivering.

Clutching him tightly, Zara rode the crest with him. The earth moved, the heavens shook, and Zara knew nothing would ever equal what she and Jamal had just shared.

"Are you all right?" Jamal asked when his

breathing returned to normal. "I didn't hurt you, did I?"

"How could anything so wonderful hurt me?"

"Nevertheless, I'd feel better if you'd take a long nap."

"I'll rest easier if you lie here beside me. I'm not ready for you to leave me yet."

"There's no place I'd rather be," Jamal said as he turned Zara on her side and fit her into the curve of his body.

Sleep came instantly. When Jamal awoke later it was full dark and the fire in the grate had burned down. He rose quietly, rekindled the fire and climbed back beneath the covers with Zara. A muffled groan slid past his lips when she pressed her buttocks against the heat of his loins. He was hard again. His sex was full and painfully heavy. Reluctant to disturb Zara's sleep, he began to ease out of bed.

"Nay, don't leave."

"I thought you were sleeping."

"As you can see, I'm not."

"I have to leave, sweet vixen." He took her hand and placed it on his erection. "See what you do to me? If I remain I can't guarantee that the randy lad between my legs will behave."

"I don't want him to behave." She ground her buttocks into his groin. "Please, Jamal."

Surrendering to Zara's plea, Jamal shifted her legs, positioned himself behind her, and eased into her slick sheath. This time he worked her slow and easy, drawing out her passion along with his. When he finally granted her release, she couldn't stop sobbing.

Alarmed, Jamal asked, "What is it, love? Why are you crying?"

She didn't dare tell him the truth, that she couldn't bear the thought of leaving him. She thanked Allah she would have his child to love. "I'm crying because I'm happy," she lied.

He didn't believe her. "You're still worried about my mother, aren't you?"

Zara shrugged. "I did so want her to like me."

"She will. Give her time. She'll come around once she realizes how much I love you. Shall we dress and go down to dinner?"

"Go without me," Zara urged. "Send something up to me on a tray. I . . . can't stand another confrontation."

He stared at her in consternation. "Perhaps that would be best. Things will look better tomorrow."

Zara gave him a sad smile. Things would never look better.

Not tomorrow, not ever.

Chapter Twenty-one

Zara's resolve to leave strengthened as the days passed. Lady Eloise found countless opportunities to throw Jamal and Lady Caroline together. The haughty blonde was invited to dinner nearly every night. One night her carriage failed to arrive to take her home and Jamal was compelled to act as escort. Another night Zara watched jealously as Caroline engaged Jamal in intimate conversation, dominating his attention for the entire evening. They looked so right together that Zara felt like an outsider.

Zara was feeling under the weather one afternoon when Caroline showed up to go riding with Lady Eloise. Using fatigue as an excuse, Lady Eloise graciously bowed out, volunteering Jamal in her stead. Zara thought Jamal didn't protest vigorously enough as he acquiesced to his mother's wishes. Zara spoke her mind while he was changing into his riding clothes.

"I can't be rude, love," he answered. "But I do intend to have a talk with Mother. Her efforts to throw Caroline and me together are becoming tedious. I promise it won't happen again. You can join us if you wish."

The last thing Zara wanted to do was squeeze her burgeoning figure into a riding habit. Her wide skirts still disguised her pregnancy, but it wouldn't be long before it became apparent that she was increasing. "I'm not up to riding today."

Jamal became immediately concerned. "Are you unwell?"

"I'm pregnant," Zara said crossly, as if that explained everything.

He sent her a tender smile. "I'm quite aware of that. During the night, when you're cuddled up against me, I can feel the babe move. I can't explain just how that makes me feel except to say that it's wonderfully satisfying."

Zara refused to be placated. "You'd better go. It isn't polite to keep Lady Caroline waiting."

"I don't give a bloody damn about Caroline. This farce has gone far enough. I haven't wanted to upset Mother, but this has got to stop."

Once again Zara felt as if she was coming between Lady Lanford and her son, and it wasn't a good feeling.

Several days passed before Zara found the opportunity to slip away. The day was bright, sunny and cold, perfect for hawking. Haroun and Jamal decided they would not find a better day to try out the pair of peregrine falcons Jamal's game-keeper had just purchased. They left early that morning.

Lady Eloise, declaring the day too fine to waste, went calling. She did not ask Zara to accompany her. Not that Zara minded. She had studiously kept out of Lady Eloise's way, not wishing to cause Jamal's mother further distress by forcing herself upon the woman.

Zara knew she'd not find a better time to journey to London. She packed only her robes and boots, which she intended to wear during the voyage, stuffing them in a pillowcase for easy carrying. Unfortunately, Zinab entered her chamber with a breakfast tray while she was packing.

"Are you going somewhere, Zara?"

Zara blanched when she saw Zinab standing in the doorway. There was no help for it now. Zinab would see through her lie, so she was forced to tell the truth. "I'm leaving."

Zinab carefully set down the tray. "For good?"

"For good," Zara declared firmly. "I can't bear seeing Lady Eloise distressed on my account. Jamal will be better off without me. Lady Caroline is the kind of wife he needs."

"You're not thinking clearly," Zinab chided. "Jamal loves you. You're carrying his child. Do you actually think he'll let you leave him?"

"I don't know," Zara said in a voice so low Zinab had to strain to hear her. " 'Tis for the best. Jamal will understand that and let me go."

"You're overwrought, Zara. Why don't you lie down? I'll ask Dr. ben Israel to look in on you."

Zara grasped her arm. "Nay, you're not to tell a soul! Promise me, Zinab. You're the only one I can trust."

"Don't ask that of me. You don't even know the way to London."

"The coachman will take us," a third voice interjected.

Both Zara and Zinab stared at the intruder, surprised to find Saha standing behind them. They'd been so intent upon their argument that they had failed to hear Saha enter the chamber.

"Us?" Zara repeated. "What are you talking about?"

"I've decided to leave this cursed country," Saha said. "I hate England. Jamal said I could leave if I was unhappy, and I am. I'm going to return to Morocco aboard the *Plunderer*. Captain Brahim promised me a place in his harem, and I'm going to accept. He's handsome and kind and can afford to keep his women in luxurious accommodations." She sent Zara a sly smile. "It took little persuasion to convince the coachman to take me to London.

"It never occurred to me that *you'd* want to leave," Saha continued. "Can't say that I blame you. I've spoken at length with Lady Lanford, you know. She'll never accept you as Jamal's wife. In time Jamal will come to hate you." This last vicious barb was rendered with a malicious smile.

"Don't listen to her, Zara," Zinab urged.

"What about Haroun?" Zara asked Saha.

Saha shrugged. "What about him? This is England and I can do as I please. Besides," she added, sending a venomous glance at Zinab, "Haroun is too taken with Zinab these days to pay attention to me."

Zinab blushed, aware of Haroun's growing fondness for her. "You do not care for Haroun. He is a good man and deserves better than you."

"I never did want him," Saha claimed. "You're welcome to him." She turned to Zara. "Are you coming with me?"

"Nay, Zara, don't do it," Zinab pleaded.

"Aye, I'm ready," Zara said, ignoring Zinab as she clutched the pillowcase to her chest.

"Lord Jamal will be angry when he catches up with you," Zinab warned.

The ladies were blissfully unaware that Jamal stood in the open doorway, his anger growing as he listened to their conversation.

"I'm *very* angry." Jamal's harsh words sent fear racing through Zara. "Leave us," he ordered, his gaze never wavering from Zara's pale face. The cold authority in his voice set the women into motion as they headed for the door.

"Saha, before you leave, I want you to know that I spoke with the coachman. Both Haroun and I agree that you should leave. Haroun awaits you by the coach. He will accompany you to London and explain to Captain Brahim. You won't be cast adrift penniless, though I know Brahim is smitten with you and will see to your welfare."

"Lord Jamal—"

"Say nothing, Saha, just leave. I wish to speak to my wife in private." Saha scurried away to join Haroun. She couldn't wait to leave this dreary place behind.

Zara held her ground beneath Jamal's withering gaze. "I thought you went hawking."

"My horse threw a shoe, forcing us to return. I saw the coach sitting outside the front door and knew something was amiss. Mother took the lighter carriage this morning. A word with the coachman confirmed my suspicions. I knew Saha wished to leave and I was going to arrange it eventually. I had no idea you intended to leave with her until I overheard your conversation."

"How long have you been listening?"

"Long enough. Did you think I'd allow you to leave with my child growing inside you?"

A muscle twitched at the corner of his mouth, the only sign of his anger, except for his outward calmness. It was unlike Jamal to be so calm.

"I hoped you'd realize that it was for your own good. I never wanted to come between you and your mother. In time you'd come to hate me."

"Let me be the judge of what's good for me. I thought you knew better than to believe Saha's vicious lies."

"You heard?"

He nodded. "You should trust me, Zara. Let me handle Mother. 'Tis time to tell her about the baby."

"You truly don't wish to be married to Lady Caroline?"

Jamal spit out a curse. "Caroline is a blueblooded snob. She perceives me as a romantic figure. She's intrigued by my mixed heritage and my wealth. Mother told her it was a simple matter to divorce in Islamic law, and Caroline mistakenly believed I'd divorce you and marry her. She is too dimwitted to realize I love you too much to let you go."

"Your mother will never accept me."

"Mother didn't marry you, I did. As soon as you and our child can travel, we'll visit all my estates and pick out one where you'll be happy. Lanford Manor has always been my favorite, but I want you to choose our home. Mother loves Lanford Manor; I suspect she'll prefer to remain here."

"I don't ever want you to be sorry you married me."

"Are you sorry you married *me?*"

"Never!"

"That's how I feel. Forget about leaving. You must have been truly distraught to think I'd let you go." He took her into his arms and nuzzled her cheek. It was impossible to remain angry with her despite her flawed thinking. How could she believe he'd be better off without her? "Promise you won't do anything foolish like that again?"

Displaying her old spunk, Zara squared her shoulders and stared at him. "I won't promise you anything, Sheik Jamal, except to love you with my whole heart."

"Will you agree to a Christian wedding, complete with guests and reception? I don't want the legality of our marriage to be questioned. Or our child's right to inherit."

Zara frowned. She knew nothing of Christianity. "Will it make you happy? Must I forsake Allah?"

"We are married no matter what religion we hold to. Allah knows we are wed, but we must show the Christian world that we are man and wife. I will not insist upon it if you are against it."

"You are right, Jamal. We must wed again to prove to the world that we are united before both Allah and the Christian God."

"Shall we go downstairs and tell Mother about the baby?"

She gave him a seductive smile. "Not now. I need to be convinced of your need for me. Make love to me, Jamal."

Jamal gave her a tender smile. "It will be my pleasure."

That night Lady Eloise invited a guest to Lanford Manor. Both Zara and Jamal were surprised to see a middle-aged man conversing with Lady Eloise in the elegant drawing room when they gathered downstairs for dinner. His distinguished gray hair and neat mustache gave him a look of quiet assurance.

Lady Eloise looked up as Zara and Jamal entered the room. "Ah, Jamal, you're here. Come and meet Lord Robert Cummins, the Earl of Durbin. Robert, this is my son, Jamal, Lord Lanford."

Jamal offered his hand, which was warmly clasped by the earl. "Durbin, pleased to meet you," Jamal said. "Do you live in the area? I don't recall meeting you before."

"I bought the Hinkley estate when I moved from Ireland a few months ago. That makes me your neighbor. I met your lovely mother at a reception given in my honor by Lord and Lady Freemont." He gave Eloise a tender smile, and Jamal wondered what was going on.

"And this must be your beautiful wife," Durbin

continued. He bowed gallantly over Zara's hand.

"This is Lady Zara," Eloise said somewhat coolly. "Jamal married her in Morocco."

"Mother," Jamal said, clenching his teeth in frustration, "I wish a word with you in private. Would you excuse us, Durbin?"

"Of course. I'll entertain your lady while you speak with your mother."

"The library, Mother," Jamal said, ushering his mother from the room.

Eloise searched Jamal's face as he shut the library door and turned to face her. "What's so important that it can't wait?"

"First, I want you to stop treating Zara like a pariah. She's my wife and will remain my wife. Second, stop creating situations that force me to endure Lady Caroline's company. Her visits must stop. It's upsetting Zara, and I won't have her disturbed at a time like this. You're making me very sorry I returned to England."

"You don't know how difficult this is for me, son. Every time I look at Zara, I see the woman whose father killed my beloved Ahab."

"Every time I look at Zara, I see the woman I love and the mother of my children. Zara is carrying my child, Mother. Your first grandchild."

Lady Eloise's delight was genuine. "A baby? Zara is pregnant?"

"That's what I said. I'm taking Zara away, where she won't be subjected to your coldness. I never imagined you could be like this. You've always been such a loving, understanding woman."

"A baby," Eloise repeated, her face softening. "It will be wonderful having a baby in the house."

"Haven't you heard a word I've said, Mother? I'm taking Zara away."

Suddenly, having a grandchild seemed more important than carrying a grudge. "Oh, Jamal, I don't know what got into me. I've been a foolish old woman. I shouldn't have blamed Zara for her father's sins. Will you forgive me? Will Zara forgive me? I want to know my grandchild."

"Of course I forgive you, but I can't speak for Zara. She was willing to leave me to keep peace in the family. Zara is proud and brave and as fierce as any warrior I've ever known, and I love her. I want you to love her, too."

"I'll try, son, truly I will."

"I'll send her in to you so you can tell her yourself."

"Jamal, about Lord Robert—"

"Later, Mother." He left before she finished the sentence.

A few minutes later Zara entered the library, wary and perturbed about her private talk with Lady Eloise. She'd been conversing pleasantly with Lord Robert when Jamal interrupted, saying only that his mother wished to speak with her in private.

"You wished to see me, Lady Eloise?"

"What I wish, my dear, is to apologize," Eloise said. "I regret our dismal beginning and wish to make amends. I had no business making rash judgments where you were concerned. May we begin anew? I know about the babe you're carrying and want to be a part of my grandchild's life. Will you allow it, Zara?"

Tears sprang to Zara's eyes. This was the kind

of welcome she had dreamed of, but had been denied. "I bear you no ill will, my lady. I never knew my mother and had no one but my father. I love him dearly and always will. Knowing that, can we still be friends?"

"Jamal loves you. That's enough for me. Your children will fill this old house with happiness and love. How can I not offer you my friendship . . . and one day, perhaps my love."

They embraced warmly, then Lady Eloise said, "Shall we join the men? Robert will think I've deserted him."

"Ah, here are the women," Robert said as Zara and Eloise entered the drawing room together. "You're just in time. Dinner has been announced." He offered Zara his arm while Jamal escorted his mother into the dining room.

Conversation flowed pleasantly. At the end of the meal, Robert cleared his throat and said, "Did you tell them, Eloise, my love?"

Jamal glanced from Robert to his mother, one eyebrow raised. "Tell me what?"

Lady Eloise blushed to the roots of her hair. "Not yet, Robert. We had other things to discuss."

"Then I insist we tell them now," Robert said. Before Eloise could express an opinion, Robert blithely continued. "I've asked Lady Eloise for her hand and she has graciously agreed to marry me. That is, if you have no objections, Lanford. I can furnish you with a complete financial report if you wish. Your mother will never want for anything. I've grown to love her dearly."

"I'd rather hear how Mother feels," Jamal said, stunned by the turn of events.

"I'm lonesome, Jamal. Robert has shown me that life isn't over for me. You have your Zara and soon there will be a child to enrich your lives. I'd like to remain close, but I want a life of my own. I love Robert and wish to marry him."

"Then we'll make it a double wedding," Jamal said with enthusiasm. "As soon as it can be arranged. Zara and I have decided to be married in a Christian ceremony. Do you mind if we make this an affair to remember?"

Lady Eloise gave Zara a watery smile. "Do you wish to share your special day with me, Zara?"

"The first time Jamal and I were married will always remain our 'special' day. I'd be happy to share the second happiest day of my life with you and Lord Robert."

They drank a toast to love and happiness, then Jamal and Zara excused themselves, leaving the newly engaged couple to their own devices.

"One never knows what to expect next from life," Jamal said once they were alone in their room. "Mother certainly is full of surprises. I had no idea she was thinking of marriage."

"Lord Robert is very handsome."

"Am I not handsome?" He preened for her benefit.

"You, my lord sheik, are arrogant beyond words. You are far too bold, but I suppose one could describe you as passably handsome."

"And you, my lovely princess, will never be tamed. Despite your sharp tongue, I've managed to survive without being slashed to pieces." His eyes sparkled naughtily. "Come to bed. I want to hold you in my arms. I might even be able to locate a set of those silver balls you're so fond of."

She stared at him. "You brought them?"

He gave her a wicked smile. "For my lady's pleasure," he said as he swooped her off her feet and carried her to the bed.

There, he made her body sing and her heart soar with the joy of being alive and being with him.

AUTHOR'S NOTE

Dear Readers,

This book is the result of my visit to Morocco. Perhaps some of you saw me on the CBS show *48 Hours*, part of which was filmed while I was in Morocco researching *Sheik*. Morocco is a fascinating country. I was intrigued with every aspect of its culture, laws and mores. During my visit, city officials were very gracious to me, treating me as a VIP. It was a wonderful experience.

I hope you enjoyed reading *Sheik* as much as I enjoyed writing it. The story is pure fantasy, though it is based on fact and steeped in the richness of Moroccan culture. According to history, Moulay Ismail was just as I described him. But my hero and heroine were created from my imagination.

The strife and hard feelings between the Berbers and Arab rulers of that time was also real. Had the various Berber tribes banded together to form a strong fighting unit, they might have become today's ruling class instead of the sheepherders and farmers they are now.

All My Romantic Best,
Connie Mason

GLOSSARY

bab...gate
cadi...chieftain
couscous...finely grained pasta
djellaba...............................outer robe worn over clothing
hammam..bath or bathing room
houri..temptress
medina...old city
kasbah...fortress
minaret..prayer tower
muezzin..prayer leader
scimitar...long curved sword
souk...marketplace

ICE & Rapture

CONNIE MASON

Winner of the *Romantic Times* Storyteller of the Year Award!

Cool as a cucumber, and totally dedicated to her career as a newspaper woman, Maggie Afton is just the kind of challenge brash Chase McGarrett enjoys. But he is exactly the kind of man she despises. Cold and hot, reserved and brazen, Maggie and Chase are a study in opposites. But when they join forces during the Klondike gold rush, the fiery sparks of their scaring desire burn brighter than the northern lights.

__4193-6 $5.99 US/$6.99 CAN

CONNIE MASON

**"Each new Connie Mason book is a prize!"
—Heather Graham, bestselling author of
*A Magical Christmas***

Love Me With Fury. When her stagecoach is ambushed on the Texas frontier, Ariel Leland fears for her life. But even more frightening is Jess Wilder, a virile bounty hunter who has devoted his life to finding the hellcat responsible for his brother's murder—and now he has her. But Ariel's proud spirit and naive beauty erupt a firestorm of need in him—transforming his lust for vengeance into a love that must be fulfilled at any cost.

___52215-2 $5.50 US/$6.50 CAN

Pure Temptation. Fresh off the boat from Ireland, Moira O'Toole isn't fool enough to believe in legends or naive enough to trust a rake. Yet after an accident lands her in Graystoke Manor, she finds herself haunted, harried, and hopelessly charmed by Black Jack Graystoke and his exquisite promise of pure temptation.

___4041-7 $5.99 US/$6.99 CAN

Dorchester Publishing Co., Inc.
P.O. Box 6640
Wayne, PA 19087-8640

Please add $1.75 for shipping and handling for the first book and $.50 for each book thereafter. NY, NYC, and PA residents, please add appropriate sales tax. No cash, stamps, or C.O.D.s. All orders shipped within 6 weeks via postal service book rate. Canadian orders require $2.00 extra postage and must be paid in U.S. dollars through a U.S. banking facility.

Name_____
Address_____
City_____State_____Zip_____
I have enclosed $_____ in payment for the checked book(s).
Payment <u>must</u> accompany all orders. ❑ Please send a free catalog.

SHADOW WALKER

CONNIE MASON

Bestselling Author of *Flame*!

"Why did you do that?"

"Kiss you?" Cole shrugged. "Because you wanted me to, I suppose. Why else would a man kiss a woman?"

But Dawn knows lots of other reasons, especially if the woman is nothing but half-breed whose father has sold her to the first interested male. Defenseless and exquisitely lovely, Dawn is overjoyed when Cole Webster kills the ruthless outlaw who is her husband in name only. But now she has a very different sort of man to contend with. A man of unquestionable virility, a man who prizes justice and honors the Native American traditions that have been lost to her. Most intriguing of all, he is obviously a man who knows exactly how to bring a woman to soaring heights of pleasure. And yes, she does want his kiss...and maybe a whole lot more.

_4260-6 $5.99 US/$6.99 CAN

Dorchester Publishing Co., Inc.
P.O. Box 6640
Wayne, PA 19087-8640

FLAME
CONNIE MASON

"Each new Connie Mason book is a prize!"
—Heather Graham

When her brother is accused of murder, Ashley Webster heads west to clear his name. Although the proud Yankee is prepared to face any hardship on her journey to Fort Bridger, she is horrified to learn that single women aren't welcome on any wagon train. Desperate to cross the plains, Ashley decides to pay the first bachelor willing to pose as her husband. Then the fiery redhead comes across a former Johnny Reb in the St. Joe's jail, and she can't think of any man she'd rather marry in name only. But out on the rugged trail Tanner MacTavish quickly proves too intense, too virile, too dangerous for her peace of mind. And after Tanner steals a passionate kiss, Ashley knows that, even though the Civil War is over, a new battle is brewing—a battle for the heart that she may be only too happy to lose.

_4150-2 $5.99 US/$6.99 CAN

THE LION'S BRIDE
CONNIE MASON

**Winner of the *Romantic Times*
Storyteller Of The Year Award!**

Lord Lyon of Normandy has saved William the Conqueror from certain death on the battlefield, yet neither his strength nor his skill can defend him against the defiant beauty the king chooses for his wife.

Ariana of Cragmere has lost her lands and her virtue to the mighty warrior, but the willful beauty swears never to surrender her heart.

Saxon countess and Norman knight, Ariana and Lyon are born enemies. And in a land rent asunder by bloody wars and shifting loyalties, they are doomed to misery unless they can vanquish the hatred that divides them—and unite in glorious love.

_3884-6 $5.99 US/$7.99 CAN